Eternal
NIGHTMARE

MAGGIE D. PURVIS

Book and Cover design by Maggie Purvis
ISBN: 979-8-9989364-0-1

Purvis Publishing LLC
First Edition: March 2025

10 9 8 7 6 5 4 3 2 1

Maggie. D Purvis

CONTENTS

BEYOND THE GRAVE 1

CALM BEFORE THE STORM 8

SLEEP DISORDER 18

COLLISION 28

THE BEACH 40

LIMITLESS 46

PREMONITION? 52

THIRTY-EIGHT SPECIAL 61

ART SHOW 69

YOU CAN'T RUN 80

DREAM SYMBOLISM 87

THE FLASHBACK 101

BALD MAN 108

KARA 117

SUNNYBROOK 124

TWO LIVES COLLIDE 138

THIS IS REALITY 154

INVESTIGATION 164

MONSTER IN A JUDGE'S ROBE 172

CONNECTIONS 180

NEW VERSION OF MYSELF 190

THE INTERVIEW 200

JANE DOE.. 209

NIGHTMARE OR MEMORY 217

REFLECTION.. 228

BLAST FROM THE PAST 235

ONE STEP AT A TIME 246

EMERGENCY PLACEMENT 257

AN US MOMENT 265

THE PHONE CALL 276

UNKNOWN NUMBER.. 293

THE VISITOR 303

THE MEETING 312

MELANIE.. 324

THE MOLE 336

THE PLAYGROUND 350

MY BABY 359

GOODBYE 367

THE WAREHOUSE... 381

THE BOX... 390

DNA 398

ARREST... 411

FINALLY 419

A PLACE OF TRUTH 429

Maggie. D Purvis

Emotions experienced in dreams are just as real as emotions in waking life, because whatever the mind believes is real is perceived as reality.

Eternal Nightmare

1

Beyond the Grave

That terrible nightmare that brought me here was still vivid in my mind. The exam chair was uncomfortable, with its hard vinyl cushion and crinkly paper cover, but at least this visit did not require the stirrups or a paper gown. I sat in the room alone, waiting for the doctor to arrive. Even though I had been going to Dr. Francis for years, I was still nervous.

She'll probably think I'm being an overly dramatic teenager and not believe anything I say. Or she'll think I'm crazy. Maybe I am. Either that, or my dead parents are haunting me.

After waiting for about half an hour, I began to doubt my decision to come. *No one makes a doctor's appointment for nightmares.* Before I could stand up to leave, the door opened, and she walked into the room.

"Hello, Grace. I haven't seen you in a while. How are things?" she asked in a cheery tone.

I looked up at her with a solemn expression on my sleep-deprived face, without saying a word.

"I know things have been a struggle since your parents died a year ago," Dr. Francis said in a soft, soothing voice. "But on the phone, you said you think the nightmares you are experiencing have something to do with their car accident?" She sat opposite me in a rolling vinyl chair, holding her clipboard.

"Yeah, they almost always involve a car accident." I paused, knowing how crazy I was about to sound. "It's almost like my parents are trying to warn me about something, get some message to me through my dreams from beyond the grave. The last one I had is still vivid in my mind, if you'd like to hear it," I offered.

"Yes, please. I'd love to," Dr. Francis said encouragingly.

I took a deep breath. "When it began, my eyes were open, but all I could see was darkness." I paused, bringing myself back there mentally. "I lay there, and I couldn't tell what was up or down. I tried to stick my hands out, but they kept hitting walls super close to me. That's when I realized I was boxed in. I screamed, but the sound was muffled. I felt like I was suffocating, like the air was running out. The first thought that came to my mind was, I've been buried alive!" I said, my voice cracking with emotion. Dr. Francis sat still, listening intently.

I took another deep breath, attempting to compose myself, then continued, "I screamed and pounded my fists against the solid surface. My voice became ragged, and I was losing the energy to even think about what to do. When suddenly... Something collides into the container I am in with a thundering crash, and the box is flying. The lid snaps open as it crashes to the ground, sending me tumbling out of it," I clamored, my voice rising as my hands imitate the motions.

"Goodness!" Dr. Francis said in a breathy whisper.

"I lie there in a daze until I realize I am in excruciating pain.

2

Looking down at my body, I see my upper right arm has snapped, the bone piercing my skin," I said, and held up my right arm as if I could actually show her the wound.

"My eyes focused on bright lights, as dust and swirls of steam floated through the air. I force myself to stand, cradling my right arm with my left, and take a couple tentative steps," I said, my tone animated. I tucked a lock of blond hair behind my ear before continuing.

"The lights are headlights from a car with a broken grill and a cracked windshield. The hood is bent, and smoke is rolling out from the engine compartment. I take a few more steps and look into the driver's seat. A young man is slumped over towards the center console. His head must have hit the windshield because there's a deep gash in his forehead. Blood is streaming down into his open eye, down the side of his nose, around the nostril, then dripping off his top lip and onto his right shoulder," I said, my voice becoming shaky.

Dr. Francis is on the edge of her seat, with intrigue written all over her face.

"I opened the door and checked for a pulse with my good arm, but he was gone. I closed the lids over his brown eyes. I fell to my knees and wept as the realization hit me. His car crashed into the box that was keeping me prisoner, and it killed him. Guilt swallowed me whole. I thought, why didn't I die too? Why did this seemingly innocent man have to die?" Tears were brimming my eyes as I thought back to the vivid imagery. Dr. Francis offered a box of tissues. I took two and dabbed the corners of my eyes.

"I muttered, 'I don't understand,' between sobs and looked

back up at him. Then..." I paused to catch my breath. Dr. Francis's eyes widen.

"He bolted upright, faced me, and screamed, 'This is your fault!'" I yelled out the words as I recalled them. Dr. Francis flinched, making me realize I needed to lower my voice.

"Blood was spraying onto me from his lips. His eyes were bulging from the sockets and boring holes into my soul," I said, shuddering. "He pointed a bloody finger in my face and yelled, 'You did this!'" I yelled as quietly as possible in the tiny room, pointing my finger at Dr. Francis as her jaw fell. She placed a hand on her heart, shaking her head.

"Right? It scared the crap outta me!" I said, agitated. "Then I woke up. I couldn't breathe. My heart was pounding. My entire body was shaking so violently, it took me a minute to focus my eyes. Exhausted, I looked over at the alarm clock on the nightstand, remembering that I last looked at the clock at three. It was now four-fifty-five."

"Wow, that's not a long sleep!" Dr. Francis said.

"Yeah, it felt like I had just laid my head on my pillow. I was in the same bed I have slept in every single night since I can remember. Yet, it felt foreign, unwelcoming, and there was no way I would be able to fall back asleep after that," I said in an irritated tone.

"I wouldn't be able to sleep after that either!" Dr. Francis said, shifting in her seat.

"That was the last straw, the last nightmare I could take. I had to do something about it. It's not just the nightmares, or that they usually involve a car accident, it's the guilt I feel afterwards. Like, I was responsible for their deaths. But instead of my parents, it's usually a young man who's killed. I don't understand!"

"Dreams can be really strange sometimes. It could be that your subconscious is trying to tell you something, but I don't think dreams always have a hidden meaning. Let's look at this from a physiological perspective," Dr. Francis jotted down some notes on her clipboard. "I'm going to prescribe a sleep aid for you. I know you are concerned about your nightmares, but it sounds like you are not sleeping through the night. It could be that your lack of sleep is causing stress, which can cause nightmares," she said with resolve.

"Hmm," I muttered. *I suppose it could be stress, or my dead parents haunting my dreams. At least she isn't dismissing me.* "I have been pretty stressed out lately, now that you mention it."

Dr. Francis' eyebrows came together. "Are you still going to therapy? Have you told Dr. Miller about the nightmares?"

I loved my therapist, but sometimes I felt that he was too quick to blame everything on my parents' death. "Yes. I am still going to therapy," I said, dabbing my eyes again. "He believes that subconsciously, I blame myself for their death, and the more time passes, the less I will have them. Since it's been a year and they haven't stopped, I started to wonder if it was something else."

"That might very well be true, but stress can create so many physical symptoms, too. Tell me about other stressors in your life," she said in a firm but gentle tone.

"Being a senior in high school without my parents has been especially hard. Everyone else in my class has been having graduation parties with their families, they will all have someone there for them when they walk down the aisle," I said, dropping my head and sobbing. "I have no one." My voice cracked.

Dr. Francis rolled her chair closer to me and grabbed my hand.

"I'm here for you. This difficult time will pass," she said, her voice soft and full of sympathy. She gave my hand a gentle squeeze, then let go. "Have you thought about what you will do after graduation?"

"My parents' estate is enough to get me through college and living expenses. I've thought about it, and I've applied to go to Loyola University and major in psychology. Especially after my parents died, I have realized how important mental health is. And now, with these nightmares, it just reassures me that I've made the right decision."

"Well, sleep does directly relate to your mental health, and almost the entire population has issues with one or the other or both comorbidly," she said, encouragingly. "Hopefully, the sleep aid and your ongoing therapy will take care of the nightmares," she added, standing up and opening the door.

"Thank you. I hope that's all it is!" I said as I walked out of the office.

"Call me if those don't work for you. Or if you just need to talk, okay?" Dr. Francis said in a firm tone.

When I got back home, I brought in the mail and flopped down on the couch. Everything was junk mail except one. It was from Loyola University. My breath caught in my throat as I opened the seal. I began reading, my mouth going from a thin straight line to a big smile in seconds. *I've been accepted!*

Excitement surged through me as I thought about all the things I needed to do. The first thing on my list was to find housing closer to the campus.

I jumped into my swivel chair and began looking for apartments. Leaving Wonder Lake would be difficult. It's all I had ever known, but at the same time, maybe moving was exactly what I needed. I was excited to start this journey into adulthood and see where life would take me.

There were a few places I wanted to go see, a couple of apartments, and a duplex, all off campus. I sent emails to inquire about viewing them all, then glanced back down at my acceptance letter and smiled. After last year, this all seemed too good to be true, like a beautiful dream I might wake up from at any moment.

2

Calm Before the Storm

I found a duplex in the Old Town neighborhood that I immediately fell in love with. Walking through it for the first time, it seemed welcoming, but I couldn't help but wonder if whatever was tormenting my sleep before would follow me here.

The inside of the duplex was clean. It wasn't very big, only one bathroom and bedroom, but it was enough for just me. I imagined trying to sleep in here and thought, *Surely, it would be better than my childhood home.* The home that held the memories of my parents' deaths. Perhaps just being in a new environment would help me sleep better.

The building itself was ancient, at least a hundred years old. They had done a good job of maintaining it and keeping it updated. I couldn't help but think about what sorts of people used to live here. Old buildings held so much history and so many secrets. I wondered if any lost souls were lingering around, too.

As I was touring the inside with the landlord, I kept hearing a faint, "mew" coming from right outside the back door. The landlord and I went to investigate and found a sad, lonely kitten with no mother in sight.

The landlord chuckled and said, "Well, looks like the apartment comes with a free cat!"

I picked up the tiny, dirty kitten, brushed the dead leaves off his fur, and he gazed at me with those blue kitten eyes. He blinked, then let out an even louder, "mew!" I knew right then that this was the home for me and my new kitten. I named him Joey, but when he was in trouble, it was Joseph—and as he grew larger and rounder, it eventually became Fat Joe. The duplex was a symbol for fresh starts and new beginnings. Little did I know it would not only be a home for my new kitten but also, a few years later, my own baby.

I wasn't looking for love. As a psychology major, there wasn't time to do much more than study. With my sleep issues and nightmares, I am realizing that I am having memory problems now, too, and I thought I should get my life together before including anyone else in it. But sometimes that's not how life works.

I was in the university library near at the start of my sophomore year, 1995. He sat absorbed in his studies at the table next to the small coffee bistro. I decided to get a cold brew.

As I walked, I fiddled with my purse, trying to get my wallet out, not paying attention to my surroundings. At that exact moment, he slid back his chair to stand up, and I tripped on the back leg of the chair and tumbled forward.

The contents of my purse spilled out and rained down onto him and the floor. I was mortified. He apologized repeatedly while helping me gather my things.

"I'm so sorry!" he said, jumping up out of his chair.

"No, it was my fault. I wasn't paying attention. I didn't sleep well," I said groggily and bent down to pick up the mess.

"I backed up right into you, though! Let me get you a coffee!" he said, then noticed my hesitation. "Please. I believe in karma. The coffee will even things out," he pleaded.

I looked into his deep blue eyes and saw kindness and sincerity. "Okay then, I'll take a sugar-free vanilla, cold brew." He pulled a chair out from the table and gestured for me to take a seat.

"I'm Grace," I said, pulling my chair closer to the table.

"Cameron. Call me Cam. It's nice to meet you, Grace," he said as he made his way to the coffee bar line a few feet away.

Less than a minute later, he came back to the table with our drinks and sat down opposite me.

I took a sip of cold brew and eyeballed him from over my cup. He was gorgeous, tall, and muscular, with disheveled, sandy hair.

"What are you majoring in?" I asked, trying to play it cool, while my mind fought hard to filter what went to my tongue. *God, he's beautiful*, I thought.

"Psychology with a minor in social work. I'll be graduating in May. You?" he asked with genuine interest on his face.

"No way! I'm a psychology major too!" I stammered.

"So, are you from here? Or did you move here for school?" he asked, holding up his disposable cup to his mouth. The steam rose into his sculpted face.

"I grew up in a quiet, tree-lined neighborhood called

Wonder Lake in Chicago and then moved here when I started at Loyola," I said, trying not to smile like a buffoon. "Where are you from?"

"I'm from Billings, Montana. I came here because of their psychology program. It's so different than home, but it's good to experience new things," he said with a wink, and I thought I might pass out right then and there.

"I would love to see Montana. I hear it's beautiful. I'll be here a while longer, though. After I graduate with my bachelor's degree in psychology this May, I plan to pursue my doctorate, and that'll take an additional four or five years to complete. Maybe after that I'll do some traveling," I said, taking another swig from my cup.

"Why did you choose psychology?" he asked, then smiled at me before taking another sip.

I paused for a moment, wondering how much to share with this stranger. He was so easy to talk to that I found myself answering all his questions without a filter.

"I believe I started having sleep issues when my parents died in a car accident, a couple years ago." I paused, thinking I shouldn't have gotten so personal already.

"That's so true, and I'm so sorry about your parents. That must have been so hard to deal with at that age," he said sympathetically as he gazed into my eyes. "My goal is to help people with mental health struggles. I hate that the subject of mental health is still taboo. It's just as important as physical health. I would really love to work with children and maybe try to tackle issues before they ruin the kids' lives," he said, his voice becoming more animated. There was a sparkle in his eyes that perfectly displayed his passion.

"Do you stay on campus?" I asked, putting my elbows on the table and leaning toward him.

"Yeah, I'm a resident advisor actually. I love mentoring the lowerclassmen. Plus, I get free housing in return for being an RA."

"Sounds interesting! I'm in a historic duplex in Old Town. It's so old, but I love living in a place with so much history and character. So many people have lived there over the years, living all sorts of different lives!" I said, then realized I had been rambling again. I couldn't help myself. The way he looked at me when I spoke made my heart melt.

I never would have imagined that a spilled purse and a cold brew would lead to a relationship, but that one chance meeting brought us together. It wasn't the most graceful start to a budding romance, but I am so glad we ran into each other. Literally.

He said my place was too far away from his early morning classes to stay with me. There's absolutely no way I would ever stay at *his* place too long. The smell of Axe body spray mixed with sweaty balls tends to stick in your nose for hours after leaving.

Even though we had our own places, things were great between us. We'd been together for two years and were planning for a future together. I just didn't know it would happen so soon.

It was August of last year, and I had just started my senior year at Loyola.

I sat on the toilet, staring at the two pink lines.

A wave of emotion swept through me as I realized the birth control pills had failed. I was pregnant.

I knew that Cameron would be supportive of me no matter what I decided to do, but my thoughts spiraled endlessly, a mix of disbelief, panic, and self-doubt.

How am I supposed to bring a child into this world when I struggle to keep my own mind together? Will my nightmares finally stop when she arrives? I didn't notice how dark and vivid they were until I found out I was pregnant.

Is there a spirit attached to me that is manipulating my dreams? Will the erratic sleep make me a bad mother? Should I even keep the baby? I've always wanted to be a mother, but is this the best time for that?

We hadn't been trying for a baby, not yet anyway, but we'd talked about it before, in those wistful, hypothetical "someday" conversations. I had known he wanted children eventually, but *eventually* wasn't now. So, when I sat him down to tell him, my heart felt like it might pound straight out of my chest.

We sat at my small kitchen table. He looked at me with those steady, deep blue eyes, his brow furrowed in concern. "What's wrong?" he asked, sensing my hesitation.

I looked up at him and put my hand on his. "I don't really know how to tell you this, so I'll just come out and say it." I took a deep breath and continued, "I just found out that I am pregnant."

His mouth fell open, and for a moment, he just stared, frozen in shock. But then tears welled up in his eyes, and a smile broke across his face like sunlight through clouds. He looked into my eyes and saw the worry and indecisiveness, and his smile faded.

"I don't know what I should do. I want to be a mother, but is right now a good time for that to happen?" I sobbed.

He placed his other hand on top of mine. "I will stand by you no matter what you decide. I know it will be a difficult journey, but I know we are strong enough to do it. I can start saving up money and move in with you as soon as I am able."

"Really? Do you want me to have the baby?" I said, my eyes lighting up.

"Ultimately, it's your decision, but yes. I would love that very much."

"It's just, I don't know. The due date will be right around the time of finals, and my research paper. What about my sleeping issues?" I said, in a regrettable whiny tone. I thought about how even people with normal sleep schedules struggled once a baby arrived.

"We can talk to the university about working around your finals schedule. I'm sure this happens a lot."

That's probably true. I can't be the first college senior to get pregnant. I'm probably not the first mother to have sleep issues either. Cam is right. He always is. I pondered my thoughts briefly. I can do this. We can do this! I love you, Cam," I said, as I wiped away my fresh tears. Then I exclaimed, "We are going to have a baby!"

"We're going to be parents!" he shouted. We both stood, and before I could say anything, he wrapped his arms around my waist and lifted me off the ground, spinning me in circles. "I'm going to be a dad!" he shouted, his voice full of so much joy that it brought tears to my own eyes.

When he finally set me down, he turned to Fat Joe, who was perched on the counter, watching us with his usual mix of curiosity and disdain. Cameron patted the cat on the head, grinning ear to ear. "You hear that, buddy? You're going to have a little brother or sister!"

Fat Joe, unimpressed, stretched lazily before placing his front paws on Cameron's chest. Without missing a beat, Cameron grabbed both of Joe's paws and started dancing with him, swaying back and forth. It was something they did all the time, a weird, goofy ritual that never failed to make me smile.

When Cameron finally turned back to me, his face was still alight with happiness, but there was a tenderness in his expression, too. He took my hands in his, his touch warm and reassuring. "I know this wasn't planned," he said, his voice steady. "But we can do this. We'll figure it out together. I'm here for you, no matter what."

He placed his hands on either side of my face and pulled me close, pressing my cheek against his chest. I could feel the steady rhythm of his heartbeat, grounding me, calming the storm of doubt inside me. He pulled back, still holding me by the shoulders, and looked at me. His tears hadn't fully dried, and his dark blue eyes sparkled with the kind of certainty I was still trying to find within myself. After getting that reaction from Cameron, the fear and anxiety calmed. I knew he would be with me every step of the way.

Fat Joe, however, had no patience for sentimentality. He pawed at us insistently from the coffee table, his way of demanding attention, and Cameron laughed as he scooped him up into his arms.

August seemed like ages ago as Cameron and I assembled the crib for the baby in my bedroom.

"Cam, can you stay the night tonight?" I asked as he was attaching the sliding gate to the base of the crib. "Please? My dreams are becoming more and more bizarre, even scary," I added.

"Yeah, I can. Your dreams have been worse than normal?" he asked, holding his hand out for me to hand him another screw.

"I thought it was stress from my senior year workload, upcoming finals, and being pregnant. When I finally drift off, my dreams are vivid—so vivid they don't seem like dreams at all. Recently, though, they've begun to change," I said.

He looked up from the crib to meet my eyes, "How so?"

"Well, for as long as I can remember, my dreams have been scary, more like nightmares. After my parents died, the theme became car crashes and death. Here lately, they are all about me being chased, held captive, and even... being sexually assaulted," I said in disgust.

"That's horrible!" he said loudly, sounding appalled.

"I had a nightmare last night about Fat Joe."

"What happened?" he asked, tightening the final screw.

I walked over and sat on the bed. "I was sitting in a chair inside a house I didn't recognize. A black and white cat came walking around the corner and sat in front of me. I thought it was Fat Joe at first, but the longer I looked, the more differences I spotted," I said.

Cam sat down beside me, listening intently.

I continued, "Instead of emerald, green eyes, they are bright

16

yellow. He's thin and skeletal, like a stray that's been starving for weeks. His ribs jut out under his fur, and his meows are weak, pitiful, almost like cries for help. It's unsettling seeing him that way. It feels wrong, like my subconscious is trying to warn me of something I don't understand," I said, getting emotional from frustration.

"I'm sure there's a doctor who will be able to help you with your sleep issues. Have you looked into a psychologist or psychoanalyst?" he asked with an encouraging tone, placing his arm around my shoulders.

My eyes caught sight of Fat Joe sauntering in and curling up in the crib Cameron had just finished assembling.

"I haven't. That's a good idea though. I've only been to general practitioners before," I said, feeling a little hopeful.

After we ate lunch, I picked up the phone book, flipping the pages until I found listings for psychoanalysts. I made up my mind I would go with the one who had the soonest availability. On my third call, I hit the jackpot. Dr. Wallace had an opening the next afternoon.

3

Sleep Disorder

Even with Cameron by my side, last night had been a sleepless one, and by four in the morning, I still wasn't tired. My eyes burned, and I could tell they were bloodshot. When I closed them, tears fell—though I wasn't crying—and it felt like the inside of my eyelids was brighter when they were shut than when they were open in that dark room. My body ached from lying in bed for hours, still unable to sleep, and there were no more sheep left to count.

Cameron got up early to go to class, leaving me with my thoughts. I was getting anxious about my doctor's appointment, and it couldn't come soon enough.

That afternoon, while sitting in a waiting room chair at the doctor's office, my hands resting on my pregnant belly, I fell asleep for just a moment. I had a nightmare.

I was walking down a dark alley downtown. The air was chilly and smelled of urine and rot. Homeless people were tucked into cardboard tents along the walls, their faces hidden in shadows. Then I heard footsteps—heavy, deliberate—and a voice shouting behind me. When I turned, a large, bald man in a leather jacket and gold chains was chasing me. He had a gun. I ran, but my feet were sinking into the pavement. Just as I tripped, he caught up to me. He raised his fist, and I found myself staring down the barrel, and then—

"Grace?"

I jolted awake, my heart pounding, my body trembling. The nurse was standing in front of me, clipboard in hand, calling my name. It took me a second to remember where I was. I glanced around the room. It was a typical, bland doctor's office, with abstract paintings on the wall, a fish tank, and a soothing instrumental CD playing.

It had been another dream. Even then, I couldn't shake the feeling that the dream had been trying to tell me something. But what?

It sounded ridiculous, but I couldn't shake the feeling that something, or someone, was watching me, in everyday life and in my nightmares. Maybe I've just seen too many ghost-hunting shows.

That was why I had come to see Dr. Wallace—another doctor in a long line of physicians I'd seen in an attempt to solve my sleep issues. It would be different this time, though, as he was a psychoanalyst who specialized in sleep disorders.

The nurse led me into the exam room, where I sat in an uncomfortable plastic chair and waited to meet my new doctor. Dr. Wallace entered the room with a clipboard tucked under his arm, pulling on a pair of thin, wire-rimmed reading glasses as he scanned my chart.

He was a kind-looking man with warm brown eyes, lanky in build and standing just over six feet tall. He appeared to be in his early fifties, with salt-and-pepper hair that was both unkempt and professional. His attire, which included a polka-dot bow tie and lab coat, gave him an eccentric Bill Nye the Science Guy vibe. I wanted to laugh at the resemblance, but I wasn't exactly in a laughing mood. I was so exhausted I couldn't even smile.

His glasses slid precariously down his nose, but he didn't seem to notice. His focus was on me, or, rather, on the words on his clipboard.

"It says here you've had trouble sleeping since childhood?" he asked, glancing up from the page.

I nodded. "Yes, I honestly can't remember a time I didn't have trouble. It's just always been... there. Some nights I do get sleep, but my dreams are so realistic, I just feel drained afterward."

His brow furrowed as he flipped through the papers. "You've tried cutting caffeine, avoiding blue light before bed, setting strict sleep schedules, and even medications." He spoke under his breath, as if talking more to himself than to me.

"Yes, that's right," I replied, already feeling the frustration rising. "Friends and family always told me it was just stress, or that I was too excited to sleep, but that's not it. Nothing works—I've tried everything I can think of, but nothing. I often wake up more exhausted than when I went to bed." My voice wavered, and I had to fight back the tears threatening to surface. "It's beyond frustrating. I feel trapped in my own body."

Dr. Wallace gave a small nod, his pen scratching across the page as he took notes. He didn't rush me or interrupt; he just let me talk.

"And now," I continued, "it's gotten worse. Ever since I found out I was pregnant, my dreams have been more vivid and frightening. They're not just dreams anymore. They feel... real. And very specific. Like they're trying to tell me something."

"Interesting," he murmured, jotting more notes. He turned to the next page of my file, clipped it back onto the clipboard, and kept writing, his glasses threatening to tumble off the tip of his nose. I found myself clinging to how he seemed to care and leaning into my words instead of dismissing them like many other doctors.

"Also, I'm having memory problems. Long term, mainly. I remember the basics, but I'm having trouble remembering any specific details of my past."

"Well, Grace, chronic lack of sleep can cause long-term memory problems. That's for sure."

Finally, he set the clipboard down and folded his hands in his lap. "Grace, based on what you've told me, you might *also* be experiencing perinatal depression. Insomnia is one of the psychiatric symptoms it can cause, though it can be difficult to say whether the insomnia is a symptom of depression or the cause of it. It's a bit of a vicious cycle."

I frowned. He was kind, but I could tell he didn't quite understand. "But that's the thing," I said. "I don't think anything caused my insomnia. It's always been there. The depression... that came later. If I could just get a good night's rest, I feel like everything else would fall into place."

He leaned back in his chair, considering my words. "I understand," he said. "It might help to think of it as your brain being stuck in a heightened state of excitement—a condition called Cortical Arousal. For most people, the brain needs to relax, to almost 'forget itself,' in order to fall asleep. Yours doesn't seem to do that. It's like your mind is stuck in overdrive. And you're right, dealing with Cortical Arousal could indeed induce depression. I have seen it many times."

There it was. A name for the thing that had plagued me my entire life. Cortical Arousal. It didn't sound like much, and it didn't feel like an answer. But at least it was something.

"Would that also cause hallucinations or visions?" I asked, then explained that I would catch shadowy figures out of the corner of my eye sometimes. "Sometimes, I feel like someone is watching me, even when I'm alone. I'll see a figure at the end of my bed, standing there and staring at me, but when I sit up, it's gone." It wasn't just my imagination. At least, I didn't think it was. What if it were a mental health issue? Or even something else—something *paranormal*, I thought.

"Sleep deprivation can cause that, and if your brain isn't shutting down properly, that would surely make hallucinations worse."

"So, you think all my issues are from lack of sleep, and my house isn't haunted by evil spirits who manipulate my dreams?" I chuckled and tried to sound like I was being sarcastic. But I wasn't.

He looked at me blankly.

I pondered the idea, but the explanation didn't sit right with me. My facial expression must have given me away. Dr. Wallace examined my face and then continued.

"There isn't exactly a cure for Cortical Arousal," he said, "but there are strategies to help manage the symptoms. Have you tried journaling?"

"Journaling?" I asked, caught off guard. "Like... keeping a diary?"

"Yes. Specifically, I want you to write down your dreams. Every detail you can remember, no matter how strange or insignificant it may seem. Keep track of emotions, familiar faces, places, smells, and the weather. Anything. Dreams often reflect what's going on in the subconscious mind. In fact, write about your everyday life, starting with your early memories. Don't be shy—write an autobiography. Constant journaling might help us uncover patterns or triggers that we can work on together."

"I don't understand how this is going to help," I admitted. "What if it's just another thing that doesn't work? What if writing down my dreams only makes things worse—what if it brings up things I've forgotten for a reason?"

He smiled a crooked smile, "And it may do just that. Since you've tried every conventional method in the book, we need to look at the unconventional. Don't be afraid of the fear. If it brings up past traumas, the only way to get over the trauma is to identify it and face it. We'll start with this, and if it doesn't work, we'll try something else. You're not alone in this, Grace," he said, ushering me toward the door. "Bring your journal to our next appointment in two weeks, and we'll go from there."

"You're right. I'll give it a try. I have to try."

When I got home, I stared at the notebook for a long time. I love creative writing, but journaling seemed like a chore, another item on the endless list of things that didn't work. But what if he was right? What if it did work? What if my dreams were trying to tell me something? I was desperate enough to try anything, even this. I had never tried journaling about my dreams before. The thought of it was both intriguing and terrifying.

I bought a new, beautiful, gold-edged journal with a faux leather cover [MΠ17] and placed it on my nightstand alongside a heavy, metal-barreled ink pen. There's something about fresh, high-quality writing supplies that makes me feel capable of anything. This will be the journal that I use to document everything, my life so far, and my dreams. At least until I see Dr. Wallace again or complete my research paper.

That night, I opened the journal and started with the basics.

February 28, 1998

Well, this is different. I haven't written in a diary since I was in middle school, but here goes: My life isn't particularly extraordinary. Not that I can remember anyway.

The details are fuzzy, like looking at a photograph that was left out in the sun too long. I can see the outline of a happy life, but so many pieces are missing. I had a happy childhood—or at least, that's what I always tell myself. The memories are blurred like pages of an old, well-loved book smudged by too many hands. I can trace the broad strokes of a joyful story, but the details, the sharp edges of faces, and specific events have faded with time.

I remember playing with other kids, but their names and faces felt like characters in a story I once loved, slipping away into abstractions. My past feels less like a life I have lived and more like a novel I read long ago—its plot clear, but its characters reshaped by every new reader who imagines them differently.

I knew I wanted to go to Loyola University Chicago for their psychology program, even though I knew it would be difficult to get in and hard to afford. Thankfully, my parents had been saving for college since the day I was born, and I was fortunate enough to land a job at sixteen at the local grocery store to help pay my way.

Loyola offers the PsyD program as well, which makes me so happy because I love it here!

The dreams leave me shaken, but I try not to dwell on them. Instead, I focus on what's real—Cameron's steady presence, the tiny flutters of life inside me, the hope that maybe, just maybe, I'll figure out how to be the mother this child deserves.

Fat Joe is curled up on my lap now as I write this, purring contentedly, oblivious to everything on my mind. I run my fingers through his fur and watch his tail flick back and forth, and for a moment, the world feels a little less overwhelming.

We're all about to face big changes—me, Cameron, Fat Joe, and the baby girl who will be here soon. And even though I'm scared, I'm also ready. Or at least, I'm trying to be. One day, one moment, one heartbeat at a time.

The next morning, I woke up on the couch with the journal clutched to my chest. My eyes snapped open as I heard shuffling. Cam was standing in front of me, holding a paper bag in one hand and a cold brew in the other. He sat down next to me.

"Morning, sunshine," he said, setting the cold brew on the coffee table. I sat upright, and he handed me the paper bag.

'Thank you," I said, opening the bag and getting a whiff of

the warm blueberry muffin.

"Did you stay on the couch all night?"

"Yeah, I must have fallen asleep after journaling last night," I forced out. My voice was groggy.

"Do you think that it's helping at all?"

"I don't know if it is helping with my nightmares, but it feels good to get my thoughts down onto paper and out of my head," I said, and took a bite out of the top of the muffin. I paused to think as I ate. "Do you think this duplex could be haunted?" I asked then, wiping crumbs off my mouth with the back of my hand. I tucked my toes under him for warmth.

He gave me a crooked smile. "I've never heard about a ghost haunting just your dreams," he said seriously. He scratched his chin while he pondered the idea. "I'm no ghost hunter, though. Are there any strange happenings besides the nightmares?"

"Every now and then, I swear I can see a figure out of the corner of my eye," I said, trying to sound convincing and not crazy. Cameron and I watched ghost-hunting shows for fun, but I wasn't sure if he truly believed in spirits. "Do you believe in ghosts, Cam?"

"I don't really know. I am open to the idea, though," he said after thinking for a moment.

"Everything I have researched has suggested that the soul is separate from the corporal body, which is why, though it may seem ridiculous, I do believe in ghosts," I said with sincerity. "Of course, I don't know what happens when we die or why a soul would choose to stay here and haunt a college girl," I added with a chuckle.

"You should investigate the history of the place. You know?

For obvious things like murders or suicides," he said, sounding more excited now. "Maybe there is a spirit trying to ask for help through your dreams."

"I would love to, but I'm not sure where to even begin!" I said in exasperation and stuffed the last of the muffin into my mouth.

"I'll help. It will be a fun Saturday adventure!" Cam exclaimed, jumping up from the couch. And with that, we were off to the courthouse and library to find anything we could about the old place.

4

Collision

After a week of searching for information about the duplex, we turned up nothing. There had been no deaths, natural or unnatural, and my nightmares and erratic sleep had not eased up one bit. It had been a week since I saw Dr. Wallace, and I had one more week to go before my follow-up appointment.

I got into the habit of journaling throughout the day. I carried the journal with me wherever I went. Even before I had seen Dr. Wallace, I started researching the link between the conscious and the unconscious mind, hoping it might give me a clue as to why I had erratic sleep issues. So, when Professor Nielson announced that we had a semester-long research paper, due at finals, I knew what topic I wanted.

Everyone always said to "write what you know," and if that's true, I was an expert on insomnia and other sleep-related problems.

I spent countless hours this semester at the historic downtown library, reading all kinds of books. Of course, I didn't limit myself to just psychology texts; I tried to think outside of the box, way outside. So, honestly, journaling about my dreams would fit swimmingly into my research paper, too. Two birds, one stone, as the saying goes.

My thoughts were all over the place. I needed to write down my theory to try to make sense of it. After making myself some tea, I sat down on the deep, fluffy couch, opened my journal, and began to write.

March 15, 1998

I don't suffer from insomnia. Instead, my mind stays active because another part of me—my soul, or perhaps my consciousness—is using it. This makes me feel like I haven't slept at all because my brain is still wide awake, going to different places, and exploring. I call myself an 'Intra' for in-between because while my body is asleep, my mind and consciousness are not. They are fully awake and aware. The idea is both terrifying and exhilarating. If it's true, then my sleep issues might have a purpose—but what does it mean for my waking life? Am I even in control?

There's an ongoing debate about whether consciousness resides within the soul or whether they are the same. For simplicity, I refer to it as my soul. If you believe in life after death, then you probably believe your soul leaves your body when you die and either goes to Heaven or Hell. While I'm not sure if Heaven and Hell are real, I do believe the soul leaves the body and continues for eternity after the body dies. I'm just not sure what happens to it.

I've been seeing a large, bald man with a gun in my dreams. Do I know him from somewhere? Was he in a mobster movie I saw when I was younger? I just can't place where I know his face from.

When I'm not being chased by that man, I'm usually dreaming of being in a car accident. I'll be driving in my dream, and headlights will come out of nowhere, veer into my lane, and we hit head-on. I wake up in a panic, drenched in sweat, my heart beating out of my chest. I don't have any memories of being in a car accident. I have no idea where these dream themes are coming from.

Something I don't understand is waiting for me there, in that nightmare realm. I'm not sure if it's a part of me or something else altogether. But I know this: whatever it is, it's just waiting for me to notice.

I closed the journal just in time to see Cam walking through the door.

"How was your day, sweet pea?" he asked happily, grinning from ear to ear.

"It was good. I went to the library and got a couple more books for my paper, then went to the gym to walk on the treadmill a while. Then I came home, ate lunch, and started writing," I said smiling up at him. "How was yours?"

"I ordered my cap and gown today! I can't believe the semester is almost up," he said with excitement. "Hey, have you eaten? I'm starving."

"Not since lunch. I lost track of time actually," I said looking at my watch, and realizing it was going on seven-thirty in the evening.

Cam sauntered into the kitchen. I heard clanging pots, running water, and a knife slicing on a cutting board. After a few moments he brought a glass of wine and a plate full of cheese, crackers, and deli meats.

"The appetizer, ma'am," he said handing me the wine, placing the plate on the coffee table, then disappearing back into the kitchen. I opened one of the books I was reading by Carl Jung while I waited. All the while, I could hear him in there whistling a happy little tune. I was fully engrossed in my book and had just finished stuffing a cracker with cheese into my mouth when he returned to the living room. He handed me a bowl of shrimp linguini and sat down. My mouth began to water at the sight and smell of it.

Fat Joe jumped up on the couch and was sprawled between us, purring like a miniature freight train. After we ate, I brought up my latest research, wanting to get his opinion. He had just taken a gulp of pink Moscato.

"Cam, do you ever think about the connection between the body and the soul?" I asked, fiddling with the pen in my hand.

Placing his wine glass down on the table beside him He raised an eyebrow. "Only every other Tuesday. Why? Is this for your paper?"

"Sort of." I pulled my legs up under me, trying not to disturb Fat Joe, who seemed downright offended by the movement. "I've been thinking about how the mind works as a bridge between the two. Like... our souls are our true essence, right? The part of us that's eternal. But our bodies are just... vessels. Temporary housing, you know?"

Cam picked up his wine glass again and angled his body toward me "Okay, Socrates. I'm listening," he said grinning.

I rolled my eyes but smiled, glad he was humoring me. "So,

when we sleep, I think the tether between the body and soul loosens. That's why we dream. Our souls are free to explore other realms. Maybe even other dimensions."

He tilted his head, the corners of his mouth quirking up. "That's an interesting take. But dreams could just be random brain activity, right? Synapses firing off while your body rests?"

"Maybe for most people." I shifted, leaning forward. "But not for me. My dreams don't feel random. They're vivid, like I'm actually there. Sometimes, they even pick up where they left off, as if they were never interrupted. It's like I'm awake in two different worlds," I said, my face and hands becoming animated.

Cameron nodded; his expression thoughtful. "Okay, so you're saying you're... what? Special?" he asked as he finished his wine and sat it on the coffee table.

"Not special." I hesitated, searching for the right word. "Aware. I call myself an Intra—like 'in-between.' I think some people have this ability to exist on two levels of awareness, awake and asleep."

He leaned back, crossing his arms. "Intra, huh? I like it. But how do you know you're not just lucid dreaming?"

"I thought about that," I admitted. "But it's more than that. In lucid dreams, you can control what happens, right? This is different. It's like... I'm a visitor in another world. I'm not in control of what happens—I'm just along for the ride. And there's something about it that feels bigger than just me. Like it's not just my mind creating it. It's... external."

Cameron's brow furrowed. "Have you ever thought about astral projection?"

I blinked at him, surprised. "You know about that?"

"Of course, I do," he grinned. "I'm a psychology major, not a caveman. I had a client during my internship who swore she could do it. She believed her soul could leave her body and travel wherever she wanted while she slept."

I sat up straighter. "Yes! That's what I'm talking about. It's not just a theory, it's something people experience. And there are so many stories out there, accounts of out-of-body experiences that line up with this idea. I've read so many accounts of people who swear they can go to other locations. Then, when their physical body wakes up, they can describe where they were."

Cameron reached over and placed a hand on mine. "Sounds like you're onto something. Sort of like a near-death experience. I heard about one where a patient was on an operating table, and their heart stopped. Their consciousness, or soul, or whatever you want to call it, separated and rose from their body. Not only did they see their body lying there, but they heard specific conversations the doctor and nurses were having. They were also able to describe some items that were sitting on top of a high shelf. They would have no way of seeing this item from the operating table or even a standing position."

"Those stories, of course, can't be proven. But there are so many, I feel like they have to be true," I said, almost in a pout.

"Don't put too much pressure on yourself to find answers. Especially since these things can't be proven scientifically," Cam said with a smile.

I sighed, glancing at Fat Joe, who let out a soft, sleepy "mrrp," as if to chime in. "I mean, I have that psychology paper that I have to finish, anyway. I figured if my research for that helps me understand what's happening to me, then all the better."

Cam nodded. "What did the new doctor say?"

"That I might have something called Cortical Arousal, which means my brain has a hard time shutting down. He thinks that I am having nightmares, memory problems, and hallucinations because I am simply sleep deprived."

"He might be right. Lack of sleep can do crazy things to the mind."

"He asked me to start journaling about my life and my dreams. On my next visit, we will go over it together. Maybe my dreams are trying to tell me something," I said, musing and finishing off my wine.

"Could be," Cam said pensively. "Or it could be just as you say, your soul or consciousness is leaving your body and goes exploring. That would mean that your brain doesn't fully shut down."

"I just feel like the truth is right there, just out of reach. If I could understand what's happening in my dreams, maybe I could make sense of... everything else." I said, trying to hold back a yawn. "So, do you think I could be just astral projecting without realizing it?"

Cameron squeezed my hand. "It's possible, but it's also hard to know for sure. You'll figure it out. You always do. But don't forget to take care of yourself in the process, even *Intras* need sleep."

I laughed; the sound lighter than I felt. "You're right. I should probably write this down before I forget."

Cameron smiled and kissed the top of my head. "That's my girl. You and your fancy journals. Don't stay up too late, okay? Your brain needs rest, too." He said, standing up and stretching.

He turned back, grabbed the wine glasses, and walked into the kitchen. I stood up and reached for my gold-edged journal, ready to capture the thoughts swirling in my mind. But before I could write anything down, shadows were forming just outside my vision. For a split second, the glow of my desk lamp morphed into two bright headlights, as if a car was heading straight for me, and I felt the sharp, terrifying jolt of an impending collision.

I gasped and stumbled backward, landing hard on the floor. My chest heaved as I struggled to make sense of what had just happened. There was no car, no accident. Just the lamp. But the vision was so real. *Too* real.

Cameron was by my side in an instant, his face a mask of concern. "Are you okay? What happened?"

"I... I don't know." My voice trembled. "I thought I saw... headlights. Like a car was coming straight at me." I said, staring straight ahead.

His hands found my shoulders, grounding me. "Hey, it's okay. You're safe. It was probably just the light messing with your eyes. Have you been sleeping at all lately?"

I shook my head, tears pricking my eyes. The look of worry on his face broke my heart. "Not enough. Dr. Wallace said I needed more rest, but every time I try, the nightmares... they're worse. And now this... What if I'm losing it?"

There was no car. My mind was racing. I have never been in a car accident, so what made me feel like I was about to crash? What is going on with me? I stayed seated on the floor for a few moments, stunned at what had just happened.

"You're not losing it," Cameron said sternly. "You're exhausted. That's all. Come on, let's get you off the floor."

He helped me to my feet, and I sank into the couch, cradling Fat Joe in my arms. Cameron sat beside me, his arm around my shoulders, and I felt a flicker of safety in his presence.

"Maybe you should write this down," he muttered, nodding toward my journal. "Dr. Wallace said it might help you make sense of it, right?" Cam asked as he stood and held out his hand toward me.

I nodded, wiping my eyes. "Yeah. Maybe it will,"

I took hold of his outstretched hand, picked up my pen, and stood. Cameron stayed by my side, his quiet strength steadying me. Even in the chaos of my mind, I wasn't alone. And for now, that was enough.

Cameron walked me up the stairs, his hand steady on the small of my lower back as Fat Joe trailed behind, his tail swaying. The house was quiet, the kind of quiet that made each step on the hardwood seem louder than it should have been. Upstairs, the shadows seemed heavier, stretching long and thin across the walls as though reluctant to settle. I told myself it was just the dim glow of the hallway night light, but something about the way they lingered made me shiver.

When we reached my room, Cameron paused in the doorway, his broad frame filling the space. Fat Joe slipped inside without hesitation, hopping onto my bed with an audible *thump* before curling up into his usual spot near the pillows. Cameron gave a small chuckle as he sat on the bed, his hand brushing the cat's fur absently.

"Go brush your teeth," he waved his hand towards the bathroom. "I'll hold down the fort."

I smiled, grateful for his presence, and stepped into the bathroom. I saw my face in the mirror. My eyes were shadowed, the faint smudges beneath them standing out starkly against my pale skin. I splashed cold water on my face before brushing my teeth, letting the mechanical rhythm calm me. Even so, a faint itch of unease lingered at the back of my mind. *What trauma did I experience that was so horrible, I made myself forget?*

When I returned to the bedroom, Cameron was stretched out on the bed, one arm draped lovingly over Fat Joe. The cat purred deeply, his compact little body vibrating with the sound. Cameron glanced up at me and grinned. "Ready to get all tucked in for bed, kiddo? I know I am!" he teased.

I rolled my eyes, but the warmth in his voice eased some of the tension I hadn't realized I was holding. "Will you stay the night?" I pleaded and batted my eyelashes.

"I can't tonight. I have an early morning," he said sympathetically.

"Then get out of my bed!" I said playfully.

"Alright, alright." He sat up. He tucked me in with exaggerated care, pulling the blanket up to my chin before leaning down to press a gentle kiss onto my forehead. "I'll lock up on my way out," he murmured, his voice dropping into a whisper. "Call me if you need anything, okay?"

"I will." My voice was soft, almost childlike, but I meant it. His presence was always like an anchor, keeping me steady when the rest of the world spun too fast. "I love you, Cam," I added, the words slipping out like a sigh.

"I love you, too." His smile was so familiar, so Cameron, that it filled the room with a fleeting sense of normalcy. He turned to Fat Joe, giving the cat a fond pat. "Goodnight, Joe Boy. Be good for her, alright?"

Fat Joe purred in response, his tail curling around himself as he formed a compact ball. Cameron stood, winked at me, and slipped out of the room, closing the door behind him. I heard his footsteps retreat down the stairs, the faint click of lights being turned off one by one, and then the soft *snick* of the front door locking.

For a moment, the house felt extremely large without him. I glanced at my journal on the nightstand, its gold-edged pages catching the light from the moon peaking in between the curtains. The hallucination of the car crash encouraged me to begin the task of journaling my dreams. This was going to be the first night that I documented everything for my research paper, and my peace of mind. I ran my fingers over the cover and made a silent promise: *I will write everything down. Every thought, every feeling, every emotion. It's all going in this journal.*

My first hour of trying to sleep was restless. I tossed and turned, trying to find that sweet spot of comfort in the tangled sheets. My mind refused to quiet. Exhaustion slammed on me like a weight, as though gravity had doubled in strength, pulling me deep into the mattress. My eyelids fluttered closed, but every time I tried to surrender to sleep, something unseen forced them open again.

And yet, even when my eyes were shut, I could *see*. The surrounding room appeared as clear as if it were bathed in daylight, every corner and shadow rendered in stark detail. I tried to tell myself it was just my mind playing tricks, some half-dream conjured by exhaustion, but the vividness of it unsettled me. Time crawled by in that half-sleep state until the glowing red numbers of my alarm clock whispered four-thirty in the morning.

As I lay there with my eyes closed—or open? I couldn't even tell anymore—I began to "look" around. The room was just as it should have been. The dresser cluttered with books and papers, the curtains slightly ajar, letting in the faintest sliver of moonlight. But my gaze soon rested on the bedroom door, and unease prickled at the back of my neck.

I was certain Cam had closed it before leaving, but now it was wide open. The blackness beyond the doorway should have been impenetrable at this hour, but instead, an impossibly bright light spilled in. It wasn't the soft glow of moonlight or even the warm hues of dawn—it was something else entirely.

I sat up in bed, my heart thudding once against my ribs before an odd calm washed over me, smothering my fear. I stood and stepped toward the door. The light grew brighter with every step, blinding and overwhelming, but I couldn't stop myself from moving closer. My feet were weightless, as though the floor beneath me was no longer solid.

When I reached the threshold, something made me glance back. My breath hitched. There I was, still lying on the bed, motionless. My body was so small, so far away, and yet I didn't panic. Instead, an unfamiliar thought rose to the surface: *this is right, this needs to be explored.*

I turned back toward the doorway and stepped through.

5

The Beach

Warmth engulfed me immediately, wrapping around me like a familiar embrace. The cool stillness of my bedroom dissolved, and my feet sank into something soft and warm. I glanced down, startled to find myself barefoot, my toes buried in golden grains of sand that were hot to the touch.

The scent of salt hit me first, carried on a gentle breeze that tugged at my hair. I froze, inhaling deeply. It was so achingly familiar, like a long-forgotten memory brought to life. My heart swelled as I realized where I was—or at least where I seemed to be.

Daytona Beach, Florida. It was a regular vacation spot I'd been to as a child. I had happy memories here, but some were not so happy, though they all seemed fuzzy and far away.

I looked up. The brightness of the sun made me wince and shield my eyes. Eventually, my vision adjusted, and the scene sharpened. The vast, glittering expanse of the ocean stretched out before me, its waves rolling lazily to the shore. The sound of them crashing against the sand was rhythmic, soothing, like a beating heart.

It was brighter, sharper, *more real* than I remembered, or than anything I'd ever seen before. The colors seemed to pulse with life, as though they might reach out and pull me into them.

The beach was alive with people. Their voices blended into a symphony of laughter, chatter, and the rhythmic smack of volleyballs being spiked across nets. Some faces were distantly familiar—people I thought I knew but couldn't quite place. Others were strangers, smiling, oblivious to the fact that they were in a different dimension from the one I had just come from. The sunlight reflected off the ocean, scattering shards of light like tiny diamonds.

Everyone around me was dressed for the beach—bikinis, swim trunks, sunglasses perched on noses or pushed up into messy, sun-kissed hair. Their bright swimsuits caught the sun, vibrant against the golden sand.

I glanced down at myself, suddenly aware of how out of place I looked. A school bag hung off my shoulder, heavy and worn. My jeans were frayed at the hems, rolled a bit at the ankles, and I held a pair of cheap, red flip-flops in my hand. The Led Zeppelin T-shirt I wore was faded, the letters cracked and peeling from years of wear. Not exactly beachwear.

Still, there was something... wrong. Something out of place, beyond my clothes. I caught a glimpse of myself reflected in the mirrored lenses of a passing man's sunglasses. I still looked like me, but not *me*. My face was paler, almost sickly. My body was thin, not in a healthy way, but frail. My heart twisted as I peered at the unfamiliar version of myself, and I turned away, the man with the sunglasses continuing without a second glance.

I looked down at my body. My skin was stretched over a

frail frame. The bones were protruding on my arms. And then I saw them—the cuts. They crisscrossed my wrists, jagged and red. What had happened to me? Where had they come from? There seemed to be old scars and fresh ones. They were painful to the touch. I didn't know if I had ever felt pain in a dream before.

The sun was heavy overhead, its heat pressing down on me, causing beads of sweat to form on my forehead. My hair clung to the back of my neck, slick with sweat, and I wiped my forehead, beads of moisture rolling down my temples. The air was so thick with humidity, like trying to breathe underwater. Everything around me—the sand, the breeze, the distant smell of salt and sunscreen—was too vivid, too real. It didn't feel like a dream.

I made my way toward the water; the waves pulling me in like a silent invitation. The last time I'd stepped into the ocean, I'd nearly drowned. I happened during one of our vacations.

The memory hit me like a slap. The water was unforgiving, snatching me under and dragging me farther and farther from the shore. Salt stung my eyes; the pressure crushing my chest, the way my arms flailed uselessly against the current. I screamed, but the ocean swallowed the sound and left me alone in its vast, suffocating embrace. I never knew how I'd made it back.

Now, the waves appeared calm, rolling rhythmically onto the shore. They didn't look dangerous; they seemed inviting. I rolled up my jeans, hesitating only for a moment before stepping into the shallows. The water was cool and soothing against my hot, sticky skin, and I waded in just to my knees. Tiny waves licked at my legs, and I took a big breath in. I longed to feel the calm of it all. The way the ocean sounded, and the light glimmered off its reflection, was relaxing, but I just could not relax.

I glanced around at the people scattered along the beach. A group of college kids nearby laughed as they crafted a life-sized naked woman out of sand. They added exaggerated curves to her figure and gave her a seashell bra, posing proudly beside her for photos.

Further down the shore, two children were locked in a heated argument over a sand bucket. The boy, wearing green swimming trunks, yanked it out of the girl's hands. She stood frozen for a moment, her waist heaving as she burst into tears. Her wails were sharp, piercing the air like tiny daggers. They couldn't have been older than six, their argument as dramatic and fleeting as only children's arguments could be.

I turned back to the water, my feet sinking slightly into the wet sand with each step. Something hard but oddly soft pressed against my toes, stopping me in my tracks. I knelt, brushing the sand away with my hands, my fingers trembling with anticipation. As I uncovered it, my breath hitched.

It was a face. A man's face, partially buried in the sand, his features contorted in an expression of terrible anger. His lips were twisting into a snarl, then his brow furrowed, and his eyes closed as though he were holding in a scream. I had dreamt about this man before, in the doctor's office.

Before I could fully process what I was seeing, something cold clamped around my wrists.

Pale, bloated hands gripped me with unnatural strength.

The skin was discolored, a sickly shade of gray blue, like the hands of something that had been underwater for too long.

I gasped, stumbling back, but the hands yanked me forward. I felt weak, my legs buckled, and before I could scream, I was pulled down to the water. My knees hit the sand, and then the waves swallowed me whole. Salt stung my lips. Water filled my nose and mouth as I fought to breathe.

My lungs burned as I struggled against the hands that were pulling me deeper. My nose was nearly touching his. His breath smelled like death. My nails scraped against the wrists that held me, but they didn't loosen. I thrashed, pulled, and kicked. Above me, the sunlight dimmed, growing fainter and fainter as the hands continued to pull me. A wave rolled in and swallowed my head as his hands held me close.

And then, just as the edges of my vision began to darken, everything vanished.

The hands were gone.

I coughed and sputtered, my knees digging into the sand as I clawed at the ground. There was no sign of the face in the sand, no hands, no struggle. Just the calm waves, rolling gracefully onto the shore as though nothing had happened.

A shadow fell over me, and I glanced up to see the little girl in the pink bathing suit standing in front of me. Her tear-streaked face was one of concern. Her small hands clasped nervously in front of her. "Are you okay?" she asked with a whimper. I almost couldn't hear her over the sound of the waves.

I opened my mouth to respond, but no words came. My chest still heaved, my pulse still raced, and I felt the sand beneath my fingers. I took a deep breath. *This is a dream. That's all. Just a dream.* Staggering to my feet, my knees wobbled beneath me, the world tilting at an unnatural angle. My vision narrowed to a pinprick; the edges swallowed by creeping darkness. Muffled sounds drifted to me—footsteps? Voices? Or was that just the pounding of my pulse?

Ahead, I saw a park bench a few feet away. In my current state, it seemed like miles.

It had the feeling of my typical dreams where I am being chased, but no matter how fast or far I ran, whatever or whoever was always right on my heels. And of course, I could see the exit sign right ahead, but I couldn't ever make it there. This was how it felt as I struggled to get to the bench.

Finally, I made my way over to it and sat down, but then in a blink, everything went black.

6

Limitless

And then I woke up.

I jolted up to a sitting position and looked down. I was in my bed. I held my arms out and stared at my wrists. They were just fine. My heart was pounding so hard I could hear it in my ears as my head throbbed. Morning sunlight filled my room, and I was relieved that the nightmare was over. That's all it was—a nightmare.

The alarm was blaring, and I knew I was safe in my bed. The soft feather pillow was beneath my head, and I heard the faint rustle of the feathers shifting inside. My toes brushed against the sheets, cool and silky, a small comfort in the stillness of the morning. My hair draped across my neck, offering just enough warmth to keep the chill away.

It felt as though I'd only just laid my head down, drifting off for maybe ten or fifteen minutes. But when I glanced at the clock, it was already eight in the morning. The alarm had been going off for thirty minutes, its insistent beeps ignored. So much for waking up early and pulling myself together—I was definitely heading to class looking like a bum. I slammed my hand down on the cancel button on the alarm clock. As I climbed out of bed, I thought about the dream, or whatever it was. The vividness of it haunted me, lingering at the corners of my mind like a half-remembered melody. I picked up my journal and wrote as much as I could remember from the dream.

March 16, 1998

It felt so real. I could feel the sand, smell the salty air, and feel the hot sunshine on my face. I had cuts on my wrists, but no clue what happened. Who was the man in the sand? I couldn't see his body, or even the rest of his head, just a face and hands. I just realized his face was the same as the one I dreamed was chasing me when I was at Dr. Wallace's office, but I still don't know who he is.

I forced myself to leave the warmth of my comfortable bed and head into the bathroom to get ready.

I slipped into a dress and flats, then stood in front of the mirror to do my hair. I picked up my brush and began to detangle my long hair. There's something about mirrors that unsettled me. It's as if they forced me to confront myself. They made me look deeper, as if they demanded to know who I really was. If I stared too long, I almost didn't recognize the person staring back. The feeling made me uncomfortable, especially when I didn't recognize myself. Maybe I was the only one who felt that way; I didn't know.

I set my brush down, holding my gaze for a moment longer before turning away. I finished getting ready, gave Fat Joe some belly rubs, grabbed a bagel, and headed out the door.

It was fall, and the air had a crisp chill to it—not cold, but brisk. I climbed into the driver's side of my sedan, pulled the seatbelt over my growing belly, and sped off toward the campus. After searching for what felt like an eternity, I finally found a parking spot, one that seemed a mile away, but, surprisingly, I was still on time.

The campus was vast but beautiful, and the professors there were always knowledgeable and supportive. One in particular, Ella Nielson, a kind and quirky woman, had been an immense help with my research. I walked about a half-mile to the psychology building and into her office for our appointment.

As I entered her office, she stood to greet me and offered me a seat across from hers. As I sat, I handed her a copy of my paper, which she skimmed through. "Your paper's fascinating," Professor Nielson said, glancing up from the draft. Her thick tortoiseshell glasses were perched precariously on the tip of her nose, and her keen gray eyes fixed on me over the rims. "But you keep referring to this other realm as 'limitless.' I wonder—what happens when something limitless turns against you?"

I frowned, caught off guard. "What do you mean?"

"Well, now..." She leaned back in her chair and tapped her pen against the paper. "You describe this 'other realm'—this dream world, this... What did you call it? The space where the tether between the body and soul loosens?"

"Yes." I was leaning forward onto my elbows, both intrigued and nervous about where she was going.

"You describe it as expansive, unbound by the laws of physics or time. Limitless," she continued. "But limitless things can be dangerous, don't you think? A limitless ocean can drown you. A limitless sky can leave you stranded, directionless. Limitless space can swallow you whole. What makes you think this realm you're so fascinated by is safe?"

I blinked, my heart sinking. I hadn't thought of it like that. My research, my *theory*, was supposed to give meaning to my insomnia, to the vivid dreams that haunted me. I thought about the beach in my last dream. The waves were rolling in, and then the angry face in the sand, staring at me, and the hands dragging me under. "I guess I assumed..." I began, but I wasn't sure how to finish the sentence. I hadn't assumed it was safe, had I?

Professor Nielson tilted her head, watching me intently. Her dark gray eyes were magnified by her lenses. "Don't get me wrong," she said, her tone softening. "I think you're onto something important here. This concept of 'Intras' you've been developing—people whose consciousness remains active even while they sleep—it's unique. But I wonder if you're focusing too much on the *freedom* of it and not enough on the *consequences*. You say it's a realm waiting to be explored. But have you stopped to consider what might already be *there*, waiting for you?"

Her words made me shiver. I forced a small laugh to cover my discomfort. "It's just a theory." I was trying to sound casual. "I haven't truly gone on any grand adventures to prove it."

"Haven't you?" she asked, lifting a brow. "You've written about how real your dreams feel, how vivid they are, how the timelines and story seem to continue the next time you dream. Isn't that exactly what an 'adventure' in this other realm would feel like?"

I opened my mouth to argue but hesitated. She wasn't

wrong. My dreams *did* feel like adventures, in a way—but they were also exhausting, terrifying. They didn't feel like something I *chose*. "I don't know if I'd call it an adventure," I admitted. "It's more like... I'm being pulled there, whether I want to go or not."

Professor Nielson leaned forward again, resting her elbows on the desk. Her expression grew serious, and her voice lowered. "Grace, let me ask you something," she pushed the glasses up farther on her nose. "When you're in this realm, do you feel like you're in control?"

I hesitated, my stomach tightening. "No," I admitted. "Not really. Usually, it feels like I'm just... along for the ride."

She nodded knowingly, as though that was exactly the answer she'd been expecting. "That's what concerns me. You call it limitless. You call it free. But if you're not in control, Grace, then who, or what, *is*?"

A chill ran through me, and for a moment, I felt like I couldn't breathe. Her words conjured images from my dreams—the face in the sand, glaring at me, the hands dragging me under the water, relentless and unyielding. I thought of the shadows that lingered at the edge of my vision when I was awake and the headlights hallucination that had sent me sprawling to the floor.

"I don't know." My voice was just above a whisper. "I hadn't thought about it like that."

Professor Nielson gave me a small, almost apologetic smile. "It's not my intention to scare you," she peered over the frames of her glasses at me, "but as a researcher—and as someone who's living this experience—you have to be prepared for all possibilities. If this other realm is truly limitless, as you say, then it's not just a place for you to explore. It's also a place where you can get *lost*. And if you're not careful, it might not let you leave."

Her words hung in the air between us, heavy and foreboding. I glanced down at the draft of my paper on her desk, the black ink on white paper.

"Do you think I should stop?" I asked, my voice beginning to quiver. "Stop researching this? Stop thinking about it? Maybe I'm just making it worse."

She studied me for a moment, her gaze softening. "That's not for me to say. But I do think you should proceed with caution. Curiosity is a powerful thing, Grace. It's what makes us human. But it can also lead us down paths we're not ready for."

I nodded, trying to process her words, but my mind was spinning. For the rest of the meeting, I had trouble focusing on what she said. Her warning echoed in my head, mingling with the fragments of dreams and fears I couldn't shake. *What happens when something limitless turns against you?* The question lingered, gnawing at the fringes of my mind, as I gathered my things and left her office.

As I walked across campus, the bright afternoon sunlight seemed too harsh, the shadows too sharp. For the first time, I felt like the world around me wasn't quite real—like I was still caught somewhere between waking and dreaming. And I wondered if I wanted to know the answers I was searching for— or if the truth would be something I couldn't escape.

7

Premonition?

After class, I met up with Cameron, and we dined at a wonderful Italian restaurant. While we waited for our food to arrive, he reached for my hand and gestured toward the spacious dance floor as the music played softly in the background. His grin widened when I took his hand, stood up, and followed him onto the floor.

There were three other couples, but it felt like the entire world had shrunk to just the two of us. The music was beautiful, made even better by the soft chatter of voices, the laughter around us, and the clink of dishes and silverware.

As we danced, I was aware of the bustling restaurant, but all I could see was him, and I knew he only had eyes for me. I lay my head on his shoulder while we danced to the rhythm. His soft hand caressed my neck, and the other rested on the small of my back; at least the best he could get around my belly. He's an amazing dancer. Me, not so much—but I danced anyway, just to make him happy. And I truly enjoyed it.

Afterward, we sat back at our table. The restaurant was quieter now, the gentle clink of silverware and the murmur of conversation fading into the background. Cameron sat across from me, watching my fork idly twirling spaghetti. I hadn't taken a bite yet, I just stared at the plate, lost in thought.

"What are you thinking about?" he asked tentatively, breaking the silence. His eyes lifted to meet mine, searching the way they always did when he was trying to figure out what I wasn't saying. There was a gentleness to his gaze, but also concern, as though he were bracing himself for an answer he wasn't sure he wanted to hear.

"Nothing," I said, taking a sip of water to momentarily avoid his stare. The lie felt heavy on my tongue, but I couldn't quite bring myself to say more. "I was thinking about the baby," I admitted after a beat, my voice quieter now. "And I think I'm still... getting used to the idea."

He nodded, setting his fork down with a soft clink. "I have been, too. It is a big deal. The baby, the future—it's everything." He paused, his hands resting on the top of the table. "I want to be ready for it all, but... I don't know." His voice softened, and he looked away for a moment. "Sometimes I wonder if we're ready for any of it."

His words hung in the air between us, heavy and raw. He let out a small, unsteady breath, his shoulders sinking. Then, as if realizing he'd let too much slip, he forced a faint smile, a crooked, fragile thing that didn't quite reach his eyes. "Sorry," he added, his fingers drumming once against the table. "I didn't mean to sound like I'm doubting us. It's just a big change."

I reached across the table and placed my hand over his. His skin was warm, but his fingers didn't close around mine right away. It was like he was somewhere else, trapped in his thoughts, until the touch of my hand seemed to pull him back, and a few moments later, his fingers curled around mine.

"It's okay." I gave his hand a gentle squeeze. "I get it, Cam. I do. This *is* a big deal. It's the biggest thing we've ever faced. And yeah, it's scary as hell." I laughed lightly, but it sounded shaky even to my ears. "I'm scared, too. Honestly? I'm terrified. But that doesn't mean we won't be good parents, even if we don't feel ready. I don't think anyone ever feels ready."

His gaze shifted back to me, his expression unreadable at first, and I wondered if I'd said the right thing. Then, his thumb brushed over my knuckles—just once, but enough to reassure me that he was still here, still with me.

"You're right, we won't ever feel ready. We love and support each other, and that will carry us through," Cam said with surety in his voice.

"You know that I've been having trouble sleeping. All of this—it keeps me up at night, running through my head on a loop. But with Dr. Wallace, well, I feel hopeful about him. I'll go back to see him in a few days. I think he is the one who is going to help because he thinks outside the box." I hesitated, searching his face. "I think... I think we can do this. I really do. Because we have so much love to give. And you..." I paused, my lips curving into a small, genuine smile. "Even with how you are with Fat Joe, I know you're going to be an amazing dad."

At that, his faint smile widened, his grip on my hand tightening as if in acknowledgement. The cat adored him, followed him around the apartment like a shadow, leapt into his lap at every opportunity, and slept curled against his chest whenever he spent the night. It had become a running joke between us, how soft he was when it came to that cat. He'd deny it every time, of course, but I'd catch him baby-talking to Fat Joe when he thought I wasn't listening.

"Fat Joe, huh?" he said, shaking his head with a soft chuckle. "That's your proof I'll be a good dad?"

"It's not just that," I was grinning now. "It's how you *are*. The way you care about people. The way you care about me. And you have the patience of a saint, honestly. I mean, you haven't killed me yet, so..."

He laughed, the sound warm and genuine, and for the first time all evening, the tension in his shoulders seemed to ease. He leaned back in his chair, running a hand through his hair as he gazed at me with something softer, lighter in his eyes.

"You give me too much credit," his smile lingered. "I'm just trying to figure it out, same as you. I don't have all the answers. Hell, I don't have *any* of the answers."

"You don't need to. We'll figure it out together," I said.

His smile faltered for a moment, turning serious again, and he gave a small nod. "Together," he echoed, his voice steady. "We can do this. Right?"

"Right," And this time, I meant it.

As we walked out of the restaurant, his hand in mine, I tried to hold on to that fleeting sense of safety. But it slipped through my fingers like the ocean's tide, retreating into a void. Everything seemed perfect, and that's how I knew it wasn't. Perfection was always calm before the storm.

Cameron drove me back to my car, which was still sitting in the campus parking lot. The lot was nearly empty now, lit by just a few orange-tinged streetlights. I climbed into the driver's seat, gave him a little wave, and headed home. The night outside was beautiful, crisp and cool, with a sky so clear the stars felt impossibly close. But as much as I wanted to enjoy it, I could feel exhaustion creeping in, weighing down my eyelids.

The drive home was uneventful, the hum of the engine and the rhythm of passing streetlights lulling me into a strange sort of trance. When I pulled into my driveway and stepped out of the car, the neighborhood was still, like the world was holding its breath.

As soon as I walked through the front door, I kicked off my heels, sighing in relief as my feet hit the cool floor. The heels clattered to the side with no ceremony. I couldn't care less where they landed. I sank onto the couch, letting my whole-body slump as though gravity had doubled the moment I'd stepped inside. My feet ached like crazy, and I rubbed them gently, wincing a little at the sore spots. Dancing was fun, sure, but high heels? Definitely not my brightest idea.

For a moment, I just sat there, letting the silence of the house wrap around me. My breathing slowed, and I closed my eyes, massaging the arches of my feet as I let the tension start to fade. But the mess around the house was nagging at me—empty glasses on the coffee table, a stray sock on the floor, a pile of mail on the counter. I couldn't relax if there was a mess around me.

Eventually, I pushed myself off the couch and started tidying up, one small thing at a time. Cleaning barefoot was oddly satisfying—something was calming about the feeling of cool tile and soft carpet underfoot, a quiet kind of freedom that was soothing in its simplicity. Cleaning was one of those mindless tasks that gave my hands something to do while my thoughts wandered, or better yet, while I tried *not* to think at all. Tonight, I wanted my brain to go blank.

By the time I finished, the house felt lighter, like it had taken a deep breath along with me. The last thing I did was take the throw blankets and put them in a chest next to the couch. When I opened the lid and examined the inside of the chest, I sensed something odd. I felt revolted and scared, but I had no idea why. I stood there in puzzlement, as if in a haze, trying to sift through memories for any clue, but there were none.

I pushed the feeling aside, telling myself that I would write about it in the journal in a moment, and perhaps the memory or the reason for the feeling would come back to me. I grabbed a quick shower, letting the hot water relax my aching muscles, and then curled up on the couch with Fat Joe. That fluffy baby was already in his favorite spot, sprawled across the cushions like he owned the place. As soon as I sat down, he climbed onto my lap, flopping against me. His warm fur and the soft rumble of his purring helped me settle a little more.

I turned on a movie, not one I was particularly interested in, but something light enough to keep me company. The screen flickered, casting a warm glow across the room. I hoped the background noise would help me wind down, but I wasn't sure it would. Sometimes, movies worked like magic, lulling me to sleep without effort. Other times, my restless mind refused to play along.

Tonight, unfortunately, seemed like one of the latter.

My mind buzzed with everything I still needed to do over the next few weeks to prepare for the baby. The to-do list seemed endless: doctor's appointments, baby-proofing the house, picking out a crib, organizing the nursery, figuring out how to be parents. The sheer weight of it all was too much some days.

My body begged for rest, but my mind refused to allow it. Like siblings who couldn't stop fighting, my body was the quiet one, retreating when overwhelmed. But my mind was the loud, bossy, older one, shouting over everything to get the last word. The moment my body tried to sleep, my mind started screaming, dragging up every little worry and fear. The tug-of-war was exhausting, and I still didn't know how to make them call a truce.

I sank deeper into the couch, my head falling back against the soft cushions. Fat Joe was sprawled across me, his front paws resting on my chest while his back paws clung to the top of my knees. He seemed absurdly comfortable, his purring a steady vibration against my skin. My eyes drifted closed, and for the first time all night, I thought I might actually doze off.

But then—

A car horn blared so loud, like it was right in front of me. My eyes flew open, but I wasn't fully awake. I was dreaming—a car was coming straight at me, its headlights blinding and growing brighter by the second. The horn screamed, sharp and unrelenting, and I couldn't move. I couldn't get out of the way.

The crash came with a deafening roar, and I jolted upright, heart pounding as I gasped for air. Fat Joe yowled in protest and leaped off my lap, his back claws digging into my knees on the way down.

"Ow! Oh, my God." My hand flew to my chest, trying to calm

the frantic beating of my heart. The realization hit me all at once; it was the TV. There was a car crash on the screen. It was part of the movie I'd forgotten was playing. "It was just the movie," I muttered to myself, still breathless. "I'm not losing it."

Fat Joe stared at me from the floor, his tail flicking in irritation. "Sorry, buddy," I winced as I rubbed the sting on my knees. "Didn't mean to scare you."

I grabbed my journal from the coffee table and scribbled down what had just happened. The dream, the headlights, the crash, the panic. It wasn't the first time I'd seen those headlights in a dream.

For the second time now, I had a shocking vision of headlights coming straight at me. What is the deal with these visions? Was I in a car accident when I was younger, and just don't remember it?

I've racked my brain trying to remember, but I couldn't come up with anything.

Maybe I was just a baby at the time. Or... Could these be premonitions of something terrible to come? I don't know. All I know is they scare me.

Earlier today, when I opened the chest to put away blankets, I had a sense of panic wash over me for seemingly no reason. I have no idea what that's about, but it was almost like I could feel what it was like to be locked inside.

I am beginning to see that journaling helps me in more ways than one. To be honest, I had to set an alarm in the morning to remind myself to do it at first. Now, it is becoming a habit. Journaling is helping me organize my thoughts in general, which is nice. It will also be a nice keepsake for years later to go back and read what I experienced during the pregnancy. Especially since I have been having memory problems.

I have to be able to look back and remember how I felt and what I thought during this precious, fulfilling, but also confusing time in my life. I am so thankful to have Cam in my life. He is my solid rock that will get me through this, and I know he will always be there for me.

I closed the journal and sighed, my hands trembling as I set it back down.

When the movie finally ended, I turned off the TV and made my way upstairs. "Cuddle time," I called, and Fat Joe's ears perked up immediately. He followed me up the stairs, his irritation apparently forgotten.

I climbed into bed, the heaviness of the day pulling at me again, and settled in as Fat Joe curled up behind my knees. His purring resumed, low and steady, and I let the sound fill the silence.

"Please, let tonight be peaceful," I whispered. I closed my eyes, let myself hope for sleep.

8

Thirty-Eight Special

What felt like only five minutes later, I opened my eyes to the sharp blare of a car horn. It echoed like a scream in the distance, jarring and out of place. I wasn't in my bedroom anymore. I was standing in the middle of a street by the beach, the asphalt hot beneath my bare feet. Everything seemed familiar, yet something was off, like I was peering through a fogged window. The surrounding colors were muted, the sunlight pale and wan, as though it had been filtered through dirty glass.

I tasted salt in my mouth, gritty and unpleasant. Sand coated my tongue, and when I spat onto the ground, it felt sticky, like something far worse than seawater mingled with grit. A breeze drifted in from the ocean, carrying with it a sour, metallic tang that turned my stomach.

Looking down, I realized I was carrying my tan, over-the-shoulder school bag again, wearing the same outfit from my last dream. The faded jeans, the red flip-flops in hand, the Led Zeppelin T-shirt. I frowned, tugging at the frayed hem of the shirt, wondering if my subconscious lacked creativity or if this outfit was trying to tell me something. Did it mean anything?

Was there some symbolism I wasn't seeing? But besides Daytona Beach, I didn't even know where I was—and yet it was familiar.

Curious, I dug into the bag, hoping it might hold some answers. In the first pocket, I found a notebook, some pens, my wallet—and then, bizarrely, a fistful of condoms. Cam and I used to use birth control before I became pregnant. There was no need for condoms now. I examined them, perplexed, before shoving them back in and zipping the pocket shut. "I hope nobody saw that," I said out loud. *Even my voice sounds a bit different. Like I've been screaming death metal music professionally or smoking cigarettes*, I thought to myself, still digging through the dirty bag.

In the second pocket, my fingers brushed against something cold, metallic, and far heavier than anything I expected to find. My breath hitched as I pulled it out. A gun.

My heart dropped, panic rising inside me like a tidal wave. Why on earth would I have a gun? Especially an old-ass revolver like this. Like I'm some sort of cowboy in an old western film. Even in a dream, it felt wrong. I couldn't remember a time when I had held a gun before. My hands trembled as I turned it over, examining the smooth steel, the dull glint of the barrel. It read ".38 S&W Special". Was it for protection? Had I used it on someone? My pulse quickened at the thought. I hesitated, then carefully fiddled with it until I managed to open the cylinder. Two shots were missing.

Two shots.

I nervously shoved the gun back into the bag, my hands clammy and shaking. I didn't want to think about what that meant. There was nothing useful in the bag—no money, no phone, nothing. Now, panic was burning my chest, but I didn't know what I should do.

Should I try to ask someone for help? Should I take the gun to the police? No. There was no point. This is a dream! My inner monologue had a point.

Instead, I threw on the flip-flops and started running.

Sprout wings and fly! This is a dream. That means I should be able to control it! I thought.

I was no good at lucid dreaming. I was not in control. But, at the same time, the curiosity was so overwhelming that I *had* to continue. I wanted to continue. I needed to explore this dream world. The need to know more was too strong. Not just for researching my paper, but for learning more about myself.

There were answers in these dreams, I knew it. Dr. Wallace's advice was my mantra, "Don't be afraid of the fear."

The highway stretched endlessly ahead of me, shimmering in the hazy heat, but something inside me told me to keep going. The road would lead me home. It had to. I felt an invisible pull towards something or somewhere. Sweat was beginning to drip down my back, and I felt so thirsty I couldn't stand it. There was a snow cone shop down the street with a line of people that seemed to stretch the entire block. What I would give right now for a snow cone.

After what seemed like miles, I saw it—a small house, weathered and worn, its blue paint peeling like old wallpaper. This was where the pull was taking me. It sat unassumingly just off the main road, almost swallowed by overgrown grass. The sight of it sent a jolt of recognition through me.

This was mine. This house, crumbling and lonely, belonged to me. I didn't know how I knew that, and I'd never seen it before, but it was a fact, as certain as the gritty salt still lingering on my tongue.

The house was falling apart. Most of the windows were cracked or missing glass altogether, their jagged edges reflecting the weak sunlight like broken teeth. Near the middle of the house, a downed palm tree rested on the roof, clearly having caused some damage. A small, sagging porch greeted me, the wood warped and uneven. Rusted nails jutted out in odd places, catching the light. On one side of the porch, a swing hung from rusted chains, swaying in the breeze. Its creaking sound was faint but persistent, like the whispered warning of an unseen presence.

"God, this is so creepy," I muttered to myself, a bitter laugh escaping my lips. My voice sounded strange, hollow, like it didn't belong to me. "Do I dare go in? What if I get shot?" I paused, considering, then shrugged. "Meh, it's just a dream. Might as well explore." I loved imagining the people or families who once lived in old houses like this; who they were, and more importantly, why they had left. "If old houses could talk," I muttered. They held so many secrets, so many clues, and so many stories.

The front door wasn't locked. It swung open with little resistance, the hinges groaning like a wounded animal. As the door swung open, I yelled out, "Is there anyone in here? I have a gun!" But there was no response. Inside, the air was thick with the scent of mildew and dust, tinged with something faintly sour. It smelled like my grandmother's attic—old and forgotten, as though the house itself had given up.

The question that was heaviest on my mind was, *was there running water?* I would drink almost anything liquid at this point.

I made my way to the kitchen. It was dingy with old, olive-green appliances straight out of the 1970s. The sink was an old cast iron with a white enamel coating that was dirty and stained. I twisted the faucet knob labeled *Cold* and held my breath. A low-pressure stream of water emerged, and a faint smile came across my face. I scooped up the water in my hands and gulped it down. The cold water was refreshing. I cupped my hands under the flow of water and splashed some on my face and neck. I was grateful I could taste it and feel it even in a dream.

There was no dining room. You would have to put a small table in the kitchen to eat. A full bathroom was off the living room. The entire house consisted of five rooms: the kitchen, living room, bathroom, and two bedrooms.

The living room was sparsely furnished, almost barren. There were no photos on the walls. There wasn't anything on the walls, not even shelves or coat hooks. I tried the light switch, but nothing happened. Of course. *Dream me never pays her bills*, I thought, a hollow attempt at humor that did nothing to ease the knot of dread coiling in my stomach.

A lone couch sat against one wall, its upholstery stained and torn, springs poking through the fabric. There was a small box TV that sat on the floor, directly in front of the sad couch. On top of the TV, there were several random pieces of aluminum foil. *That's odd*, I thought.

The walls were bare, smeared with dirt. In the corner, a small fireplace stood cold and empty, its stone hearth filled with only a few logs. Outside, I'd noticed a neat pile of firewood stacked by the house, a strange contrast to the neglect that defined the rest of the property.

I stepped outside and made my way to the fence, a misshapen chain-link structure that had been patched and re-patched with random pieces of wire. I picked up a couple of logs and brought them inside, setting them on the well-used, smoke-stained hearth. I didn't need a fire for heat, that was for sure. But I thought maybe I could use the fire to cook something if I wanted, as the range was electric.

That's when I realized I had no way to light the fire. No matches, no lighter. I rummaged through my school bag again, hoping for some magical solution, but found nothing useful. In the kitchen, there were several empty lighters. *How helpful.* Sighing, I abandoned the quest to light the fire and sank onto the couch. The springs groaned under my weight, but I didn't care. My limbs felt heavy, my mind clouded with the oppressive weight of the scene that surrounded me.

I knew this was a dream. The thought circled in my mind like a mantra, a reminder that none of this was real. Still, it was so vivid, so uncomfortably real. It was like watching a bleak sitcom of my life, only I was the star, and the title might as well have been *Misery*. Sadly, that title was already taken.

I kept trying to control aspects of the dream. I tried snapping my fingers and flying to New York or simply conjuring up a damn snow-cone, but nothing worked. I was not in control. This was not a lucid dream, that was for sure.

The couch was pushed back against the east wall. The gaping holes in the roof from the fallen palm tree were in the center of the room. I leaned back, the musty cushions swallowing me, and stared up at the cracked ceiling. There were brown water stains, and the plaster was missing in a few spots. The place was dirty and smelly, but for some reason, it felt like home.

What was my subconscious trying to tell me? Was there a hidden message in this place, in the peeling paint, the rotted wood, the missing bullets? My eyelids grew heavy, my body sinking deeper into the couch as exhaustion took over. *Just a moment of rest*, I thought. *Just a moment to gather my thoughts.*

I closed my eyes, letting the silence wrap around me like a weighted blanket. I let sleep take me. After what seemed like minutes, I woke with an unnerving feeling in my gut. The room was dark now, as if hours had passed.

I suddenly realized what the feeling meant. I felt the unmistakable sensation of being watched. The hair on the back of my neck stood on end.

My gaze darted to the corner, where the fireplace sat filthy and unused. At first, it seemed empty—but then I saw it.

A figure hunched low and shadowed. It was difficult to distinguish it from the darkness surrounding it. This figure wasn't like a typical shadow, it was blacker than one. It made my skin crawl. I pulled my feet up off the floor and tucked them under me.

I couldn't look away.

It wasn't moving, but its presence was like a hand pressing against my chest. My breathing quickened, and my pulse thundered in my ears. I couldn't move, couldn't scream, and my whole body trembled. It felt like sleep paralysis.

And then, without warning, it stood up.

I gasped as the figure began to step forward, its movements slow and deliberate. Its face was shrouded in darkness, but I could see the faint gleam of its watchful eyes, piercing through the haze of the dream. They sent a shiver of pure terror straight into my soul. He, or *it*, was wearing a black robe that almost touched the floor.

He lunged at me.

I screamed in terror and bolted upright, my breath catching in my throat—and then the figure vanished.

9

Art Show

I woke up in my bed, gasping for air, heart pounding. It took me a few moments to realize I was safe in my bed and that had been just a nightmare. I turned on my side and grabbed the journal. I wrote everything down that I could remember while it was fresh in my mind. Then, at the end, I added a small note.

Was that the same large man I dreamed about before? What does he want? This presence felt different somehow. More authoritative, more controlling. He was pure evil.

As I lay there, comfortable in my nest of blankets and pillows, Fat Joe started crying for his breakfast. He always starts telling me about it at precisely eight in the morning, his pitiful yowls filling the room as his paw patted my face from the nightstand. His silly personality solidified the fact that I was safe now. I groaned, swatting at him half-heartedly, but he wasn't deterred. His little black nose twitched as he leaned closer, sniffing at my cheek like he was checking to see if I was even alive.

"Alright, alright," I muttered, my voice still thick with sleep.

I looked over at the alarm clock and then back at him. His big, green eyes were staring back at me, full of determination. "You've got a built-in alarm clock, don't you?"

He meowed in response, loud and demanding, then hopped onto the bed and sat squarely on my ribs, as if to emphasize his point. With a sigh, I pushed myself upright, ruffling his fur as I swung my legs over the side of the bed.

"You win, buddy. Breakfast it is."

Fat Joe raced ahead of me as I shuffled toward the kitchen, his tail flicking with purpose. I grabbed his food bowl and filled it with kibble, smiling as he immediately buried his face in it. "You eat better than I do, you know that?" I said, shaking my head as I leaned against the counter.

It was eight sixteen now, and I needed to get moving. My day wasn't packed, but it was full enough. Just a Molecular Biology lecture and lab, which wouldn't be so bad, except for the fact that I could barely concentrate. My mind kept wandering— to the baby, to all the things I still needed to do, to the sleep I desperately needed but never seemed to get. I knew I was sleeping because I was dreaming. I just never felt rested.

I sighed and headed to the bathroom to get ready, my reflection in the mirror stopping me for a moment. My hair was a mess, my eyes a bit puffy from another semi-restless night, and I could see the faintest outline of dark circles forming. "Lovely," I mumbled sarcastically, splashing cold water on my face to wake myself up.

After class, I decided to run a few errands, checking off some last-minute baby items from my list. I found myself weaving through aisles of tiny socks, bibs, and bottles. My cart filled quickly with things, though my heart ached to grab something sentimental, like a soft stuffed animal or a tiny, pink dress. I reached out to touch one of the baby outfits on display, feeling the soft fabric between my fingers. She was going to be here soon, and the thought filled me with both excitement and a nervous flutter in my stomach.

By the time I got home, my arms were full of shopping bags, and I was already thinking about collapsing on the couch for a bit before diving into more tasks. But when I rounded the corner to my front door, I froze.

Cameron was standing there, waiting for me.

He looked... breathtaking. I almost didn't recognize him. He had dressed up for some occasion, in a sharp black suit that hugged his frame, his red tie standing out like a vibrant splash of color. His dark hair was combed neatly, but not overly so—it still had that messy, boyish charm that always made my heart skip. And in his hands were a dozen red roses, their petals soft and full, like they'd been plucked straight from a romantic painting. He was so put together that it made me feel even more frayed.

I stood there for a moment, staring like an idiot. My mind scrambled to figure out why he was there and why he was dressed like that. Then it hit me. The roses. The suit. Oh, my God—our anniversary. We celebrated the day we ran into each other at the coffee stand as the start of our relationship.

"Hi!" His smile was slow and sweet, like he was waiting for me to catch up.

"Oh," I breathed. Guilt stabbed at me as I realized I'd

completely forgotten about it. "Oh my God, Cam. I... I'm so sorry."

"For what?" he asked, his smile widening as he stepped forward, offering me the roses. His tone was light, teasing. "For forgetting? Don't worry, I figured you might. You've had a lot on your plate lately."

I accepted the flowers, burying my face in them to hide the blush creeping up my cheeks. Their fragrance was sweet and calming, a stark contrast to the chaos that seemed to be running my life as of late. "You didn't have to go through all this trouble," I said, glancing up at him.

He tilted his head, his expression softening. "Of course, I did. It's our anniversary. And I wanted to make sure you had something to look forward to today."

I swallowed hard, feeling a lump form in my throat. It wasn't just the flowers or how he looked at me. It was the fact that he knew me so well, knew how overwhelmed I'd been, how much I needed this little reminder of love and normalcy.

"That's why you took me out dancing yesterday," I said, sighing, the realization just dawning on me. "You were trying to make it special."

He chuckled, reaching out to tuck a stray strand of hair behind my ear. "Well, spaghetti's not exactly fine dining, but I thought it'd hold us over until tonight."

Tonight. The art show. It all came flooding back to me—the plans we'd made weeks ago, before my life turned into a blur of doctor appointments, research papers, and the recent nightmares.

"I almost forgot about the art show," I admitted, my voice

small.

"You didn't almost forget," he teased, his grin turning playful. "You *completely* forgot."

I laughed, despite myself, the sound breaking through the haze of guilt and exhaustion. "You're right," I shook my head. "I did. But now I remember, and I couldn't be more excited."

His eyes softened at that, and he leaned in to press a gentle kiss to my forehead. "Go get ready. I'll wait right here. Tonight's going to be special. You deserve that."

I stood there for a moment, clutching the roses to my chest and looking at the man who somehow loved me, even when I felt like a total mess. "Thank you."

"Always," he replied, his smile unwavering.

As I headed inside to get ready, I felt a little lighter, like some of the weight I'd been carrying had finally been lifted. For the first time in days, I wasn't thinking about to-do lists, nightmares, deadlines, or everything that could go wrong. I was just thinking about Cameron—and how lucky I was to have him.

I changed into a sleek, black, sleeveless dress that hit just above my knees, and we were off to the museum. The night was beautiful—clear skies without a cloud in sight, and every star was shining brightly. It was magical.

The art at the show was beautiful and intriguing. Every time I visited a museum, I left feeling inspired, eager to create something of my own. There were so many people. As I wandered through the exhibits, something tugged at me, telling me there was a painting I needed to see. I made my way through the crowd and stopped in front of a painting that seemed almost alive.

It depicted a vast, stormy ocean under a blood-red sky, palm trees violently blowing to the right, and a single male figure standing on the shore. A large, looming, dark figure. The figure's face was obscured, but something about it was familiar, tugging at my memory.

Staring at the painting, I slipped into a sort of trance. I could hear the wind rustling through the palm trees. I heard the waves crashing onto the rocks in the distance. The gallery around me began to fade out. The murmur of voices faded into an eerie silence. The walls, floor, and ceiling of the gallery dissolved into darkness, leaving only me and the painting.

As I stood there unable to look away, unable to blink, the dark figure in the painting seemed to move closer to me. It wasn't a trick of the light, nor an illusion. He stepped forward. I couldn't move. He came closer still. I was frozen in fear. My feet were anchored to the floor, eyes peeled open, unable to blink. My heart pounded against my ribs, a frantic drumbeat of alarm. The darkness clinging to his form stretched and bled into the space between us. And then he reached for me.

A cold, unnatural hand emerged from the painting, crossing the threshold between art and reality. His fingers wrapped around my throat. A strangled gasp tore from my lips as my lungs seized, panic clawing up my chest. I tried to scream, but no sound came. My hands shot up, gripping at the phantom fingers, but they were solid. Too solid. I could see now that he was wearing a black robe. His evil, gray eyes burned holes in my flesh as I tried to escape.

Suddenly, a voice shattered my spiral.

"Are you ready to leave, Grace?" Cameron asked, jolting me

out of the trance and back to reality.

"Y-Yes, yes, please," I said, nodding dramatically to shake the feeling out of my head.

While we were driving back to my duplex, I couldn't stop thinking about that painting. Why did I feel drawn to it? Who was that figure? His face terrified me, but I didn't know him, at least I couldn't remember him. He made me feel like he wanted me dead. After Cameron parked, he walked me to my door. As I was unlocking it, he stood there, staring at me as if he couldn't get enough.

"Please come in with me?" I pleaded, knowing what his answer would be. I couldn't tell him I was scared of my nightmares and that a man in a painting tried to kill me. I didn't want to seem childish.

"You know I have those early morning classes, and my dorm is right there on campus. I have been packing, though. I should be able to move here in a few days," he said with reassurance.

I couldn't wait for him to move in. I knew I would feel better just having him near me, especially at night.

I glanced up, and he pulled me close by the waist, kissing me like it was the last time he would ever see me. He cupped my face in his hands, running his fingers through my hair. He always kissed me like that, and it was such a comforting feeling. It's nice to be kissed with that kind of love every day, to know that I was truly cherished by someone who needed me. I placed my hand on his cheek, kissed him softly, said goodnight, and went inside.

Once inside, I locked the door behind me. I leaned against

the door, letting out a sigh. I already missed him. I slipped off my heels and made my way upstairs. I unzipped the dress and let it crumple to the floor, then threw on one of Cam's old T-shirts, and crawled into bed. Fat Joe was already taking up fifty percent of it, looking annoyed at me when I asked him to scootch. Reaching for the book on my nightstand, I picked up *The Psychology of the Unconscious* by C.G. Jung, a book I was nearly finished with. Jung, a Swiss psychiatrist, had delved into dreams, mythology, and literature to explore the human soul, mind, and spirit.

The room was silent, save for the soothing hum of Fat Joe's purring and the rhythmic ticking of the clock. Although the book was fascinating and my mind was doing cartwheels, my eyelids grew heavy. As I drifted off, the moonlight painted soft shadows across the walls and ceiling. Fat Joe's purring slowed, his warm body nestled against my leg. The wind whistled outside like a storm might be rolling in.

I heard a faint creak, like the sound of a rusted chain swinging in the breeze. The image of that old porch swing in my dream popped into my head. My eyes shot open, but there was nothing. Just shadows. Just silence. Still, my heart wouldn't stop racing.

The shadows on the walls seemed to shift, almost imperceptibly, as though the moonlight had decided to play tricks on my tired mind. I took a deep breath and closed my eyes again, forcing myself to relax. It was just my imagination. Just the lingering residue of that eerie painting, stirring up something deep in my subconscious.

Then I felt it.

A subtle weight. Light, like a single hand pressing down on the end of the bed.

My body stiffened, and my eyes snapped open. Fat Joe hissed, a low, guttural sound I'd never heard from him before, and bolted from the bed, his claws clicking against the hardwood floor as he disappeared into the shadows of the hallway.

The weight was gone.

I sat up, every nerve in my body buzzing. My heart hammered so loudly I could hear it echoing in my ears. I studied the spot where Fat Joe had been moments before, where the bedspread was now perfectly smooth.

Maybe I had imagined it. Maybe I was just tired, my overactive mind twisting the silence into something sinister.

I glanced at the clock: thirteen past one in the morning. The room was quiet, save for the faint rustling of the trees outside my window and the whistle of the wind. I leaned back against my pillow, closing my eyes again and letting out a shaky breath.

And then, just as sleep began to pull me under, I heard it again.

Not a creak this time. Not the faint rustle of the wind.

A whisper.

My name.

Soft. drawn out. As if it were being carried on the wind from somewhere far away.

"Grace..."

My eyes flew open, my body frozen, my breath caught.

The room was empty.

But the shadows seemed deeper now, pooling into the

corners like spilled ink, and for the briefest moment, I could have sworn I saw the faint outline of a figure standing near the window. Tall, dark, and obscured, like the man from the painting.

I blinked. The figure was gone.

The whisper, though, lingered in the air, wrapping itself around me like a thread tightening with every breath I took. I grabbed my journal and wrote:

Because our investigation into the duplex turned up nothing, I am stumped. There have been no deaths on either side. There have not been any murders, suicides, or even natural deaths, which I found odd since the building was at least a century old.

Maybe there is a spirit attached to me from somewhere other than the duplex. Because tonight I thought the figure in a painting at the art gallery was going to kill me. At home, I heard my name being called and felt a presence sitting on my bed. Even Fat Joe reacted.

Sometimes I see a figure wearing a black robe. I have seen him in my dreams and in visions. This entity is different from the bald man. He is more frightening, and instead of just fear, I feel hopeless.

Maybe it was time for a priest and a sage cleansing.

I closed the journal and, as my heavy eyelids betrayed me once more, dragging me unwillingly into sleep, I swore I could hear the faint sound of waves crashing in the distance. Waves— and the low, haunting creak of a rusted chain swinging in the breeze.

10

You Can't Run

All of a sudden—*bam*! I was back in the old house. The shift was so abrupt, I was like Alice being shoved into a tiny door as I was continuing to shrink. Or like I was unknowingly dropped into a pool blindfolded. My ears were ringing, like the aftermath of an explosion, and a deep chill seeped into me, gnawing at my bones. The house seemed worse than before, as if time itself had picked it apart piece by piece, leaving behind a skeleton of rot and ruin.

I was in the center of the living room. The floor creaked beneath me, each sound sharp and deliberate, like the house wanted me to know I wasn't alone. The windows rattled in their frames, their cracked panes smeared with streaks of grime and something dark, like oil, or perhaps something worse.

The smell hit me harder this time—a rancid, suffocating stench that filled my lungs and clawed at my throat. It was a thick, invasive odor, not just of something rotting, but of something *wrong*. I pulled my shirt up over my nose, but it didn't help. It never did. It was the kind of smell that once it invaded your nostrils, there was no getting rid of it.

The sky above was visible through the gaping holes in the roof, but the air offered no comfort. Angry, black clouds churned, restless and alive, a storm brewing with no intention of mercy. The air was heavy with the kind of stillness like a predator holding its breath, waiting for you to step just one inch too far. I knew the house had a secret, and I wanted to find out what that secret was.

I moved forward towards the kitchen cautiously, but the house didn't feel like it wanted me there. The walls seemed to watch me, their peeling paint curling like dried skin, revealing layers beneath. The stains on the floor, dark and ominous, seemed to spread with every step I took, creeping closer like spilled ink seeping through paper.

On the dirty kitchen floor sat two empty bowls. I guessed food and water bowls for a dog or cat, though I had not seen any animals. The silence pressed down on me, thick and oppressive, making it hard to breathe.

I told myself to turn back, to leave, but my legs moved on their own. The filthy wood planks groaned beneath my weight, each step a reluctant cry, like the house was warning me to stop.

The hallway was darker than it should have been, even with the holes in the roof. Shadows stretched unnaturally, twisting along the walls and ceiling like living things. My bedroom was at the end of the hall. The door was open a sliver.

When I stepped inside, it was like walking into a storm. Random, filthy spoons and lighters covered the nightstand.

Papers were scattered everywhere, pages of something torn and shredded, the jagged edges curling in the damp air. The walls were covered in writing—frantic, overlapping scrawls in uneven lines. I tried to read the words, but they shifted under my gaze, the letters twisting and rearranging themselves into unintelligible gibberish. A few stood out, though, clear and cutting: *IT'S YOUR FAULT. YOU CAN'T RUN FROM THIS.*

YOU ARE GUILTY.

I glanced down and saw the unmade bed, but it seemed like it had recently been slept in. A memory flashed into my mind. One minute, I was standing by the bed staring at it, and the next minute was like I was in another dimension altogether. It was a memory of me being assaulted.

I was held down on this very bed by an older man with greying hair. He looked like the man in the painting at the art gallery. He had intense, gray eyes that stared daggers into me as he held me down. They were pure evil. I remembered the struggle to free myself. I was scratching and kicking and pulling at his clothing. He was vicious and unrelenting. He didn't stop until he was satisfied he was empty. When he opened the door to leave the bedroom, he told a large bald man standing watch, "She'll do just fine."

I snapped out of it. My thoughts were swirling. The large bald man. He was the same one in previous nightmares. Who are these men? Do they exist only in this dream world, or do I know them from somewhere? There was only one thing I knew for sure. I had been sexually assaulted by the man with the gray eyes. This was too real to ignore.

I was broken out of this horrible spiral by a faint sound. A cat's meow.

Sitting on the edge of the mattress was a black-and-white tuxedo cat, thin and sickly, its fur patchy and dull. It looked like Fat Joe, but something about it was wrong—its eyes, bright and gold, fixed on me with an unnatural intensity, as if it knew something I didn't. What did cats symbolize in dreams? One book I remembered reading said that cats often symbolized a sense of threat, deception, or hidden dangers. Their unpredictable nature and sharp claws could represent a fear of someone in your life who might be malicious, or a part of yourself that feels potentially destructive.

I sat down, and the cat immediately jumped into my lap, its purring vibrating my body. As I stroked its fur, I could feel every sharp ridge of its spine. The sensation made my stomach churn. I sat there, trying to make sense of what was going on, when the light from a broken window hit something shining on the floor near my foot, halfway under the bed.

I reached down and picked it up. A small key. It didn't look like a house key, but maybe a locker or padlock key. The frail cat sniffed the key, hissed, and jumped down. What could the cat sense that I could not? I wondered why it was here. It seemed so out of place. I studied it for a few moments before throwing it in the drawer of the nightstand. It didn't make sense, but nothing here seemed to make sense.

I stood and walked around the room. The cat's eyes followed me. I wasn't sure if he was worried about me or if he was cautious of me. The damp carpet squished under my shoes, making the worst sounds. The smell of mold and rot was overwhelming now, coating my tongue, crawling into my lungs.

The closet door stood ajar, dark and waiting. Something

pulled me toward it, like a string tied around my wrist, dragging me forward. My hand shook as I reached out, gripping the edge of the door and pulling it open.

The clothes inside looked familiar. Although they looked like they belonged to someone else, someone I didn't recognize. Skintight dresses, miniskirts, and trashy-looking high heels, the ones they sold at the sex stores that were a foot tall. They smelled of mildew. My fingers brushed against the fabric, and I yanked my hand back, my skin tingling with a faint, unpleasant warmth. Thoughts were running through my mind, trying to make sense of it all. *The clothes, the gun, the condoms. Am I a prostitute? This really is a nightmare.*

A soft noise made me spin around. The bathroom door was open now, though I didn't remember opening it. The mirror above the sink caught my eye, the fractured glass throwing jagged reflections across the room. On the back of the toilet were two crusty spoons. *Why?*

I stepped closer to the mirror, my breath hitching as I studied myself.

It wasn't me.

It was worse than my reflection on the sunglasses at the beach. The mirror pointed out everything wrong. It was unsettling. The face in the mirror was mine, but it was different. My skin was pale and waxy, my eyes sunken, shadowed with dark circles that made me look half-dead. A bruise bloomed across my cheek, purple and swollen. My normally shiny and full strawberry blonde hair hung in limp, uneven strands, matted with something sticky. I looked so... old.

Then the reflection moved—but I didn't.

Its mouth twisted into a sneer, its teeth sharp and too many.

"This is real," it hissed, the voice distorted, grating like nails on glass. *"He's gone, and it's your fault."*

The words hit me like a blow, and I stumbled back, shaking my head. "Who?" I whispered, my voice wavering. "I don't know what you're talking about!" I yelled.

The mirror rippled, the glass shifting like water.

And then, behind me, in the reflection, I saw... him.

The man who was buried in the sand on the beach. He was the bald man I saw standing guard outside my bedroom door during my assault. His face was gaunt and waterlogged, his eyes black pits that seemed to pull the light from the room. His lips were blue, and when they moved, no sound came out.

His hand rose, slow and deliberate, reaching for me through the glass.

I spun around, my heart in my throat.

The room was empty.

Still, I could feel him. The air pressed against me, heavy and cold, suffocating. The smell of rot was unbearable now, choking me, clawing at my insides.

Somewhere behind me, the cat let out a piercing yowl, and I ran.

The hallway stretched unnaturally long, the walls narrowing as I stumbled out of the room. The sound of footsteps followed me, heavy and deliberate, each one louder than the last.

I ran as fast as I could down the creaky hallway. When I reached the front door, it wouldn't open. My hands fumbled with the metal doorknob. It was slick with something cold and sticky. The footsteps grew closer, the air thickening around me like a noose tightening.

I closed my eyes, squeezing them as tight as I could. I rested my forehead against the door in utter despair and screamed.

"Wake up! *Wake up!*"

11

Dream Symbolism

And then, just like that, I was back in my bed.

My body jerked upright, drenched in sweat, my breaths ragged and shallow. Fat Joe was curled up beside me, his soft purring the only sound in the room.

But I could still feel the man's presence, lingering like a shadow, just out of sight. And I swore, as I stared into the darkness, I could still smell the faint, sickly scent of rot.

I couldn't take these nightmares anymore! I had been sleeping through the night, but this was almost worse than not sleeping. My follow-up appointment with Dr. Wallace was coming up soon, and I could not wait. My dreams were getting scarier by the day. I had to go to class, even though I was shaken. Learning something new always calmed my nerves. I got up, got ready, and left.

I had class with Professor Nielson, and I wanted to update her with the paper and the nightmares I had been having. I told her about the latest book I was reading, *The Meaning of Psychology for Modern Man* by Carl Jung.

"What do you think about this?" I asked her after the class

ended. I opened the book to the page I had dog-eared and handed it to Professor Nielson.

"From what I understand, Carl Jung is emphasizing that dreams should not be dismissed as meaningless. Even though they can seem confusing, it's more likely that we lack the understanding to interpret them properly. Since we spend about half our lives in the unconscious, including sleep and dreams, and our conscious and unconscious minds influence each other, it's essential for psychology to take dreams seriously. Unconscious experiences can be just as important, or even more impactful, than our waking ones," I said, hoping I was understanding it clearly.

Professor Nielson leaned back in her chair, her thoughtful gaze drifting to the window for a moment before settling back on me. She adjusted the thin chain of her reading glasses, which dangled around her neck, and leaned forward, resting her elbows on the desk.

"Yes, that's the basic gist of it. That's a lot to unpack, Grace," she said, her tone soft but probing. "Dreams often have a way of blending the symbolic with the personal. What constant figures or places are in your dreams?

"There's a shack of a house, a large, bald man, a man with gray eyes, and a cat," I said, wondering where she was going to go with this.

"Let's start with the house. What does it look like? How do you feel when you're in it?"

I hesitated, trying to articulate the heavy, suffocating dread that clung to me in those dreams. "It's rundown—decaying, even. It's... cold," I said, my hands fiddling with the cord on my hoodie.. "Not physically, but emotionally. Like something terrible happened there, and the house won't let it go. It feels alive in a way, and it doesn't want me there. But at the same time, I feel drawn to it, like I have to keep going deeper, even though I don't want to."

Professor Nielson nodded, a faint frown creasing her brow. "Houses in dreams often represent the self—your psyche, your inner world. A decaying or dilapidated house might suggest parts of yourself or your past that feel neglected, abandoned, or damaged. That pull you feel to go deeper? It could be your subconscious urging you to confront something buried."

I shifted uncomfortably in my seat, her words hitting closer to home than I'd expected. What terrible thing did I bury in my past?

"And the cat?" I asked, eager to move the conversation along. "It looks like my cat, Fat Joe, but it's... not him. It's sickly, thin, like it's near death. But it's affectionate. Almost clingy."

Her lips pursed as she considered. "Yes, cats are complicated symbols," she pointed and waved her index finger in the air. "They can represent intuition, independence, or even mystery. But in your dream, this cat seems weak and sickly. That could symbolize something in your life—or within yourself— that feels neglected, fragile, or vulnerable. The fact that it resembles Fat Joe might be your mind borrowing a familiar, comforting image to embody this... whatever it is."

"It doesn't feel comforting, though," I admitted. "It feels wrong. The cat certainly looks neglected. It's like it's trying to tell me something, or warn me of something, but I don't know what."

"That's worth exploring. Dream figures often act as messengers. They may embody feelings or truths that you're not consciously ready to acknowledge." She paused, her tone growing more serious. "Now, let's talk about the men. You said there's a large, threatening, bald man. And there's another man with gray eyes. Tell me more about them. How do you feel in their presence?"

"Terrified," the word spilled out before I could stop it. "But with the bald man, I feel... guilty. Like I've done something wrong, even though I don't know what it is. He never says anything, but the way he looks at me—it's like he knows something I don't. Something awful. And it feels like he blames me for it." I paused, considering whether I should tell her more about the other man and what he did to me. It just felt so personal. Even though it was a dream, it made me feel ashamed. Finally, I just said, "The other man feels like pure evil. He makes me feel violated," I didn't want to explain further. Just thinking about him made me shiver and want to puke. I didn't understand why my reaction to a dream figure would be so visceral in waking life.

"Feeling violated could be interpreted as you not giving free rein to your emotions or urges. If you see yourself as a victim, the dream could represent a lack of integration or acceptance."

I nodded, though my mind was spinning. Lack of integration made sense because I didn't have any close relationships except with Cam. I wasn't involved in any community activities or extracurricular activities here on campus. Maybe I should. Maybe this was just all about me feeling like a loner.

Professor Nielson's expression didn't change, but her eyes sharpened, studying me intently. "A large, threatening figure in a dream often represents an aspect of yourself or your life that you feel overwhelmed by, or afraid to confront. It could be fear, shame, anger, or even a memory you've repressed. The fact that he's familiar yet unknown suggests he's tied to something deeply personal, something your conscious mind hasn't fully recognized yet."

I swallowed hard, my hands tightening around the cover of the book in my lap. "He doesn't feel like part of me. He feels... separate. Like, he doesn't belong there. Like he's invading my dreams."

"That could mean he represents something external." Her voice was calm but firm. "Someone or something in your waking life that you feel threatened by. Or it could mean that your mind is externalizing a deep, unresolved fear, giving it form so you can confront it. Either way, his presence is significant."

She leaned back, folding her hands in her lap. "Grace, dreams don't just come from nowhere. They're not random. They're born from the interplay of your conscious and unconscious mind, your thoughts, experiences, and emotions. If this man keeps appearing, if the house keeps calling you back, it's because there's something your mind wants you to address. Something it won't let you ignore."

Her words sent a shiver down my spine. "But how do I figure out what it is?" I asked. "How do I make sense of it?"

"That's the challenge," she said with a small, knowing smile. "Dreams speak in symbols and metaphors, not plain language.

It's up to you to decode them. Start by reflecting on your waking life. Are there areas where you feel overwhelmed, guilty, or afraid? Are there memories or emotions you've been avoiding? The more you dig, the clearer the connection might become." She drummed her fingertips on the desktop.

"What about the book?" I asked, gesturing to *The Practical Use of Dream Analysis*. "Do you think it could help?"

"Absolutely. Jung's work is a powerful tool for understanding dreams. But remember, no one can interpret your dreams for you. Not Jung, not me. Only you know your mind. The symbols in your dreams are drawn from your life, your experiences. Trust your intuition as you work through them."

She paused, then added, "And don't be afraid of the fear. Sometimes, the things that scare us the most are the things we need to face to move forward."

Her words hung in the air between us, heavy with implication. She said the same thing as Dr. Wallace. I nodded again, clutching the book tighter as if it could anchor me. "Thank you." Though I wasn't sure if I felt comforted or more afraid.

As I walked out of her office and into the crisp afternoon air, her final words echoed in my mind: *Don't be afraid of the fear.* But as I thought of the house, the cat that looked like Fat Joe but wasn't, and the man's sunken eyes, I couldn't help but wonder—what if fear was the only thing keeping me safe? What if I was not ready to find out what it all meant?

After class, I grabbed a sandwich and headed to the library to work on my research paper. The library had been quiet that afternoon, but not the kind of quiet that calmed me.

It was the thick, weighty kind of silence that made my thoughts louder. The long aisles of books seemed to stretch endlessly, the smell of old paper mixing with the faint, sterile scent of the building itself.

I sat at a corner table tucked away near the psychology and metaphysics section, surrounded by a fortress of open books, printed articles, and my own scribbled notes. My laptop hummed beside me, its screen cluttered with highlighted PDFs and half-finished paragraphs of my paper. The sandwich I'd bought earlier sat untouched on a napkin, the bread drying out as I lost myself in the research.

"Intras," I whispered under my breath, my pen tapping against the tabletop. The word felt strange in my mouth, foreign yet oddly familiar. It was just an idea for now, a label I'd given to the concept I was trying to piece together. Something that tied the threads of insomnia, vivid dreams, and the psyche into one cohesive theory.

I flipped through another book I'd pulled from the shelf, one on dream symbolism and Jungian archetypes. My eyes skimmed over the words of a summary of Jungian dream interpretation. The basic premise is that in dreams, figures who appear as strangers yet feel familiar are often projections of the dreamer's shadow self. They may embody repressed aspects of the psyche—fears, desires, or memories—that the conscious mind is unwilling to confront.

I paused, the words prickling at the back of my mind. The man in my dreams, the one who loomed in the shadows of the decaying house, flashed in my memory. The way he stared at me, silent but accusing. That horrible, gut-wrenching familiarity. Was he some kind of projection? A shadow self? Or was he something else entirely?

I scribbled the quote into my notebook, my handwriting jagged from the speed of my thoughts. The pages of my notes were chaotic, filled with fragmented ideas: connections between the unconscious and the body, the interplay of fear and memory, the strange phenomena of insomnia-induced hallucinations. But none of it felt solid yet. It was like trying to put together a puzzle where half the pieces were missing—or worse, where the image on the box didn't match the pieces at all.

I leaned back in my chair, rubbing my temples. The baby kicked hard against my ribs, pulling me back to the present. "I know, I know," I murmured, placing a hand on my stomach. "You're tired of sitting here, huh?"

The gentle movement beneath my hand reminded me why I was doing this. It wasn't just about me anymore. The nightmares, the insomnia, the strange, creeping sense that my soul was unraveling—it wasn't just mine to deal with. There was someone else now, someone growing inside me, someone I had to protect. If there was even a chance that my dreams were more than just a side effect of stress or hormones, I had to figure it out.

I glanced around the library, at the rows of books were both comforting and overwhelming. I'd already spent hours combing through passages on dream analysis, the psyche, and the body's connection to the unconscious. My back ached, and my legs were stiff from sitting too long. But there was still so much more

I needed to uncover.

I closed the book in front of me—*Dreams: The Mirror of the Soul*—and sighed. The stack of books I hadn't touched yet loomed at my side like an unspoken challenge. I checked the time on my phone and winced. *Four hours. How has it been four hours already?*

The baby kicked again, this time harder, as if to scold me. "Okay, okay, I hear you," I muttered, standing up slowly and stretching. My joints popped in protest. I packed up my notes and tucked a few books into my bag to check out, their titles heavy with promise: *Sleep and the Psyche, Consciousness Beyond the Body*, and *Nightmares: A Window to the Soul*.

As I approached the checkout desk, a librarian glanced at my belly and smiled. "Someone's keeping you busy," she said, nodding toward my stomach as she scanned the books.

"You have no idea," I replied, forcing a small laugh.

Before leaving the campus, I wanted to visit the chapel and maybe get advice from one of the chaplains. I had always admired the building with its graceful steeple and stained-glass windows. As I drove closer to the location, the more confused I became. The road leading to the chapel was lined with cherry blossom trees, but there were none in sight. *Did they cut them down to plant something new?* I wondered.

I knew I was on the correct road, as I always passed it on my way to the psychology building. Baffled, I continued driving and reached the parking lot. A chill shot through me. I turned my head back and forth with enough force that my ponytail hit the side of my face.

The chapel was gone.

It hadn't been torn down. It was as if it had never been there. I sat in silence for a moment, questioning my sanity. *What is wrong with me? I know it was here! What is happening?*

I told myself that I must have been mistaken, and I was just in the wrong place. I drove around the campus a few minutes longer, but the chapel was nowhere to be found. *It's just pregnancy brain. It has to be. I need to rest. That's all this is, exhausted pregnancy brain*, I thought as I drove out of the campus.

The drive home was a welcome reprieve. I rolled down the windows, letting the cool evening air sweep through the car, and turned the radio to my favorite pop station. The music filled the space surrounding me, its cheerful energy a sharp contrast to the dark, heavy thoughts still swirling in my mind.

But even as I tapped my fingers against the steering wheel in rhythm with the song, I couldn't shake the feeling that the answers I was searching for weren't in the books I'd borrowed. They weren't in the theories of Jung or the scientific explanations of REM cycles and sleep studies.

They were in the shadows of my dreams. In the man who stared at me with silent accusation. In the decaying house that pulled me deeper every night.

And the only way to find those answers was to face them.

But how do you confront something you don't understand? How do you face something that might not even be real?

As I drove down the winding road, I realized I didn't have an answer. Not yet. But I was determined to find one. Even if it meant going back into the uncertainty of the nightmares that grew darker and scarier by the night.

When I pulled into the driveway, the first thing I noticed was Cameron sitting on the front porch steps. He wasn't scrolling through his phone or checking his watch like he sometimes did when waiting for me. Instead, he sat perfectly still, looking thoughtful, his elbows resting on his knees and a small black box in his hands.

For a moment, I just stared at him through the windshield. My heart skipped a beat. *Is that...? No, it couldn't be. Could it?*

He stood when he saw me, a warm smile spreading across his face, the kind of smile that made my world feel steady, even when it wasn't. The late-afternoon sun cast a golden glow around him, like a spotlight. He was wearing a crisp white button-up with the sleeves rolled halfway up his forearms, and the sight of him took my breath away. He looked like he had walked straight out of a dream—the good kind, not the kind that left me waking in a cold sweat.

"I've been waiting for you," he said as I stepped out of the car. His voice was calm, but I could see the way his fingers fidgeted with the box. His nerves betrayed him.

I didn't respond right away, I couldn't. My mind was spinning, and I was very aware of everything around me. The crunch of gravel under my shoes as I walked toward him. The cool spring breeze brushing against my skin. The faint scent of roses drifting toward me from the bouquet that sat on the porch railing.

When I reached him, he took a deep breath, like he was gathering all the courage he had. Then he sank to one knee.

My breath hitched. I hadn't expected this—not today, not like this. I had been dreaming of this day for nearly two years.

Now, here it was after I had experienced the most visceral, terrifying nightmare just last night. I felt like I might fall apart at any minute!

"Grace," he began, his voice steady despite the flush creeping into his cheeks. "These past three years with you have been the best of my life. You're my partner, my best friend, the person I want to build my future with. And now, with our baby on the way... I know I want us to be a family. Not just two people raising a child, but a real family. Forever."

My chest tightened, emotions welling up so fast I thought I might burst. He opened the small black box, revealing a stunning, white gold ring with a heart-shaped diamond. The way it caught the light, sparkling in the fading sunlight, made my breath catch.

"Will you marry me?" he asked, his blue eyes searching mine, filled with so much love and hope my knees went weak.

For a moment, I couldn't speak. Tears blurred my vision, and I had to bite my lip to keep from completely breaking down. A part of me felt like I didn't deserve this. This man, this love, this happiness. Another part of me was scared. *What if I never found out what was causing the nightmares?* I was scared of what the future held. *What if I dragged him down with me into the throes of insanity?*

Most importantly, I was scared of failing him, of failing our baby. But he took hold of my trembling hand in his. His hand was strong and confident, and above all the fear, I felt something stronger.

I felt hope.

"Oh, Cam! Yes," I whispered, my voice trembling. "Yes, of

course."

His grin widened as he slipped the ring onto my finger, his hands warm and steady against my own. The fit was perfect, as though it had been made just for me. He stood, and before I could say another word, he pulled me into his arms, lifting me off the ground in one swift motion.

I laughed through my tears as he spun me around, the world a blur of golden light and pure joy. "I love you," he whispered into my ear before setting me back down. His hands moved to cup my face, his thumbs brushing away the tears on my cheeks.

"I love you, too," I said, and I meant it with every fiber of my being.

And then he kissed me. Not the sweet, gentle kind of kiss we usually shared, but the deep, passionate kind that made my heart race. The kind that felt like a promise.

For a moment, everything else—the dreams, the stress, the uncertainty—melted away. All I could feel was him, his warmth, his love, his certainty.

When he finally pulled back, he rested his forehead against mine, both of us breathing hard. "You've made me the happiest man alive!" His voice was full of wonder. I glanced down at the ring on my finger, the diamond catching the light as if it were alive.

"And you've made me the luckiest woman," I replied, barely containing my joy.

I wanted my baby to have a real daddy who would always be there for her. He would always have been her dad, but now he would be a constant presence in her life, and that made me the happiest person in the world. He kissed me passionately, one more time, and we went inside.

That evening, after the whirlwind of emotions had settled, we lay together in my bed. My head rested on his shoulder, and his arm wrapped securely around me. The ring on my finger felt unfamiliar, but in the best way—like a symbol of a new chapter, one I hadn't quite dared to imagine before.

"Cam, I am starting to get worried about the nightmares, though. I feel like I'm going crazy. I think we should delay the wedding until after I figure out what is happening to me." I whimpered, looking up at him with glossy, tear-filled eyes.

"Nonsense. I am here for you. We will figure it out together. You aren't going crazy. I can promise you that," Cam said in a steady, confident tone.

His hand rested on my growing belly, his thumb tracing lazy circles over the fabric of my shirt. "I'll take care of you," he murmured into my hair, his voice barely audible. "You and her, forever."

I believed him. Or at least, I wanted to. I know he would do anything in his power to keep me and the baby safe.

But what if he couldn't? What is he was too good to be true?

12

The Flashback

When I woke up, it was day, and the little house was well lit from the windows and the numerous holes in the ceiling. I went into my bedroom to read the walls. Some of it looked like poetry, or maybe song lyrics.

I was just starting to read when a glimmer of light hit my eye. It was a beam of sunlight that hit a photo frame. It was lying face down on the nightstand. I picked it up.

The frame was silver and covered in dust. It was a photo of me and a man—a good-looking man. We seemed genuinely happy.

The photo must have been a few years old; I appeared to be younger. I opened the frame to check the back of the photo and prayed there was more information. It read: "Grace and Joseph on their three-year wedding anniversary." I turned the photo over and touched his face with my finger.

I remembered him.

Memories flooded into my mind without even trying to think. It was like I was standing still while the world rushed around me in fast forward for a moment, and then it stopped, and all that remained were memories. I closed my eyes and let the memory swallow me whole, and again, I felt like I was being transported into another dimension.

I remembered the first time I stepped inside, back when we were just kids. I remembered we helped his grandma Edna paint the house together when we were only teenagers, and we had just started dating. The house had belonged to her for decades. Years later, Edna left the house to Joseph. We moved here after the wedding. We did everything together.

We went to school together and got married right out of high school. For my birthday one year, he gave me a cat, the cat that looked exactly like Fat Joe but with gold eyes. Joseph said his name was Captain Cheetos because he found his way into an open bag of them and hardly saved any for us. The long fur on his face was covered in Cheeto dust. We mostly called him Cappy for short.

On our third wedding anniversary, our friends surprised us with a beautiful party downtown. The night was magical, filled with laughter, music, and the kind of love that still felt fresh and intoxicating after all these years.

But as the hours passed, the drinks piled up, and exhaustion set in. I'd had far too much, but Joseph was worse off. That fool could barely stand, let alone walk. With the help of a friend, we managed to get him into the passenger seat of my car. I promised her I was fine. I thought I was fine.

The night air was heavy, a thin veil of mist clinging to the streets. The radio played one of my favorite songs, its melody wrapping around me like a blanket. I reached down for just a second to turn the volume up.

Just a second.

When I glanced back up, blinding headlights filled my vision. Panic surged through me as I swerved hard, slamming on the brakes. The car spun violently, skidding out of control before smashing into a curb. The next thing I knew, we flipped down into darkness and landed with a sickening crash.

For a moment, everything was still.

My heart pounded in my ears as I thought of Joseph, praying he was okay. The car was on its side. The side Joseph was on. But if I was alive, surely, he was too. It was hard to move. My neck hurt, but I forced myself to look over at him. When the car landed, it fell onto jagged metal spikes jutting up from the ground. They were those thin metal posts used in wire fencing. One had shattered the passenger window and impaled Joseph.

He was gone. Just like that.

At the hospital, they patched me up and ran tests. I felt their hands on me—gentle, efficient, detached—but my mind felt distant, like it had left my body. I heard their voices, muffled and blurry, as though they were speaking underwater. Words floated around me: "lacerations," "fractures," and "monitor closely." I didn't care. I wanted to scream at them to stop, to let me go, but my body was too weak, too broken. So, I let them do what they needed to, numbly staring at the glaring fluorescent lights above me.

That's when they told me that I had been pregnant.

Pregnant, and I didn't even know.

The words didn't register at first. The Doctor—mid-forties,

silver hair, tired eyes. His voice was so soft, so careful, as though I might shatter if he wasn't delicate. I hated his voice.

"You were between six and eight weeks along. I'm sorry, Grace, but the baby didn't survive the accident."

My breath caught, but I couldn't cry. I couldn't speak. My mind raced, trying to catch up with the words he'd just spoken. Pregnant? How had I not known? How had I not felt it? And now, it didn't even matter, because the baby was gone, just like Joseph.

In one night, I lost everything—Joseph, our child, and the future we had been building together.

I sat in the hospital bed, utterly alone.

The room was cold—too cold. The thin hospital blanket draped over me did nothing to warm me, and the scratchy fabric of the gown clung uncomfortably to my bruised skin. The sterile, chemical scent of antiseptic filled my nose, sharp and suffocating. Machines beeped in the background, their steady rhythm a cruel reminder that life went on. Even though mine had fallen apart, and maybe I no longer wanted to live.

The Doctor was gone now, replaced by silence. My hands trembled in my lap, pale and bruised from the crash. I focused on them, at the faint lines of dried blood under my fingernails, at the hospital bracelet looped around my wrist. It bore my name, Grace Christopher—printed neatly in black ink, as though I were still a person who existed in the world, someone who mattered. But I didn't feel like a person anymore. I was a shell.

I let my head fall back against the pillow, staring at the ceiling tiles as tears slid down my face, warm and relentless.

They wouldn't stop, no matter how hard I tried to swallow them back. My chest felt heavy, like my ribs were caving in. I couldn't breathe.

Why didn't I see the headlights sooner? Why didn't I stop drinking earlier? Why didn't I just stay home that night? The questions pummeled me, each one sharper than the last. There were no answers. Just the suffocating weight of what I'd done.

Joseph's laugh echoed in my mind, unbidden. That loud, goofy laugh he couldn't hold back when I told a joke that wasn't even that funny. I remembered the way he'd ruffled my hair when I was mad at him, the way his voice softened when he said my name. I remembered how he looked that night—smiling, carefree, so alive.

And then I remembered his face after the crash. Blood smeared across his cheek. His chest was motionless. His beautiful brown eyes stared at nothing.

A sob escaped my throat, ragged and broken. I clenched my fists so hard my nails bit into my palms, but the pain wasn't enough. Nothing would ever be enough.

The door to the room opened quietly, and a nurse stepped in, her shoes squeaking against the polished floor. She was young, maybe just a few years older than me, with kind eyes and a clipboard tucked under her arm. She stopped when she saw my tears, hesitating for a moment before stepping closer.

"Grace," she said kindly, "can I get you anything? Water? Another blanket?"

I shook my head, not trusting my voice.

She nodded, her expression filled with sympathy. "I'll check back later, okay? Take your time."

And then she was gone, leaving me alone again. I didn't want sympathy. I didn't deserve it. I didn't deserve another blanket.

When I closed my eyes, I saw the headlights again, bright and blinding. The car was spinning out of control, the jolt of impact, the world flipping over and over until it all went still. I saw Joseph, lifeless and crumpled in the seat beside me, and the jagged shards of guilt bury themselves deeper into my chest.

The baby. My baby. My child that would never have a name, never take a breath, never be held in my arms.

My hand moved instinctively to my stomach, resting on the soft curve beneath the hospital gown. I didn't even know. I didn't know. And now, I never would.

I was supposed to be a wife. A mother. Instead, I was a murderer.

The guilt was unbearable, a weight that pressed down on me until I thought it might crush me completely. I deserved it. I deserved every ounce of this pain.

But the worst part was the silence. Joseph wasn't there to comfort me, to lie to me and tell me it wasn't my fault, like he would have done. The baby wasn't there to remind me that life went on. There was no one, just the cold, empty hospital room and the steady beep of the machines.

My eyes focused on the wall, my vision blurring, my mind screaming for something, *anything*, to make it stop. But nothing did. Nothing could.

I didn't know how long I sat there, staring at nothing, lost in the storm of my thoughts. Time had no meaning anymore. The emergency room was busy. People crying, injured and bleeding, people waiting to be seen, and nurses running down the hallway. The world around me was in fast-forward mode. The nurses running down the hallway became blurred, white streaks moving past me. The crying and voices talking in the background faded to a long, drawn-out hum—then it stopped.

Suddenly, I was back in the bedroom. That horrid smell was back in my nose, and I was confused about what the hell had just happened. *What was that? A dream within a dream?* I had not woken up yet because I was still in the little house, holding the framed photograph.

13

Bald Man

I was on the edge of the bed in the old house. My eyes were filled with tears, and I felt immense guilt—even though the tragedy that occurred was in another dimension, or maybe it was something that happened in a past life.

Either way, my brain believed it happened to me. I seemed to be carrying the weight of that night. My reflection didn't lie. I *had done* this. Joseph was gone because of me, and no amount of punishment would ever make it right. I had tried to atone. The scars on my wrists were from attempts at ending my life. I had tried several times to end it all, but someone always "saved" me, dragging me back to this unbearable existence.

Maybe it's God's will. Maybe I was meant to suffer, to feel every ounce of the pain I had caused. But I didn't know how much longer I could bear it.

Tears were blurring my vision as I reached into my bag and pulled out a worn wallet. There were no identification or credit cards. There wasn't any money inside—just a business card tucked into one of the pockets. It read *Dr. Theodore Cameron, Psychologist,* accompanied by a headshot. The man in the photo bore an uncanny resemblance to my boyfriend Cameron, though he was older, with piercing light blue eyes.

They said that when you dreamed, your brain couldn't come up with a new face that you had never seen. My brain wanted to see Cameron everywhere, I supposed. Flipping the card over, I saw a date scrawled on the back—tomorrow at ten o'clock—circled with the word *Meeting.* Did that mean I had spoken to this Doctor to make an appointment? If time worked the same way here as it did in the waking world, that meeting would come up fast.

The house reeked—a sour, putrid stench that seemed to seep into the very walls, clinging to every surface. It began as a faint odor, one I could almost ignore, but since the first day I had dreamed of this place, it had grown unbearable. Every breath was thick with it, the kind of smell that made bile rise in the back of my throat. I could no longer pretend it wasn't there. I *had* to find the source.

The main bathroom was the worst offender. The closer I got to the cracked door, the stronger the stench became, until it was so overwhelming that my stomach churned. My hand shook as I pushed the door open. The hinges creaked like a warning. The smell hit me like a physical blow, making my eyes water. For a moment, I stood frozen in the doorway, breathing shallowly through my mouth.

At first, the bathroom looked the same as it always did—dim, grimy, a perfect picture of neglect. The mildew in the corners had grown thicker, and the peeling wallpaper hung limply from the walls like sagging flesh. But the smell was worse here, far worse.

I stepped in and turned toward the tub. The shower curtain hung limply from rusted rings, its once-white plastic now yellowed and brittle. My gut twisted as I reached for it, my fingers brushing the sticky material.

Was there something behind the curtain? I asked myself.

I yanked it back.

My breath caught, a strangled gasp escaping my lips, and I felt ill. There, slumped in the bathtub, was a corpse. He was the bald man I had seen on the beach and in the reflection of the mirror.

The man was lying in an awkward, crumpled position, his head tilted at an unnatural angle. His skin was waxy and bloated, mottled with shades of purple, green, and sickly yellow. Flies buzzed around his body in lazy loops, their wings a faint hum in the oppressive silence. Maggots were writhing all around his face. The smell hit me with full force, and I gagged, staggering back a step.

A single bullet hole marred his forehead, a blackened wound crusted with dried blood. It looked like he'd been dead for days, maybe longer, but that wasn't the most horrifying part.

I *knew* him.

I didn't know where I knew him from, but his face tugged at something deep in my memory. His sharp features, now swollen and distorted, were distinct. The buzzed haircut with a balding crown. The expensive leather jacket that clung awkwardly to his bloated frame. The polished shoes, scuffed, but still gleaming. Even his watch—sleek, silver, far too fancy for a man rotting in an abandoned house—looked familiar.

Who was he?

My stomach flipped as I forced myself to step closer, every instinct screaming at me to run. I couldn't. Something about him demanded my attention, like he held answers I didn't yet know I needed. My hand trembled as I crouched down and reached into his pockets. The leather of his jacket was damp and sticky, and I had to fight the urge to retch as my fingers brushed against something cold and solid.

I pulled it out—a small, clear baggie filled with fine, white powder. Coke.

For a moment, the world tilted. My pulse quickened, a sharp, staccato rhythm that seemed to echo in my head. The bag felt too familiar in my hand, like it belonged there. The smell of the corpse faded into the background as another sensation crept in, something sharper, more insistent.

I knew what to do with it. I *needed* it.

The realization hit me like a punch to the gut. This wasn't just some random dream logic filling my hands with a foreign object. I *knew* this powder, knew how it would feel, how it would taste, how it would rush through me like liquid fire. My body remembered, even if I didn't want it to.

My mind screamed at me to drop it, to leave the bag, the bathroom, the house—but my legs carried me out on autopilot. The smell followed me as I stumbled back into the living room, but it was fainter here, less suffocating. The air felt clearer, the stench diluted. I sank onto the sagging couch, the baggie still clutched in my hand.

My hands shook as I examined it, the white powder almost glowing in the dim light. The logical part of my brain, the part that knew this was a terrible idea, that knew nothing good could come from this, was drowned out by the other part. The part that was desperate, hungry, and aching.

"One quick shot," I muttered to myself, my voice hoarse and trembling. "Just one."

The ritual was muscle memory. I didn't question where I found the tools or how I knew the exact motions. My body moved on its own, guided by instincts I didn't want to acknowledge. The moment the powder hit me, the rush was immediate.

It slammed into me like a wave, electric and euphoric, racing through my veins and lighting up every nerve. My limbs felt light, my chest warm, my mind soaring above the horrors of the house. For a moment, everything was perfect. Blissful.

But then it wasn't.

My high shifted, twisting into something darker. Details of the room grew sharper, the shadows deeper, until I thought the house was watching me. The air thickened again, pressing down on me, and the stench of rot came roaring back with a vengeance.

The couch was too soft beneath me, like it was swallowing me whole. I tried to stand, but my legs felt heavy, uncooperative. My breath came in short, shallow bursts, and my chest tightened as panic set in. The cocaine acted like a memory enhancer. The room felt instantly smaller as a memory invaded my mind. The Memory flashed in my mind, vivid and haunting. It was all I could think about. I knew who he was.

His name was Lenny.

I remembered being on the street, turning tricks for him. I

remembered all the abuse he had inflicted on me.

One night, it was worse than normal. He was furious because I hadn't brought in enough money. He accused me of hiding some from him. He sneered as he reminded me that I owed him for "protecting" me out there.

When we got back to my house, his anger exploded as we stood in the living room in front of the open bathroom door.

"Where is it, bitch? Where's the rest?"

"That's all there is, I swear, Lenny."

He hit me open-handed against my face with such force, I stumbled backward.

"Don't you lie to me, whore! I will ask you one more time. This is your last chance," he said as he popped the knuckles in each hand. "Where. Is. The. Rest?" He emphasized each word slowly.

"I gave you everything!" I cried.

His fists began slamming into my head like I was a punching bag. He said, "You're disposable. You know that? You are trash!"

I kicked him hard in the groin, his howl of pain giving me just enough time to grab the gun from my bag. My head was spinning from the pain. His brow furled, and his teeth clenched together.

He lunged toward me. My hands shook as I pointed the thirty-eight Special at him. I pulled the trigger, I didn't hesitate.

One shot to the chest. He stumbled backwards into the bathroom. I stepped forward and refocused, aiming again, just in case. He looked down at his chest, "You bitch!" he snarled through his clenched teeth. Spittle and blood sprayed out.

He started to come at me a second time.

I pulled the trigger again. This time, the bullet hit him on the forehead. He stumbled back again. His knees caught the side of the tub, and he collapsed backward.

He didn't move, his body draped over the tub like a wet towel. I grabbed his ankles, tucked them into the tub, under the faucet, and closed the curtain.

Adrenaline coursed through me, but it wasn't enough to keep me conscious. Moments later, I passed out.

I remembered that the next day, reality struck me like a freight train. I knew I needed help. Not the kind the cops would give—they'd only see a drug-addicted prostitute who killed her pimp. I didn't want to go back to prison. I wasn't ready for judgment.

After I killed another human being, I just couldn't live with myself. I flipped through the phone book, and I found the name: Dr. Theodore Cameron. Something about "psychologist" next to his name felt like a lifeline. His photograph was on the ad with a phone number. He had a strong face with striking features. His eyes were so trustworthy and kind. Maybe he could help me make sense of everything, help me move forward.

When I met him at his office, I was a bundle of nerves. But his calm demeanor and kind eyes put me at ease. He didn't interrupt, didn't judge. He just listened. I told him everything, even the part I thought I should have kept buried: how I killed Lenny, my pimp.

Dr. Cameron didn't flinch. Instead, he leaned forward, his voice steady and reassuring. "I'm going to help you work through this. Let's take it one step at a time."

Before I left his office, he handed me a business card with

the date of our next session circled. It felt like the first solid step on a path I wasn't sure I deserved to walk.

Then everything went black.

The flashback was finally over, and I was back inside my dream. I was still standing in the living room like a zombie, high on cocaine. How many layers of dreams could there be at one time?

The couch was old and sagging but oddly inviting, its worn fabric soft against my skin. In front of it sat a coffee table cluttered with an overflowing ashtray. Cigarette butts and ashes were scattered across the table and even onto the floor—a chaotic little monument to neglect.

I sank into the couch and let my body give in. The heaviness pulled me under, and I passed out. It was a serene, dreamless sleep.

Suddenly, I woke up, choking, gasping for air. My eyes flew open, and there he was. Lenny. His massive hand clamped around my neck, squeezing with terrifying strength, while his other fist slammed into my face over and over. Panic surged through me as I kicked, scratched, and thrashed against him. I tried to scream, but no sound came out. My lip split open, warm blood trickling down my chin. The pressure on my throat was unbearable. The world went dark.

When I came to, he was gone. The room was silent except for my ragged gasps for air. *It was just my imagination. A hallucination. Right?* I thought. My legs trembled as I forced myself up and stumbled to the bathroom. Each step felt like my knees might give out beneath me.

In the bathroom mirror, I braced myself for the sight of bruises and blood. But there was nothing. No marks on my neck, no blood on my lip. My reflection stared back at me, unscathed yet haunted.

Shaken, I returned to the couch and collapsed. It was all in my head. Hopefully, the meeting with Dr. Cameron would be soon. Time had no meaning here. Cappy jumped up beside me, his warm, little body pressing against mine. His soft purring radiated through my chest like a soothing hum. He stared into my eyes, his gaze steady and calming. At that moment, I swore he was telling me it was okay, that it was safe now.

I believed him. So, I closed my eyes.

14

Kara

When I opened my eyes next, Cameron was lying next to me in my bed, looking into my eyes and caressing my arm, and then my big belly. He seemed so happy, and everything was all so perfect that I was scared it was too good to be true. My dreams had been so intense and realistic that I was starting to get confused about what was real and what was a dream.

Last night's dream was like a nightmare within a dream. It had all felt so incredibly real. *How does my dream-self feel just as real as my waking self?* At times, my dreams seemed more real than reality. I was sleeping for longer periods as well, almost as if my brain didn't want to wake up sometimes. I was coming unraveled to the extent that Cam would have to knit each strand of me back together.

Cameron studied my stunned expression with a curious tilt of his head. "Everything alright?" he asked, his voice soft with concern.

"Yeah," I replied, shaking off the haze of my thoughts. "Well, no, not really. I've just been having these crazy dreams— disturbing, vivid ones. Last night I dreamed I was in a shack of a house, which is a recurring dream of mine. Then, while in the dream, I have almost like a flashback of a memory to a car accident that kills my husband; his name was Joseph. When I got to the hospital, they told me I had been pregnant, but I lost the baby in the crash. Then the flashback ends, and I am back in the little worn-down house, and find a corpse in the tub. This brings another flashback of him beating me, so I shot him."

"Holy cow!" Cam blurted out. "That is one crazy nightmare," he said with surprise.

"Right? It was like a nightmare within a recurring dream. It felt so real, as if they were my own memories bubbling to the surface."

He nodded and raised an eyebrow. We got up and made our way to the kitchen.

"What if they *are* your memories? You said your past is foggy," he said inquisitively while starting a pot of coffee.

My brow furrowed as I pondered what he just said. "One would think they would remember at least snippets of crazy events like that though!" My voice was animated and had a tinge of sarcasm.

He didn't press further. Instead, he poured me a steaming cup of coffee. Over breakfast, we talked about setting a date for the wedding. We agreed it should be after we graduate and after the baby gets here, so we wouldn't have to juggle the chaos of school, new baby, and wedding planning all at once. I tried to push the lingering anxiety of the dream, or nightmare, or whatever it had been, out of my mind. I had too much to do to dwell on it. I had to keep telling myself that none of it was real. It was all from stress; I was sure of it.

I had to get moving. Today's to-do list was packed: Ordering graduation essentials and finalizing details for the party Cameron and I were throwing to celebrate. We wanted it to be unforgettable, the biggest party ever. I hoped all our friends would make it.

The day was gorgeous, one of those perfect, breezy days that made you want to stay outside forever.

After I did my shopping, I went home and hopped online. Cameron and I chatted online for a while, and then I fell into the rabbit hole of wedding dress photos. I already had my dream dress picked out—a stunning gown being held for me at the boutique. It was pricey, yes, but I told myself it was worth it. You only got married once, right? I could already imagine myself walking down the aisle, all eyes on me in that dress.

I went into the kitchen to make myself a sandwich. I just realized I hadn't eaten anything since breakfast. I was so wrapped up in wedding plans that I didn't realize I was hungry until now, and it was nearing six in the evening. I grabbed some deli meat and cheese out of the fridge and set them on the counter.

Then, a searing pain surged through my gut, but within a few seconds, it was gone. *Was that a contraction?* I wondered. I hoped not, as I was only at thirty-two weeks. I forgot about my hunger completely. *I need to pack a hospital bag just in case*, I thought. But I didn't know how much time I had at this point. Another sharp, stabbing pain hit me. I grabbed my belly and leaned over in pain. I walked upstairs to my bedroom as carefully as I could manage.

Another contraction came. Panic surged inside me as I

fumbled for the phone on my nightstand, my hands trembling so badly that I nearly dropped it. I managed to dial Cameron's number, my voice shaky and uneven as I blurted out the words I never imagined would come so soon: "It's happening. The baby—she's coming."

As I hung up the phone, I was interrupted by another sharp, unexpected pain tearing through me. These were contractions. This one was worse than the last, and the time between them was shortening. The sensation was so sudden and intense that it stole my breath. I gasped, doubling over, clutching my stomach as if holding it could somehow stop the pain. Then I felt it—a dampness spreading down my legs. It hit me like a jolt of electricity. My water had broken.

Cam arrived in the blink of an eye, his face pale but resolute, like a soldier preparing for battle. He didn't waste a second, guiding me into the car with a mixture of urgency and care. As he sped toward the hospital, one hand gripped the wheel while the other held mine. His thumb brushed gentle circles over my skin, a soothing gesture that spoke louder than any words could.

"Everything's going to be okay." His voice was steady and calm, like a lifeline in a storm. I clung to those words. Cam never lied to me—if he said it would be okay, I believed him.

When we reached the maternity ward, chaos and calm collided around me. The pain was all-encompassing, a primal force that seemed determined to split me apart, but the nurses moved with practiced efficiency, their presence reassuring despite the storm raging inside my body. They ushered me into a room, and though they offered me something for the pain, it hardly made a dent in its overwhelming intensity.

Through it all, Cameron never left my side. His hand remained clasped in mine; his gaze locked on mine with an unshakable resolve that made me feel like I wasn't alone in this battle. "I love you," he whispered, his voice thick with emotion. "I'm so proud of you."

His words wrapped around me like armor, shielding me from the fear that threatened to creep in. They gave me the strength to keep going when I thought I had none left.

Hours passed in a blur of contractions that felt like waves of fire, each one crashing through me and leaving me gasping for air. At some point, time lost all meaning; all I could focus on was the unbearable pressure and the singular thought cycling through my mind: *Let this be over.* I screamed through the pain, clutching Cameron's hand so tightly I worried I might break it. But he never flinched. His steady presence was my anchor as I pushed with everything I had.

And then, finally, a new sound filled the room—the sharp, beautiful cry of new life. My entire world narrowed to that one perfect moment as they placed her on my chest. She was tiny and rosy. Her face scrunched with indignation, her lungs already announcing her arrival with incredible strength. She was crowned with a rare full head of soft, light-brown hair, and as I gazed at her, I knew she was perfect.

For years, I'd had her name chosen, holding it close to my heart, waiting for this exact moment. "Kara Melody," I whispered, tasting the name for the first time as I cradled her in my arms. It was magical, like saying it aloud finally brought her fully into being. She was everything I'd imagined Kara would be—soft, sweet, and precious. My heart swelled with the thought of calling her "KaraMel," a nickname I'd been saving for her long before I had ever met her.

The nurses wrapped her in a soft pink blanket and handed her back to me. As I held her, her cries softened until she was quiet, her wide, curious eyes locking onto mine as though she already knew me. Time seemed to stand still as we gazed at each other, the feeling of her in my arms grounding me in a way I'd never felt before.

Cameron leaned over, brushing a tear from his cheek as more streamed freely down his face. I hadn't even noticed that I was crying, too. We were a mess of emotions—pure, overwhelming love, fear of failure, and relief that she was here. When the nurses carefully lifted her from my arms to take her to the nursery, a pang of loss struck me so sharply I almost protested. It felt too soon to let her go, even for a moment. She was so tiny, I couldn't help but be overly protective of her.

"She'll be safe, but she needs to go to an incubator so her lungs can get good and strong," one of the nurses assured me kindly, her voice calm and understanding. They brought me to my room, where a bed was waiting, freshly made with crisp, cool sheets. I was so exhausted I could hardly think, yet part of me resisted the idea of sleep. How could I rest after something so monumental, so life-altering?

"You need to rest now, love," the nurse said. Cameron pulled up a chair beside me, his hand finding mine like it had so many times that night.

"She's perfect," he murmured, his voice filled with awe. I nodded, tears still threatening to spill as I let myself sink into the bed.

The room was bathed in moonlight, soft and silver, streaming through the bare branches outside the window and casting delicate shadows across the walls. The air was cool and crisp, carrying the earthy scent of freshly cut grass through the slight crack in the window Cameron had opened for me. The breeze kissed my skin, refreshing and soothing, and for the first time since the night began, I felt at peace.

I closed my eyes, the sensation of the smooth sheets against my skin grounding me in the moment. Cameron's hand stayed clasped in mine, his warmth a constant reminder of the life we'd just brought into the world. My heart felt incredibly full, like it might burst from the love and promise that now surrounded me. In that quiet, moonlit room, the world felt soft and new, and I let myself drift into sleep.

But then came the bird. Its harsh, repetitive squawking shattered the stillness. It sounded like a crow, perched just outside my window, and its relentless cries were impossible to ignore. With a sigh, I reached for my earplugs, slipping them in to muffle the sound.

Cameron leaned over and kissed my forehead, his presence calming me amidst the frustration of the noisy intruder. "I love you," he murmured.

"Goodnight, Cameron. I love you, too," I whispered back, my voice soft with affection. Finally, cocooned in the comfort of the sheets and the quiet hum of his presence, I closed my eyes and attempted to sleep while the bird cawed repeatedly, rhythmically.

15

Sunnybrook

CAW! CAW!

The harsh cry of a crow pierced through the void of sleep, ripping me awake. Except it wasn't a crow—it was my alarm clock, blaring at half past nine for some inexplicable reason. My head throbbed, my heart raced, and for a moment, I couldn't make sense of where I was. The couch beneath me was stiff and uncomfortable, and my blanket was tangled around my legs. Why had I set an alarm? I couldn't remember.

The noise grated on my nerves until I finally reached over, slamming the button to silence it. *Peace at last.* My chest heaved as I sank back down, the relentless screech now replaced by the muffled hum of distant traffic outside.

On my chest, Cappy was curled in a small, fragile ball of warmth, his fur like silk under my fingertips. I absently ran my hand through his soft coat, his purring vibrating against my ribs like a quiet metronome, steady and soothing. My head was foggy, as though my thoughts had been plunged underwater. Everything about the morning felt... off. Like I was walking on the fringes of reality, not quite awake, not fully dreaming.

I tried to shake the sensation, focusing instead on Cappy's little face, his half-lidded eyes blissfully shutting into slits. But then, I saw them.

Legs. Someone's legs were standing directly in front of me.

My stomach twisted.

Blinking hard, I forced myself to look up, my pulse quickening.

Dr. Cameron stood there, dressed in khakis and a light blue button-down shirt that matched his eyes. His tall frame was relaxed, his face unreadable except for the faintest hint of amusement. He tilted his head to one side, his pale blue eyes studying me like I was a puzzle he was trying to piece together.

"Do you talk in your sleep often?" he asked lightly, but his question carried an unsettling undercurrent of curiosity, as though he already knew the answer.

"Was I sleeping?" I croaked, my voice hoarse and my thoughts sluggish. The words tasted strange in my mouth.

Instead of answering, he leaned down and offered his hand. He pulled me to my feet, his grip firm but too calm, too controlled. I swayed as the room tilted off kilter, the edges of my vision swimming.

"What's going on?" I asked, my words trembling as they left my lips. "Where are we going? How... How did you get into my house?"

"The door was unlocked," he said smoothly, as though that explained everything. "We have an appointment."

I stumbled after him as he led me toward the door. "No!" My voice was rising as panic began to creep in. "The door wasn't unlocked. It couldn't have been. I locked it. I *know* I locked it."

Dr. Cameron paused and turned to face me, his expression softening, though his tone remained unshakable. "Grace," his voice was low and steady. "You've been forgetting little things like that. Don't you remember? You've been... distracted."

The words slapped me like ice water. *Had I?*

My memories slipped through my fingers like smoke, impossible to grasp. I couldn't remember locking the door. But I also couldn't remember leaving it unlocked. The certainty I thought I had was shattered into pieces, leaving only doubt in its place. But in truth, I couldn't remember caring at all since this was a dream and nothing mattered.

"No," I whispered, shaking my head hard, as if I could will the confusion away. "You're twisting this. Something's not right."

We stepped outside. The sunlight hit my face like a punch. I raised my hand to shield my face from the light while Dr. Cameron grasped my other arm and led me over to a parked car.

I hardly noticed the man seated in the passenger seat of the car until I was climbing into the back. He hadn't said a word, hadn't moved an inch, his face a mask of blank indifference. His presence was chilling, as though he were a shadow given form, watching, waiting. I slid into the backseat without protest, the quiet tension heavy in the air as we drove. The drive probably took seven minutes, but to me it felt like ages. Time seemed to have no meaning in dreams.

I was curious to see where we were going, but at the same time, this dream was too frightening. *To hell with my research. I needed to wake up!* I thought. I wasn't in control at all, and no matter how hard I tried, I couldn't wake myself up from this nightmare.

The car crept forward through a pair of towering iron gates, their rusted hinges groaning as they swung inward. My stomach twisted into a tight knot as I read the words on the sign: Sunny Brook Institution. The name sounded deceptively cheerful, like it belonged to a cozy retirement home, or a bed-and-breakfast. But nothing about the place felt cozy. Not the peeling paint on the sign, not the iron of the gate, and certainly not the suffocating feeling that began to settle over me as we drove deeper into the grounds.

Am I being committed? The question repeated in my mind, gaining weight with every turn of the car's wheels. *Is this involuntary? Do I have a choice?*

Part of me wanted to yell at Dr. Cameron, to demand answers, to insist that I didn't belong here—that this was all a terrible misunderstanding. But another part, quieter but insistent, whispered back: *Do you really know that? Don't you remember feeling like you're coming undone?*

The conflict churned inside me, a clash of panic and reluctant acceptance. I hated the idea of being here, of being trapped in some sterile institution like a crazy person. But at the same time, I couldn't deny the exhaustion pressing down on me, the constant noise in my head that never let up. The nightmares had become unbearable, relentless. I hadn't felt like myself in weeks—months, maybe. *Maybe this is what you need,* that quiet voice insisted. *Maybe you're too far gone to fix this on your own.*

I clenched my hands in my lap as the car rolled further down the gravel drive. The tires were crunching loudly in the stillness. The grounds of the institution unfolded before me, a strange mix of beauty and foreboding.

The garden was the first thing I noticed, too vibrant, too perfect. Beds of vivid flowers lined the pathways, their bright reds, yellows, and purples a startling contrast against the muted grays and browns of the massive building ahead. Roses, daisies, tulips—all blooming in neat little clusters, as if nothing in the world could ever touch them. But the perfection of it felt artificial, staged, like it had been curated to distract from the truth of the place.

The tall trees that bordered the garden were imposing, their thick trunks like silent sentinels. Their branches stretched out wide, casting dappled shadows over wooden benches scattered beneath them. For a moment, I could almost convince myself it was peaceful here. The kind of place where someone could sit under a tree and read a book or simply close their eyes and breathe.

But the building looming ahead shattered that illusion.

It was enormous, a hulking structure of weathered stone that seemed to watch us as we approached. Its facade was lined with tall, narrow windows, most of which were dark, their glass smudged and cloudy. A few were cracked, faint spiderweb patterns etched across their surface. The stone itself was worn and pockmarked, the kind of aging that spoke of decades— maybe centuries—of use.

The closer we got, the more oppressive the building felt, as though it were absorbing all the air around it. It towered above the picturesque gardens like a predator lying in wait, its corners sharp, its roof steep and severe. Vines crept up its sides, but instead of softening its appearance, they only made it seem more alive, more menacing. Like the building was part of the landscape, rooted deep into the earth, immovable and inescapable.

It's just a building, I told myself, though my chest tightened as I stared up at it. It's just stone and glass. It can't hurt you.

But the nagging voice in the back of my head whispered something darker: You don't get to leave places like this. Not until they decide you're fixed, and what if you are irreparably damaged?

Dr. Cameron pulled the car to a stop in front of the building, the tires kicking up a faint cloud of dust. My breath hitched as I focused on the heavy double doors. They were made of dark wood, thick and reinforced with metal bands. The doors seemed like they were meant to keep people in as much as keep others out. He glanced over at me, his expression unreadable. "We're here," he said simply, as if this was a normal trip, arriving at a coffee shop or the movies and not... this.

I swallowed hard, glancing back at the gardens, the trees, the flowers. They appeared so inviting, so safe. But they were a lie, weren't they? Just a distraction from what this place really was.

You do need help! that quiet voice in my head reminded me again, more insistent now. You've been spiraling, Grace. Maybe this is the only way to stop it.

But another part of me, the part that felt more like the real me, was screaming. You don't belong here. You're not crazy. You don't need this kind of help. They've got it wrong. Dr. Cameron's got it wrong.

"Grace?" His voice pulled me from my thoughts. He was studying me, his tone calm but firm. "Let's go inside."

I nodded, though my body felt disconnected, like I was moving through water. My legs were shaky as I climbed out of the car, the crunch of gravel underfoot too loud in my ears. The other man—the silent one—wearing white scrubs, was already waiting for me, standing by the car door like some kind of guard. His face was as blank as ever, his eyes cold and distant, like he didn't see me as a person but as something he'd been tasked with managing.

I hesitated, glancing back at the gates. They were still open, but they felt like miles away now, like they'd already closed in spirit.

The man gestured for me to move, his silent authority suffocating. Reluctantly, I followed Dr. Cameron toward the massive building, each step heavier than the last.

I tried to focus on the gardens, on the flowers, trees, and benches. I tried to convince myself that this place wasn't as bad as it seemed. *It's peaceful here,* I told myself. *People get better in places like this. You'll get better here.*

But as I crossed the threshold of the stone building, the cool air inside rushed over me like a whisper of death. The voice in my head grew louder, angrier: *No, you won't. This isn't a place for getting better. This is a place in your mind where you'll be forgotten—because this is a dream! What if Professor Nielson was right? What if I get lost in here and never wake up?*

Dr. Cameron walked beside me as we entered the building, the other man flanking me on the opposite side. I felt caged between them, unsure of what awaited me in this strange, enormous place.

Walking into the lobby almost gave me a bout of vertigo. The ceilings were so high! There was an ornately carved, dark wooden staircase in the center. On either side of the lobby, two large hallways split off into north and south wings. We headed down the north hallway to what I discovered to be my new accommodation.

The small, sterile room felt like a cage. The walls were painted a pale, washed-out green that was supposed to be calming, but only made me feel more uneasy. Bars on the tiny window cast long shadows across the floor, cutting the dim light into jagged stripes. The narrow bed, with its thin blanket and single pillow, was pushed against the wall, as if someone had decided that any kind of comfort here was a luxury.

I turned to Dr. Cameron, who stood in the doorway, watching me. His expression was gentle, but there was a tension in his posture that didn't match the softness in his eyes. I felt like I was being studied like a bug under glass. Behind him, the other man lingered silently, his face blank and unreadable, yet his presence was oppressive. He hadn't said a word during the entire drive, and now he stood like a shadow, filling the doorway with his bulk.

"What is this?" I asked, my voice trembling. "You said this was an appointment. An appointment for *what*? Why does this feel like a prison?"

Dr. Cameron stepped into the room, his hands raised in a gesture of calm. "It's not a prison, Grace," he tried to sound soothing. "It's a place where you can feel safe. A place where we can help you."

I scowled at him, my chest tightening with panic. "Help me? I don't need *this*! I'm just tired, that's all! I've been having nightmares, sure, but this—" I gestured to the room, to the bars on the window, to the shadow of the man in the doorway. "This is insane!"

"Grace," he said tentatively, taking a step closer. "We spoke about this at our last meeting. You agreed then to come here. You told me yourself how the nightmares have been getting worse. How you're not sleeping, how you're seeing things you can't explain. You said you feel like you're losing control. You called me and asked for my help. Do you remember any of that?"

I opened my mouth to argue, but the words got caught. Had I said that? It sounded familiar, but everything in my head was tangled, like trying to piece together fragments of a shattered mirror. My thoughts were foggy, my memories slipping through my fingers like sand. "I—" I began, but I couldn't finish the sentence.

"Exactly." His voice was gentle but firm, as though he were explaining something to a child. "This isn't about punishing you or locking you away. This is about understanding what's happening to you. We're going to figure this out together."

I started crying and shaking my head in disbelief. I looked up at him through the tears, searching for something, anything, that would tell me what was real.

He sighed, his calm demeanor faltering for the first time. "Grace, I need you to trust me. Just for now. Let me help you. Rest here, just for a little while, and we'll talk more later. You'll see—it's not as bad as it seems."

But it was as bad as it seemed—or even worse. The walls felt like they were closing in, the sterile air pressing against my skin. I glanced around the room again, my gaze lingering on the barred window, the narrow bed, and the thin blanket. It was like I was being buried alive. I needed Cam and Kara. I needed everything to go back to normal.

"Just for now," he repeated, stepping back toward the door. "You're safe here. I promise."

Off to the side was a tiny, cramped room—barely bigger than a closet—with nothing but a toilet and a sink. The stark simplicity of it all made the air feel thick with unease.

Dr. Cameron handed me a paper cup filled with water and emptied three pills from a plastic pill box into my hand. My mind immediately thought of *The Matrix*. Will one of these pills show me for sure what was real? What if I didn't want to know? I was scared to know. The fluorescent light above him buzzed, casting sharp shadows across his face. His voice was soft, deliberate, as though he were speaking to someone on the edge of a precipice.

"Everything will be alright," he promised, his eyes steady. "You can rest now."

I was desperate to believe him. Dr. Cameron had a calm demeanor that made me feel like everything really could be okay, just like Cam. But part of me was too terrified to truly believe in anything. I examined the small, white tablets in my shaking palm, their edges glinting under the light.

And then, against every instinct screaming at me not to, I tipped the pills into my mouth, took a sip of water, and swallowed them down in one smooth motion. The bitterness of the pills lingered on my tongue for a moment, then quickly faded. I handed the empty cup back to him and lay down on the bed, tucking my legs under the blankets.

Almost immediately, a heavy drowsiness swept over me, wrapping itself around me like a thick, weighted blanket. The edges of sleep pulled at my limbs, my head, and my thoughts. I barely registered the cool sheets beneath my skin as I sank into the narrow bed, my body folding into the softness like I hadn't slept in years.

Through the fog, I heard Dr. Cameron quietly leave the room, the faint creak of the door followed by the unmistakable metallic click of the lock sliding into place. That sound, a tiny, innocuous noise, echoed loudly in my mind, reverberating like a bell in a silent cathedral. My heavy eyelids fluttered once, twice, before giving in completely to the overwhelming pull of sleep.

For what felt like hours, I was lost in a black void. There were no dreams, no flickers of thought, just a thick, enveloping darkness that was more like an abyss than sleep. I floated there, weightless, my mind blissfully empty.

I'd always wondered if it was possible to dream inside a dream, and somewhere, in a fleeting moment of lucidity, the thought bubbled to the surface: *I should add that to my research paper. I need to talk to Cam about this. He will know what to do.* But even that faint whisper of logic was swallowed by the darkness.

When I finally opened my eyes, I was in a deep fog. I was disoriented and didn't recognize my surroundings. I sat there for a few moments trying to get my bearings. My head and eyes began to clear.

The sterile room greeted me like a cruel joke. I had woken up in the same place where I had fallen asleep. The faint chemical smell of disinfectants still lingered in the air, and the sunlight filtering through the small, barred window was dim and weak.

My body felt heavy, like it had been weighed down with lead, and for a moment, I couldn't quite tell if I was awake or if this was just another layer of the dream. I was shaking but I wasn't cold, and my body ached all over like I had been hit by a bus.

At the foot of the bed was a tray of food. The faint smell of lukewarm soup and bread wafted toward me, stirring my stomach into a growl despite the fog clouding my thoughts. My movements were sluggish as I pushed myself upright, my muscles stiff like I'd been lying there for days. That's when I noticed something else: my wrists, no longer raw and stinging, were now cleaned and wrapped in crisp, white bandages. I must have slept so deeply; I hadn't felt them doing this. How long had I been out?

Confusion prickled at the edges of my mind, as if I were trying to grasp a thread that kept slipping through my fingers. Slowly, I lifted my arm, noticing for the first time the hospital bracelet dangling loosely around my wrist.

The details were printed in sharp, clinical black text: Christopher, A. Grace. Age: 32. Daytona Beach, Florida. ID #435643. Date of admission: 03/20/2008.

I studied the bracelet, blinking as if that would somehow rearrange the letters and numbers into something that made sense. Was I *that* disoriented? Thirty-two? That couldn't be right. I was twenty-two. It's not 2008, it's 1998! And Daytona? I'd never lived in Daytona Beach. Chicago—that was home. I was sure of it. My childhood, my family, and my entire life had been rooted there. The chaos of crowded sidewalks, the frigid winters, and the skyline.

But Daytona? My connection to it was flimsy, like a ghost of a memory trying to slip back into my awareness. I'd visited several times, years ago, on childhood vacations. That was it. It was sunny, sandy, and generic, the opposite of the gritty, bustling city I loved. Why would my mind conjure up this place?

The bracelet didn't belong to me. The ID number, the age, the location—it all felt like someone else's story. And yet, the words stared back at me with an undeniable certainty.

I thought of Chicago again, searching for clarity, trying to anchor myself. I pictured the scenes I knew so well: the Wrigley Field crowds, the L trains rattling through the air. I remembered watching *Adventures in Babysitting* over and over as a kid, loving how Chicago was alive, like it could swallow you whole. I'd always related to the nerdy girl with glasses in the movie, the one who never quite belonged, the one stranded downtown, scrambling to find her way home. That was me, wasn't it? Chicago wasn't just where I lived; it was part of who I was.

But the bracelet... The sterile walls of this hospital... The faint scent of saltwater in the air... They were all telling a different story. My thoughts swirled into an incoherent mess. *Who was rewriting my life? And why couldn't I remember?*

The door creaked open, breaking my spiral, and Dr. Cameron entered with Cappy in his arms. The cat from the house. Even though he wasn't Fat Joe, my heart still leapt at the sight of the cat, who had been with me during my nightmares.

"Cappy!" I breathed, my voice cracking as I reached out. He squirmed in the doctor's hold before leaping onto the bed and curling into the crook of my arm. The warmth of his small body grounded me for a moment, and I buried my face in his fur. His scent, comforting and familiar, was enough to calm the trembling in my hands. His purring was faint, uneven, a shadow of the steady hum I knew by heart.

"I missed you," I whispered, fighting back tears. He didn't feel like *my* cat, but he had been with me during all those nightmares. He was a familiar comfort to me. His fragile body pressed against mine, and the ache inside me deepened. If this were a dream, it was too cruel. And if it wasn't, what had happened to him?

Dr. Cameron's voice broke through the quiet moment. "I couldn't leave him at your place. He'd miss you too much."

My place. The phrase hung in the air like a splinter. The dilapidated shack the cat had been living in. My head swam as he set down a tray of food and water for Cappy. He bent and set a small litter box in the corner of the room. I was grateful he brought the cat here. Now I wouldn't be utterly alone. Then Dr. Cameron stood, walked back over to me, and handed me something else—a photograph.

16

Two Lives Collide

The second I saw it, I froze.

It was Joseph.

The ache in my chest sharpened into something unbearable. My breath caught as I traced the image with trembling fingers. He was smiling—God, that smile. Warm, crooked, so uniquely *him*. I could practically hear the low rumble of his laugh, and feel the way his presence had always filled a room.

"Joseph," I whispered, hardly recognizing the sound of my voice. The name spilled from my lips like a prayer, desperate and hollow. Memories flickered in my mind, like glimpses of sunlight through a cracked door. His face. His laugh. The feel of his arms around me, solid and safe. But there were holes, too— jagged, empty spaces in my memory where the rest of him should've been. Where *we* should've been.

Dr. Cameron's voice was steady and professional. "We have a session in an hour. Bring the photo." I nodded, though I couldn't pull my eyes away from Joseph's face. My fingers curled tighter around the photo, as if letting go would make him vanish. Was he real or imaginary?

The confusion in my head surged again, stronger this time. What part of this was real? What was a dream? And why did the two feel so indistinguishably tangled, like threads knotted together in a way I couldn't unravel?

If this were reality, why did it feel like a story I didn't belong in? Why did I feel like I had swapped bodies with some stranger? What if that were possible? I thought again about my research paper and how consciousness could leave the body, as during astral projection. What if my soul were in someone else's body? If that were true, who was in mine, and how did we switch back?

If it was all just a dream, then what part of me was being held here, unable to wake up?

Cappy's weak purring was the only sound in the room as I sat there clutching the photo, my thoughts spiraling into that question over and over.

What was real? And what had I already lost trying to figure it out?

The lock clicked behind me as the nurse shut the door. I sank onto the bed, gripping the photo of Joseph as if it were the only thing tethering me to myself. But even as I stared at his face, the edges of the room blurred. The dream—or whatever this was—was swallowing me whole, and if I didn't wake up soon, I might never wake up at all.

My mind and heart felt like they were being split down an invisible seam. One half of me remembered and loved Joseph— the warmth of his smile, the sound of his laugh, his dark brown, soulful eyes, the way he used to hold me like I was the only thing in the world that mattered.

But the other half clung desperately to Cameron and Kara. I *knew* them. I loved them. Kara was my baby, *our* baby, and that was real. It had to be real. I felt the pain of giving birth to her just yesterday. That pain and joy of her birth had to be real.

Or was it?

My head had been a mess long before Kara was born—dark thoughts, memory lapses, dreams so vivid they bled into my waking life. But now? Maybe the drugs they'd given me at the hospital when I went into labor, or maybe the drugs I had been given here, made things more distorted. What if the medication was keeping me asleep? What if this wasn't real, and I just needed to wake up?

"I have to wake up," I muttered, the words gaining urgency. My heart thudded painfully. "I *have to* wake up."

Panic surged as I stumbled to the window of my room. Throwing it open, I screamed into the air, my voice frayed with desperation. "This is a dream! Wake up, Grace! Wake up!"

But nothing happened. The world outside remained steady, immovable. No flickering, no dissolving, no sudden break in the illusion. If this *was* a dream, it wasn't listening.

Frustration swelled up into my throat like a dam about to burst. I spun around, rushing to the door. My fists pounded against it with a frantic, uneven rhythm. "I need my baby!" I screamed, my voice cracking under the weight of my fear. "Where is Kara? Give me my baby!"

Behind me, Cappy let out a sharp, mournful meow. His voice cut through my hysteria, bringing me back from my panic for just a second. I turned to look at him, his thin body perched on the bed, his gold eyes fixed on mine. He seemed so real, so solid, so heartbreakingly present.

But how could he be? How could *any* of this be real when none of it made sense? My two lives were colliding, overlapping, and I didn't know which one to trust.

The door opened, and the male nurse stepped in, a small paper cup in his hand. Inside were pills—red, white, green—a kaleidoscope of chemicals designed to silence my screaming thoughts. He smiled, but the expression didn't reach his eyes. There was something cruel in the curve of his lips.

"Time for your medication." His voice was smooth but cold. "Something to help you relax, Grace."

"I don't need to relax! I have to wake up!" I snapped, stepping back as he approached. My voice was sharp, rising into a growl. "I need my baby! Where is she? *Where is Kara*?"

His calm demeanor didn't falter as he held out the cup. "Take your medication, Grace."

I slapped his hand away, the pills scattering across the floor like tiny, colorful beads. Anger surged through me as I glared at him, my chest heaving.

"You are not listening! This is a nightmare! You can't keep me from Kara!" I shouted. My fists were clenched. I raised one fist upward. I was going to get back to Kara, no matter what it took. He couldn't hold me here. I started towards him with my fist in the air.

His face hardened. Without warning, he grabbed my arm, his grip bruising my flesh. I thrashed against him, struggling to break free, but he was stronger than he looked. Before I could scream again, I felt the sharp prick of a needle in my skin.

"No!" I gasped, but it was too late. Whatever he'd injected me with was already working, spreading a sluggish heaviness through my limbs. My strength ebbed away, and he guided me back to the bed with surprising gentleness. Even when he strapped my limbs down with leather straps, he was careful not to hurt me.

"Sleep, Grace," he murmured, his voice fading into the growing fog.

The world tilted, darkened, and I sank into unconsciousness.

When I opened my eyes again, everything was blurry, but the piercing sound of a baby crying cut through the haze like a knife. My breath hitched as I blinked, focusing.

Kara.

Tears immediately brimmed in my eyes, and it felt as though my heart would explode. Cameron stood by the bed, cradling her in his arms. My heart surged at the sight. She was real. She *had* to be real. The tears ran down my face as he pressed a kiss on her chubby cheeks, murmuring to her.

"She's beautiful," he said, his voice cracking with emotion.

He turned and handed her to me, and the moment her weight settled into my arms, I felt whole again. She wasn't crying anymore, just making soft cooing noises as her wide, curious eyes gazed up at me. Her tiny hand was curled around one of my fingers.

I leaned down, pressing my cheek against hers, inhaling her sweet baby scent. My baby. My Kara.

But then, something shifted.

I glanced back at Cameron. My love, my rock—and froze.

His face... it was changing. His youthful features aged before my eyes, wrinkles deepening around his eyes, gray streaking through his dark hair.

No.

He wasn't Cameron anymore. He was *Dr. Theodore Cameron.* The man in the white coat, calm and clinical, was watching me with those cold, calculating eyes.

"No," I whispered, shaking my head. "No, no, no!"

I sat up as quickly as I could manage and turned back to Kara, clutching her closer, desperate to block him out. But then she gasped—a sharp, choking sound that sent a bolt of terror through me.

"Kara?" I said, my voice was trembling.

Her tiny body convulsed in my arms, her skin losing its rosy warmth. It turned pale, then gray, then an unnatural, sickly white. She was shrinking, her soft, chubby cheeks collapsing, her limbs withering.

"No!" I screamed, watching helplessly as her small body began to crumble into ash.

I clutched at her, trying to hold her together, but the ash slipped through my fingers, scattering onto the floor. A hollow wail tore from my throat, raw and primal. "No! Please, no!"

Dr. Cameron's voice broke through my anguish, calm and unshaken. "It was just a nightmare, Grace. You're safe."

"Safe?" I spat, trembling with rage and grief. "You took her from me! You killed her!"

He stepped closer, his gaze steady, detached. "Grace," he said, his tone infuriatingly measured, "you're not well. Let us help you."

"I don't need help! I need my baby! I need to wake up!"

But as I thrashed and screamed, I felt the familiar sting of another injection. The heaviness returned, pulling me under.

When I woke up again, my chest ached with profound grief. My face was damp with tears, my throat raw from screaming. Cappy was curled against me, his fragile body a small comfort. His gold eyes stared into mine, filled with an unspoken sorrow.

I sat up slowly, my movements mechanical. The straps on the bed had been removed, but the room still felt like a cage.

When the nurse arrived to escort me to Dr. Cameron's office, his tone was sharper this time. "Let's go," he snapped, his patience clearly worn thin.

I hesitated, my body stiff, my mind screaming for me to fight, to resist.

"Now!" he barked. "Or do you want me to sedate you again?"

Reluctantly, I stood. Cappy meowed inquisitively as I left him behind, echoing in my head as I stepped out of the room.

The office smelled of old books and woodsy cologne, the kind that clung to the air in antique shops or forgotten libraries. It wasn't unpleasant—if anything, it was oddly calming—but that only made the tension inside me coil tighter. Something about the stillness of the room felt too carefully arranged, as if I were stepping into a set piece instead of something real. Cold sweat formed on my brow, and my pulse quickened.

Dr. Cameron motioned for me to sit in a cushioned velvet fabric chair. He sat across from me in a high-backed chair upholstered in cracked leather, his posture as steady and composed as ever. The faint glow of a desk lamp cast soft shadows across his face, deepening the lines at the corners of his mouth and eyes. The shadows on his face made him look less trustworthy. I glared at him, trying to decipher his intentions.

In his hands, he held a large, weathered book. The cover was dark leather, scuffed and faded, the edges worn with age. Gold embossing on the spine caught the light, though the letters were too faded to read.

He turned the book toward me, his movements deliberate and smooth, as if he were handling something precious.

"How are you feeling now, Grace?" Dr. Cameron asked.

"I'm not entirely sure, Dr. Cameron," I said with a hint of sarcasm. I was still seething about the interaction with the nurse earlier, still mad that I was here and not with Cam and Kara. I needed them, but I was also beginning to tire from fighting whatever this was.

"Do you remember this?" he asked, his voice low and gentle, like a father coaxing a frightened child. But I wasn't comforted. His question wasn't light; it was heavy, thick with implication.

I peered at the book. It tugged at the edges of my mind, familiar in a way that made my skin prickle. It was very large and seemed more like a three-ring binder. The worn, scuffed cover, the bent corners, even the faint musty scent—all of it struck a chord that felt both intimate and alien.

"I..." My voice wavered, almost inaudible, as I tried to speak. I wanted to say yes, to name the book, to make this moment solid, tangible. But the truth pressed harder against me, cold and relentless: I didn't know. Not for certain.

"No," I whispered finally, my hands clenching the armrests of the chair. My nails dug into the fabric. My unease was eating away at me.

Dr. Cameron's expression didn't change—neutral, thoughtful, unreadable. I didn't like that. He didn't seem disappointed, but there was a weight to his silence that made my stomach twist. I felt like he was trying to trick me.

The tension in the room thickened, and I felt a rising urge to escape. Not just from him, but from everything. From this place, this moment, this maddening blur between what was real and what wasn't.

And then a thought slithered through my mind, cold and dark: What if Dr. Cameron wasn't real at all? Maybe that's why I felt so on edge, and why I didn't trust him.

What if he was something else—something *other*?

One of those shadowy figures from folklore, the ones that pinned you down in your sleep and whispered nightmares into your ears.

Shadow people. The Hat Man. The Hag.

Demons in the guise of doctors.

Maybe he wasn't here to help me. Maybe he was a figment conjured by my fractured mind, or worse, some malevolent entity trapping me in this world for reasons I couldn't understand. How could I possibly tell the difference in the state I was in?

My breaths came quicker, shallow, and uneven.

He doesn't believe me. He doesn't want me to leave.

I could feel my pulse pounding in my ears as paranoia took hold, whispering sinister truths in my head. Maybe Dr. Cameron wasn't trying to help me. He was the reason I was here. Maybe he wanted me trapped in this reality forever, locked away from Kara, from the life I so desperately wanted to return to.

Or... was this the life I was trying to return to?

My nails bit deeper into the fabric of the chair as my mind spiraled. If this place isn't real, then the harder I fight, the more I risk staying. I thought about those horror stories, the ones where people get stuck in lucid dreams because they can't stop resisting. After all, the very act of wanting to wake up only strengthens the dream's hold.

Is that what this is? Is he some kind of gatekeeper, here to test me? To punish me?

"Grace?" His voice cut through my thoughts like a scalpel, precise and piercing. My eyes snapped to his, startled.

He was watching me intently now, his gaze no longer calm but sharp, probing, as though he could see the storm raging in my mind.

I swallowed hard, my throat dry. Maybe I needed to play along. Maybe the only way to escape this place, to wake up, was to convince him I trusted him. I needed to make him believe that he was in control.

"Yes." The word tumbled out too quickly. My voice was cracking, but I pushed forward. "I remember. I think..." I let the sentence trail off, vague and uncertain, as if I were searching for the memory.

His head tilted, and a flicker of something showed in his eyes as he glared at me—was it interest? Or was it suspicion?

"Do you?" he pressed. His tone was still gentle but now tinged with curiosity.

I nodded, forcing myself to hold his gaze even as my pulse thundered inside my ribs. "It's... it is familiar. I think I've seen it before."

His lips curved into the faintest hint of a smile, but it wasn't warm. It was clinical, measured, like he was cataloging my reaction for some unseen record. His eyes narrowed as if he were trying to see my thoughts through my skull.

He set the book on the table between us and opened it, flipping through the pages with a deliberate slowness that made my skin crawl. The sound of the paper—thick, more like cardstock—seemed to echo in the stillness. I didn't want to touch it or look at it. I wanted this all to be over.

He picked the book back up, closing it as he did. He handed it to me, the feeling of it familiar in my hands. My fingers brushed against the worn cover as I opened it. It was a scrapbook, the pages thick with memories. The sight of the photographs had pulled out memories buried deep in my mind. It was as if every time I saw a different photograph, another filing cabinet in my mind would open and scatter documents all over.

There were pictures of me as a baby, a little girl, and images from high school. As I flipped through, my chest tightened. There were photos of my wedding to Joseph, pictures of Cappy as a kitten, and snapshots of the house we'd once called home. The house that now seemed like it was near collapse, where Dr. Cameron found me.

"It belonged to your mother," Dr. Cameron said, his voice softer than usual.

"My parents both died when I was in high school. We all lived in Chicago. This isn't real." I yelled, trying to make him understand.

"After I had met with you at my office, I searched your name online and was able to find your childhood address. I went there hoping your family still lived there. I had no idea. I knocked on the door, and your mother answered. We spoke for a good while. She told me that after your car accident, you spiraled into depression. When you were convicted of vehicular manslaughter and went to jail, she said you were like a zombie," he said in a calming voice, then continued,

"She said she wrote you hundreds of letters, but you never responded. Then, when you got released from jail, you refused her help, turning to drugs and alcohol. She showed up at your house a few times, trying to offer support, but you were distant and cold. She could tell you were high out of your mind.

"Then one day, she said she went to your house for a visit, but you were gone. She tried again a few times, but you weren't at the house. She thought you took Cappy and left. She hadn't heard from you and was worried sick."

I looked him in the eyes as he said these words, trying to decipher if he was telling the truth. His eyes were full of concern and honesty. I didn't say a word, still processing the information.

"She had no idea that you were back at that house, barely surviving. She gave me the photo album in hopes that it would help jog your memory. She wanted to come herself, but she was very ill the last time we spoke. She wanted you to get well and paid for your stay here."

I held the photo album close. "This…" I choked out, my voice barely audible. "This is my life?"

Dr. Cameron nodded slowly, his gaze unreadable. "Yes, Grace. It is."

I pulled my hand back as though the book had burned me. The room spun, and I gripped the chair to steady myself.

How could my life—*my* life—be laid out so neatly in this book? Was this proof that I was still dreaming? That he was controlling everything?

Or was this proof that this was real, and the life I wanted to wake up to was the dream?

Tears blurred my vision as the lines between the two worlds blurred even further. I didn't know what was real anymore or who I could trust. Could I even trust myself?

I glanced up at Dr. Cameron, my voice faltering. "Am I... Am I dreaming?"

His expression softened, but there was something unsettling in his eyes. He reached forward, placing his hand over mine. His touch was warm, steady, too real.

"No, this is reality. You're safe, Grace," his voice was gentle. "That's all that matters."

I flipped to a page near the middle, where a photograph of me as a twelve-year-old stared back at me. I was at the beach in Daytona, grinning awkwardly in a faded swimsuit. Mom was sitting beside me. Memories were beginning to pop up like fish to their food. It was as if my memory had been jump-started by the sight of these photographs.

"Mom! Yes, that's her! That was the day I got caught in the current," I said with some excitement.

The memory was like a knife twisting in my gut. I continued, "The cold waves dragged me under. I was flailing my arms as I screamed for help. I remember my mom sitting on the sand, her headphones in, completely absorbed in her book. She didn't hear me screaming. She didn't see me choking on seawater until I finally dragged myself back to shore.

"We'd moved to Daytona shortly after my dad ran off with another woman. I never saw him again after that. He disappeared, leaving a void that my mother and I didn't talk about. She dealt with it in silence, losing herself in her novels, while I silently wondered what it was about me, or us, that wasn't good enough to make him stay."

Another photo caught my eye: me, Joseph, and Cappy on my birthday. Cappy was just a kitten, a hyperactive little ball of fur, that Joseph had given me as a gift. He was like a black cotton ball with eyes and claws.

I smiled and said, "I remember how chaotic it was trying to snap that picture. Cappy was bouncing off the walls, chasing a fly, and in his excitement, he'd leapt from the back of the couch onto the drapes, pulling them down in a tangled mess. My mom, ever the problem-solver, dangled a cat toy above the camera to grab his attention. It worked—for a second. You can see the photo caught him staring wide-eyed at the toy, just before he launched himself off the couch and climbed up her legs in pursuit."

I laughed to myself at the memory, but the sound quickly faded as I turned to the next page.

There was another photo of me, alone.

"It was my birthday again, but this one came after Joseph's death." I wasn't smiling in this photo. No one in the photo was. I continued, "My mom had tried to make the day special, but I remember thinking that I'd never celebrate anything again," I said as I wiped away tears with the back of my hand.

That was the last photo I had from that time. Everything after that was a blur, a haze of pain I didn't want to feel. I closed my eyes, the flood of memories pulling me under. I began to cry, but I needed to tell my story. I tried to compose myself.

"As you know, I spent time in jail for manslaughter. Nine years. I got out when I was twenty-nine and became hooked on drugs. Alcohol stopped being enough to forget. When I ran out of money, the cravings didn't stop. That's when I met Lenny. He said he could help me, give me what I needed—if I worked for him. All I had to do was turn tricks. He made it sound simple, like a business arrangement. Legitimate, even.

"I told myself I didn't have a choice. I had nothing left. Every night, I came home to the run-down house and poured my pain onto the walls, writing and writing until my fingers cramped. It was the only way I could escape. I created Grace—the Grace I wanted to be. A girl who was loved, who was pregnant, who had a future. She had a boyfriend who adored her and a life that made sense."

Dr. Cameron handed me a tissue.

"I didn't want to live in my reality anymore. The more I wrote, the more her world became real to me. I dreamt of her every night, slipping into her life like a second skin. I clung to her story because it was easier than facing the wreckage of my own," I told him in between sobs. But now, as I focused on the photos in the scrapbook, the lines between what was real and what I'd created blurred even further.

"Your mind did what it's supposed to do when it deals with trauma. I blocked it out completely. That's the mind's way of protecting you. I've been trying to find relatives who could visit you, maybe help jog your memories, and someone to help ground you in the present, but your mother was the last of your family."

Almost not letting him finish, I blurted out, "Where is she? Can I see her?"

"Grace..." He hesitated, his voice cracking. "I hate to have to tell you this, but your mother passed away last night. Pancreatic cancer. I'm so sorry."

His words hit me like a punch to the gut, the air leaving my lungs in a sharp gasp. My grip on the scrapbook tightened, my knuckles turning white as the memories rushed in all at once, crashing over me like a tidal wave. I wish I could remember her. I wish I could have been there for her. I began to grieve that loss, and I could feel a void growing in my heart.

17

This is Reality

Joseph's smile. Kara's tiny hands. My mother's laughter. The feeling of Cam's arms around me. They all seemed so real. So did the cold straps that had once bound me to a bed in detox at the jail so long ago. So did the faint hum of fluorescent lights in this office. So did Dr. Cameron's hand on mine, keeping me anchored in the present.

"What's real?" I whispered. My hands shook as I clutched the scrapbook tighter, as though it could answer my questions. "What's real, and what's just a story I've told myself?"

Tears blurred my vision, hot and unrelenting. My mother was gone. The one person who'd still tried to save me, even after I'd pushed her away, was gone.

Dr. Cameron moved to my side, his voice soft but steady. "This pain is real, Grace. But it doesn't have to define you. You've been running from it, but now you've stopped. That's the first step. You don't need to run anymore. Now that you know the truth, you can begin to heal. It will take time, and it won't be easy, but you can do it."

I couldn't stop crying, the weight of my grief crashing over me. "I can't," I choked out. "I don't know how to move forward. I've lost everything."

"You haven't lost everything," he said, his hand covering mine. "You still have yourself. And now that you understand your past, you can decide what your future will be."

I peered up at him through blurry eyes, and for the first time, I thought I saw the faintest glimmer of tears in his. He was real. And for now, that was enough.

"Take some time," his voice was firm. "Think about everything we've talked about. When you're ready, we'll figure out the next step. Together."

"I want you try to socialize with the other patients in the day room," he said, "it might help you feel connected to the world again."

I nodded, not because I agreed with him, but because I didn't have the energy to argue.

I clutched the scrapbook like a lifeline as I stood. My memories were overwhelming, but somewhere, buried beneath it all, was the faintest flicker of hope. Because, for once in what seemed like a lifetime, I could finally see a small piece of truth.

I returned to my room with heavy steps, the intensity of the day pressing down on me like a thick fog. My hands trembled as I closed the door behind me, the soft click of the latch louder than it should have been in the silence. The room felt smaller than it had that morning, the walls closer, the air thicker—but it was real.

Cappy greeted me from the bed, his thin, black and white body curled up in a loose ball. His gold eyes blinked up at me, weary but watchful, as though he'd been waiting for me all day.

I scooped him up, cradling him against my chest, and the warmth of his body soothed the ache inside me. His fur was soft against my cheek as he nuzzled into me, his purring steady and low, like a small, constant heartbeat.

"I'm going to be alright now," I whispered, the words trembling on my lips and tears running down my face like a waterfall.

In response, Cappy licked my cheek, his rough tongue dragging over my skin in a series of deliberate strokes. It wasn't just affection—it was comfort, reassurance. He was telling me, in the only way he could, that he believed in me. That even now, in the mess of all my uncertainty and pain, he still trusted me.

I held him tighter for a moment, then set him down on the bed. Without hesitation, he hopped off and padded over to his food dish. The soft crunch of kibble broke the silence, and I realized with a pang of gratitude that he'd waited for me. He'd sensed something was wrong. He had been holding back, staying close to me, putting my well-being ahead of his own. Now that I was calmer, steadier, he finally let himself eat.

That simple gesture unraveled something in me. My throat tightened, and tears welled up in my eyes. Cappy had loved Joseph, too, in his way. He had grieved in the silence of this room, just like I had, just like I still was. But now, he was here with me. He'd stayed loyal and unwavering, and I couldn't let him down.

I sat on the edge of the narrow bed in my room, staring at the pale green wall in front of me. It was the same shade as the walls in every other part of this place, probably chosen because someone decided it was "soothing." It wasn't. It just made me feel smaller, like I was fading into the background, becoming part of the furniture.

The window above my bed had bars on it, but that didn't matter. I didn't feel trapped because of the bars—I felt trapped because of the exhaustion, the fog, the constant ache in my chest that never seemed to go away. I tried to tell myself that things would get easier now that I wasn't living in a dream world. But it was difficult to believe in myself at the moment.

I thought about Docor Cameron suggesting that I socialize. I knew what he was trying to do. He wanted me to engage, to build bridges between myself and other people, to pull myself out of this fog. I *wanted* to want that, but I didn't. Not yet. It was hard to trust others right now.

The thought of walking into that room, filled with strangers, their stories likely just as broken as mine, made my chest tighten. *Will they see the cracks I try to hold together with brittle, frayed threads? Will it remind me too much of my own fractured mind?* I was drained, physically and emotionally. *How can I connect with anyone when I feel so disconnected from myself?* I knew Dr. Cameron was right and that the only way to get over the fear of being around other people was to do it. I had to open myself up again and let people in.

I tried to imagine what the day room looked like. I pictured a space with mismatched furniture, maybe some games. I imagined it being full of people who were screaming, hurting themselves, or maybe wanted to hurt me. There would be some sitting silently, and some muttering to themselves. Others could be trying to find slivers of connection in a place that felt so inherently isolating.

I thought about shuffling in awkwardly, every movement weighed down by the thick haze of fatigue, unsure if I could handle a simple conversation, let alone the invisible weight of someone else's pain.

At the same time, I wanted to believe Dr. Cameron might be right. Somewhere deep inside me, I craved connection, craved the feeling of belonging to the real world again. I missed normalcy. I missed easy conversations over coffee. I missed being someone who could laugh without thinking too hard about it. I missed being someone who didn't feel like a stranger in their skin.

But wanting to connect and having the energy to do it were two very different things. I didn't know how to find the strength for even a small step toward that.

Still, I reminded myself I'd endured worse. Somehow, that thought comforted me. I'd endured sleepless nights, weeks of haunting dreams that left me shattered, months of feeling like I was unraveling while trying to pretend everything was fine. I'd endured the sharp edge of loneliness, endless doubt, and the fear that I was losing my grip on what was real. I'd been through all of that, and I was still here. That had to count for something, didn't it?

I told myself that maybe tomorrow I'd have the energy to leave my room, even if just for a little while. Maybe tomorrow I'd venture into that day room, take a look around, and see what was waiting for me there. It wouldn't fix anything overnight, I wasn't naïve enough to believe that. But maybe, just maybe, it could be a start. For now, though, all I could do was let myself rest. Rest, and hope that the fog would lift enough for me to see tomorrow a little more clearly.

I sat down on the bed, tucking my legs beneath the covers, and Cappy jumped back up onto the bed after finishing his meal. He curled up on my lap once more, his purring returning as a soft rhythm in the quiet. I stroked his fur absentmindedly, my fingers tracing the sharp curve of his spine.

Outside, the sky was darkening, the last traces of daylight fading into deep indigo. Through the window, I could see the branches of the trees swaying in the wind. Their brittle limbs scraped against one another, casting long, eerie shadows on the walls and ceiling. They were like skeletal fingers playing a mournful tune on an invisible piano, the wind their only accompaniment.

I shivered, but not from the cold.

"I'll be alright," I murmured again, this time almost as if I were trying to convince myself. The words hung in the air, soft and uncertain. It seemed like the truth hovered just out of reach, elusive and fragile. I had spent so much time believing that this wasn't real, that I could wake up from this nightmare and find myself somewhere else, *someone else*. A woman who wasn't grieving. A woman who wasn't fractured. A woman who could hold her baby in her arms.

But sitting here, with Cappy's steady warmth on my lap, I felt the heaviness of the truth beginning to press down on me. There was no waking up from this. There was no other reality waiting for me on the other side of this pain. I wasn't trapped in a dream, and Dr. Cameron wasn't some shadowy demon keeping me imprisoned.

This was it.

I was awake. This was my life, my reality.

The realization settled over me like a heavy blanket, stifling but inevitable. There was no escape from the pain, no hidden exit door to a brighter, easier version of my story. If I wanted to move forward, I had to do it here, in this world, with the pieces I had left. It was going to be a long, painful process to put my pieces back together. I knew that.

I looked down at Cappy, his gold eyes half-closed, his purring soft and content. He was my anchor, the last link to the life I'd had before, the life with Joseph. Cappy loved both of us, but now he needed me just as much as I needed him.

"I'll be alright," and this time the words felt a little more solid, a little more real.

The wind outside picked up, rattling the windowpane, and the shadows on the walls shifted like ghosts in a restless dance. I watched them for a long time, my thoughts circling like the wind outside.

Doubt lingered in the corners of my mind, dark and stubborn. Was this acceptance? Or was I giving in? Was this the beginning of something new, or was it the beginning of the end?

The thought made my chest tighten, but I shook it off. I couldn't focus on that now. All I could do was take one moment at a time, one breath at a time.

Cappy stretched out beside me, his small body pressing against my side. His loyalty, his quiet presence, was enough to remind me that I wasn't alone. Not entirely.

I leaned back against the pillows, my gaze drifting to the window once more. The branches swayed in the moonlight, their skeletal shapes shifting and curling. They seemed like they could crumble at any moment, brittle and fragile. But they held on, bending with the wind, refusing to break.

"I'm so sorry, Cappy," I whispered, the words barely audible over the sound of Cappy's purring.

He stood and began making biscuits on my stomach as if to say, "I forgive you. It's not your fault." Tears rolled down the sides of my face for so long, I wondered if they would ever stop.

And as the shadows danced on the walls, I closed my eyes, letting the reality of this world settle over me like a second skin. It didn't fit perfectly yet—it still chafed in places, rubbed raw against the memories of the life I'd lost. But it was my reality.

For better or worse, it was mine.

I lay down on the bed, staring at the ceiling as the immense exhaustion pulled at me. Falling asleep here had become almost mechanical; they always made sure of that. Every night at exactly half past nine, the male nurse I'd grown all too familiar with came by, his heavy footsteps echoing down the hallway.

His name was Ben. He was a muscular, stout man who looked like he should be a bouncer, not a nurse. In his hand, like clockwork, he had a small paper cup with my sleeping pill, Trazodone. By ten, I was always out, floating into a chemically induced sleep. No fighting it. No resisting it.

As my body succumbed to the pull of the medication that night, my mind plunged into the abyss of nightmares. They weren't just fleeting, nonsensical dreams; these nightmares were vivid, raw, *alive*. They tangled themselves around me, dragging me deeper and deeper into memories—or was it all fiction?—until I couldn't tell where one ended, and the other began.

I dreamed of burning. My body shook violently as I detoxed from years of cocaine use, the imagery grotesque and unrelenting. My skin was clammy and cold, but inside I was on fire. I twisted my torso over the edge of the bed and retched into the trash can. My head throbbed, the pain so sharp and relentless it felt like my skull was splitting open. My temples pulsed with every beat of my heart, and my vision blurred as the world around me slowed to a crawl.

Am I in Hell? I thought. My voice was no louder than a whisper in my dream. I moaned, the sound guttural and raw. *I think I've finally hit rock bottom.*

The words escaped my lips like a confession, a painful truth I could no longer deny. *I have nothing! I have nobody!* I tried to scream, to release the ache building inside me, but the pain swallowed my voice, reducing it to a feeble croak.

I sat up slowly, the memories, or dreams, of being Grace from Chicago clinging to me like cobwebs. Kara. Her rosy cheeks. Her soft skin against mine. Those moments felt so vivid, so heartbreakingly real, that it almost felt like Dr. Cameron was lying to me. But he wasn't. I knew now, deep down, that this was my reality. He was trying to help me. He was real.

I longed to escape this endless torment, to drift into a dream where I wasn't *me*. Where I wasn't the broken woman on this bed, the addict, the grieving widow. I longed to stay asleep forever, to dream that I was Grace from Chicago. Grace, the woman with the perfect baby girl, Kara Melody. Even though I knew it wasn't real. I *knew* that world was warm. It was tender. It was *blissful.*

Thomas Gray was right when he said, "Ignorance is bliss."

I wished I'd never uncovered the truth, wished I could slip back into the beautiful lie of that dream world. It would have been easier. Simpler. But there was no going back, now. I had seen through it, and like a mirror shattered, I couldn't piece it together again.

And yet... wasn't it better to live in that lie than face this bleak, relentless reality?

18

Investigation

When I woke up the next day, it was almost lunchtime. The sunlight filtered weakly through the window, casting pale beams onto the green walls. I felt groggy, like I hadn't slept at all. Maybe I hadn't. I didn't know anymore. How could I, when my dreams felt like entire lifetimes stretching on for decades? In one of our sessions, Dr. Cameron told me they were nothing more than fragments of a spiral that began twelve years ago.

Twelve years ago. I was only twenty when Joseph had died. That was a lifetime ago. I had been arrested and spent nine years behind bars. After that, I just didn't know how to start over. I had spent all those years constructing a fantasy world that felt so real that I believed it. I didn't want to see my reality, which was a drug addict forced into prostitution and abused for years. I didn't want to be reminded of my guilt for killing Joseph, for killing our baby. But I did. I had to face these facts, no matter how difficult it was.

A knock at the door pulled me from my thoughts, and the nurse entered with my lunch tray. The meal was simple—a sandwich, some fruit—but I couldn't bring myself to eat much.

I took a few bites, more for Cappy's sake than my own. He had been watching me from his spot on the bed, his gold eyes steady and filled with quiet concern. When I put the fork down, he padded over and let out a soft meow, nuzzling my hand.

"I'm okay," I whispered to him, offering a faint smile.

He blinked slowly at me, as if to say, "I'm glad," and for a moment, my chest didn't feel quite so hollow.

But the moment didn't last.

About an hour later, Nurse Ben returned, this time to escort me to my session with Dr. Cameron.

"I am so exhausted, though!" I groaned, the words spilling out in frustration. I just felt so emotionally raw. "I want to take a nap!"

Nurse Ben didn't answer, but the sharp look he gave me spoke volumes. It was the kind of look that said, "Try me." Reluctantly, I relented, letting out a long sigh as I stood up.

I patted Cappy on the head before I left, and he let out a soft meow, his version of "See you later." His small gesture of loyalty was enough to nudge me forward, even though my steps were slow and heavy.

The hallway was as cold and lifeless as always. The walls were painted in the same dull green, the floors an uninspiring shade of slate. Everything about this place seemed designed to suck the life out of you, to keep you from feeling anything at all.

By the time I sat down in Dr. Cameron's office, I was already exhausted.

The session began as it always did, with his calm, steady voice coaxing me to talk. I resisted at first, frustration bubbling up in me. "Why do you even care?" I demanded, my voice breaking. "I'm in my own personal hell. I don't even know who I am anymore. You can't possibly understand the rage I feel inside me for what was done to me, for what they made me do."

Tears streamed down my face as I spoke, and Dr. Cameron leaned forward. He had a box of tissues in his hand. His expression was soft, patient, as he said, "That's why we have these therapy sessions, Grace. It will take time, but you can trust me. I just want to help you."

I took a tissue from the box and wiped my eyes. I wanted to argue, to push him away, but the words didn't come. His tone was steady, and part of me clung to it like a lifeline.

"I've never seen a patient with so much trauma," his words cut through my tears. "And yet here you are, Grace. Still alive. Still fighting. You have been through not only a single traumatic experience, but several. You're here for a reason, and you are stronger than you think."

The truth of his words was like a punch to the chest. I *was* still here. Somehow, through all the loss, the grief, the self-destruction, I was still breathing.

"Your spiral began with your accident. Which you say cannot be an accident because you broke the law. You said that you were drinking, and you shouldn't have gotten behind the wheel. But Grace, you have paid your debt to society with your incarceration for this lapse in judgment.

"Then you continued to punish yourself after being released from jail. You have paid every single day for the death of your husband and unborn child. It's time to stop punishing yourself and to get to know who you really are. Do you think Joseph would want you to keep punishing yourself? Or would he want you to move on and find happiness again?"

"I don't know. I feel like I don't deserve to be happy at all." I said, pausing and wiping the tears from my face, "I mean, I want to be happy and live a normal life. A life like I had before. But I am scared I will never find that again. I've lost everything."

"You need to talk about yourself," he continued, his voice unwavering. "Not just the loss, but who you are. What makes you, *you.* That's how we'll find you again, Grace."

It was painful to open up, like ripping off a bandage that had fused to my skin, but I did it. Slowly. Hesitantly. And it helped, more than I thought it would.

Amid all the chaos, I began to see something I hadn't noticed before—pieces of myself that were still intact. Tiny fragments of the person I used to be. Memories of hobbies, interests, and things that once brought me joy. They were small, almost insignificant, but they were there.

At that moment Dr. Cameron's goal became clear to me: to help me focus on those pieces, those small but vital parts of me, instead of drowning in the sea of loss and guilt that had consumed me. There was still something left of me. It wasn't much, but it was mine. And maybe it was enough to start over.

A week later, I sat down with Dr. Cameron in his office. He wanted to talk to me about something important.

Dr. Cameron's expression was calm but serious as he sat across from me during our morning session. His hands rested on his desk, fingers interlaced, as though bracing himself for my reaction.

"I need to let you know that the criminal investigation into

Lenny's death has begun," he informed me, his voice steady but heavy with what he was saying. He studied my face for a reaction.

The words hit like a sudden gust of wind, sharp and jarring. My chest tightened. Lenny. Just hearing his name brought back flashes of the violence, the fear, the chaos. I could still feel the bruises on my skin, his fists, his rage. Most of all, I could feel my guilt. I didn't say anything. I could only nod.

"The house is a full-blown crime scene," Dr. Cameron continued. "The detectives have cordoned it off with yellow tape stretching to the trees by the curb."

I stayed silent, taking in the information. I closed my eyes, picturing it in my mind: my house, now under the harsh scrutiny of strangers in uniforms. It wasn't even a home, not really. It was a prison, a trap where I'd been bound by fear, by addiction, by Lenny.

Dr. Cameron stood, walked over to me, and put a hand on my shoulder. "For the first week of your hospital stay, I refused to let the detectives speak with you. You weren't ready. You needed time to stabilize. But now..." He paused, leaning towards me. "I believe you're strong enough to talk to them."

His words sank into me slowly, like a stone dropped into deep water. My stomach churned, but I nodded. I trusted Dr. Cameron now, and if he thought I was ready, I had to believe him.

"Alright, if you think I'm ready."

"I'll call them back and let them know. I understand this might not be the easiest thing for you. But you can do it. Just tell them the truth."

The detectives arrived that afternoon. Mark Schammel and Bethany Berry stepped into Dr. Cameron's office, their presence sharp and professional. I was already sitting in my usual spot—the surprisingly comfortable armchair that had become my reluctant haven during sessions—but I felt anything but comfortable.

Schammel was an older man, somewhere in his mid-fifties, with a weathered face that spoke of years of hard cases. His black suit was immaculate, his pressed white shirt and blue tie lending him a no-nonsense air. When he spoke, his voice was gruff, with the faint rasp of someone who'd smoked for decades, or maybe still did.

Berry, on the other hand, was younger, mid-to-late-thirties, with striking green eyes that held an unexpected warmth. Her auburn hair was pulled back into a neat bun, and she wore tailored black slacks and a simple, brown button-down blouse. Her presence felt softer, more approachable, as though she could see right through my defenses without making me feel exposed.

Dr. Cameron introduced them, then stepped back and stood by the bookshelf on the far wall, a silent but steady presence.

Schammel wasted no time. His tone was direct and serious. "Miss Christopher, we're here to get your statement regarding the events leading up to Lenny's death. We understand this is difficult, but we must hear everything you can remember."

I glanced at Berry. Her expression was empathetic, and when she spoke, her voice was gentle. "Take your time. We're here to listen. Whatever you can share will help."

Tears welled up as I began to speak. The words came slowly

at first, but as I recounted the horrors of my life with Lenny, they began pouring out in a rush. I told them everything—the beatings, the relentless control, the fear that had consumed me. I told them how I had tried to fight back, how I had defended myself with my fists, but it was never enough.

"And then..." I paused, my voice hitched. "And then he lunged at me." My hands gripped the arms of the chair as the memory surged back, raw and vivid. "I panicked, and I—I shot him. Twice." My voice broke on the last word, and I hung my head, guilt choking me.

"Is that *everything* you can remember, Miss Christopher?" Schammel asked abruptly.

"Yes." I continued, "I didn't want to hurt him," I sobbed. "I didn't want to hurt anyone! But that's all I seem to do—hurt people."

For a moment, the room was silent except for my ragged breathing.

"I hated him," I admitted, my voice cracking. "But I also... needed him. Isn't that sick? He was the reason I had food to eat, and the drugs I thought I couldn't live without. I hated him for what he did to me, for what he made me do, but without him..." I shook my head, my voice dropping to a whisper. "I don't know if I would have survived. How do you reconcile that? He was someone who was both my tormentor and my lifeline."

Berry leaned forward, her green eyes locking onto mine. "It's complicated, but we're here to find the truth. You've been through hell, Grace, and none of this is your fault. Your strength speaks louder than your circumstances." They explained that the investigation was still in its early stages. The scene was being processed, interviews were being conducted, and they would be in touch as the case progressed.

Before leaving, Detective Berry handed me a business card. "Call me if you think of anyone we should talk to or if any other details come back to you," she said in a professional but empathetic tone.

She hesitated, as if debating whether to say more. Then she added, "We know Lenny was a violent pimp. Other girls he abused are coming forward. But he was small-time—a pawn in a much larger game. There are bigger players in this ring, and we need your help to take them down."

Her words lingered in the air as she gathered her briefcase. I nodded, gripping the card. "I'm remembering more every day. But some memories I can't trust."

"That's understandable. It might take some time, and that's alright."

As Berry left the room, I sat frozen, her words pressing down on me. *Your strength speaks louder than your circumstances.* Did it? Could anyone really look past the fact that I'd spent years lost in a dream? That I'd built an entire world to escape the wreckage of my real one? The doubt crept in like a shadow, curling around my chest and squeezing tight. *If I can help take down the people who put others through what I went through... Maybe it's a chance to redeem myself.* I thought.

But can I? What if they don't believe me? What if I am not strong enough to tell my story in court? I don't trust my own memories. How can I expect a judge or jury to believe them?

19

Monster in a Judge's Robe

After meeting with the detectives, I decided to take a leap and explore the day room. My heart was pounding before I even stepped into the hallway, the walls seeming to press in closer the farther I walked. The air felt heavier out here, or maybe it was just my anxiety. New places, new faces, they still set my nerves on edge. I focused on each step, trying to keep my breathing steady as I followed the faint murmur of voices and the hum of the television down the corridor.

When I reached the doorway, I paused, only peeking my head inside. The day room wasn't as chaotic as I'd feared. A few tables were scattered across the room, some with jigsaw puzzles in various stages of completion and others stacked with board games. Plastic chairs surrounded the tables, their surfaces scuffed and dull from years of use. A couple of plastic rocking chairs sat near the far corner, the faint squeak of one of them moving back and forth punctuating the silence. The walls were lined with bookshelves, crammed full of old paperbacks and hardcovers, their spines cracked, and their covers faded.

Mounted high on one wall was a TV with a visible scratch running diagonally across the corner. The channel was set to Classic Television Network—CTN—and *The Brady Bunch* played on low volume. I felt a flicker of familiarity, a brief flash of warmth. *The Brady Bunch.* My mom used to put it on when I was little, usually while folding laundry or doing something in the kitchen. I couldn't help but linger for a moment, watching as Marcia and Greg argued about something trivial.

My gaze shifted to the people in the room. At a table near the window, a girl was hunched over, drawing. She appeared to be young, maybe nineteen or twenty, and her long, black hair fell like a curtain around her face. I could only catch glimpses of her work from where I stood, but what I saw was impressive—sharp lines and intricate details that hinted at real talent. She moved her pencil swiftly and her hand steady.

As if sensing my stare, the girl glanced up, her eyes meeting mine for a split second before darting back down. She shifted in her seat, letting her hair fall farther over her face like a shield. The message was clear: "Don't come any closer."

I averted my gaze, not wanting to make her uncomfortable. My attention landed on a man sitting at a table near the center of the room. He was older, maybe in his late sixties, and plump, his belly stretching over the waistband of his khakis. What remained of his hair was nearly white, the bald crown of his head shiny under the fluorescent lights, highlighting the wispy hairs that remained on top. He sat facing me, playing cards by himself. *Solitaire*, I guessed.

Something about him felt... different. Inviting, almost. His round face broke into a wide smile when he noticed me, his rosy cheeks nearly swallowing his eyes as they crinkled with warmth. It wasn't the strained or empty kind of smile you'd expect in a place like this. It was genuine, as though he was truly glad to see me.

I hesitated, unsure if I should approach him. My anxiety tugged at me, urging me to stay put, to keep my distance, and retreat to the safety of my room. But something in his expression gave me the courage to step forward.

I walked past the young girl, who was still hiding behind her curtain of hair, and stopped in front of the older man's table. My voice wavered as I asked, "Do you want a card partner?"

His smile widened, and he motioned for me to sit. "Name's Frank, little lady," he said, his voice warm and gravelly, like someone who'd spent years laughing and talking a little too loudly. He adjusted the wire-framed aviator glasses perched on his nose, pushing them up with one thick finger. "And you are?"

"Grace," I replied, sliding into the seat across from him. "It's nice to meet you, Frank."

"Grace," he repeated, nodding as if testing how the name felt in his mouth. "Pretty name. Strong name." He began gathering the cards into a neat stack, shuffling them with surprising dexterity. The sharp snap of the cards as they slid together was oddly comforting, satisfying.

"Gin rummy okay with you?" he said as he shuffled.

"Yes, I love rummy. I remember playing with my mom when I was young."

I glanced around the room as Frank dealt the cards. The girl was still hunched over her drawing, her pencil moving

174

furiously across the page. I had caught a better look at her sketch as I walked by—a striking image of a bird in flight, its wings spread wide, each feather rendered with intricate care.

Frank's voice brought me back to the table. "So, what's a young lady like you doing in a place like this?" he asked, his tone teasing but not unkind.

I hesitated, unsure how to answer. How did you explain something you didn't fully understand yourself? "Just... trying to figure things out," I said finally, keeping my tone light.

"Aren't we all," Frank said with a chuckle, his round belly shaking. "Well, you picked the right place for it. Nothing but time to think around here."

The way he said it made me pause. His words carried a weight beneath their surface, an unspoken truth that lingered in the air between us. *Nothing but time.*

He didn't press me further, and for that I was grateful. But something about his easy demeanor tugged at me, made me wonder about him. He seemed so... normal. Sweet, even. Not the kind of person I'd expect to find in a place like this.

"And what about you?" I asked, my tone light but curious. "What's a nice guy like you doing here?"

Frank let out a chuckle, his round belly shaking with the effort. "Nice guy, huh?" he said, pushing his glasses up the bridge of his nose again. "Don't let the dimples fool ya, little lady. I've got my fair share of ghosts."

The way he said it—half-joking, half-serious—sent a shiver down my spine.

"Ghosts?" I echoed.

Frank leaned back in his chair, his smile fading just enough to reveal something beneath it—a flicker of pain or maybe regret. "Not the kind you see in the movies. Not the sheet-wearing, chain-rattling kind. No, the ones I've got... they're quieter. Harder to shake. They don't scream at you in the night, but they don't let you sleep much, either."

I didn't say anything, unsure if I should push or let the silence settle. But Frank didn't seem to need much prompting.

"You ever hear of intrusive thoughts?" he asked, looking at me over the rim of his glasses.

I nodded slowly. "I think so. Like... thoughts you don't want, but you can't stop them?"

Frank snapped his fingers and pointed at me. "That's the kind. Only for me, they don't just stop at thoughts. They're more like... commands."

He paused, as if deciding whether to say more, and then sighed. "I'll tell you something, Grace, because you seem like a good kid. You ever had a thought so dark, so awful, that it scared the hell outta you? The kind of thought that makes you wonder if you're even still yourself?"

My stomach tightened at his words. "Yeah," I admitted quietly.

Frank's gaze softened, and for a moment, he looked older, tired in a way that had nothing to do with his age. "Well, imagine having those thoughts all the time. Imagine your brain whispering things to you—things you'd never in a million years want to do, but the thought just... sticks. You try to push it away, but it's like pushing water uphill. The harder you try, the more it pushes back."

I swallowed hard. "What kind of things?" I asked before I

could stop myself.

Frank's smile returned, but it was smaller this time, sadder. "I used to think I was a monster," he said quietly, as if confessing a long-held secret. "The things I'd think about... hurting people, hurting myself. And the worst part? It didn't feel like me. It felt like someone else had crawled into my brain and started pulling the strings. But it was me, Grace. It was always me."

A heavy silence settled over the table. The hum of the television filled the background, but it sounded miles away.

"What did you do?" I asked cautiously.

Frank glanced down at the cards, flipping one absentmindedly between his fingers. "At first? I did nothing. I hid it. I smiled. I told everyone I was fine, even when I wasn't. But then..." He trailed off, his hand tightening around the card. "Then one day, I couldn't fight it anymore. I didn't want to hurt anyone, but I was so tired of the noise, of feeling like I couldn't trust myself. So, I checked myself in here."

I blinked. "You... checked yourself in?"

Frank nodded, his glasses slipping down his nose again. "Oh, sure. People think you've gotta be dragged kicking and screaming into a place like this, but sometimes... sometimes you're the one who walks through the doors. Because you know if you don't, you're not gonna make it."

His honesty felt like a punch to the gut. I didn't know what to say, so I just sat there, staring at him as he shuffled the cards again.

"You know the funny thing?" he said after a moment, his tone lighter now, almost amused. "Turns out, I'm not a monster. I've got a condition. Obsessive-compulsive disorder, with a side helping of something they call Harm OCD. It means my brain gets stuck on the worst possible thoughts and won't let go, even though I'd never act on them in a million years."

"That's... a thing?" I asked, surprised.

"Oh, it's a thing, alright," Frank said with a grin. "And let me tell you, once I found out there was a name for it—something other people had, too? It was like being let out of prison. Turns out, the thoughts don't make you bad, Grace. What makes you bad is acting on 'em. And I haven't. Not once."

I felt a strange mixture of relief and sadness as he spoke. Relief because Frank wasn't the monster he'd once thought himself to be, and sadness because he'd spent so many years believing otherwise.

"So now I'm here," he said, spreading his hands. "Trying to get better. Trying to trust myself again. And you know what? I'm starting to think I might actually be okay one day."

His words hung in the air, and I felt something stir inside me, something almost like hope.

"I'm glad you're here, Frank."

Frank's smile returned brighter this time. "Me too, little lady. Me too."

I glanced around the room again, my gaze lingering on the girl by the window. She was still lost in her drawing, but her shoulders were tense, as if she could feel my eyes on her.

"She doesn't talk," Frank said, following my gaze. "I think she's a kind of savant—amazing artist. Every time I come in here, she is there in front of the window, drawing. I try to catch a glimpse of her work when I walk by. She is really good."

"What's her name?" I asked.

"Don't know. She's real shy. Came in about two weeks ago. Just started showing up here with that notebook of hers, drawing like her life depends on it."

I glanced back at her, curiosity prickling at the corners of my mind. Her hand moved quickly, almost frantically, across the page. Whatever she was drawing, it wasn't just art—it was something more, something urgent.

"You'll see," Frank said, his voice drawing my attention back to him. "Everyone here's got their story. Some of 'em'll tell you, some of 'em won't. But if you stick around long enough, the stories have a way of finding you."

His words hung heavy in the air as we started the game, the soft buzz of the television and the faint scratch of the girl's pencil the only sounds filling the room. I tried to focus on the cards, but my mind kept drifting back to what Frank had said— and to the girl in the corner, drawing as though the world depended on it.

20

Connections

The weeks blurred into months, passing faster than I could process. The regimented days, the steady rhythm of therapy, and the growing familiarity with the hospital's routines created a structure I hadn't realized I so desperately needed.

Slowly but surely, the staff were tapering me off my medications, and for the first time in years, I was beginning to sleep normally again. My body, once used to constant exhaustion, didn't know how to respond to actual rest. The nights felt less like an endless spiral and more like a quiet reprieve.

I felt safe.

Except for the nightmares now and again. The difference now was that I knew they were nightmares. They couldn't hurt me any longer.

They didn't visit as often now, but when they did, they hit just as hard. Twisted visions of Cam and Kara—the versions of them I had created in my stories—morphed into grotesque creatures, their eyes black voids, their mouths stretched unnaturally wide as they screamed accusations at me.

There were other dreams too, Lenny appearing in dark alleyways, his face illuminated by the glow of a lighter as he hissed threats at me; violent clients who took pleasure in tormenting me; the memory of the accident, blood, shattered glass, the unmistakable crunch of metal. My mind wouldn't let me rest.

From the beginning, Dr. Cameron encouraged me to journal my dreams, feelings, and thoughts. He said they might hold clues to my subconscious—secrets, fears, and memories tangled together in the fog of my mind. Journaling was hard at first. I had to learn to write what was real instead of my fantasy world.

May 5, 2008

I am no longer twenty-two-year-old Grace from Chicago, researching for her psychology paper. The year is 2008, and I am thirty-two years old. I spent nine years in prison. I have to be honest with myself so I can heal.

Putting pen to paper felt like exposing a wound, but over time, it became second nature. It became my lifeline. I wrote feverishly, pouring the chaos of my nights onto the pages of a faux-leather book with gold-leafed edges. The book reminded me of something from my dreams—a strange echo of the life I had once imagined for myself.

One chilly evening, wrapped in a hospital-issued blanket, I flipped through the journal, rereading entries from when I first arrived. It was like retracing my steps through a labyrinth, looking for clues I hadn't noticed before. My breath fogged the cold air as I skimmed the pages, my eyes landing on an early entry:

> April 15, 2008
> I had a nightmare about a man named William.
> His last name had been hazy in the dream—Smithwick? Smithick? But his presence was unforgettable. He wasn't just any man. He was a controlling, sadistic man, the kind who seemed to take pleasure in hurting me. He didn't seem like a typical John and acted above all of that. I can still vividly recall the dream: his hands around my neck, squeezing until my vision blurred and my lungs screamed for air, only to release me just before I passed out, laughing as he started again. His laughter was cold, hollow— like something ripped straight out of a horror film.
> But the detail that stood out the most, the one that makes my skin crawl even now, was his wardrobe. He wasn't dressed like the other clients. He wore a judge's robe. The image brought me back to the nightmares I had of him. He was always this dark, looming presence that made me feel violated and hopeless, and now I know why.

My heart began to race as I read and reread the entry, the words blurring together. This wasn't just a nightmare. I remembered him assaulting me in my own bed while Lenny waited just outside the door. It had been *real*. The memories were fragmented, jagged like broken glass, but one detail solidified in my mind: *a heart-shaped birthmark, right on his groin.* I remembered seeing that when he assaulted me.

Assault didn't even come close to describing what he did to

me. He defiled me. My stomach twisted as I stared at the page.

Had my rapist actually been wearing a judge's robe? Or had that been something my mind made up?

The question echoed in my mind over and over, growing louder with each repetition. My pulse pounded in my head as I stood, gripping the journal. I needed answers. There was only one way to find out if this had been just a dream. I asked Nurse Ben if I could go to the computer room, and while he wouldn't let me go alone, he escorted me there without complaint.

The hospital's computer room was dimly lit, the hum of old monitors filling the silence as I logged on. My fingers trembled as I typed, "Judges in Daytona Beach." The search results loaded slowly, each passing second stretching into an eternity.

And then, there it was.

His name jumped off the screen like a monster in a 3D movie: William S. Smithick. Judge. Seventh Judicial Circuit. Division 8. Felony Criminal Court.

My breath caught, and the world seemed to tilt. He was *real.* This man, this monster from my dreams, was real. There was a photo of him on the bench, holding up his gavel. His expression was smug, so full of himself, and he had a smirk on his face that made me feel nauseated. Memories flashed through my mind. I remembered his voice. *He* is *the one who said, "She'll do just fine," after raping me while Lenny stood watch!*

Dr. Cameron let me use the phone to call Detective Berry. My hands shook as I dialed her number, the receiver slick with sweat. When she answered, my mouth went instantly dry.

"This is Grace Christopher." I finally managed. "I remembered something."

"Yes, what is it, Grace?"

"Lenny, he worked for a guy. His name came to me the other night. He raped me," I said as my voice cracked.

"And his name?"

"Judge William Smithick."

There was silence on the other end for a good five seconds. Then she said, "Okay. That is... wow. Are you sure?"

"I looked up his name to see his face before I called. I am sure. He has a heart-shaped birthmark on his groin area. If that helps."

She listened quietly while I rambled on, her tone serious as she promised to look into it. There was another emotion emanating from her voice over the phone, though—a hint of fear.

That night, it took forever to fall asleep, even with the medication. My mind raced with possibilities, memories surfacing like debris after a storm. I couldn't tell where my nightmares ended and reality began, but one thing was certain: something dark from my past was clawing its way to the surface.

The next morning, as Nurse Ben was leaving my room after bringing my medications, Frank shuffled over to my door, his slippers scuffing against the linoleum floor. His oversized cardigan hung lopsided over one shoulder, and his glasses perched precariously on the tip of his nose. Seeing him always made my heart happy. He carried something in his hands, a crooked grin stretching across his face.

"I got a gift for your kitty," he announced proudly, holding up what appeared to be a handmade toy. He'd crafted a long, dangly pom-pom out of mismatched yarn, strung onto a thin dowel rod with a loop of nearly invisible crafting cord. The care he had poured into it was evident in every uneven strand of yarn and the knotting of the cord. I couldn't help but tear up at the sight of it. Frank was so kind. I was thankful for his friendship.

"Oh, Cappy will *love* it! Thank you, Frank," I said, scanning the room for Cappy's telltale black and white fur.

Frank's grin widened as he unrolled the cord and dangled the pom-pom over the edge of the bed, lowering it just enough to brush the floor. "Let's see if he's hiding," he murmured, a conspiratorial edge to his voice.

As if on cue, Cappy lunged out from under the bed in a blur of fur and claws, swiping wildly at the pom-pom with both paws. His tail fluffed like a bottle brush, and his eyes glowed with predatory determination. Frank let out a laugh, warm and unrestrained, and tugged the cord, teasing the pom-pom just out of reach. Seeing them play together tugged at my heart.

"Look at that! Got ourselves a jungle cat in here!" Frank exclaimed, his weathered hands jerking the toy back and forth. Cappy, emboldened, leapt high into the air, his claws snaring the yarn and dragging the pom-pom down in one final, victorious swipe. He landed with a thud, his head high as he paraded his "kill" onto the bed. With one last jump, he flopped onto his side and gnawed at the pom-pom like a prize he'd earned, his hind legs kicking furiously.

"You're a good boy, Cappy," Frank said, reaching over to scratch behind the cat's ears. Cappy purred so loudly it rattled the bed frame.

"You're welcome to play with him anytime, Frank," I offered, watching the genuine joy on his face as he stroked Cappy's head. "He really likes you."

Frank nodded, standing upright with a creak of his knees. "I like him, too. He's got fight in him. I respect that."

When we left the room, I propped the door open so Cappy could socialize, too. He loved visiting the other patients and getting all the pets his little heart desired. Together, Frank and I walked toward the dayroom. Frank called it our "social hour," but more often referred to it, with a mischievous twinkle, as "fraternizin' with the other curators of chaos."

His words felt even more apt tonight, as the faint murmur of a sitcom theme song echoed down the hall.

The day room was already half full when we arrived. Art Girl sat in her usual spot in the far corner, hunched over a sketchbook, her hand moving furiously across the page. She barely glanced up as we walked in, her hair falling in tangled curtains around her face. On the mounted television, *I Love Lucy* played at a low volume, the canned laughter providing a strange juxtaposition to the murmurs of conversation around the room.

Frank and I stopped for a moment, letting ourselves get caught up in the TV show. Lucy was on one of her classic antics, fumbling with jars in a factory assembly line. Frank chuckled quietly beside me, muttering something about "the good ol' days."

Then a sharp, piercing cry shattered the air behind us.

We turned to see Art Girl wailing, her voice raw and wild, like an animal caught in a trap. She rocked back and forth on the worn-out couch, her fists pounding against her temples. One of the newer patients—his name escaped me—was jumping up and down a few feet away, clutching her pencil in his hand. His laugh was high-pitched and staccato, like a child who didn't realize the gravity of his actions.

I had never heard her voice. Her screams were shocking, blood-curdling. It was upsetting to see her in a meltdown. I needed to help her. All the other patients turned and glared.

"Damn it," Frank muttered under his breath, already shuffling a step forward. But I was quicker.

I crossed the room toward the boy, who was probably around fifteen, keeping my steps measured and my voice calm and steady. "Hey. That's her pencil, isn't it?"

The boy froze mid-jump, his face scrunching into a puzzled frown. He stared at the pencil in his hand, then over at Art Girl, whose cries had devolved into gut-wrenching sobs. I looked at her. Her fists were still beating against her head, her body folding inward like she was trying to disappear. I was scared she might hurt herself badly. I turned back to the boy.

"I know you didn't mean to upset her," I continued softly, crouching a bit to meet the boy at his eye level. "But she really needs that pencil. It's hers. There are lots of other pencils you can use, you know."

He stared at me, his lip quivering, as if deciding whether to trust me.

"It's okay. You're not in trouble. She's not mad at you. She just misses her pencil. It's her favorite, you see," I said, looking directly into his eyes and smiling.

Behind him, Art Girl let out another loud wail, and his head whipped toward her. Something flickered in his eyes—guilt, maybe, or confusion. He shuffled a step closer to her, his movements slow and deliberate, and placed the pencil back on the table in front of her with care. My eyes went back to her, hoping this would be enough.

"I sowwy," his voice was barely a whisper. "I sowwy."

Art Girl's cries softened almost immediately. Her hands dropped away from her head, and she reached for the pencil, clutching it in both hands like it was the most important thing in the world. She didn't look up at the boy or at me, but her rocking stopped. Slowly, she lifted the pencil to the page and resumed her furious sketching; her strokes were heavier now, more purposeful. A wave of relief fell over me.

When I stepped back, she glanced up at me briefly, for a second. Her eyes didn't quite meet mine, but the faintest smile tugged at the corners of her lips before she returned her focus to the paper.

"You handled that well," Frank said as I rejoined him by the television. His tone was casual, but there was a note of approval there that wasn't lost on me.

"Thanks," I murmured, my eyes drifting back to Art Girl. She was in her world again, her pencil flying across the page as if nothing had happened.

"Come on," Frank said, patting my shoulder lightly. "Lucy's about to burn down the kitchen or somethin'. You don't wanna miss this."

I smiled and turned back to the television, but my mind lingered on Art Girl and the boy, the quiet storm that had just passed, leaving behind its usual calm. In a place like this, you took those moments as they came and hoped they stuck.

21

New Version of Myself

A few days later, Detective Berry returned with a photo array. The sheet contained six faces—older white men, each with salt-and-pepper hair, clean-shaven faces, and dark, penetrating eyes. My stomach tightened as I scanned the images, but I didn't need to hesitate.

My finger shot out, trembling, to the fourth photo. My finger hovered over the photo for a split second before pressing down, trembling as it touched the glossy surface. Seeing his face made me want to vomit. I swallowed and cleared my throat.

"That's him," I said, meekly. My heart pounded in my ribcage, so loud I was sure Berry could hear it. The air in the room felt thin, like I was breathing through a straw. His face was burned into my memory—the cold, empty eyes, the cruel twist of his lips. I could still feel his hands around my neck, his laughter echoing in my ears.

"That's him," I repeated, louder this time, my voice shaking but with certainty. "I'll never forget those eyes. And I can't say for sure he was *the* top dog, but he was calling the shots for several pimps under him. Lenny was just one of his many minions, and..." I paused, feeling my eyes prick. "He had to approve every girl himself. 'Give her a test drive' is what he called it. He raped every girl that was recruited. Then he would assign the girls to their pimp."

Berry nodded, her expression both serious and empathetic. "Thank you, Grace. We found Lenny's phone in his back pocket, and we have been analyzing it. We are trying to see if there are any victims that he called so we can track them down. The more witnesses, the better."

"That would be good if there were others who could corroborate my story. I hate to think of how many girls he has done this to. I wish I were the only one," I answered.

"Grace, I need to ask you something. If this case goes to trial, would you be willing to testify about what happened to you and the abuse you endured?" Berry asked in a steady but sympathetic tone.

I hesitated for a moment, my confidence wavering under my circumstances. "Yes. I'll do whatever it takes to help, but... would I even be a credible witness? I mean, I'm here, in a mental institution," I added, my cheeks flushing with embarrassment.

Berry leaned forward, her voice steady and filled with conviction. "Grace, with Dr. Cameron testifying that you've recovered from your delusions and regained your memory, absolutely, you'd be credible. You've been through unimaginable trauma. Anyone with a shred of humanity would understand why you're here," she said with gentle confidence.

Her words settled over me like a warm blanket, softening my doubt.

"Also, in Lenny's case, it was clearly self-defense. The DA

will not be moving forward with any charges against you. We've had the crime scene clean-up crew at your place, so when you go back home, there will be no trace of him left," she said as she stood to leave.

"Oh, thank God—and thank you. I couldn't have cleaned that myself," I groaned, fake gagging as if I was about to throw up. She shook my hand, gave me a knowing, empathetic smile, and walked out the door.

That night, I sat by the small window in my room, the cool glass against my fingertips. Outside, the moon was high and bright, its silver light cutting through the shadows of the hospital courtyard. For the first time in what felt like forever, I felt... calm. Not happy, not at peace, but calm—a fragile, fleeting kind of calm that could shatter with the slightest misstep. But still, it was there.

Cappy curled up beside me, his gentle purring a steady metronome in the quiet. My journal lay open on my lap, blank pages stretching out before me like an invitation. For once, the words didn't come. My mind was too full of the day's revelations. Smithick. The name felt like a jagged piece of glass lodged in my throat.

Somewhere out there, he was living his life—judging others, issuing sentences, wearing his robe like a shield of righteousness. The thought made my skin crawl. He was a monster hiding in plain sight, and now that I'd named him, I I'd become part of something bigger than myself. Bigger than the nightmares that still clung to me. Bigger than the small, broken life I'd lived until now.

But even as I told myself I was ready to testify, to help bring him and the others like him down, a cold dread settled deep in my heart. Smithick wasn't just a judge. He was powerful. Connected. I was sure he knew how to keep people silent—how to make them disappear.

What if he still remembers my name?

The thought sent a chill racing down my spine. My fingers tightened around the pen, and before I realized what I was doing, I'd scribbled a single sentence on the blank page:

What if he comes for me?

I stared at the words, my breath catching. For all the progress I'd made, all the hope I'd started to feel, the truth was inescapable. The past wasn't done with me yet. It had claws, and it was still digging into me, refusing to let go.

The fight wasn't over.

It was only just the beginning.

As the days passed, life in the hospital began to even feel less like a prison and more like a sanctuary. Frank and I played cards together almost every day. He felt like the stepfather or uncle I never had. I even grew close to Nurse Ben, who had once strapped me down during one of my worst episodes. Now, he joked with me during meals, his dry humor a welcome distraction from the seriousness of my recovery.

But despite the bonds I was forming, I knew I couldn't stay in the hospital forever. I didn't *want* to stay forever. I wanted to stand on my own again, to rebuild my life outside these walls.

Dr. Cameron was supportive. He helped me see I wasn't

defined by my past. He reminded me that I could start fresh, that life could still be good. He believed in me even when I didn't believe in myself.

One day, during one of our sessions, I confessed my true passion. "I've always wanted to be a writer," I said quietly. "I don't care if it's novels or newspaper columns or anything in between. Writing is what I've always wanted to do. It's the one thing that's ever felt... right."

Dr. Cameron smiled, his kind eyes meeting mine. "Then you should do it. You *can* do it. But you'll have to keep sorting through what's real and what's fiction in your life. It'll take time. But you're already doing the work, Grace."

In our sessions, I began sharing passages from my journal, reading aloud the entries that blurred the line between dream and reality. He helped me untangle the threads, guiding me as I separated memories from fantasies. It was like unraveling a knotted ball of yarn—slow, frustrating, but cathartic.

"You've made incredible progress," Dr. Cameron said one day, his voice full of pride. "I think you're ready to leave soon. But I want to make sure you're truly ready—not just to avoid falling back into old habits, but to start building the life you deserve. And I'll be here to help you, every step of the way."

The thought of leaving terrified me, but it also filled me with hope. I felt like the future wasn't a black void. There was light on the horizon.

But I didn't know if I was ready to chase it. The hospital had become my safe place. It was my security blanket that I knew I had to eventually give up, but how would I know when I was ready to do that?The next morning, sunlight filtered through the blinds, streaking the room with soft gold. I rubbed the sleep from my eyes and swung my legs over the side of the bed, feeling the chill of the linoleum beneath my feet. That's when I noticed it—a folded piece of paper lying just inside the door, as if someone had slipped it underneath during the night.

Curious, I bent down and picked it up. The paper was thick, almost like cardstock, and as I unfolded it, I let out a small gasp. It was a drawing—a stunningly intricate and lifelike portrait of Cappy. Every detail was there: his tufted ears, his inquisitive whiskers, the sharp glint of mischief in his gold eyes. It wasn't just a drawing; it was Cappy, as vivid as if he were staring back at me in the flesh. At the bottom, in small, careful handwriting, was a signature: "Janie."

Janie. Art Girl's name was Janie.

The realization hit me with a kind of quiet warmth, the way the first sip of coffee did on a cold morning. It felt like a gift, a thank you for yesterday, but in truth, I was the thankful one. She'd let me in, even a little, through this drawing. Maybe now, I thought, she would let me see a bit more of her world—a world that seemed so vivid in her art, yet so guarded in everything else.

Before heading out, I propped my door open for Cappy, who was stretched out on the bed, his tail flicking lazily. He watched me leave with mild interest, then went back to snoozing.

The day room was quiet when I arrived, the usual early-morning haze still hanging in the air. Frank was already there, perched in his favorite rocker in front of the TV. The opening theme of *M.A.S.H.* played softly, and he hummed along, out of tune but content. Janie was at her usual spot in the corner, hunched over her sketchpad, her hand moving furiously across the page. Her hair fell in messy waves around her face, and she occasionally pushed it back with an impatient flick of her hand.

I walked over to Frank, holding the folded paper like it was something precious. "Look!" I said quietly, trying not to disturb Janie's focus. "Her name is Janie! She drew this."

Frank adjusted his glasses and took the drawing from me, his face lighting up as he examined it. "Well, I'll be damned," he said, his voice full of admiration. "That's our Cappy, all right. Look at that—the little rascal's got that 'I'm about to pounce' look in his eyes." He adjusted the paper, holding it farther away, then closer, as though trying to find the perfect focal distance.

"Janie," he said, almost to himself. "That's a pretty name."

I glanced over at her, still deep in her work. For a moment, as if sensing my gaze, she looked up. Our eyes met, and she smiled—not the faint, fleeting smile from yesterday, but something warmer, more intentional. Then, just as quickly, her eyes dropped back to her sketchpad, her pencil moving in quick, confident strokes.

I hesitated; the folded paper was still in my hand. I wanted to go over, to thank her in person, to tell her how much the drawing meant to me. But I also didn't want to intrude. Her space felt sacred, and I was afraid of stepping into it uninvited.

Before I could decide, Cappy came bounding into the room, his black and white, fluffy fur a blur as he skidded across the floor. He darted past me and leapt onto the old couch beside Janie. She froze for a moment, her pencil hovering above the paper, then slowly reached out to pet his head. Her touch was tentative at first, almost unsure, but when Cappy tilted his head into her hand and let out a loud purr, she relaxed.

She patted her lap, inviting him to climb up, and Cappy, never one to resist attention, happily obliged. He curled up in her lap, his tail wrapping around his body, and let out another contented purr as she stroked his back.

Something about the moment gave me courage. Taking a deep breath, I began walking toward her table, each step careful and deliberate. As I reached the chair across from her, I stopped.

"Is it okay if I sit here?" I asked quietly, not wanting to disrupt the quiet rhythm of her space.

Janie paused, her hand still resting on Cappy's back, and glanced up at me, but her eyes still avoided mine. Her eyes were calm, curious. After a brief moment, she nodded, the faintest smile playing on her lips, then returned her focus to her drawing.

I sat down slowly, placing the folded paper on the table in front of me. "Thank you so much for the drawing, Janie," I said, keeping my voice low and steady. "I love it. It's so beautiful. His name is Cappy, by the way."

Janie's hand paused mid-stroke, and her lips curved into a bigger smile. She didn't look at me this time; her gaze stayed fixed on Cappy, who was now stretching luxuriously in her lap, his paws kneading the fabric of her jeans.

For a long time, I sat across from Janie, watching her draw, feeling the steady rhythm of her pencil against the paper like a calming heartbeat. It was a rare moment of stillness, of quiet connection in a place that's not always calm. Sitting there with her, and with Cappy purring contentedly in her lap, something shifted in me. It was subtle, almost imperceptible, but it was there—a sense of possibility. A tiny voice, tucked somewhere deep inside, whispered, "Maybe you're ready for more than this."

I wasn't sure where that thought came from or why it struck me then, but it stayed with me all day, lingering in the corners of my mind like sunlight through an open window. It wasn't until much later, when I stood in my room again and glanced at Janie's portrait of Cappy on my dresser, that I realized the truth: I had spent so long surviving, I had forgotten what it felt like to *live*.

Which was why, when Dr. Cameron brought up the idea of me speaking to the local newspaper about starting a writing job, I didn't immediately recoil in fear. Instead, I thought about Janie's bravery, her quiet way of letting people in—piece by piece, line by line. Maybe I could try that too. Dr. Cameron said it would help me in my recovery journey. So today, I took a step I never imagined taking only a few months ago. I set up an interview for a job at the local newspaper. Dr. Cameron had recommended this particular paper because he knew the owner.

Dr. Cameron, ever thoughtful, arranged for one of the nurses to pick out a professional outfit for me. It was a sleek, black pencil skirt paired with a matching blazer, a crisp white button-down shirt, and modest black heels. As I slipped into the ensemble, an unfamiliar but welcome sense of confidence fell over me. I actually looked like someone with a purpose.

Standing in front of the mirror, I buttoned the last button on the jacket and paused to take myself in. For the first time in years, I was beginning to recognize the woman staring back at me. My hair was still flat and lifeless, its color dulled by everything I had endured, but it was clean and combed. My figure was slim but no longer fragile, and my skin was pale but for once, there was no trace of drugs or alcohol in my body.

My slate was clean—a fresh start I hadn't thought possible. And as I stood there, I realized I wasn't just dressing for an interview. I was stepping into a new version of myself.

22

The Interview

That interview was the most nerve-wracking thing I'd done in years. I was full of the kind of nervousness where your stomach churned and you couldn't quite tell if you were about to cry, faint, or throw up—or maybe all three.

Before this new chapter of my life, I hadn't cared much about what I did or the consequences that followed. There was a certain freedom in apathy, as dangerous as it was. But now, everything felt different. My new life *depended* on this. I couldn't afford to mess up.

My palms were clammy, and I could feel a tremor running through my entire body. I tried to remind myself to sit up straight as I waited in the small, brightly lit office where the interview was being held. A potted plant by the window drooped, its leaves curling, and for some reason, I fixated on it, thinking it mirrored how fragile I felt. The air smelled of printer ink and freshly brewed coffee, but nothing could soothe my nerves.

Then the door opened, and in walked Maddie Piper, the

owner of the newspaper herself. She wasn't just any staff member to greet me—they'd sent *the boss*. My throat tightened.

"Call me Maddie," she said firmly, and gave me a warm smile as we shook hands. Her grip was firm but not crushing, the kind of handshake that said, "I know exactly who I am."

Maddie was petite and middle-aged, with sharp, rectangular glasses perched on her nose and a halo of dark, curly, bobbed hair that seemed to defy gravity. She wore a tailored blazer over a floral blouse, and her confidence seemed to fill the room. She had the air of someone who had seen her fair share of battles but had come out of every one of them stronger. Yet there was something approachable about her, too—a quiet kindness beneath the authority she carried.

She began the interview with a series of standard questions, her tone friendly but probing. As she spoke, she absentmindedly twirled a strand of her curls around her finger, a habit that made her feel almost disarmingly human.

"Have you ever worked for a newspaper before?" she asked, her voice bright but laced with curiosity.

I cleared my throat. "No... No, ma'am, I've only written school papers... and, um, as a hobby."

Her lips quirked up in a wry smile. "Please don't call me ma'am. It makes me feel old. Maddie is just fine."

I nodded, my face burning with embarrassment. "Yes, ma," I stammered, wincing internally as the word "ma'am" slipped out. "I mean... Maddie. Yes, Maddie."

She chuckled and moved on, asking about my writing experience and my goals. The questions were simple enough, but each one felt like a tightrope I had to walk without falling.

My palms dampened against the fabric of my skirt, and my mind raced for the right words. For a brief moment, all I could hear was the rushing sound of my heartbeat in my ears. *What if I mess this up? What if she sees right through me?*

I hadn't gone to school for journalism. I didn't have a polished portfolio or years of experience. The only credentials I could boast were a stint on the high school newspaper and helping put together the yearbook, both of which felt like a lifetime ago. Impostor syndrome hit me hard, and I felt devastation for all the time I had lost—the years I had wasted on destructive habits instead of building a career.

But then, somewhere in the chaos of my thoughts, I heard Dr. Cameron's voice: "You've come so far, Grace. You're stronger than you think."

I took a deep breath, steadied myself, and answered Maddie's next question. My voice wavered at first, but as I kept talking, it grew stronger, steadier. I told her about my love for storytelling and how I'd always found solace in writing, even at my lowest points. I admitted my lack of formal training but explained that I was eager to learn, to grow, to prove myself.

Maddie listened intently, her eyes sharp but not unkind. I could tell she wasn't someone to be underestimated. Beneath her approachable demeanor was a steely resolve. This was a woman who had likely spent years fighting to prove herself, whether because of her petite stature, her glasses, or the wild halo of curls that might have made her an easy target as a kid. Whatever had shaped her, it had left her resilient.

When the interview ended, Maddie stood and shook my hand with a firm grip. "I'll be in touch," she said, her smile giving nothing away. Her words lingered in the air as I walked out of the office, my heart racing but full of cautious optimism.

Two days later, Dr. Cameron called me into his office. As I walked in, I saw a boyish grin on his face. He held the phone receiver in his hand.

"The phone is for you. It's Maddie Piper."

"Hello? This is Grace Christopher." I listened intently... "That will work for me. Thank you so much!" I handed the phone back to Dr. Cameron and looked at him, stunned. For a moment, the words didn't feel real, like they were coming from a dream I'd soon wake up from. My mind scrambled to catch up.

"I got the job. I got the job!" I exclaimed. The realization hit me all at once, like a tidal wave crashing over me, and the excitement, gratitude, and disbelief swelled inside me.

Before I could stop myself, I threw my arms around Dr. Cameron in a grateful hug. The thought occurred to me that this was not very professional. He was my doctor, but I wanted to show him how much this meant to me. He stiffened for a split second—likely not expecting it—then relaxed and gave me a soft pat on the back.

"Thank you," I whispered, my voice breaking as I blinked back the tears that were already threatening to fall. I felt so safe next to him; I wanted to continue the hug, but I reluctantly let go.

He chuckled lightly, stepping back, but still smiling at me. "*You* did this, Grace," he said with quiet pride. "You've earned this. Every step of it. Don't you forget that."

His words hit me harder than I expected, and I nodded,

swallowing the lump in my throat.

"I should probably leave tonight, then," I said, my voice tinged with bittersweetness. Saying it aloud made it feel real, and a pang of sadness crept into my chest. Leaving this place, this odd sanctuary that had been both a refuge and a battleground, felt both liberating and heartbreaking.

"You can stay here, you know, until you are back on your feet financially. Your mother paid for a year in advance."

"I need to do this on my own, but thank you," I said quietly.

Dr. Cameron gave me an understanding nod. "Take the time you need to say goodbye."

I nodded again and quietly left his office, my footsteps echoing in the hallway. The familiar hum of fluorescent lights above and the faint chatter from the day room drifted toward me as I made my way there. I paused just outside the door, letting the moment settle over me.

This is it.

I stepped inside, scanning the room for the faces I had come to know so well. Frank was perched in his favorite rocker, half-watching the TV, half-dozing, as usual. Across the room, Janie sat in her corner, hunched over her sketchpad, her pencil moving with purposeful precision. Cappy was curled up beside her on the old couch, his tail twitching occasionally as if he were dreaming.

I decided to go to Janie first. Her world was quieter, and I knew she wouldn't interrupt her work for just anyone. But this was different.

I approached slowly, sitting down across from her at the small table. Her focus remained on her drawing—whatever world she was building in graphite seemed to have her full attention. I pulled a folded piece of paper from my pocket and slid it across the table toward her.

"Cappy and I have to go," I said softly, my heart squeezing as I spoke the words. "My phone number and address are on that paper. If you're ever able to visit us, you're welcome anytime. Dr. Cameron has my number, too, so if you ever need me, you just let him know, and he can call me."

Janie's pencil strokes slowed until they stopped completely. She didn't look up, but I noticed the way her shoulders hunched, the way her breathing changed. And then, a single tear fell onto the corner of her paper, spreading out in a small, dark bloom.

My chest tightened as I watched her, unsure of what to say or do. "We will both miss you," I managed, my voice barely above a whisper. "Can I give you a hug?" I asked, almost sheepishly.

For a long moment, Janie didn't move. Then, slowly, she set her pencil down and stood. She kept her head down as she took a small step toward me, her hands fidgeting with the hem of her oversized sweater. I reached out timidly, not wanting to startle her, and wrapped her in a soft, gentle hug.

"It's going to be okay," I murmured, my voice steady despite the tears that were now freely falling down my face. "I'll visit you, and I'll bring you more paper and new pencils, okay?"

Janie's arms stayed limp at first, but then, slowly, she lifted them and hugged me back. It was brief but meaningful. When I pulled back, she looked up at me—*really* looked at me, her eyes meeting mine for the first time since we'd met. She gave me a small smile, one that felt like a rare and precious gift, and nodded.

I smiled back, trying to hold on to the moment.

Behind me, I heard a familiar voice. "What's going on here?"

I turned to see Frank standing across the room, his face a mixture of confusion and shock. He shuffled closer, his hands gripping the sides of his cardigan as if bracing himself.

"Cappy and I are leaving this evening," I said, forcing a smile through my sadness. "I got that job I told you about at the local newspaper."

Frank's eyes widened. "You're going to be a newspaper woman?" he asked with a beaming smile. Then his smile faded, and he stared into my wet, glassy eyes. I could see tears welling up in his.

"You're leaving?" he asked, his voice trembling, and his chin beginning to dimple.

I nodded, feeling my tears threatening to return. "I can't thank you enough for being my friend here. I'll miss you so much, Frank."

His lip quivered, and he looked down, blinking hard. "I'll miss you and Cappy both," he said, his voice thick with emotion. "You've got to promise me something, though."

"Anything," I said earnestly.

"You have to promise me you'll visit," he said, his voice growing stern. Tears were falling now, but his tone carried the same playful gruffness I had come to love.

"I promise," I said, meaning it with every fiber of my being.

Frank pulled me into a bear hug, the kind only someone of his size and warmth could give. His embrace was comforting, steady, and safe—exactly what I needed at that moment.

As we embraced, he whispered, "You'll look out for yourself, won't you? And I'll look out for Janie like she's my own granddaughter."

I nodded, swallowing hard. He glanced down at Janie, who had gone back to her sketchpad but was watching us out of the corner of her eye. She glanced up briefly and gave Frank a small smile, one that seemed to reassure him in a way words never could.

"I love you both," I said, my voice breaking as I turned to leave. My feet felt heavy, like every step toward the door was weighted with memories, but I forced myself to keep going.

As I reached the door, I turned back for one last look. Janie was already lost in her drawing again, but Frank stood where I'd left him, his hands resting on his hips, his eyes still damp.

"Don't forget your promise," he called after me, his voice cracking.

"I won't," I said, smiling through my tears.

And with that, I stepped out of the dayroom, leaving behind the people who had become a second family.

I walked in somber silence back to my room to pack, my heart racing with anticipation, but breaking at the same time. It didn't take long—my belongings were few, just enough to fit into a single duffel bag. Cappy, as always, watched me with mild interest, his tail swishing lazily as I moved around the room.

Dr. Cameron had arranged for a cab to pick me up, and when the time came, he handed me some money for the ride, another gesture of kindness I wouldn't forget. I stepped outside, the crisp afternoon air hitting my face, and opened the cab door.

As I slid into the back seat, Cappy climbed in beside me, curious but surprisingly calm for a cat in a car. He pressed his little paws against the window, his gold eyes wide as he watched the world pass by. His tail flicked occasionally, betraying his curiosity.

I glanced back at the institution as the cab pulled away, its brick walls and barred windows growing smaller in the distance. I had been here for nearly seven months now. This place had been my sanctuary, my safe harbor in the storm, but it was time to move forward.

As I focused on the road ahead, my duffel bag on my lap and Cappy beside me, I couldn't help but feel a strange mix of emotions—nervousness, hope, fear, excitement. Finally, something was going right in my life. A fresh start was waiting for me, and I wasn't going to let it slip away.

This time, I thought, *I'll get it right.*

23

Jane Doe

When we got home, the state of the place hit me like a slap. Papers littered the floor, and a fine layer of dust coated everything. This wasn't how I wanted to start my new chapter, but at least the crime scene cleaners took care of the worst parts for me, in particular the bathroom.

With renewed determination, I rolled up my sleeves, picked up every last piece of clutter, and swept the floors until they gleamed. The next day was the start of my new job, and I refused to wake up in a mess.

Fortunately, the newspaper office wasn't far from my house. I could walk to work until I saved enough for a taxi—or better yet, maybe a car of my own one day. The future didn't seem like a dark unknown anymore. It felt like a chance. It was hard to put words to what I was feeling, but I finally figured it out—it was hope.

I crawled into bed, pulling the worn blanket snugly around me as Cappy jumped up, meowing insistently. He pawed at the covers until I lifted them, letting him burrow underneath to curl up against my side. The fall chill seeped through the house, biting at my skin. With all the holes in the roof over the living room and the cracked windows, the insulation was a joke. At least there were no holes over the bed. Every gust of wind made the house creak and groan, like it was alive and in pain. In hindsight, I should have stayed at Sunnybrook until the weather warmed up, but the creepy sounds would fit right in for Halloween.

I tried to sleep, but excitement over the next day kept my thoughts racing. The eerie sounds didn't help either, each creak or whistle of wind keeping me on edge. I could hear the chains of the swing rattle and creak. When there was a gust of wind, it would bang against the house with a crash, making me jump out of my skin. Lying there in the dark, I found myself talking to Cappy, his soft purring the only thing making me feel safe.

Before I knew it, the first rays of sunlight started creeping through the broken blinds. Sleep had eluded me, but it didn't matter. If I drifted off now, I'd risk oversleeping and missing my first day, and I was too creeped out to sleep.

Instead, I swung my legs over the side of the bed and stood, stretching away the stiffness of a restless night. A strange thrill filled my chest—Christmas was around the corner in a couple of months, and for the first time in years, I had something to celebrate. Starting this new job wasn't just a paycheck; it felt like a gift, the best one I'd received in a long, long time.

When I arrived at work, Maddie wasted no time introducing me to my new coworkers. The faces were unfamiliar, and I was quietly relieved—this was my chance to start fresh, with no past weighing me down. The building was small and easy to navigate, which helped ease my first day jitters.

The newsroom buzzed with energy. Desks and cubicles filled the space, each one alive with conversation, laughter, or the quick cadence of phone calls as reporters chased down leads. The hum of voices and the clatter of keyboards felt strangely comforting, like I was part of something important.

Maddie led me to my very own cubicle, tucked neatly in the middle of the chaos. It was modest but functional, and the office chair was surprisingly comfortable. It was a space I could make my own.

Not long after, Maddie stopped by to check on me, a warm smile on her face. She handed me a small stack of forms.

"Once you get these filled out, let me know. I'll have your first story assignment ready soon." Her words made my pulse quicken, not with fear, but with excitement. This was it—the start of something new.

Maddie stopped by my cubicle toward the end of the day, her sharp eyes scanning the draft.

"This is good work," she said, her tone firm but encouraging. "Tighten up the second paragraph, and it's ready for print."

Her words stayed with me all afternoon. It wasn't a glowing review, but it was enough. I was good enough. When I got back home after my first day, I picked up my journal and wrote down my thoughts.

October 25, 2008
My new job is going surprisingly well. My first story wasn't

groundbreaking, just a short piece about the city's upcoming spring festival. But as I typed the final sentence and hit "save," a strange sensation washed over me. Pride. It had been so long since I'd felt it, I almost didn't recognize it. The house will take time. There is so much to do, but the house is like me, getting a fresh start.

I closed the journal and took some pajamas out of the dresser, then made my way to the bathroom. I opened the door and immediately fell backwards.

Lenny was lunging at me. The bullet wound was gushing blood and streaming down his face. His teeth bared in a sneer.

I screamed and pushed my feet against the floor to back away further. He came closer still. I could see maggots going in and out of the bullet hole. He leaned down, his forehead nearly touching mine. I couldn't move, couldn't scream. I couldn't even blink. One of his eyes had rolled back into his head. The other was cloudy. The maggots on his face slithered over his unblinking eyes. I let myself fall backward to the floor and covered my eyes with my arms.

But nothing happened. The only sound was my ragged breaths and heartbeat. I lowered my arms and opened my eyes, blinking rapidly. There was nothing there. Nothing but an empty bathroom.

Weeks turned into paychecks, and there was something deeply satisfying about earning honest money from writing—something I was proud of. The feeling of depositing those checks and knowing I'd earned them with integrity was priceless.

With a bit of extra cash, I treated myself to taxis on the days when the Florida weather decided to rage. Whether it was pouring rain, freezing cold, or suffocating heat, I no longer had to walk into work looking like a drenched rag or, worse, sweating like a sinner in church—hardly the professional vibe I wanted to project.

I started saving a little from every paycheck, slowly building a fund to fix the roof. Until then, I put a tarp over the gaping holes and threw myself into cleaning, painting, and gradually piecing the house back together. The kitchen got a cheerful coat of pale yellow, and after hours of scrubbing, the floor was unrecognizable—a small victory in what felt like a sea of needed renovations.

The bathroom, though, was a bigger challenge. The thought of taking a bath or shower in *that* tub made my skin crawl—it was still haunted by the memory of Lenny. A replacement was high on my wish list, but for now, it would have to wait.

The bedroom was the worst of all. The stained, threadbare carpet had to go, no question. And the walls, covered in my frantic scribblings from a darker time, were like a diary of my torment. Before painting them over, I read them. I had to confront the chaotic thoughts I'd once scrawled in desperation. It felt like a necessary step, a way to acknowledge the past before I could fully embrace the future.

I bought a dusty turquoise tub of paint for the living room. The color was so soothing and fresh. *I need to paint the bedroom this color, too, because I need to do anything and everything to heal right now,* I thought. Seeing the old, worn-out, dingy walls being covered with this new paint was very satisfying. A clean slate for me and my humble abode.

I was in the middle of painting the living room when a knock at the door interrupted me. I opened it to find Dr. Cameron standing there, holding a cat bed. Before I could say anything, he smiled and said, "I knew you were fixing up the place. I thought Cappy might appreciate a new bed, too."

I couldn't help but smile back as I motioned for him to come inside. "Thank you, Dr. Cameron. That's very thoughtful. Please come in!"

"Oh, please, call me Theo. I'm not your doctor anymore," he said and handed me the cat bed with a warm smile. "By the way, I have referred you for outpatient treatment from a colleague of mine. His name is Dr. Bill Watson, and he is an amazing therapist," he added, handing me a business card with my new doctor's information, and stepped inside.

I was glad he referred me to someone he trusted. I had to continue going to therapy. I knew that. Medication alone was not going to heal these wounds. It was just the band-aid.

"You don't want to be my doctor anymore?" I asked.

"Well, I... do, I mean, I will, if—"

I cut him off and teased, "You're in such a hurry to get rid of me!" I said sarcastically and winked at him.

"No, it's just the opposite," he blurted out. "I would like to see you more often, just not as your doctor," he said a bit sheepishly for a grown man.

I glanced down at myself and realized I probably was a mess—paint splattered across my clothes, my hair pulled into a messy ponytail, and a few smudges of color on my face. I probably looked like I'd just wrestled a can of paint and lost. *He wants to see more of this?* The thought amused me.

"Would you like some lemonade?" I asked while trying to tidy up my appearance a little. Of course, he had seen me at my absolute worst, there was only moving up from there.

"I probably shouldn't stay. I just wanted you to have a welcome home gift," he said sweetly, and with a bit of hesitation.

I put my hand on his forearm, "I would like to show you the progress I have made on the house. I am proud of myself."

He nodded, and I quickly went into the kitchen to grab two cups. I was parched from all the work I'd been doing. When I returned, I placed the glasses down on the coffee table with a sense of satisfaction, like this small act of hospitality made everything feel a little more normal again.

Cappy jumped up onto the couch between us and started meowing at Theo, as if demanding attention. He reached over and patted him on the head while asking how everything was going. We chatted for quite a while, and afterward, I gave him a tour of the house, proudly showing off all the improvements I had made. When we finished, Theo took my hand with a soft smile and said, "I don't want to take up too much of your time. I should get going and finish up some work."

I smiled back, feeling a little reluctant to see him go. "Feel free to come by anytime, whether it's checking on me or just to visit. I would like to see more of you, too."

He smiled and nodded. "I am so proud of you and what you've accomplished, Grace. We'll have to do this again soon. If you would like."

We walked to the door together, and he waved goodbye as

he got into his car. I stood in the doorway, watching him drive off, the image of his face lingering in my mind. He was an attractive man, about eight years older than me, successful, and genuinely kind. I couldn't help but think about what it would be like to have someone like him in my life. *I feel so at home when I am near him. I wonder if he feels the same about me. He might be just flirting, with no intention of following through,* I thought.

Shaking myself out of my thoughts, I picked up the paintbrush again and went back to work, letting the brush strokes clear my head. When I finished, I carried the new cat bed to my room and showed it to Cappy. He sniffed it briefly before completely ignoring it and jumping up on the bed beside me, as he always did. We settled in, and soon enough, we were both asleep, the quiet of the house wrapping around us like a blanket.

24

Nightmare or Memory

Valentine's Day was quickly approaching, and I had to write a piece for work about the holiday—its origins, popular spots in town, and other related things.

When I was younger, I always dreaded Valentine's Day. Back then, I was the stereotypical nerd—glasses as big as my cheeks and a mullet so bad it should have been a crime, all because my parents thought it would be "cute." I always wanted a Valentine, just like everyone else, but rarely had one. The only exception was when I was with Joseph.

I spent the day driving around in the company car, gathering information about the best restaurants and hotel, spa, and salon packages—basically, everything you needed for the most romantic day of the year, all ready to be featured in our paper.

Once back at the office, I wrote up my piece and left it on Maddie's desk, since she had already left for the day. After work, I stopped by the coffee shop for a hot mocha. As I waited for my order, I sat on one of the benches outside, enjoying the chilly air, watching the world go by. It was amazing how quickly life could get so busy. We rushed through everything, caught up in the chaos, and forgot to stop and appreciate the little things.

I promised myself I would never let that happen again.

I walked home holding the hot cup in both hands, feeling content after a simple but pleasant workday. I wasn't expecting anything special when I flipped through the stack of mail, but the red envelope stopped me in my tracks. My breath hitched as I slid my finger under the seal, careful not to tear it. Inside was a Valentine's Day card, simple and understated, but the words written in Theo's neat handwriting struck me with a force I didn't anticipate.

Grace,

I hope you're doing well. Keep up the amazing progress and don't forget—you've got people rooting for you. I'll stop by soon to see how the house is coming along.

-T

Tears pricked at the corners of my eyes. It wasn't romantic, not really, but it was thoughtful in a way I hadn't experienced in years. Someone cared—not because they had to, but because they wanted to. I cared about him tremendously, and while I knew he cared about me, I wasn't sure whether he would pursue a relationship with me or not.

I smiled, thinking about how much progress I'd made. My house was beginning to look like a home again. With the next paycheck, I was hopeful I'd have enough to cover the deposit for the new roof, at least for the first installment on the payment plan.

After feeding Cappy, I spent some time tidying up and then called a few roofing companies to get price quotes and inquire about financing options. Some of them wanted to visit the property, so I scheduled appointments. Since my house was small, with only two sides, the cost wasn't as steep as I'd feared. I might even have some of the deposit money left over—maybe enough to put a down payment on a car.

After a quick shower, I went to bed, feeling exhaustion settle over me. As always, after declaring it was "Bedtime!" Cappy followed close behind, his small paws padding softly against the floor. He let out a quiet, contented meow as he climbed under the covers, curling himself into a warm ball against my side. His rhythmic purring was like a lullaby, and within moments, the pull of sleep became too strong to resist.

But my mind betrayed me.

As soon as I drifted off, I was tormented by another nightmare.

I jolted awake, my heart hammering as my alarm clock blared beside me. The sound was sharp, jarring, pulling me violently out of the dream's grip.

Cappy stirred beneath the covers, letting out a soft, confused meow as he stretched. I sat up, clutching my chest as I tried to steady my breathing. My skin was damp with sweat, and my hands trembled as I reached for my journal on the nightstand.

I grabbed my journal and wrote everything down I could remember.

219

Jan 28, 2009

The dream swallowed me whole, dropping me into its dark depths without warning. I was no longer in my bed, no longer safe. I was standing in a dimly lit room, the air thick and stifling. The floor was cold beneath my bare feet; the texture was smooth like concrete. Shadows pooled in the corners, heavy and oppressive, and the only source of light came from a single, swaying bulb overhead, casting sharp, jagged shapes across the room.

In the center of the room was a wooden box that was old and splintered, like something pulled from the attic of a decaying house. It was long and narrow, barely wide enough for someone to lie down inside. It resembled a coffin.

I could hear her before I saw her.

The screams ripped through the air, high-pitched and full of terror.

"Please! Let me out! Please, I'll be good, I promise! I'll be good!" The voice was young—too young. A child's voice, trembling and raw with fear.

Judge Smithick stepped out of the shadows, his looming figure illuminated by the flickering bulb. He was dressed in his black judge's robe, the fabric billowing as he moved, but his face was far from dignified. His eyes were cold, devoid of humanity, and his lips twisted into a cruel smirk.

"You'll stay in there," he said, his voice low and deliberate, each word dripping with malice. "You'll stay in there until you learn to behave. Until you're a *good girl*."

The girl's screams grew louder, more desperate, and I could see the box shake as she thrashed inside, her small fists pounding against the wooden lid. The sound was deafening, a frantic rhythm of panic and helplessness.

I wanted to move, to do something, but my body refused to obey. My feet were rooted to the floor, my limbs heavy and unresponsive, as if they had turned to cement.

"Please!" she sobbed from inside the box, her voice cracking. "I'll be good! I'll be good! Please, don't leave me in here!"

Smithick crouched beside the box, his movements slow and methodical, like a predator savoring its prey. He ran a hand over the lid, his fingers tracing the grain of the wood with an almost reverent touch.

"Good girls don't scream," he said, his voice soft now, almost soothing. It made my skin crawl. "Good girls don't cry. Be quiet, and I'll think about letting you out."

The girl's sobs quieted to muffled whimpers, but the box continued to tremble as she trembled inside it.

"Good," Smithick murmured, standing upright and brushing off his robes as though he'd done something noble. "Now, let's see how long you can keep that up."

He turned toward me suddenly, his cold eyes locking onto mine as if he had known I was there all along. A sick grin spread across his face, slow and deliberate.

"Don't think I've forgotten about you," he said, his voice echoing unnaturally in the room. "You've been in the box before, haven't you, Grace?"

The words sent a jolt of terror through me, sharp and electric. Memories—or were they fragments of the dream? —flashed through my mind. A tight, suffocating space. The scratch of splintered wood against my skin. The sound of my own screams echoing back at me, unheard.

I opened my mouth to respond, to deny it, to scream, but no sound came out. My throat was dry, my voice stolen.

Smithick stepped closer, his towering form blocking out the light. The shadows swallowed me as he leaned in, his breath hot against my ear.

"You remember, don't you?" he whispered, his voice dripping with cruel satisfaction. "You remember what it felt like to be in the dark. Alone. Helpless. Just like her."

The girl's screams erupted again, louder this time, raw and frantic. "Please! I'm sorry! Let me out!"

The sound became deafening, reverberating through the room until it was all I could hear. I clamped my hands over my ears, but it didn't help. The sound seeped into my mind, into my chest, making my heart pound violently.

The box began to shake harder, violently, as if the girl inside was clawing her way out. The wood groaned under the strain, and cracks began to spider-web across the surface. I could see thin, pale fingers poking through the gaps, reaching, clawing.

"Help me!" she screamed.

I finally found my voice. "Stop!" I shouted, my throat burning as the word tore out of me. "Stop it! Let her out! Please!"

The cracks in the box deepened, the wood splintering as the girl's cries grew more desperate. And then, with a deafening snap, the lid burst open and that's when I woke up.

Was this a nightmare? Or was it a memory?

As I scrawled those final words, two questions burned in my mind, and those two questions sent a shiver down my spine.

Have I been in the box before? Is this twisted scene something I lived through and buried so deeply that it only now clawed its way to the surface?

I peeked at Cappy, who was now watching me intently, his gold eyes full of quiet understanding. He climbed into my lap, pressing his small body against mine, and I stroked his fur absentmindedly as I tried to make sense of it all.

I didn't have an answer. Not yet. But the terror of that dream, the vividness of it, made one thing clear: I needed to remember. Because if it *was* a memory, then someone else might still be trapped in the box, screaming for help.

The next day after work, a few roofing companies came by to give me estimates. After weighing my options, I chose one and picked out the shingles I wanted. They assured me they'd start as soon as they had all the necessary materials. True to their word, they were up on the roof in no time, tearing off the old layers and replacing everything from scratch, including the plywood.

I felt a wave of relief when they managed to get the new plywood in place the same day they started, especially since it rained that night. Thanks to their hard work, I stayed dry inside.

A few days later, the new roof was finished. I paid the balance due, and to my surprise, I still had nearly seventeen hundred dollars left over. There was a used car lot about five blocks away, so I decided to check out what they had. The lot was fairly spacious, with shiny, newer cars up front and older, more worn vehicles tucked in the back. I headed straight to the back, hoping to find something I could afford to buy outright.

There, I spotted a 1990 hatchback that clearly hadn't been treated with much care. The mismatched parts, severe hail damage, and cigarette burns in the faded upholstery made it look like it had seen better days. Still, I figured it was worth a shot, so I asked to take it for a test drive. Shockingly, it drove perfectly fine.

When I got back, I popped the hood. The engine looked surprisingly clean—no oil leaks or messy spills on the ground beneath it. There was no price listed, so I offered a thousand dollars, and to my surprise, the dealer agreed.

I drove the car home, feeling a surge of pride. Tomorrow, I'll finally be able to drive myself to work. With that thought in mind, I walked down the hall, into my bedroom, and fell into a peaceful sleep.

The following day, I woke up feeling a sense of accomplishment. I felt like a sixteen-year-old again with her first car. It sat proudly in my driveway, as if it were a badge of my progress. It wasn't perfect—far from it—but it was mine. For so long, I'd lived in survival mode, never daring to think about the future. But now, with a roof that didn't leak, a car to call my own, and a steady job, I could finally see a glimpse of stability. A real life.

As I got ready for work, Cappy perched on the windowsill, his tail swishing idly. He watched me zip up my boots, his gold eyes filled with curiosity. "Gotta go to work, buddy," I said, scratching his chin before grabbing my keys. "Don't get into too much trouble while I'm gone."

The drive to work felt almost surreal. I'd spent so long walking that being behind the wheel of that old car felt like a luxury. It had a working radio and a cassette player that I had not tried since no one had cassette tapes anymore. The heat worked, the AC not so much, but it got great gas mileage. The car rattled annoyingly when I hit a pothole, and the rearview mirror tilted downwards with every bump, but I didn't care. I cracked the windows open a bit, letting the crisp morning air fill the cabin as I hummed along to the radio. I felt... normal.

When I arrived at the office, Maddie greeted me with a stack of assignments. "Morning, Grace," she said, her sharp eyes peering at me over the rim of her glasses. "Feeling ready to tackle the day?"

I nodded, flashing her a confident smile, still excited about my luxury drive over. "Absolutely."

She handed me a folder, her lips curving into a small grin. "Good. I've got a feature story for you. The city's hosting a charity gala next month, and I want you to cover it. Interviews with organizers, photos, the whole nine yards. Think you can handle it?"

A charity gala? That was a far cry from the fluff pieces I'd started with. My chest tightened, but I nodded again. "I'll do my best."

"Good. I wouldn't have given it to you if I didn't think you could," she said, then turned and walked briskly toward her office.

The rest of the day flew by in a blur of research and phone calls. By the time I got home, the sun was setting, casting a warm, golden glow over the neighborhood. I parked the Fiesta in the driveway, its chipped paint gleaming in the fading light. It was beautiful. As I stepped outside, I felt my phone vibrate. I had a missed call from Theo. I checked my voicemails. I hoped and prayed he wanted to take the relationship past the friend zone. I checked to see if he left me a message, and he did.

"Hello, Grace. I just wanted to check in on you. I would love to know how you are doing. I would also love to take you to dinner, if that is something you would be interested in. Let me know."

I smiled, the warmth from his words spreading through me like a soft fire. It wasn't flashy or overly sentimental, but it was thoughtful, just like him. I was excited about my life for the first time since Joseph died. I had never thought I would be happy again. I didn't think I deserved to be happy.

Cappy meowed at me and sauntered into the living room. I followed him and sat down on the couch. He jumped up on my lap and curled up into a round ball.

I turned the TV on at a low volume, but I wasn't paying attention. I found myself replaying the last few weeks in my head. The progress I'd made, the connections I'd built, and the life I was slowly piecing together. It wasn't perfect—not yet—but it was mine. I was proud of myself, and I was feeling accomplished.

I reached for my phone, typing out a quick text to Theo:

Dinner sounds perfect. Let me know when.

When I looked back up from my phone, there was a news report on the TV. A young female reporter was following a man who had just been arrested at the courthouse. She walked alongside him, shoving the microphone to his mouth. I grabbed the remote to turn up the volume.

"... where a prominent circuit court judge has been arrested on suspicion of prostitution," she said, looking at the camera, her hair windblown across her face.

"Judge Smithick, what can you tell us?" She asked, looking at him as she walked.

"I'm trying to stay strong despite the lies. You know what they say, 'courage is grace under pressure.'" He said with a smirk, looking directly into the camera. "I'll be home before you know it."

I sat there, mouth agape, as he was placed into the police car in handcuffs.

I turned off the TV, feeling both elated and angry at his arrogance. That smug comment made my skin crawl. I felt relief that he was behind bars, at last, for now.

I leaned back against the cushions, letting the sound of Cappy's purring fill the quiet. The world seemed lighter, like the weight I'd been carrying for so long was finally starting to lift. I thought about going to dinner with Theo. That gave me something good to look forward to.

Tomorrow would bring its own challenges, its own uncertainties. But for now, I allowed myself to rest, knowing that Smithick was exactly where he needed to be.

24

Reflection

Theo followed through with taking me to dinner. He drove me to a popular steakhouse. Inside, the atmosphere was cozy and intimate. The booths all had high backs, which helped lessen the noise. Midway through the meal, Theo grinned at me. "What?" I asked playfully.

"You look lovely tonight," he said, smiling.

I blushed. "Thank you, you look very handsome too! That blue shirt makes your eyes really pop."

"Maybe I should take it off then. That sounds painful!" he said with a wink, cutting into his steak.

A puzzled look swept across my face for a moment, until I understood, then I laughed harder than I had in a long time. I had to wipe away tears that came rolling down my cheeks.

"It's so good to see you smile," he said, taking a sip of his red wine.

I smiled back at him as he finished his last bite of steak. "I feel like you know everything there is to know about me, but I hardly know you," I said, intrigued. "Tell me three things: What is your special talent, greatest accomplishment, and your favorite hobby?"

"Oh boy," he said in a long, drawn-out sigh. "I'll have to think about the talent. My greatest accomplishment was getting my doctorate in psychology. No one else in my family even went to college," he said proudly and took another drink. After setting his now empty wine glass down, he continued. "My favorite hobby would have to be cooking. I'm always trying new things and putting strange things together to see if they work," he said with wide eyes, his voice becoming louder.

"I would love to be a good cook, but even boiling water is a struggle," I said, chuckling. "And the talent? You have to have a secret talent!" I prodded, looking up to see that the waitress had brought the dessert.

He looked down at the table and pondered the question for a moment, then looked back up at me with bright eyes. "I can name the ingredients in a dish by taste. I guess it's my palette that has a special talent," he said, taking a small bite of chocolate cake. While he chewed, his gaze turned upward, and his eyes narrowed. He raised his hand and pinched his chin with his thumb and forefinger in deep concentration.

Then he said, "Ah, yes! Besides having the standard eggs, flour, sugar, milk, butter, and baking powder..." his voice was smug, but he had a grin plastered to his face. "This not only has cocoa powder, but also chocolate pudding, chocolate chips, cinnamon, and sour cream for moisture."

We both laughed, and I wished that moment would never end. Even if this never developed into a long-term romantic relationship, I was happy having him as a friend.

Over the next few months, we continued spending time together. When I wasn't with him, I was at my cubicle at the newspaper.

Working for a newspaper had its perks, but it wasn't without its burdens. I'd gotten used to being in the know about big stories before the public, but it also meant I was often assigned stories that hit even closer to home.

One gorgeous day in late May, I walked into work. Maddie was waiting at my cubicle, leaning casually against the divider. I could see it in her eyes before she even spoke—she had a story for me, and not the kind you could finish with a smile.

"There's been a horrible accident," she said, sliding a file onto my desk.

My stomach sank.

"A drunk driver," she continued, her voice brisk. "She hit a family head-on. Two fatalities. I want you to cover it."

I nodded stiffly, opening the file as Maddie walked off to her office. I could feel my pulse quicken as I scanned the details, each one hitting me like a physical blow.

The drunk driver was a woman, alone in her car. She hadn't been wearing a seatbelt, and she'd been thrown from the vehicle, skidding along the asphalt. Somehow, she was still alive, though badly injured. The family she hit wasn't as lucky. They'd been driving home from one of the kids' basketball games. The drunk driver's SUV hit them head-on with such force that the family's car was thrown into a telephone pole.

The father and mother in the front seats were killed instantly. The impact caused the hood of their car to become unhinged, slicing through the air like a guillotine. I stared at the report in horror as I read the words describing how it severed the adult's heads.

In the back seat were two children: a five-year-old girl and her six-month-old baby brother. The kids survived, but barely. They were cut up and bruised, their small bodies battered from the crash.

I closed the file, swallowing the bile rising in my throat.

Maddie didn't know. She didn't know what I'd been through, what it was like to lose everything in a single moment of reckless tragedy. All she knew was I was a recovering addict who did time for manslaughter. She didn't know about Joseph, the crash, or my baby. And I wasn't about to tell her.

Later that day, I sat in a hospital room, across from the woman who had caused the crash. She was in her mid-thirties, with a gaunt face and hollow eyes. Her hands trembled as she cradled a styrofoam cup of lukewarm coffee. Tears streamed down her face as she spoke, her words broken and raw.

"I didn't mean to hurt anyone," she sobbed, her voice hardly audible. "I just... I just wanted it all to stop."

I swallowed hard, her words cutting too close to home.

She told me she'd been depressed, that she'd decided to drink and drive to kill herself.

"I thought... if I could just go fast enough, I could hit something, and it would all be over," she whispered, staring down at her shaking hands. "I didn't see them. I didn't see the car. And now..." Her voice broke into a choked sob. "I killed their parents. I ruined everything."

I wanted to look away, but I couldn't. My stomach twisted

231

in knots as she cried. I knew what it was like to want the pain to end so badly that you'd do anything to escape it. I understood her desperation.

But understanding didn't excuse it.

Those children had lost everything in an instant because of her recklessness. They would grow up without their parents. They would carry scars, emotional and physical, for the rest of their lives.

I clutched my notebook, my pen trembling in my hand. I tried to focus on the words, to capture the details of her story, but all I could see was *my* crash. The blood. The shattered glass. Joseph. My baby. I pressed the pen to the paper harder, as if that could force the memories away. The end of the day couldn't come soon enough, and when five o'clock hit, I was on my way.

When I got home, I took my laptop into my bedroom and stayed up all night writing the story. Cappy tried to help several times by lying on the keyboard, or stretching in front of the screen so I couldn't see, but ended up curling up next to me and falling asleep. For me, sleep was out of the question, not after that interview, not with the memories it had dredged up. I poured myself into the piece, trying to channel my grief, my anger, my guilt into the words. For a moment, I wondered if there had been a piece written after my accident. Maybe I didn't want to know.

When the sun began to rise, I was almost finished. The soft light spilling through the window felt surreal, like a reminder that life went on even after tragedy. I closed my laptop and walked into the bathroom for a quick shower before work.

After my shower, I walked out of the bathroom while drying

my hair with a towel. Cappy followed me into the kitchen, letting out a cheerful meow as I poured myself a bowl of Rice Krispies. I wrapped the towel around my hair tightly. I smiled, offering him the last bit of milk from my bowl. He lapped it up eagerly, his tail flicking with satisfaction. For a brief moment, his simple joy lightened the heaviness in the room.

At work, I handed the story to Maddie, who scanned it quickly, nodding in approval. "This is good. Very thorough. You turned it around fast."

I nodded silently and returned to my cubicle, where I tried to focus on my next assignment: piecing together the comics section. But my mind refused to cooperate.

All I could think about were those kids. The way their lives had been ripped apart. The fear they must have felt, the loss they would carry with them forever.

I thought about my own life after Joseph's accident, how I'd drifted aimlessly, untethered, with no one to care for me, no one to pull me out of the darkness.

I couldn't let that happen to them.

They deserved better. They deserved a home, love, stability—all the things I'd failed to give my own child.

The thought hit me like a bolt of lightning: *I could be that for them.*

On my break, I grabbed my phone and went out to sit in my car. I called Theo, one of the few people I trusted. We talked through the logistics, and the hurdles. Proving that my past was behind me would be the hardest part. But Theo suggested I start by signing up to be their foster parent. "The government will help with the costs. It'll give you a chance to prove yourself before actually adopting," he said.

"That sounds like a plan. Would you like to come over tonight? I thought we could watch a movie or something."

"I would love to. I will be there. See you soon," Theo said.

I hung up, staring at the computer screen in front of me, but not seeing it. The idea burned in my mind, too bright to ignore.

The rest of the day was a blur of exhaustion and caffeine. I made trip after trip to the break room, refilling my mug until the bitter taste of coffee coated my tongue. By lunchtime, my body was running on fumes, but I forced myself to walk to the burger joint down the street.

As I sat at the small plastic table, poking at my baked potato and chicken nuggets, I thought about the kids again. I didn't know their names or their faces, but I felt their pain like it was my own.

I wasn't the same person I'd been all those years ago. I'd clawed my way out of the wreckage of my past, and if I could do that, maybe I could give them a future.

It wouldn't be easy. Nothing worthwhile ever was.

But I owed it to them, to myself, to Joseph, and to the baby I'd lost.

26

Blast From the Past

When I got home, Theo was on my porch holding a rose.
"Hello, Grace. This is for you," he said as he handed me the freshly cut red rose.

"Thank you so much. It's beautiful!" I took the rose and scrunched my nose in its petals.

"*You* are beautiful, Grace," he said sweetly, a boyish grin emerging on his lips.

My face reddened. "Thank you," I said shyly.

"We can go out to the movies if you would like, or would you rather stay here?" he asked.

"Would it be okay if we just stayed here? I would rather be with you than surrounded by strangers."

"Staying here sounds perfect."

I unlocked the door, and we went inside. I walked into the kitchen to put the rose in a vase with some water as Theo stood in the living room by the front window, looking out.

"I see you got a car."

"Yes. It's ugly as sin, but it runs fine," I replied with a little giggle. We sat down on the couch and talked for a while. I sat with my hands on my knees and was facing forward. He had the arm closest to me on the back of the couch and had his body facing me. I could tell he was no longer my doctor, but how serious was he?

I offered to put on a movie because when movies were playing, people got comfortable and before they knew it, they were cuddling. I didn't have a huge selection, but I had the movie *Big* with Tom Hanks, and everyone loved *Big*. I hoped.

The movie started playing, and I was right, he started getting comfortable. He stood up and took off his coat, then draped it over the arm of the couch. When he sat back down, he sat very close to me and put his arm back on the back of the couch.

Thankfully, the sound of the TV smothered the sound of my beating heart. I leaned back, my arm against his side, my head resting on the couch. A few moments later, he took his arm off the back of the sofa and wrapped it around me. Now it was clear, I wasn't imagining it, he was interested in me. But why? After everything I'd done, how could anyone be? I put my head on his shoulder and forced the doubt away. *He* asked *me* out. *He* made the first move.

You knew you were having a good date when the movie faded into the background and all you could think about was body language. If I put my hand here, would he hold it? Should I grab his? Our faces were close, my forehead nearly touched his chin. Should I look up and wait for a kiss? Kiss his cheek? Or just keep watching the movie?

His arm tightened around me, and my heart skipped a beat. I felt safe.

I peeked up at him, and he was already looking down at me, his eyes soft and full of something. Hope, maybe? Time seemed to slow, the world narrowing to just the two of us.

"Theo..." I began, my voice just a whisper.

But he closed the distance, his lips brushing against mine in a kiss that was gentle but steady, like he was afraid to rush me but couldn't hold back anymore. It was perfect, and for a moment, the rest of the world fell away. All of my thoughts evaporated. We sat there completely still for a moment, one perfect moment, but the movie was ending.

"I should get going, but I had a lot of fun tonight. I would like to do it again, if you feel the same way," he said as he stood and stretched his long arms out.

"Yes, please, I would love to. Thank you for coming over and keeping me company. Next time we should go to the video store down the street and rent something." I stood, and we walked to the door.

"A lazy night in with a few movies, snacks, and you. That sounds perfect," he said, caressing my cheek, then bent slightly to kiss me. "Have a good night, Grace."

I walked him out the door and watched him until he was in his car and driving off. I was extremely tired now, but excited about Theo. Instead of obsessing over him, I begrudgingly went to bed.

I lay in bed, staring at the stained ceiling, willing sleep to come. The house creaked with every gust of wind, each noise pulling me further from much-needed rest. My mind wouldn't stop spinning—images of the children in the back of that crushed sedan, crying for their parents, filled every corner of my thoughts.

I turned onto my side, curling into myself. Cappy meowed and curled against my stomach as if trying to comfort me. "It's okay," I whispered, though I wasn't sure who I was trying to convince, him or myself. I tossed and turned for hours on end. I had to get some sleep, or I wouldn't be able to function at work the next day. It was midnight, and I had to be up by eight o'clock at the latest.

I took some melatonin hoping that might help. The last time I noticed the clock, it said half past one in the morning, but I fell asleep after that. I was in the middle of the most beautiful dream, until my alarm started going off and ruined it. I wrote down the dream, trying to wake myself up.

May 24, 2009

I dreamed that I was in a park on a hot summer day, and there were children all around me. They were laughing and playing and wanting me to play with them. I turned the merry-go-round for them. I was running and getting dizzy, but I kept running. I felt pure joy. I have so much love to give, and I know I was meant to be a mom.

I wanted to call in and continue that beautiful dream, but I needed the money. I hit the snooze button a few times too many, so I had no time for a shower or coffee. I threw some clothes on, brushed my hair and teeth, and ran out the door.

I arrived at work right on time and got situated in my cubicle. There was a text on my phone from Theo.

> I got an interview for you with the director of the foster care facility for after you get off from work at 5:30 pm. I will be there waiting for you. I miss you!

Now, I was excited. My house was completely remodeled except for my room. I would get to it eventually, but painting over the scribbles almost felt like I would be erasing part of myself. There was an extra bedroom that was big enough for two children. The baby could sleep in my room, and when he was old enough to want his own room, maybe we could move to a bigger house.

Theo was behind me the whole way. He said I would make a great mother. He met me at the foster care facility for the interview. I was really glad that he came with me because he had been my doctor. He knew first-hand how far I had come and that I hadn't had a delusion since I was under his care. I sat in the agency's waiting room, my hands gripping the armrests of the chair so fiercely my knuckles turned white. The clock on the wall seemed to tick louder with each passing second, mocking me.

What if they say no? What if they look at my past and see nothing but failure?

As if reading my mind, Theo placed a reassuring hand on my shoulder. "You're going to be great," he said, his voice steady and confident. "They'll see what I see—someone who's ready to change lives."

We walked into the office, hand in hand. A plump woman with greying hair stood to greet us and motioned for us to sit in the two chairs opposite her.

"I'm Pamela. You must be Grace and Theo," she said, sitting back down.

"Yes, thank you for meeting us," I said, anxious to get to the point of our meeting. "So, do the children have any family they can live with?"

"Their father was an only child whose parents passed away five years ago during Hurricane Frances. Their mother was estranged from her family, but we are still trying to reach other family members. But for the moment, we do need emergency housing for them," Pamela said in a professional, yet hopeful tone.

Pamela also said foster care was possible, but to adopt, they'd prefer a married couple, and of course, it would be expensive. Theo looked at Pamela in the eyes and in a confident but kind voice, said, "When she is ready to adopt, she will be married, and we'll have the money." He glanced at me and smiled. I smiled so big it felt like my ears should be on the top of my head. I grabbed his hand and held it tight.

At the end of our meeting, Pamlea said that I would potentially get the kids in a few days. The agency would send someone by to look at my house and make sure it was satisfactory for the emergency foster placement.

Theo and I left the office and were standing in the hallway. I hugged him tightly and kissed his cheek.

"Thank you so much for this. I need to go to the store and buy some things for the spare bedroom, if you would like to come."

"Actually, I have to get back to work. I took an extra-long lunch break for this. I will see you soon, though," he said, disheartened. He placed his hands on the side of my face, leaned in, and kissed me.

I ran to the store to buy bedding, and I needed a dresser for the girl's room. The children had clothes and some personal items from their house that they could bring, so at least I wouldn't need to start from scratch. I just wanted everything to be perfect. Those kids needed a clean slate as much as I did.

As I loaded the car with shopping bags, a car pulled up beside my driver's side door. I saw the driver get out of the car and begin walking toward me to go into the store. I continued placing items into the car. He stopped and stared at me. It was enough to make me feel like I was being watched, so I turned to look. He was still staring.

"Can I help you?" I asked.

"Karamel, is that you?" he asked with a smile.

My mouth dropped. The air around me felt like it was closing in. My mind reeled, like clothing tumbling inside a dryer. That had been my street name. I had forgotten I went by Karamel. "My name is Grace," I said and turned abruptly to get into the car.

"It's Jason. I know it's you. Don't you remember me?"

I did remember him. Tall, lanky, and covered in tattoos. The only different thing was that his long, raven black hair had been buzzed short. He had been one of my clients who was not cruel. He had been gentle and treated me more like a girlfriend than a prostitute.

"That part of my life is over, and I would like to keep it in the past," I said abruptly, trying to hide my fear and anger.

"That's understandable. I know Lenny didn't treat you good.

I'm sorry I didn't do anything about him. I liked you, you know? I just want to know how you are," he said as if genuinely concerned for me.

"I'm working on myself every day," I said, remembering that I liked him back then as well. Back then, being with him was an escape. He made me feel normal.

"I am so glad to hear. You look good. Happy. I don't know if I saw that in you before. Say, I work at the bar on Evergreen, *The Rusty Knob*, if you ever need to talk. About anything," he said eagerly.

"I'll keep that in mind, Jason," I said and got into the car. It was probably a bad idea to socialize with people from my past, even the ones who were good people. At the same time, it would be nice to talk to someone who knew me back then. Someone who knew what I had gone through.

We had met through Lenny, of course. Jason was looking for companionship more than sex, but we had that, too. He was lonely at the same time I was, and we had become very close. I hadn't even remembered him until I saw his face, and the memories came flooding back.

That evening, I had the TV on in the living room while I cleaned. I liked having background noise while I did housework—it made the quiet feel less suffocating. I wasn't paying attention until a phrase caught my ear.

"... an unsolved homicide."

I hesitated, my grip tightening on the broom handle. I continued sweeping, but my focus was no longer on the dust collecting in the pan.

"The victim is yet to be identified," the anchor said. "The medical examiner estimates she has been dead for approximately a year and is somewhere between fourteen and twenty years old. Jane Doe is a white female with dark blonde hair."

I abandoned my broom and turned toward the screen. The image of a blurred, grainy crime scene flashed in the background behind the anchor.

"By the time she was found, she had mummified," the newscaster continued. "Her eye color and weight could not be determined, but she did have this distinctive mark on her buttocks. If you recognize this mark or have any information, please call the Daytona Police Department at—"

I muted the TV.

That mark.

A strange weight settled on me as I inched closer to the screen. It wasn't a birthmark or a tattoo. It was something else— something intentional. The edges were rough, uneven, like whatever had seared it into her flesh hadn't been handled with care.

It was a scar.

No, not just a scar. A brand.

My breath hitched as I studied the image. I knew what I was looking at. It was crude, almost careless, but unmistakable—a half-moon shape combined with a rhombus, like a diamond stretched from tip to tip. Like the letter D, but with a jagged, sharp-edged diamond in place of the straight line.

My stomach plummeted. I'd seen that brand before.

Demetrie.

His name came to me like a whispered curse, like the ghost of every broken girl I'd ever known. He was a monster, the kind who thrived on power, who didn't just own his girls—he possessed them. And when he did, he left his mark.

To most, the brand might look like a burn, an accident, maybe even self-inflicted. But I knew better. I'd seen it before, years ago, on girls who wouldn't—or couldn't—talk about what had happened to them. Some of them had worked my track. Some of them disappeared.

I grabbed my journal, my fingers trembling as I sketched the mark from memory. I needed to talk to Detective Berry. This had to be connected to my case. Demetrie was still out there, still leaving his signature on girls like they were nothing more than livestock.

I pulled my phone from my back pocket and dialed Berry's number from her card. The line rang once before someone else picked up.

"Daytona Police, this is Detective Schammel."

I frowned. "Oh, um, I was trying to reach Detective Berry. This is Grace Christopher."

"She stepped out to grab some food. I can help, though. What's going on, Miss Christopher?"

I hesitated. Schammel had worked with Detective Berry on Lenny's case, too—I just didn't feel as comfortable with him, but he might still be able to do something.

"I saw the news," I said, forcing my voice to stay steady. "About Jane Doe."

"What about her?" he said sharply.

"She has a mark on her skin—a brand. I recognize it. Seeing

it jogged a memory. A pimp named Demetrie uses it on all of his girls. I know because some of them worked my block."

Silence.

Then: "That is interesting." His tone was unreadable. "I've heard of pimps branding their girls before, but I've never actually seen it."

I clenched my jaw. If he'd never seen it, he hadn't been looking hard enough.

"I hope this helps get her identified," I pressed.

"This is very helpful," he said, though the words felt stiff. "Thank you, Miss Christopher."

The line went dead.

I lowered the phone, my pulse drumming in my ears. Something in his voice—it wasn't just disinterest. It was something else.

Annoyance. Like I'd touched on something he didn't want to deal with.

Maybe I was reading too much into it. Maybe he was just having a long day.

Or maybe he knew something I didn't.

27

One Step at a Time

Two days passed without any news from the adoption agency, and I was beginning to think they had found family members to take the children. I was getting ready to go out to dinner with Theo when my phone rang.

"Hello, this is Grace."

"Hi there, this is Sarah Ward from the adoption agency. I am the social worker for the children needing emergency placement," she said in a professional tone.

"Yes! How are they?" I asked excitedly.

"They are doing as well as can be expected. I'd like to do a home visit in a couple of days to see where they will be staying. Will Friday at five o'clock work for you?"

"That's perfect. Thank you, Sarah."

I hung up the phone, my heart soaring. As I finished getting dressed, there was a knock at the door. I was so excited I nearly ran to open it, grabbing my purse on the way.

"Wow, you look amazing!" Theo said, with wide eyes.

"Thank you, so do you!" I said with a wink and stepped outside. "I just got the best news! I have the home visit with the social worker on Friday at five," I said, practically squealing.

"That's awesome. Let me know if you need help with anything!" Theo said enthusiastically.

We walked to the car, and he opened the passenger door for me.

We went to a nice little bar and grill that had a live band playing. We ate as we listened to the slow jazz playing. I looked into Theo's eyes and saw love and protection, and I thought I couldn't be happier than I was at that moment.

When we got back to my house, it was late, and we both had early mornings.

"Just stay here with me. Go to your apartment in the morning to change," I begged as we walked up to the front door,

He leaned in and kissed me as I was trying to open the door. I left the keys in the lock and wrapped my arms around him, kissing his neck. As he kissed me, he turned the key without looking and opened the door.

"I love you. I want to be with you," he said, panting and unbuttoning his shirt.

"I love you, too," I said softly. His hands were all over me, tearing at my dress. I hadn't felt this feeling in so long, I let him do all the work.

The couch was right there, and we fell into it, not even bothering to go to the bedroom.

The next morning, we got up early so he could run to his place, shower, and get clean clothes. I kissed him goodbye, wearing only his undershirt. When he got to his car, he looked up at me, smiled, and blew me a kiss. My heart was still pounding from the night before. I showered, got dressed, and left for work.

It was an uneventful, slow day. I didn't mind because I was up in a cloud thinking about Theo. *Nothing could spoil this day.* I thought. I was excited for what life had in store for me. I had already hit rock bottom, so there's only up from here. The clock finally hit five in the evening, and I headed back home.

I was still in a great mood until I got home from work and saw a dark sedan parked in front of the house. Detective Berry stepped out of the passenger side of the vehicle, and I knew then it was an unmarked police vehicle. As she began walking towards me, a wave of dread flooded over me. Memories surged through my mind even though I tried to fight them. We met each other on the porch.

"Get ready to testify," she said, sounding annoyed.

"What?" I snapped.

"Smithick turned down the damn plea bargain. He wants to go to trial. I don't understand why a judge thinks he will be able to get out of this one," she said with exasperation in her voice.

"I have so many questions! Would you like to come in and have some coffee or tea?" I asked.

"No, thank you, Grace. I don't have time. I just wanted to let you know what's going on so you can prepare yourself," she said sullenly, clearly annoyed at the situation.

"Am I the only witness?" I asked nervously.

"No, there are two other girls who worked for Smithick who have come forward—Melanie and Sasha. And according to Melanie, she was in charge of luring the girls into being trafficked. She was forced to, rather, by Smithick," Berry said with a hint of disgust. She turned her head back towards the car.

"I better get going, Schammel is waiting, and he's been bitchy lately."

Thinking about Schammel reminded me of our strange phone conversation, and I wondered if anything had come from it. "Detective Berry? Did Detective Schammel tell you that I called last week?"

"No, he didn't," Berry answered, her voice stern and filled with worry.

"You know that mummified Jane Doe they found a while back? The homicide victim?"

Detective Berry's interest was piqued. "Yes."

"I recognized the mark on her. It's a brand; a letter D that her pimp Demetrie gives all his girls. I called your number, and he picked up. He said you were out for lunch. I just wanted to make sure you knew."

"He must have just forgotten," she said, not sounding like she believed it. "This is good information. I'll see if I can contact some of the other girls to get an ID. This also gives us a suspect to look into after we've had nothing to go on for so long. I mean, this case is so cold it has fucking icicles. Thank you, Grace," she said as she turned and walked back to the unmarked car.

I stood on the porch, gripping the shopping bags full of bedding and children's supplies, as Detective Berry walked back to the unmarked car. My mind buzzed with everything she'd told me. A trial. Smithick. Melanie and Sasha. Girls being trafficked. The words circled in my head, overlapping with old memories I didn't want to confront. My stomach churned as nausea crept up on me, but I forced myself to breathe through it.

The sound of the cruiser's door shutting brought me back to the present. I waved half-heartedly as the car drove away, disappearing down the street. As soon as it was gone, I unlocked the door and stepped inside, setting the bags on the couch. My hands were trembling. The thought of testifying made my chest feel tight. I had been trying so hard to put Lenny behind me, but now he and Smithick were back, dragging me into the darkest parts of my past.

I paced the living room, running my hands through my hair as my thoughts spiraled. Could I do this? Could I stand up in court, in front of Smithick, and lay everything bare? The humiliation, the fear, the memories I'd buried as deep as I could—it would all come rushing back. And worse, it wouldn't just be him in the courtroom. The jury, the lawyers, the reporters—they'd all see me as the woman I used to be.

No, I thought, shaking my head. That's not who I am anymore. I've changed. I've worked too hard to let them reduce me to my worst mistakes.

I stopped pacing and examined the room. My eyes landed on the bags of bedding, then over to the rose Theo had given me. A faint smile tugged at my lips despite the storm of emotions inside me. This wasn't just about me anymore. If those other victims were brave enough to testify, then I could, too. If I could face this trial and help bring down Smithick, maybe I could give future generations a safer future—a world where monsters like him couldn't hurt them.

I took a deep breath and walked into the kitchen. Cappy meowed loudly, rubbing against my legs. His gold eyes were full of concern—or maybe he just wanted dinner. Either way, his presence was grounding. I knelt and scratched behind his ears, feeling a bit of the tension leave my body.

"It's going to be okay," I whispered, both to him and to myself. "One step at a time."

I stood up and reached for my phone, dialing Theo's number. He answered after the second ring, his voice warm and steady, instantly easing my nerves.

"Hey, Grace. How's the shopping coming along?" he asked.

"It's done," I said, smiling despite everything. "But Detective Berry was waiting for me when I got home. There's going to be a trial. Smithick refused the plea bargain."

Theo let out a low whistle. "That's unexpected. I thought he'd take the deal to avoid dragging this into court."

"Me too," I admitted, leaning against the counter. "Berry said they'll need me to testify. I just... I don't know if I can do it. What if I freeze up? What if he looks at me and I can't speak?"

"You can do this," Theo said, his voice filled with quiet conviction. "You've been through hell, Grace, and you've come out stronger on the other side. This isn't just about the past, it's also about protecting the future from that monster. Those kids you're taking in, they're part of that future. You're not just fighting for yourself anymore."

His words hit me hard, like a door unlocking in my mind. He was right. I wasn't alone this time. I had Theo, Cappy, the kids—people who believed in me, who were counting on me.

"I'm scared," I admitted, my voice low and breaking.

"I know, but you don't have to face this alone. I'll be there every step of the way. We'll prepare together, and when the time comes, you'll be ready."

251

A lump formed in my throat, but it wasn't from fear this time—it was gratitude. "Thank you, Theo. For everything."

"Always. I love you, Grace" he replied, his tone soft but unwavering. "Now, go take care of yourself. You've got a few big days ahead of you, with the kids coming and all."

"I love you, too! See you soon!"

I hung up, feeling a little steadier, and like my heart was floating. I grabbed the bags from the living room, my arms straining under the weight as I made my way to the spare bedroom. The wood floors creaked beneath my feet, the sound familiar and comforting in a way that made it feel more like a home instead of a house.

The spare room was small, barely more than a closet. It was down the hall, between the bathroom and my room. The hardwood floors were scuffed, but the walls had a fresh coat of paint. The furniture was mismatched—a dresser I'd found at a thrift store, a twin bed frame I'd dragged out of the basement, and a small, wooden bookshelf with scratched white paint. It wasn't much, but it was a start.

The sun hung low in the sky, its warm golden light streaming through the cracked blinds. Dust motes floated lazily in the air, and for a moment, I stood there, watching the way the light softened the room. It was like the beginning of something new.

Setting the bags down, I began unpacking. The bedding came first—a soft quilt in shades of blue and yellow, cheerful and bright. I smoothed it over the mattress, tucking in the edges with care. Next came the pillows, one with a striped case, the other solid yellow. As I fluffed them and placed them neatly at the head of the bed, I couldn't help but imagine a child lying there, reading a bedtime story or drifting off to sleep after a long day of play.

I opened another bag and pulled out a few small items I'd picked up earlier: a stuffed rabbit with one ear that was perpetually droopy, a set of toy cars with different colors of paint, and a set of markers and coloring books. I arranged them on the bookshelf, stepping back to admire the way they brought a little life to the space.

With each item I unpacked, the room began to feel less like a forgotten corner of the house and more like a haven. A place where two kids, two little lives that had already been through so much, could feel at home.

I worked until the light outside faded, the warm glow giving way to deep purple shadows. As I hung light curtains over the window, I caught my reflection in the glass. My hair was messy, my face tired, but there was something different in my expression.

Excitement. Real and true excitement.

I paused for a moment, leaning against the windowsill, and let myself picture it: the kids playing in this room, their laughter bouncing off the walls, filling the house with a kind of energy I hadn't felt in so long. I imagined the five-year-old girl spinning in circles, her giggles contagious, while her baby brother gurgled happily on the bed.

The thought made me smile, a real smile, not one of those hollow ones I used to force when I was pretending to be okay. I felt like I was building something worth fighting for. Something real.

The dresser was my last task. I lined the drawers with fresh contact paper and placed a small lamp on top, its soft, yellow light bathing the room in a cozy glow. I added a picture frame— empty for now but waiting for a photo of the kids. It felt symbolic, like a promise to myself that one day this house, this room, would hold memories.

By the time I finished, the room wasn't perfect, but it was ready. Ready for a new chapter, for new possibilities.

After much contemplation, I decided to head over to the Rusty Knob and see if Jason was there. I wanted to ask him if he knew anything about Smithick or the other girls who worked for him. When I got there, it wasn't terribly busy. It was a typical dive bar with a couple of pool tables, darts, TVs showing different sports, and a long bar that was the length of the building. Jason stood behind the bar, serving a couple at the far end. He smiled when he spotted me and motioned for me to sit near him at the bar.

We talked for a couple of hours. He was drinking some amber beer, and I drank a light beer with lime. I had forgotten how funny he was. He was always able to take my mind off things with his humor.

After I had a couple of beers in me, I felt relaxed. I decided I wanted to tell him what happened. "I killed Lenny," I told him.

He set his mug down on the table. "Really? How? What happened?" He asked in shock.

"We were at my house, and he was punching me. I kicked him in the nuts. Then he lunged at me, snarling like a bull. I had taken the gun out of my bag and shot him," I said as controlled as I could manage. I didn't want to start crying in a bar. "I just couldn't take his abuse anymore. He would have killed me!" I said raising my voice.

Jason's jaw dropped. "That's crazy. That asshole deserved everything you dished out. I wish I had done it years ago, but apparently you have bigger balls than me," he said with a smirk.

I took another sip of my beer. "So, Lenny worked for a guy named William Smithick, who is a circuit court judge. Did you ever meet him or any of his other guys?"

"No, never," he said shaking his head. "I never used any other escorts, either. You were the first and the last for me. Do you have to go to trial for Lenny?"

"The police interviewed me about Lenny, and I told them everything. After doing some investigating, the detectives told me it was clear self-defense, and that case was dropped," I said, peeling the label from the beer bottle. "I told them about Smithick's drug and prostitution ring, too. So, they opened a new investigation into him and his crew. Smithick turned down the plea bargain. So, there will be a trial eventually," I said with a sigh.

"Yeah, of course. Being a judge, he probably thinks he is above the law and can outsmart everyone. I would love to hear the outcome of everything. Can we keep in touch?" He asked casually, pulling out his phone.

We exchanged phone numbers before I left.

That night, I curled up in bed with Cappy nestling against my side. The house was so quiet, the only sounds were the soft rustling of the wind through the trees and the faint hum of the refrigerator. I stared up at the ceiling. My thoughts raced with everything that had happened and everything still to come.

The trial loomed large in my mind, a dark cloud of uncertainty. I thought of Theo, his unwavering support, a lifeline I never thought I would have. And the kids—the thought of them both thrilled and terrified me. *What if I am not good enough? What if I can't give them the life they deserve?*

Cappy shifted, pressing closer, his purring a steady rhythm against my side. I reached out and stroked his soft fur, grounding myself in that moment.

I could feel the fear creeping in, that familiar urge to run away from anything getting too overwhelming. But this time, I didn't want to run. Because now, I wasn't merely surviving. I was moving forward.

The spare room, with its mismatched furniture and hopeful little details, felt like a metaphor for my life—imperfect, pieced together, but full of potential. And as I drifted off to sleep, Cappy's warmth anchoring me, I allowed myself to believe, for a moment, that maybe I was capable of creating something good. Something whole.

I turned onto my side, wrapping my arm around Cappy, who purred in his sleep. "One step at a time," I whispered, the words a promise to myself.

The fight would begin soon. But tonight, I let myself rest. For once, I didn't dream of the past—I dreamed of the future. Of hope. Of family. Of a life worth living.

28

Emergency Placement

I hardly slept last night. I was so excited it felt like my mind and my heart might explode. I wasn't sure how to even express my feelings because it was a mix of excitement and doubt. *Will the house be good enough for them? Will they even like me and want to stay?* So many thoughts raced through my mind as I raced around the house, making sure everything was absolutely perfect for the social worker's visit.

It had to be good enough for the social worker. I hoped and prayed it was so they could stay.

Theo should be here any minute, I thought to myself as I popped the second batch of chocolate chip cookies into the oven. The first batch had already come out and was cooling on a baking rack. The house smelled amazing, and everything was as child-proof as it could be, and I was ready. Just then, there was a knock at the door. I opened it to see Theo, holding a fresh bouquet of gorgeous wildflowers.

"Welcome!" I squealed.

"It smells and looks amazing in here, Grace!" he said as he handed me the bouquet that I had already squished up into my face, smelling the aroma. I filled a vase with water and put the flowers in.

"This will make a great centerpiece for the dining room table. The perfect final touch!" I said excitedly.

"I agree! Can I help with anything?" he asked as he hung his jacket on the wall hook.

"No, they should be here any moment now," I said, patting the cat hairs off my white shirt and khaki pants. "Do I look alright?" I asked in a panic.

"You look lovely." Theo put his arm around my shoulders and kissed my forehead. "No matter what happens today, just know that I am proud of you. And if it doesn't happen today, that doesn't mean that it will never happen, okay?"

"Alright," I said, looking him in the eyes. He had a way of putting me at ease, and I knew that whatever happened was meant to be. *Que será, será*, I thought to myself.

A car pulled up in front of the house, and at the same time, my phone rang. It was Detective Berry, telling me the trial date had been set for February 3rd of next year. With that, the blood drained from my face. I hung up the phone. There was knocking on the door, but it did not register with me. Theo answered and introduced me to the social worker and the kids, which made me snap out of it.

The social worker named Sarah Ward put her hand out to shake mine, and I did so with a smile. "Grace Christopher. Thank you for coming."

"Sarah Ward. I am the social worker assigned to the case. We are still reaching out to family members to see if anyone can take them," she said in a monotone voice, judging my very existence.

The baby boy was in his car seat, fast asleep. "His name is Michael," Sarah said in a whisper. I got down on my knees to say hello to the little girl.

"My name is Grace. What's your name?" I asked in a low but chipper voice.

"Emily," she said with little emotion and standing perfectly still.

"Do you like chocolate chip cookies, Emily?" I asked enthusiastically. Her eyes widened, and the softest smile began to emerge on the corners of her mouth with a hint of caution.

"Yes," she said, and her smile widened. I stood and went into the kitchen and grabbed a plate of cookies, then brought them into the living room where we stood.

"Help yourself!" I glanced at Emily and Sarah and gestured to the cookies. "Theo, would you like to give Sarah a tour of the house, and I can stay with Emily and the baby?"

I crouched down to see if the baby had stirred yet—he hadn't. He seemed like an angel, with his porcelain skin and rosy cheeks. My eyes became glassy as I gazed at him, fighting the memories of the baby I had lost and trying to stay calm. I turned to the TV, turning it to a cartoon channel to distract both Emily and my mind. I sat gently on the couch next to her, not wanting to startle her. She held her cookie with both hands and took small, polite bites. My heart ached for her. *What must she be going through? How much of this does she understand?*

A few moments later, Theo and Sarah came back to the living room in mid-discussion about Theo's work. "I have seen everything I need to see. Everything looks like it is in order. Are you prepared to take the children now?" Sarah asked as she made notes in her portfolio.

"I am!" I said, gleaming.

"I just want to remind you that this is an emergency placement only. Hopefully, we can find someone from her family to take them. I'll be in touch." She handed me her card, shook my hand, and turned to leave. Theo walked her to her car.

When Theo came back inside, Emily was curled up beside me on the couch, her tiny frame leaning barely against my arm. Her guard was still up—I could feel it in the way her shoulders tensed every time I shifted—but she hadn't moved away. I considered that a victory.

"She's warming up to you," Theo whispered as he sat on the armrest of the couch, careful not to disturb the moment. I nodded, smiling at Emily, who was still focused on the cartoon on the TV.

Fatigue was beginning to set in for me, but I could see Emily's energy starting to brighten, her eyes darting curiously around the room. Just then, there was a soft thud behind us. Cappy had emerged from his usual perch on the windowsill, landing gracefully on the floor and padding over to investigate our visitors.

"Emily, this is Cappy," I said, keeping my tone light and warm. The black-and-white cat sat a few feet away, his gold eyes watching Emily with interest, his tail flicking lazily.

She turned her head slowly to look at him, her lips slightly parted. "Is he... yours?" she asked quietly, her voice almost too soft to hear.

"He's yours too now. Cappy loves making new friends, don't

you, buddy?"

Cappy meowed in response, as if on cue, and I felt Emily's tiny body relax beside me. She slid off the couch and crouched down on the floor, reaching a hand out cautiously. Cappy sniffed her fingers, then rubbed his head against her palm, purring loudly. Her lips curved into a real smile this time, small but unmistakable, and my heart swelled.

"He's soft," she said, stroking his fur.

"He likes you," I said, watching as Cappy flopped onto his side dramatically, inviting her to rub his belly.

Emily giggled—a sound so sweet and pure it made my chest ache. Tears stung the corners of my eyes, but I blinked them away quickly. I didn't want to overwhelm her.

"Cappy's been the boss around here for a while," Theo added. "But I think he just gave you the job."

Emily peeked up at him, still smiling, and then back at the cat. "He can stay the boss," she said simply, and the three of us laughed.

Meanwhile, Michael had begun to stir in his car seat. I leaned forward to check on him, and his tiny fists flailed for a moment before he settled again. "He's still sleeping like a champ," I said with a smile, brushing a strand of hair out of my face.

The evening passed in a blur of small, quiet moments like that. Emily explored the house cautiously, her steps tentative but curious. She held my hand when I showed her the room I had prepared for her—a cozy space with soft bedding, shelves full of books, and a small, stuffed bunny perched on the pillow.

Her fingers tightened around mine when she saw it, but she

didn't say anything. Instead, she walked in and sat carefully on the edge of the bed, as if testing its softness.

"It's your room. You can make it your own."

Her eyes darted to mine, searching for something. I wasn't sure if she found it, but after a moment, she nodded.

Back in the living room, Theo picked up Michael, who had finally woken, and cradled him with the kind of ease that made my heart flutter. He cooed softly to the baby, who responded with wide, curious eyes and a gurgling sound that almost resembled a laugh.

"You're a natural!" I leaned against the doorway, watching them.

"I've had some practice with nieces and nephews," he said with a wink, as he rocked Michael.

Later, after Emily had fallen asleep in her new room and Michael was dozing again in his crib, Theo lingered in the doorway, watching me tidy up the kitchen.

"Are you sure you don't want me to stay the night?" he asked, his voice low and careful.

I looked up from the sink, meeting his steady gaze. The offer was tempting—more tempting than I wanted to admit. But I needed to prove to myself that I could do this, that I could be strong for these children.

"You can if you want to, but I'll be fine. Really."

He stepped closer, placing his hands on my shoulders. "Of course, I want to. You're amazing, you know that?" he said, his voice full of warmth and pride.

"I don't feel amazing," I admitted with a soft laugh. "I feel... terrified."

He nodded, brushing a stray hair out of my face. "That's how I know you're going to be great at this. You care enough to be scared."

I swallowed hard, his words settling into my chest. He kissed my forehead, lingering for a moment before stepping back.

I checked on the kids one last time—Emily was sound asleep, clutching the stuffed bunny to her chest, and Michael was like a cherub in his crib. Cappy had stationed himself on the armchair in the living room, his eyes half-closed but watchful, as if he'd taken it upon himself to stand guard.

Theo and I sat down on the couch, and I finally let myself exhale. I leaned against him, feeling his breath and heartbeat. The fear and doubt were still there, humming beneath the surface. But so were hope and determination.

I glanced at Cappy, who blinked at me lazily. For the first time in a long time, the house felt like a home. And I knew, no matter how difficult the road ahead might be, I wasn't walking it alone. I picked up my journal and wrote every detail of the day so I could remember it for the rest of my life. Then we went to bed.

May 29, 2009

This is the first night the kids are with me. I am scared, but so excited about the future. Emily is so sweet. She is a little shy, but that is to be expected. Michael is a tiny, precious angel. I do hope they find their family, because that is always best if it is possible. I hope I can be everything they need me to be for now. Theo has been such a supportive partner in all of this. He makes me so incredibly happy.

29

An Us Moment

Time began to speed up with two kids in the house. They had been with me for a few months now. I felt like it was working out. I was so very thankful that Maddie allowed me to work from home most of the time. I brought the kids with me to do research out in the field. I wrote my reports from home and submitted everything electronically.

Every other week, the kids and I would all go visit Frank and Janie. Frank's face would light up when he saw us coming. Janie was not used to children at all. After overcoming her initial shyness, Emily was a little loud and rambunctious, but Janie enjoyed sitting next to Michael and showing him different toys or her drawings.

I was busier than ever, but I was loving every minute of it. I was excited for fall. I loved the crispness in the air, the color-changing leaves, sweaters, and hot chocolate. I was excited to take the kids to the pumpkin patches and decorate for Halloween.

Theo came by after work to take me and the kids to dinner. When he came through the door, I was getting my shoes on and watching the news. There was a story about a local murder that had happened the previous night.

"We have just been told they have identified the young woman as seventeen-year-old Sasha Woods. She was found on Old Mill Road, shot execution style, last night, September 28th. If you have any information ple—" I shut off the TV.

Was that the Sasha I think it was? That isn't a very common name. I didn't know for sure, but it could be the same Sasha who was going to testify at Judge Smithick's trial. I didn't want to say anything to Theo that would ruin our night. I let that sit in the back of my mind until I could call Detective Berry.

We ate dinner at a burger place where kids ate for a dollar. They always had an older gentleman out in the lobby making balloon animals for the kids. Emily wanted a monkey, and he smooshed and squeaked the balloon together until it appeared to be a pink monkey with a very long tail. Emily squealed with joy. The table had a placemat for Emily to color, and she sat quietly coloring while Theo and I talked.

The burger joint was buzzing with the usual chaos of families and kids, the air filled with the scent of sizzling fries and ketchup, punctuated by the occasional squeak of balloon animals made by the man near the entrance. Emily was fully engrossed in the placemat in front of her. Michael was babbling happily in his highchair, his chubby hands slapping at a toy car that Theo gave him to keep him occupied.

Across the table, Theo caught my eye and smiled—one of those smiles that made the noise of the restaurant fade into the background. He seemed so calm, so steady, so... *Theo.*

"You're quiet," he leaned his elbows on the table. "What's on your mind?"

I shook my head and forced a smile, pushing the news report I'd seen earlier to the back of my mind. "Nothing important. Just trying to soak it all in." That was true. I was trying to soak in everything that had happened recently. My life felt so perfect that I was scared.

"Good," he said, his grin widening. "Because I've got something important to say, and I need you to pay attention."

My heart skipped a beat. He was smiling so it couldn't be bad news. He had that look in his eye, the one that always spelled trouble or mischief.

"Oh no," I said, narrowing my eyes at him playfully. "What are you up to?"

Before I could react, Theo stood up. *Stood up* in the middle of the restaurant, right next to our table. My stomach flipped. *What is he doing?*

"Theo, sit down," I hissed, my cheeks already burning.

But he ignored me, clearing his throat dramatically.

"Ladies and gentlemen, if I could have your attention for just a moment!"

The room quieted, and I froze in place, torn between mortification and the tiniest bit of curiosity. Even the balloon artist paused mid-twist, holding what looked like the beginnings of a giraffe.

"I don't mean to interrupt your delicious dinners," Theo continued, his voice steady but with a playful edge, "but I have something very important to say to a very special woman sitting right here at this table."

The kids' table next to us erupted into whispers of "Is he gonna do it?" and "He's gonna propose!" Emily glanced up from her coloring, wide-eyed, while Michael stared at Theo like he was the most fascinating thing in the world.

"Grace," he said, turning back to me. His voice softened, but it carried just enough to be heard over the muted clatter of forks and the hum of the restaurant.

"You are... everything. You're the strongest, most incredible woman I've ever met. Watching you take care of these kids, balancing work, life, and everything in between—it blows me away. Every single day."

I felt my throat tighten, my cheeks still hot as everyone stared at us, but Theo wasn't done.

"You make me laugh when I need it the most. You're kind, patient, and just the right amount of stubborn. And don't even get me started on how good you are at making chocolate chip cookies."

A smattering of chuckles rippled through the restaurant. I could see one of the servers grinning from behind the counter.

"Before you, I didn't know what it meant to feel... whole. You've given me so much—love, a family, a purpose. And I don't want to spend another second of my life without you by my side."

I blinked rapidly, my vision blurring as tears threatened to spill over. Then, to my utter disbelief, he pulled something out of his pocket—a small, black velvet box. He knelt on one knee, right there beside the table, with a diamond ring sparkling under the fluorescent lights.

"Grace," he said, his voice steady and filled with all the love

I'd ever felt from him, "will you marry me?"

The room went silent. I heard Emily gasp quietly beside me. Even Michael seemed to sense the gravity of the moment, his tiny hand gripping the corners of the high-chair tray.

For a moment, all I could do was stare at him—this man who had been my rock, and my partner. He had literally saved my life. He had seen me at my worst. Here he was, standing—well, kneeling—in a burger joint surrounded by balloon animals and crayons, asking me to be his, forever. And it was the most perfect, beautiful, *us moment* in the world.

"Yes," I finally said, my voice tentative. Then louder: "Yes, Theo. Of course, yes!" I couldn't believe what was happening and thought I might pass out from sheer joy.

The restaurant erupted into cheers and applause. Emily clapped her hands and giggled, while Michael squealed happily, not entirely sure what was happening but delighted by the noise.

Theo slid the ring onto my finger, grinning like a kid on Christmas morning. Then he stood, pulling me up and into his arms, and planting a kiss on my forehead as everyone around us cheered.

"I can't believe you just did that, here," I whispered, laughing through my tears.

"Why not here?" he said, his voice low and teasing. "What better place than where Emily met her pink monkey, and Michael got his first taste of French fries?"

I laughed harder, wiping my eyes. He was right; this place, as quirky as it was, would forever hold a special place in my heart.

Emily tugged at my sleeve. "Does this mean Theo's going to live with us forever?" she asked, her little face full of hope.

I crouched down to her level, pulling her into a hug.

"Yes, sweetheart, it means he's going to be with us forever."

"Good," she said simply, holding her balloon monkey tight.

As I sat back down, sliding the ring onto my finger properly and taking it in under the warm light, I felt a deep sense of peace settle over me. The past few months had been a whirlwind, and the road ahead wasn't going to be any easier But with Theo and these two little ones by my side, I knew we could face anything together.

"Alright," Theo said, picking up a French fry with a grin. "Now, who wants ice cream? My treat!"

Emily cheered, Michael babbled happily, and I couldn't stop smiling. This was the beginning of the rest of our lives—and I couldn't wait for all the quirky, chaotic, beautiful moments to come.

The ride home was quiet. Partly because we had all expended our energy at the restaurant, and partly because everything just felt right. There was no need to fill the silence with words. I was still in shock. *I am going to be Mrs. Grace Cameron,* I thought. After everything I had been through, it was almost too perfect, like a too-good-to-be-true scenario, and in the back of my mind, I was scared. I tried to push those feelings to the far corners of my mind, but the feeling never fully went away.

By the time we arrived home, the stars were already out, scattered like tiny pinpricks of light against the darkening sky. Michael, fast asleep in his car seat, his little fists clenched around the edges of his blanket. Emily, as usual, fought sleep tooth and nail, insisting she wasn't tired even as her head nodded forward with each bump in the road.

After carrying Michael to his crib and tucking Emily in with her favorite stuffed bunny, Theo and I grabbed a couple of beers from the fridge and collapsed onto the couch. My shoulders sank into the cushions, and for the first time all day, I let myself exhale.

"Finally," I muttered, taking a sip of my beer.

"Finally," Theo echoed with a tired smile, leaning his head back and closing his eyes.

The house was quiet, the hum of the refrigerator in the kitchen the only sound. We sat in comfortable silence, but the peace didn't last long. My phone rang, its shrill tone cutting through the stillness. I groaned, fishing it out of my pocket and glancing at the screen. It was Detective Berry.

"Hello. This is Grace," I said, raising my eyebrows at Theo, who had a "what now" expression plastered on his face.

"Hey, Grace. Did you see the news?" Berry's voice was low and composed, the kind of tone people use when delivering bad news.

"I did," I replied, a knot forming in my stomach. "I was wondering... was it the same Sasha? Do you know who killed her? Smithick is still in custody, right?"

There was a pause on the other end of the line.

"Yes, it was the Sasha that was set to testify," she said with a depressing sigh. "Yes, he's still in custody," Berry said. "But he has plenty of goons who could have done it for him. We haven't caught the guy yet, so we can't say for sure why she was killed.

She was still involved in prostitution and drugs—it's such a high-risk lifestyle. It's hard to say whether her death was connected to the trial or if it was just... that life catching up to her. We're still working on it, though.

"Smithick has been a real peach, too. He's been running his mouth, threatening to sue all of us. Laughing like this is some kind of game. He knows exactly what he's doing. He is cruel and smart, which is a dangerous combo."

"Yeah, a scary combo. I am terrified that he will bond out."

"Me too. I just wanted to let you know. And Grace..." She paused again. "Be safe out there."

Theo's eyebrows shot up, and he leaned forward, watching me intently as I replied. "I will," I said, forcing a calmness into my voice that I didn't feel. I reached over and placed my free hand on Theo's, squeezing it. "Theo will keep me safe."

"Good. Let me know if you see or hear anything suspicious, okay?" Berry said, her tone softening.

"I will. Please let me know if you find anything out about Sasha's case," I replied, my voice faltering.

"Will do. Goodnight, Grace."

"Goodnight," I said and hung up, placing the phone on the coffee table as though it had suddenly become unbearably heavy.

"What's going on?" Theo asked, his tone gentle but laced with concern.

I took a deep breath, running my fingers through my hair. "It's about Sasha. The Sasha I told you about, the one who was going to testify at Smithick's trial. She was killed last night. I saw it on the news. Berry was calling to let me know."

Theo's brow furrowed, his jaw tightening. "You think her death wasn't random?"

"The police don't know yet," I said quickly, trying to reassure him. "Smithick is still locked up, but Berry said he has people on the outside. It could have been one of them. Or it could have been something else entirely, maybe a drug deal gone wrong." I tried to smile, but it felt hollow, forced. "We don't know for sure, so there's no point in jumping to conclusions."

Theo didn't look convinced. "Grace..." he said, his voice trailing off as he searched my face. I wondered if he thought I was being too emotional.

"She was only seventeen," I blurted, cutting him off. My voice wavered, and I swallowed hard, fighting back the lump forming in my throat. "She was still a kid, Theo. Figuring out her life. She didn't deserve this."

Theo shifted closer, his hand moving to caress my cheek. His touch was warm, grounding. "I'd like to stay tonight," he said calmly, his eyes steady on mine.

I nodded, his presence making it a little easier to breathe. "I'd like that too," I whispered.

He smiled, his thumb brushing against my cheekbone. "You know," he paused, "we don't need two houses anymore. And since my place is a glorified bachelor pad..."

"You should just move in here," I finished for him, my lips quirking into a small smile.

"Yeah, my apartment is, well... It's no place for kids. No yard for them to play in, no room for them to grow. I'll start moving my things over. Or..." He paused, his head tilting as he considered the thought. "We could look for a new place.

Something that's just ours. Michael's going to need his own room soon, and Emily would love a bigger backyard."

The idea warmed something deep inside me, a spark of hope for a future that felt more stable, more real. "We'll figure it out," I said, leaning over to kiss his cheek. "But for now, let's just go to bed. I'm beat."

"Fair enough," Theo replied, finishing off his beer and setting the empty bottle on the table.

I stood and grabbed his hand, pulling him up with a smile, as if I had the strength to lift him myself. He chuckled, letting me tug him to his feet, and together we meandered to the bedroom.

As we climbed into bed, the weight of the day settled over me like a blanket. I told myself everything was fine. Sasha's death was tragic, yes, but it was more than likely a drug deal gone wrong. Or something else completely plausible, nothing to do with Smithick's trial.

And yet, as I lay there in the darkness, the thought wouldn't stop nagging at me. *What if it did?*

I opened my journal and wrote down my thoughts.

September 29, 2009

What did Sasha know? Was this random, or did Smithick have her killed? Am I imagining a connection where there is none? Who else might be in danger? Could I be next? What if it is a message—to me, to anyone else thinking about standing up to him?

In the back of my mind, the unease simmered, a quiet storm brewing beneath the surface. Sasha's face—young, hopeful, scared—flashed in my mind, and I wondered if she'd known it was coming. If she'd been afraid in those final moments.

The room felt colder, the shadows longer and darker than they should have been. I turned to Theo; his steady breathing was a comfort as I nestled closer to him. His arm wrapped around me protectively, and for a moment, I allowed myself to feel safe.

30

The Phone Call

The morning sun pierced through the slit between the curtains like a laser, warming my face and pulling me from a deep, dreamless sleep. Theo's heavy arm was still draped over me from behind, anchoring me in place. His steady breaths against the back of my neck provided a strange kind of comfort, like I was tethered to something solid, something safe. Cappy was curled into a ball in front of my hips, his soft fur brushing against my fingers.

Normally, being hemmed in like this—trapped by another person's weight—would make me feel suffocated, even panicked. But this morning, with Theo, it felt different. It was nice. Peaceful. When I was lying next to Theo, I felt like I could let my guard down, even if only for a moment.

Outside, the crisp bite of autumn was seeping in, slipping through the cracks in the windows and settling into the bones of the house. The air smelled different this time of year—earthier, touched with a hint of decaying leaves. It was the kind of scent that made me think of change, of endings and beginnings, all tangled together like the fallen branches in the yard. I didn't want to leave the cocoon of blankets. But the heaviness refused to let me rest. Every time I closed my eyes, I saw Sasha's face.

A life snuffed out in a way no one deserved.

I slipped out of bed as quietly as I could, careful not to wake Theo. He lay on his side, one arm tucked under the pillow, his breathing slow and steady. The kids were still asleep, the house silent except for the faint creak of the floorboards beneath my feet as I moved. I made my way to the kitchen and started a pot of coffee. The kitchen was dim, the only light coming from the muted glow of the stove clock.

As I waited for my coffee, I sent Jason a text, asking him if he was awake and could talk.

Yes, I'm awake.

I filled a mug with steaming coffee and stepped out onto the porch so as not to wake anyone else. The air outside was a little humid, but there was a chilly breeze. The birds were singing happily. I dialed Jason's number.

"Are you alright?" he asked, his voice filled with concern.

"One of the witnesses in Smithick's case was murdered two nights ago. I'm worried, but I am safe," I replied.

"Let me know if you need anything. I know you have a boyfriend, but he might not understand this like I do. He doesn't know how dangerous these people can be. Do you have a gun?"

"I did, but the police took it as evidence in Lenny's case, and I still haven't gotten it back yet."

"You should probably get one."

"Detective Berry doesn't know if it is connected or not. She had a dangerous lifestyle. So, it may have been a coincidence," I said nervously as I paced around in the porch. "That's what I am trying to tell myself anyway. I should probably get going. Theo will wake up soon."

"Come see me tonight at the Rusty Knob. We can talk more then. I have something for you," he said calmly.

"Okay, I will stop by later."

I went back inside with my now tepid coffee. I dumped it out and refilled my mug. I knew Michael would wake up soon, so I made his bottle, leaving it on the counter. I took a slow breath, trying to steady my nerves, and decided to search for answers. Setting my mug on the counter, I grabbed my phone and typed Sasha's name into the search bar. The results flooded the screen, familiar headlines and images flashing in front of me. There was the original report from the local news station, the one I'd seen when the story broke. Sasha's smiling face stared back at me, frozen in time, stuck as a seventeen-year-old girl forever.

My stomach twisted as something caught my eye—a smaller article buried beneath the others. It was one of those early reports released before they had identified her body, a plea for information. The article included photos of Sasha's tattoos and other identifying marks. I clicked on it, enlarging the images until they filled the screen.

Most of the marks were typical—tattoos, birthmarks, and surgery scars. One mark stood out among the others. It appeared to be Demetri's brand.

I grabbed my journal and compared it with the one I had

sketched when I learned about Jane Doe. It matched. It *matched.* The implications tightened around my chest like a vice. If she was killed because Smithick wanted her dead, Demetrie might work for Smithick.

For a moment, I couldn't think. Couldn't breathe. While I tried to gather myself, I wrote down my thoughts.

September 30, 2009
Why? Why would Demetrie kill her? Was it punishment? Did she defy him somehow? Or was this connected to something bigger—something darker? And what about Smithick? Was Demetrie one of Smithick's puppets? How did it all fit together?

I snapped a photo of my sketch and took a screenshot of Sasha's mark, then typed a quick email to Detective Berry:

"The mark on Sasha is Demetrie's mark. It's the same one that was on Jane Doe back in October of last year. Can you find out if he works for Smithick?"

The words blurred on the screen, but I forced myself to hit "send."

If Demetrie works for Smithick, then it is *all connected,* I thought. I picked up my mug and was holding it in front of my face, warming my hands and thinking.

The sharp trill of the phone shattered the silence, and I jumped, nearly spilling my coffee. My heart pounded as I grabbed it, the screen lighting up with Berry's name.

"Hello?" My voice came out thin and shaky.

"Grace, it's Berry." Her tone was brisk, professional, but there was an undercurrent of something else. Tension, maybe. I set my mug down on the counter, my fingers tightening around the phone.

"Did you get my email?" I asked.

"Yes, I did." Her voice was clipped, and I caught the edge of frustration. "It's possible Sasha's death was unrelated to the case, but—" She exhaled sharply. "Grace, I need to tell you something. Smithick posted bond."

The words hit me like a blow. My mouth became instantly as dry as the Sahara. I couldn't even speak for a few moments. "What?" I finally managed. I couldn't keep the edge out of my voice. "How? Why would a judge even *consider* giving him a bond?"

"He has no priors, and his defense team argued he was a 'pillar of the community,'" Berry said, the sarcasm in her voice sharp enough to cut glass. "The judge set his bond at half a million dollars. Pocket change for someone like him."

A chill ran through me. "So, he's out? Just like that?" I shrieked. My heart felt like it was playing the bongos in my chest.

"I'm afraid so. We just don't have physical evidence. But I'll keep looking into the brand. I've started questioning some of the girls. A few of them are saying Demetrie works for Smithick. But we need evidence that he was paid by him and wasn't just a 'self-employed entrepreneur,'" she said with all the sarcasm possible. Then, she added, "We even got a warrant for his phone, but it had nothing incriminating on it. He must be using a burner that we didn't find. But if I find out anything—anything at all—I'll let you know."

"Thanks," I murmured, though the word felt hollow. My confidence was fading fast.

"Stay safe, Grace. And watch your back."

When I hung up, I tried to convince myself it was fine. But the thought brought little comfort. Denial was flimsy armor, and I could feel it cracking. *Did Smithick know I was a witness too?* He knew where I lived. I tried to push those thoughts out of my head, distracting myself while making a bottle for Michael.

Theo's footsteps broke through my thoughts. He came into the kitchen with Michael balanced on his hip, both of them still soft with sleep. It was his day off, and he was excited to spend it with the kids. Michael's round, rosy face and Theo's grin was as tired as it was genuine.

"The bottle's on the counter, nice and warm for Mikey," I said, forcing a smile as I took a sip from my mug. "And the coffee's hot and strong, just for you."

"Perfect," Theo said, handing Michael his bottle and setting him in the highchair. Michael grabbed it eagerly, smiling as he drank, while Cappy leapt onto the table and begged for milk. Michael grinned and hugged his bottle tighter, unwilling to share.

"What are you going to do today?" I asked.

"I'm planning on taking them to the zoo," he whispered and put his finger up to his lip, signaling it was a secret.

"That will be fun!" I whispered. "I'm going to head into the office in a bit to finish some projects."

For a moment, the scene felt almost normal. But the weight in my chest didn't lift. It couldn't. Not with everything hanging over us.

As we sat at the table, I heard little feet pattering. Emily came out lazily, walking down the hall into the kitchen, rubbing her eyes with one hand and holding her stuffed bunny in the other.

"What do you want for breakfast?" I asked, knowing what the answer would be.

"Cereal!" she yelled as she jumped into the chair at the table. It's always cereal. She would eat cereal three times a day if I let her. After pouring the cereal and milk into the bowl, I grabbed my purse, kissed all of them goodbye, and walked out the front door. I sat in my car for a moment, trying to stay composed, but the feeling of dread would not leave.

After everything that had happened, the fear lingering in the back of my mind had grown into something sharper, more insistent. It wasn't just anxiety anymore; it was the grim acknowledgment that things could spiral further out of control. I couldn't afford to pretend that I was untouchable—not with Smithick out on bond, not with Demetrie's shadow looming over Sasha's death. I decided to take another step to protect myself.

As I sat in my car, after some Internet searches, I made a call to a lawyer. I didn't let myself second-guess the decision, though my hands shook as I held the phone. I asked them to draft a will and specified every detail: who would care for the kids, who would inherit the house, even who would take in Cappy.

As we went through the details, I felt an ache settle inside me. It was surreal, planning for a world without me in it. I asked if I could come by later to pay for everything. They said that was fine, and that it could be delivered to the house in a couple days. By the time we hung up, my throat was tight, but the feeling of unfinished business had lifted, just a little.

Still, I knew it wasn't enough. I needed to go further. If something happened to me, people needed to know the truth. And there was only one person I trusted to help me tell my story.

I drove to the office with a sense of purpose, though my nerves churned as I gripped the steering wheel. The newsroom was buzzing with quiet activity when I arrived, the hum of keyboards and low murmurs creating a backdrop of urgency. Maddie was at her desk, her short, brown hair tucked behind her ears as she scrolled through something on her screen. She glanced up as I approached, her warm brown eyes immediately narrowing in concern.

"Grace?" she said, standing to greet me. "What's going on?"

"I need a favor," I said, forcing my voice to stay steady, but I was unsure if I succeeded. My hands were clammy, and I clasped them tightly to keep them from trembling.

"What is it?" Maddie asked, her brow furrowed. She gestured to the chair across from her desk, and I sat down, suddenly aware of how dry my mouth was.

I took a deep breath, then another. "I need you to interview me," I said finally, my voice cracking. "About what I went through before I came here. About Smithick, the abuse, the drugs—everything." The words felt heavy, like dragging stones out of my chest one by one. "I need you to record it. Write it. Hold on to it—just in case."

"In case of what?" Maddie asked, her concern evident. I had told Maddie about some things in my past once I felt comfortable around her. She knew I had been abused by my pimp and that I had shot him and that's why I had spent time in prison. She had no idea that my pimp worked for Smithick, the judge who was all over the news for being the leader of a sex trafficking ring.

"In case something happens to me. My pimp Lenny worked for Smithick. I was assaulted by Smithick on more than one occasion, and now, I have agreed to testify against him." My throat tightened around the words. "If I don't make it through this, I need you to get the recording to Detective Berry and blow the lid off everything." My voice wavered, and I stopped to swallow, the lump rising in my throat. "People need to know what's really going on. They need to know who these people are and what they've done."

Maddie leaned back in her chair, her expression softening. She didn't rush to respond, and I was grateful for that. Her calm presence was a balm to the storm raging inside me. After a moment, she reached out, placing a hand lightly on my shoulder.

"Of course, I'll do anything I can. I am so sorry that happened to you." She squeezed my shoulder. "You're brave for doing this, Grace. I know your actions will help bring him down and help other girls who are in the same situation you are."

I let out a shaky breath, relief mingling with fear. "I've written out a sort of script I plan to go by, and you can ask questions during the recording if something isn't crystal clear. And I'll email you everything I have, my notes, my journal entries, anything I can remember that might help. I just... I just need to get it all out there." My voice broke again, and I clenched my jaw, willing the tears to stay back.

Maddie grabbed a tissue from the box on her desk and handed it to me. Her voice was soft, but there was a determination in it that reassured me. "You're doing the right thing. This story needs to be told, Grace. No matter what."

I nodded, blotting my eyes with the tissue. "Thank you," I whispered. "Thank you so much. We just have to hold on to the story for a while because Smithick is out on bond, and it is far too dangerous for all of us."

She gave me a small smile and then leaned forward, her hands folded on the desk. "Let's start with this: how much time do you need? Do you want to do this over several days, or should we just go for it all at once?"

The practicality of her questions steadied me. "I think all at once is best," I said after a moment. "I want to get it all out before I lose my nerve."

"All right, send me the script and notes tonight. We'll set up a time when you're ready."

I stood, reaching out to hug her. "Thank you, Maddie," I murmured into her shoulder. Her embrace was firm, reassuring.

As I left the office, the sunlight outside felt too bright, too sharp against the cool autumn air. The conversation replayed in my mind, over and over. This was the right thing to do, I knew that. But it also felt like I was sealing a door behind me, locking myself into a fight I wasn't sure I was ready for.

The fear was still there, a cold knot in the pit of my stomach, but now it was tempered by something else. Resolve. If they came for me—if they silenced me—I'd make sure the truth lived on.

I drove to the lawyer's office and paid for the draft of the will. It wouldn't be ready for a few days, but at least it was there and paid for. Then I went to the Rusty Knob to see Jason. His thin frame was leaning on the bar, smoking a cigarette. He came over and offered me a beer.

"Thanks. Irish Red, please. I need this tonight," I said as I perched up on the barstool. "Smithick posted bond."

"What? How is that possible?" He asked, as anger filled his face.

"He is well-connected. That's all there is to it. I can see him getting away with all of this because of his status and network," I said, taking a sip of my beer. The jukebox was playing some terrible country tune, but it was loud enough to drown out our conversation.

"He can't get away with trafficking and abusing girls! It's just not right. I don't claim to be a saint, but people who abuse the vulnerable need to all burn in Hell," he grunted, his voice getting louder than the bar crowd. He took a shot of whiskey and slammed down the shot glass.

"They need to be stopped, somehow," I cried. Tears were stinging the inside corners of my eyes.

"Well, I know how to stop him," he said, as he motioned me to look behind the counter. As I did, I saw him pull an automatic pistol out of the front of his jeans. He leaned in closer and said, "We can give all the victims the justice they deserve ourselves. Eye for an eye style."

My eyes fixated on the dark silver metal, the wooden handle, and the barrel. I had so much rage inside me I knew I could pull the trigger. To see his face the moment he would know it was over, and that my face would be the last face he would ever see, would be horrifically satisfying.

But that was not who I wanted to be anymore. I had to think of Theo and the kids. I couldn't just go off Rambo style.

Jason could see my hesitation. He added, "It's here if you want it. No one else has to know, and I'd be glad to help you blow that motherfucker away."

"No, I couldn't do that. I am trying to get my life back together," I said with conviction. "I just wanted to talk to you because you understand. Sometimes I feel like Theo is so positive and chill about everything that he isn't taking this seriously. Either that or he thinks that I'm overreacting," I said as I stared into my beer glass, wishing it were a crystal ball.

"You aren't. Both of your lives could be in danger. Let me know what I can do to help," he said with urgency in his voice.

"You are listening, that makes me feel better in itself." Especially since Theo basically said that everything's going to be alright. I didn't know how he could be so calm with all that's going on.

"Well, you were there for me during a dark time in my life, and I want to be there for you, as well. So, let me know if there is anything you need." I remembered that dark time. He wanted to die. He was contemplating suicide. He had called for an escort simply to have someone to talk to.

"I will let you know. Thank you for listening to my rant."

That evening, after the kids had gone to bed, worn out from their day at the zoo with Theo, I curled up in my favorite armchair with my gold-leafed journal. The small lamp beside me cast a warm pool of light over the pages, cutting through the dimness of the living room. Beyond its glow, the house was quiet, peaceful, but I couldn't shake my sense of unease that had been simmering beneath the surface all day.

Theo was stretched out on the couch, his legs propped up on the armrest. Cappy was curled into a tiny black and white fluff ball on his lap, purring loudly enough that I could hear it from across the room. Theo absentmindedly scratched under Cappy's chin as he read one of his psychology journals. Every so often, he'd pause and glance at me, a small smile tugging at the corners of his mouth, as if checking to make sure I was still there, still okay.

The sight of him sitting there, with the cat nestled against him like a living, vibrating blanket, made me smile despite myself. This life, this house, these moments of calm with Theo and the kids—it was more than I'd ever dared to hope for. I felt like I was finally in a place where I could be happy. The thought made my heart ache with longing and fear. I wanted this happiness to last.

But no matter how hard I tried to settle into the life I'd built here, my past wouldn't let me rest. Happiness always felt like it came with an asterisk, like a reprieve rather than a permanent state. There was always something looming beyond the edges of the light, threatening to pull me back under.

My hands hovered over a journal entry dated a few weeks ago. I hesitated before turning to it, knowing exactly what it contained. My fingers traced the page, the memory already clawing its way to the surface. It had been a dream—or maybe it hadn't. Some memories had buried themselves so deeply that they resurfaced in fragments, slipping through my mind like water through a sieve.

September 8, 2009

In this dream—or memory—Smithick wasn't the poised, commanding judge I'd seen in courtrooms and newspaper profiles. He wasn't dressed in a robe or wielding a gavel. Instead, he was in what appeared to be a warehouse, shadowed and cavernous, with the sickly yellow glow of industrial lights casting long, eerie shapes on the walls. He had a whip in his hand—an instrument he used with cold precision. And he loved to use it. His face, usually so composed in public, was twisted with cruelty. There was no pretense of civility here.

I wasn't alone. There were other girls with me, so many of them. Sasha was there, along with girls I didn't recognize. Most of them seemed heartbreakingly young, barely out of their teens, if that. They cried, they pleaded, their voices raw with desperation. But Smithick didn't care. He relished their suffering, feeding off it like it gave him life. The sound of the whip cracking against skin still echoes in my ears, even now.

I closed the journal abruptly, my breath hitching. The leather cover felt too warm in my hands, and I set it aside quickly, as though it might burn me. My chest tightened, and I exhaled slowly, forcing myself to stay calm.

The house was quiet. It was the kind of silence that pressed in on me, until my thoughts became deafening. I peered at the journal for a long time. The memory lingered like a bruise. *How many girls has he hurt?* I wondered. The question sat like a stone in my gut. It seemed so unfair, so impossible, that a man like Smithick could continue to live his life unchecked, his crimes hidden behind the veneer of wealth and power. He seemed untouchable.

Untouchable, but not invincible.

I had to find a way to stop him. I didn't know how yet, but the thought of doing nothing—of letting him destroy more lives—was unbearable. The image of the gun at the bar flashed in my mind. It was a silent reminder that I could at least defend myself, Theo, and the kids. But would Theo allow a gun in the house?

I barely noticed Theo get up until I felt his hands on my shoulders. His touch was firm but gentle, his thumbs pressing into the knots of tension in my neck. I hadn't realized how tightly I'd been holding myself until his strong hands started to ease the tension.

"You're so tense," he murmured, his voice low and soothing. He bent down, brushing his lips against my temple. "You should come to bed. You need to relax."

I placed my hands over his, squeezing them lightly before tilting my head to kiss his cheek. "I will. Just a few more minutes."

He gave me a knowing look but didn't argue, retreating to the couch. I glanced at the journal again, but the thought of opening it was unbearable. Instead, I reached over to turn off the lamp.

As my fingers brushed the switch, my phone buzzed on the coffee table, the sound shattering the fragile quiet. The screen lit up with an unknown number. I stared at it, unease prickling along the back of my neck. My thumb hovered over the decline button. I should ignore it. I didn't owe anything to strangers calling at odd hours.

But curiosity—and dread—got the better of me.

"Hello?" My voice was quieter than I intended.

For a moment, there was nothing. Silence, heavy and oppressive. Then, I heard static. And beneath it, breathing. Slow, deliberate breathing. My heart leapt into my throat as a cold sweat broke out on the back of my neck.

"Who is this?" I said, my voice quivering now. The breathing didn't stop. My pulse pounded in my ears as I gripped the phone tightly. Then, as abruptly as it had started, the line went dead.

"Wrong number?" Theo asked from the couch, his voice cutting through the thick silence.

"It went dead," I whispered, my throat dry. "All I could hear was breathing." My hands were trembling as I set the phone back on the table. "It's probably nothing," I added quickly, trying to convince both him and myself. But the words rang hollow.

As I turned off the lamp and stood, something caught my eye. Movement—or at least, I thought it was movement—just beyond the front window. A shadow, slipping through the darkness. My heart lurched, and I froze, staring at the glass until my eyes burned. *Maybe it was a reflection in the glass?* I leaned in, my forehead almost touching the glass, and cupped my hands around my eyes to get a better view.

But there was nothing. No movement. Just the empty yard,

bathed in pale moonlight, only my eyes playing tricks on me. I needed sleep, even though that seemed like an impossible task.

I walked to the bathroom to brush my teeth, telling myself that everything was going to be alright. Entering the bedroom, I pulled off my sweatshirt and jeans, letting them drop to the floor. I climbed into bed beside Theo, curling into his warmth like it was the only thing keeping me tethered to reality. His steady breathing soothed some of the tension coiled in my chest, but my mind refused to quiet.

It's just your imagination, I told myself, squeezing my eyes shut. It's just your mind playing tricks on you.

But deep down, I wasn't so sure.

31

Unknown Number

The next morning, I woke to the warm, savory aroma of breakfast and the sound of soft footsteps entering the room. Theo and Emily appeared at my bedside, carrying a tray laden with two perfectly cooked eggs, golden-brown sausage links, and a stack of fluffy pancakes. Emily's face was lit up with excitement, her cheeks pink with pride.

"Did you make the pancakes, Emily?" I asked, propping myself up on one elbow, my voice still scratchy with sleep.

"I put the face on him!" she squealed, her giggle bubbling out as she pointed to the smiley face made of banana slices and blueberries on the top pancake. The smile was crooked, endearingly so, with one blueberry a tad off-center, but her joy in it was contagious.

"Oh, this is so nice. Thank you!"

Theo bent down to kiss me on the forehead. "Your job this weekend," he announced, his tone a mix of mock-seriousness and playfulness, "is to do absolutely nothing."

"Nothing? Not even playing?" I asked, raising an eyebrow and glancing at Emily. Her eyes widened, sparkling with anticipation, her mouth dropping open in an exaggerated gasp as she turned to Theo. She didn't say a word, but her expression screamed: *You wouldn't dare say no.*

Theo gave in with a snicker. "Okay, okay, fine. I guess I'll allow that."

"Yay!" Emily shouted, leaping up onto the bed. Her stuffed rabbit, one ear perpetually floppy, bounced in her arms. As she landed, the rabbit's long, floppy ears waved in the air, catching the attention of Cappy, who was curled up like a fluffy loaf on Theo's pillow. His sharp, gold eyes widened as he followed the movement, his pupils expanding until they were inky black saucers. Slowly, he crouched down, his back end wiggling as he prepared for the ultimate attack. Emily noticed him and let out a high-pitched laugh, shaking the rabbit's ears even more.

"Look, Cappy!" she said through her giggles.

And then—springing like a coiled-up jack-in-the-box, Cappy launched himself into the air, his paws batting at the rabbit's ears with lightning precision. He latched onto the rabbit with mock ferocity, gnawing at its plush ears like they were his mortal enemy. Emily dissolved into hysterics, and soon the whole room was filled with laughter—Theo's deep chuckles, my breathy giggles, and Emily's squeals mixing into a symphony of joy.

I caught myself watching Cappy, my laughter fading into something softer, quieter. His coat was so much healthier now, a silky, glossy black that shimmered in the morning light. He'd gained weight, his body now sturdy and robust, no longer the frail, sickly creature I'd found, or rather, neglected. He was healing, but a pang of worry twisted in my stomach. I couldn't shake the thought that none of us—Cappy included—would truly be safe until Smithick was behind bars where he belonged. I had a long way to go before I could feel like I was truly healed.

As if sensing my unease, Theo stepped out of the room, saying he needed to check on Michael in his playpen. I turned my attention back to the tray of breakfast, cutting into the pancakes, while Emily eagerly helped herself to the banana slices. She giggled as she popped the last one into her mouth and then scooted closer to my side, pressing herself against me with childlike affection. She draped her small arm over my stomach and rested her head against me. The simplicity of her love made me smile—but beneath it, worry churned.

What if my past is putting her in danger? What if I can't protect her? My mind spiraled, imagining the shadows of my old life creeping closer to this fragile happiness.

Before I could sink too far into those thoughts, my phone buzzed on the nightstand, cutting through the quiet hum of the room. My heart clenched as I glanced over, my stomach tightening when I saw the words "Unknown Number" flashing across the screen. My breath hitched, the memory of the last call rushing back—the eerie silence, the faint sound of breathing on the other end.

Should I answer? My finger hovered over the screen. *If it's important, they'll leave a message*, I reasoned, swallowing the lump in my throat.

The phone buzzed a final time and fell silent, but the ominous tension in the room lingered. I waited, heart pounding, for the sharp *ding* of a new voicemail.

It didn't come.

I got up and got ready for the day, keeping comfort as my top priority. Leggings, an oversized T-shirt, and a messy bun. It was simple, cozy, and practical. As I came back into the living room, I saw Emily sprawled out on the floor with Cappy, who was still batting at the stuffed bunny. Emily was still dangling it above his head. His sleek, black fur glinted in the sunlight streaming through the window, and Emily's giggles filled the room every time he made a clumsy leap for the toy.

Michael was content in his playpen, lying on his back with a bottle in one hand and a stuffed animal clutched firmly in the other. A squeaky toy—one that might have actually been for a dog—lay nearby, emitting the occasional high-pitched squeak whenever his foot kicked it. The sound should've been annoying, but in the warmth of the moment, it was endearing instead.

Thank goodness it was the weekend. But as much as I appreciated Theo's insistence that I relax and do "absolutely nothing," sitting still wasn't an option for me. The idea of having idle hands—of letting my thoughts run rampant with worry— made me restless. I needed to stay busy. I grabbed my coffee mug and headed into the kitchen for a refill.

The smell of coffee and pancakes lingered in the air, mixing with the rich, twangy sound of a Johnny Cash record spinning softly on the turntable. Theo stood at the sink, washing dishes, his movements fluid and efficient. As I poured fresh coffee into my mug, he crossed the room and wrapped his arms around me from behind. The warmth of his embrace caught me by surprise, and I laughed as I tried not to spill the coffee.

"You okay?" he asked, his voice low and comforting.

I nodded. "Just keeping my coffee supply up. You know me."
I was worried he could see right through me. I hadn't told him
that I ran into one of my old clients, and that we were texting
and even meeting in a bar. What would he think, knowing that
I was hanging around an old John from my past? I definitely
hadn't told him I was considering getting a gun for protection.

He smiled and kissed the top of my head before going back
to the sink. Something was grounding about him, his steadiness,
his ability to make everything feel a little less overwhelming
with a single touch. It brought me out of my swirling thoughts
of revenge and back into the laid-back Saturday with family.

I carried my mug into the living room and curled up in the
armchair. I pulled my legs up into a cross-legged position,
balancing my laptop on my thighs, and let out a slow breath. It
was time to look into the adoption process. Just in case it came
to that.

I looked at the search bar for a moment, my fingers
hovering over the keyboard as questions flooded my mind.
Would they approve of me, knowing my history? Could I even
afford it? How long will the process take, and what hurdles will
I face? I knew I'd come so far—I was clean, stable, and
supported by the people I loved—but the shadow of my past
loomed large. No matter how much progress I made, it was hard
to shake the fear that it might still define me in the eyes of
others.

I typed in the first few words of my search, but my thoughts
spiraled before I could hit enter. Theo's footsteps caught my
attention as he walked into the room. He paused beside me,
resting a hand on my shoulder. I peered up at him, my heart

heavy with uncertainty.

"Do you think we're ready?" I asked.

He didn't answer right away. Instead, he knelt beside me, his hand warm and steady on my shoulder. "We need to set a wedding date first," he said, his voice calm but firm. "I want to be able to show them that we're stable, that this relationship is serious, and that any kids we bring into this home are going to be loved and cared for. We need to show them how solid we are."

He gave my shoulder a reassuring squeeze, and I nodded. "You're right," I admitted, though the thought of planning a wedding added yet another thing to my ever-growing list of worries. "So... what are you thinking? Do you want something big and fancy? Because I don't. But if you do, we can compromise."

Theo chuckled and shook his head. "No, nothing big or fancy. That's not my style. Just close friends and family. Simple. Intimate."

I let out a breath I hadn't realized I'd been holding. "Since I don't have any family, that's easy. Really, the only person I'd need to invite is Maddie."

"What about people from work?" he asked.

I hesitated. "There are some nice people, sure, but I'm not exactly close with anyone except Maddie. Honestly, I was closer to a few people at Sunnybrook than I am with anyone at my job now. Is that sad?"

"No," he said, shaking his head. "It's just how life is sometimes. But if you want, I can look into whether any of those people are still around."

"Just Frank and Janie. We were close at Sunnybrook."

"Oh yes!" Theo exclaimed. "You were like the Three Musketeers."

"If the Musketeers were psychotic, OCD, autistic, and off their meds," I said laughing.

Theo laughed softly, "Sounds like a fun party! For now, let's figure out the wedding. What do you think about next fall? I know fall is your favorite time of year."

The idea lit a spark in me, cutting through my worries. "That would be amazing," I said, smiling at the thought. "It would give me something to look forward to... And something to plan, instead of constantly worrying about testifying against Smithick."

He gave me a knowing look. "That's exactly why I suggested it."

I felt a flicker of hope. A fall wedding, a new chapter, something beautiful to balance the ugliness of the past. Maybe this was exactly what I needed.

I closed the laptop, took a sip of coffee, and was about to get up and help Theo clean up when my phone buzzed. I pulled it out of my pocket and saw the words "Unknown Number" and showed it to Theo. "I have still been getting calls from an unknown number. They called this morning, but I didn't answer. I was hoping they would leave me a voicemail, but they didn't." Theo snatched the phone out of my hand and answered it.

"Hello?" he said firmly and waited. "Who is this?" No response. Only breathing and then the dial tone. He handed the phone back to me and shrugged.

I let out a sigh. "It's probably nothing, but it is creepy."

"Even though it says, 'unknown number,' the phone company might still have records for it. Call Detective Berry and see if the police can trace it, just in case."

"It would make me feel better if she traced it and it was nothing," I said as I pulled up my contact list and tapped on Berry.

"Hello?" Berry answered on the second ring.

"Hey, Detective Berry. I was wondering if you could do me a favor to put my mind at ease. I know you're busy, but I am paranoid that this may have something to do with Smithick's case."

"What do you need? What is going on?" she asked with intensity.

"I keep getting calls from an unknown number that is just breathing, and then they hang up. It has happened three times now. I would feel better if you took a look and were able to tell me that they were all unrelated or some kids were being stupid."

"It depends on what kind of service provider they are using. If someone uses an internet service like a messenger application, I won't be able to see the number, but I'll look into it. Also, I need to tell you..."

Berry hesitated, her voice lowering. "We found Sasha's phone. It had been wiped, but our tech team was able to recover fragments of text messages. One of the conversations mentioned Smithick."

My stomach twisted. "What kind of messages?"

"They're vague, but it sounds like she was getting cold feet about testifying. Someone was pressuring her to stay silent, threatening her, we think. We're still working to identify who she was texting, but Grace... this wasn't random. Whoever killed her was sending a message. Unfortunately, Smithick is smart and uses a burner. Demetrie probably does as well."

My pulse spiked, my coffee completely forgotten. My free hand gripped the counter so tightly that my knuckles hurt. "Do you think I'm in danger?" I asked, my voice quivering.

"We don't have any concrete evidence pointing to you, but if Smithick's people are trying to silence witnesses, you should be cautious. Lock your doors. Be aware of your surroundings. And don't hesitate to call me if you feel unsafe. In the meantime, I will check on that unknown number and see if it is connected."

I nodded, even though Berry couldn't see me. "I will. Thank you for letting me know."

After I hung up, I stared out the living room window. I picked up my journal from the side table and wrote:

October 1, 2009

I have gotten three "unknown number" calls. No one ever speaks, but I can hear breathing. They creep me out! Those calls must be related. They just have to be. Did Sasha get these hang-up calls before they started threatening her?

My mind was spinning like water about to go down the toilet. The sun was passing mid-sky now, spilling golden light over the backyard. It was a perfect autumn day—birds flitting from branch to branch, dew shimmering on the grass, the world so calm and normal. But the storm inside me raged on, impossible to ignore.

32

The Visitor

Later that afternoon, I took the kids to the park, hoping the fresh air would help clear my head. Emily squealed with delight as she raced ahead toward the swings, her princess dress billowing behind her. Michael babbled happily in his stroller, kicking his legs as he reached for the leaves fluttering down from the trees.

Theo had insisted on coming with us. He stayed close by my side, his presence steady and reassuring. As the kids played, he placed a hand on the small of my back, his touch warm through the cool fabric of my sweater.

"What did Berry say? I only heard bits and pieces. You look worried," he said softly, his eyes searching mine.

I hesitated. I didn't want to burden him with my fear, but it was too heavy to carry alone. "They found Sasha's phone. She was being threatened before she died."

Theo's expression darkened, his jaw tightening. "And you think it's connected to the trial?"

"It has to be," I said, my voice trembling. "And if they went after her, what's stopping them from coming after me? They know where I live, you know?"

Theo's hand moved to my shoulder, pulling me closer. His voice was steady, resolute. "Grace, listen to me. I won't let anything happen to you or the kids. Do you hear me? We'll take every precaution. We'll get security cameras, locks, whatever it takes. You're not facing this alone. Before I go to work on Monday, we will get some security cameras and an alarm set up. I don't want you to be home alone without it."

His words should have comforted me, but the fear had already taken root, burrowing deep into my chest. *Maybe I should ask Jason to get me a gun for the house, just in case.* I had to be able to protect us and the kids.

My mind instantly went to Melanie. She was another one of the girls who agreed to testify against Smithick. I wondered where she was, if she was safe, what she knew, and if she would remember me. I vaguely remembered her and knew that she was one of the older girls who helped lure new, young girls into being trafficked in Smithick's ring, but she had a different pimp than I did, so we ran in different circles.

I need to be able to help connect the dots. "What do we have besides memories?" I said out loud as I searched through my journal for any clue. "We need physical evidence!"

I called Detective Berry and asked her if she could get Melanie and me together. "Maybe she can jog my memory," I told her.

"I don't like the idea of having the only two surviving eyewitnesses together in the same location, unless you both come to the station, where I can be with you." She paused, "But *if* she agrees to meet you, *and* if you both come to the station, I will make that happen."

"That would be fine with me," I snapped, almost not letting her finish. "Let me know when, and I will be there." I hung up the phone, not knowing how to feel.

What if she didn't help me remember anything? What if I was putting her in danger by asking her to meet me? I called Maddie and told her what was going on. I wanted to meet with Melanie before I did my interview with Maddie, in case I remembered more. It was the weekend, and I had no clue when Melanie would be able to meet with me.

A few hours later, Detective Berry called to let me know that Melanie could meet with me on Monday at six o'clock in the evening. I thanked her and told her I was looking forward to it.

"I am meeting Melanie at the police station on Monday at six," I told Theo, while we put Emily to bed. Michael was already fast asleep. Emily was waiting patiently to read a story with Theo, who sat on her bed.

"I'll drive you," he said quietly.

"You don't have to do that."

"I do. You going anywhere alone right now makes me nervous. I do think it is a good idea to talk to her, though. It might be good for your healing. Was she the one who lured you?" he asked.

"I know she was in charge of new acquisitions, but I just can't remember her. Maybe when I see her face, I will," I answered. "I'll be on the couch when you are done with your story."

Theo threw his arms around my waist and buried his head in my stomach. When he finally released his grip, I leaned down and kissed his forehead. He smelled of his recent shower. He looked up at me and put his hands on the sides of my face, pulling me back for a kiss on the lips. I wanted this moment to last forever.

I made my way to the living room and took my phone off the side table. I wanted to update Jason and see if he could think of any questions I should ask.

"Hey, Grace. How are things?"

"I'm going to meet with Melanie, another witness, at the police station on Monday at six o'clock. Hopefully, she can help jog my memory. Could you help me think of good questions to ask her?"

"Let me think about that," he said. I heard him take a puff of his cigarette, "Ask her when she got out. If it was recently, she might have information on locations."

"Yeah, that's a good point."

"You might ask her if she knows of any other names of people involved. By the way, I've been casing Smithick's house. I know his schedule. Maybe we could meet up and see where he goes? You know, to find his lair," Jason said with excitement, like a kid talking about going to the park or the movies.

"I'm not sure I would feel comfortable doing that," I said sternly. But I have been thinking about getting a gun for protection. Could you help me with that?" I asked, then added, "My past will probably prevent me from getting one the legal way."

"Sure thing. Just let me know when you want to meet."

It was late in the afternoon on Sunday, and we had just arrived home from the park. Theo was in the kitchen making snacks for the kids when there was a knock on the door. I opened it a crack and peeked out. I saw the social worker, Sarah Ward standing there, looking forlorn. My stomach sank as I opened the door and welcomed her inside. Theo met us in the living room holding Michael. Emily sat at the kitchen table coloring.

"I'm sorry to drop in unannounced, especially today, but something has come up."

"Is everything okay?" I asked, not sure if I really wanted to know.

"We had someone walk into the office yesterday asking about the kids. A relative on their father's side. She lives out of state and is only here for the weekend. She wants to meet them," she said with a hint of irritation.

"Really? It has been months, and no one has come forward. Can they still do this after all that time?" Theo asked with annoyance in his tone. We had both grown so attached to them already.

Sarah sighed, "Yes, we still have to run our checks on her, but the court is always in favor of giving priority to family. I am sorry, I know this is upsetting. You can have the meeting at a public place, or here if you would like," she said, in a calming tone.

"What do you think, Theo?" I asked, not trusting myself to make the right decision, "Would it be better to meet here?"

"I think so," Theo said.

"Alright, I will go pick her up at the hotel and bring her here. I will stay for the whole visit," Sarah said and turned toward the door. Theo opened it for her. As he shut it, he looked at me and let out a big sigh. We both stared at each other for a while in total shock and dismay.

"I can't believe this is happening!" I said, my chin beginning to quiver.

Theo took me in his arms and held me tight. I started to cry but blinked away the tears. I couldn't let whoever this was see me crying. They would be back soon. Theo put Michael in his walker. He would be content in there the whole meeting. I went to check on Emily, still sitting at the kitchen table.

I sat down in the seat next to her. "Sweetie, we're going to have a visitor soon, and they want to meet you and Michael."

"Who is it?" she asked without looking up from her drawing.

"Someone who says they are related to you. They're just here to visit."

Emily's eyes darted up at me with intensity. "Will we have to go with them?" she asked.

"Not today. But after the agency checks to make sure she is your family, then you both will go with her," I said, trying to smile. "She will be here soon, okay?"

"Okay," she said and went back to drawing.

Nearly thirty minutes later, Sarah Ward was back with a woman. I opened the door for them and invited them inside.

"Would either of you like something to drink?" Theo asked. "We have bottled water and lemonade."

They both shook their heads. She looked nice enough, but I was already silently judging her. *Why come forward now? What does she want out of this?*

"Grace, Theo, this is Sherri."

"Hi, there. Have a seat." I motioned to the couch and armchair. Sherri sat on the couch and Sarah in the armchair. Theo took the spot on the couch furthest from Sherri, and I was content to stand.

"Can I hold him?" she asked, pointing to Michael. I gave Sarah a glance. She nodded. I rolled Michael closer to the couch, picked him up, and sat him in her lap. Then, I walked over to the doorway to the kitchen. "Emily, would you please come in here and meet your visitor?"

"I don't want to," she pouted and wrapped her arms around herself. I walked over to her and crouched down.

"I know. Meeting new people is scary, even for me. So, let's be brave together and go meet her."

Emily got up, took my hand, and walked into the living room with me. Michael looked up at Sherri's face and began to squirm.

"Emily, this is Sherri, she is your aunt. She is in town until tomorrow and wanted to meet you and Michael," Sarah said soothingly.

"Can you say 'hello,' Emily?" I asked.

"Hi," she quipped. She was still holding my hand as we stood near the couch.

"Hello, honey," Sherri crooned. "I haven't seen you in so long. You were just a baby the last time I visited you. We were really close before I moved to North Carolina," she said sweetly.

Emily stared blankly. Sherri reached forward to touch her, and Emily recoiled, grabbing my hand. Michael was full-blown crying at this point, flailing around in her lap. Sherri's eyes widened, and her face displayed a look that I couldn't distinguish at first.

"Were you and her dad close?" I asked as I walked over to take him from her. I wondered for a moment if I should continue letting her struggle, but decided against it. Once I had him in my arms, she wiped the tops of her legs as if to dust off cat hair. Then I realized what her facial expression was. Disgust. It was obvious to me that she was not used to handling children.

"Oh yes," she said after she finished patting the invisible filth off her. "Before I moved, we would go to the lake every summer. He loved fishing so much that he never wanted to leave. And the family reunions were always a hoot," she said with a chuckle.

Emily squeezed my hand so hard, I thought she might break it. "She's a liar," Emily said in a hushed tone.

Sherri's smile disappeared. "Maybe this visit is a bit much for today. I'd better get going," Sherri said nervously and stood to leave. Sarah stood as well and gave me a look that said, "something's not right here." Theo opened the door and walked them back to the car. Sherri seemed in such a hurry. I turned back around and looked at Emily.

"What did she lie about, sweetheart?" I asked, kneeling, and taking both of her hands.

"Daddy grew up in Arizona. We lived there until last year," Emily quipped. I could tell from her expression and tone of her voice that she was telling the truth, even though fear remained in her eyes.

I paused for a moment, then the meaning of what she said hit me. "I guess there aren't many lakes around there, huh?"

"No," she said in a tone that screamed "Of course not!" and

310

walked back toward the kitchen. Theo came back inside, shut the door, and locked it. I had assumed Emily wanted to continue drawing at the table. I followed her. "Please don't make us go with that lady!" she said and started crying. I dropped to my knees and wrapped her in the biggest hug I could manage. Theo came in, hearing the cries, and began to caress her hair.

"Oh, baby. I really don't know what is going to happen," I said into her ear as tears began to roll down my face and onto her cheek. I didn't know how to comfort her in that moment. Theo tapped my shoulder, and I let go. He opened his strong arms up to her, and she threw her arms around his neck. He lifted her little body off the ground and held her tight.

All I knew was, Monday couldn't come fast enough. The minutes leading up to the meeting felt like they dragged for an eternity.

33

The Meeting

By the time Monday evening arrived, I was a tangle of nerves. Theo wouldn't be home from work until half past five. Michael was in his bouncer, happy as a clam. Emily was watching cartoons with him in the living room. I was pacing behind the couch, trying to think, when my phone rang.

"Hello?" I asked.

"This is an automated call from the Volusia County Jail. An inmate, Jason Marrow, is trying to contact you. Press one to accept the call."

My stomach twisted in knots as I pressed the number one. What had he done? "Jason?"

"Grace, I can't talk long—"

"Why are you in jail? What happened?" I asked frantically.

"Smithick caught me casing his house and called the cops. I was just trying to watch what he was doing, and I saw something."

"What was it?"

"I was in my car across the street last night, and I saw a dark sedan park about a half block away. A man got out. Smithick came out of his front door, and they both went to the left side of the house. They were behind some bushes, but I had a direct line of sight. Smithick handed the guy a thick manilla envelope, and he glanced around before taking it. Then he nodded and walked back to his car."

"What did the man look like?" I asked.

"I couldn't see much. It was getting dark out. He wasn't wearing a uniform, just something casual. I couldn't see his face. But I am fairly certain his car was one of those unmarked cars that police sometimes drive. I actually pulled out my binoculars and tried to catch his plate number, but as I was focusing them, Smithick yelled. 'Hey!'

"I dropped the binoculars and tried to act casual. He pulled out his phone. As he dialed and got on the phone, he was walking toward me. He told whoever was on the other line the description of my car, my plate number, and that he had seen me casing his house for a week.

"I said, 'You're crazy, I'm just waiting for my girlfriend to come out for our date,' and I started the car to leave. He jumped in front of my car and threw his hands out like he wanted a fight. I thought about just running the bastard over, but then I saw the flashing lights."

"You shouldn't have gone there. He is dangerous!" I said.

I heard a deep voice in the background say, "Wrap it up!"

"I know. That's why I had to call you. I had to warn you not to trust the cops. He's got 'em on payroll. I gotta go, but I'll get a bond set tomorrow, and I'll be out. Be careful!" The call ended, but my fear was now ramped up to one hundred.

Detective Berry had arranged for us to meet in a private

room at the police station, a safe, neutral space where Melanie and I could talk without worrying about being overheard.

Theo had insisted on driving me, and though I told him I'd be fine, I didn't argue. The thought of walking into that station alone, knowing I'd come face-to-face with someone from that dark chapter of my life, sent waves of unease through me. I spent the entire drive fidgeting, twisting my engagement ring around my finger until Theo finally reached over and squeezed my hand.

"You don't have to do this, Grace," he said, his eyes darting from the road to me. "No one would blame you if you backed out."

But I shook my head. "I *do* have to do this. If Melanie can help jog my memory or knows something that can help us take Smithick down, then I can't walk away. Not now. Not after everything."

He nodded, his grip on my hand tightening briefly before letting go. "Just remember, I'm proud of you. No matter what happens in there."

I didn't trust myself to respond without my voice cracking, so I gave him a weak smile and turned to stare out the window.

The city blurred by. Streetlights were flickering on as the sky faded to a dusky blue. "I've been thinking," I mumbled, looking down at my lap. "Maybe I should get a gun... for protection," I whispered. "The police still have mine after they took it for evidence."

"I would rather not have one in the house. Especially with the kids," he murmured quietly, glancing back to see if Emily was paying attention.

"We can get a safe," I said, raising my voice. "I just don't feel safe."

"It's not a good idea. I don't want you to get one, Grace. Please tell me you won't," he said in the most serious and worried voice I have ever heard from him.

"It's six. I need to get in there," I said, avoiding the conversation. If he won't agree, then maybe I should get one without him. I don't need permission to protect myself, I thought.

"I'll stay here with the kids." He gave me a reassuring nod. "We'll be right here when you're done," he said as he parked the car in the lot beside the station. Michael was fast asleep in his car seat, and Emily was happily playing with a princess doll, hardly noticing me step out of the car.

Detective Berry was waiting for me right inside the lobby. Her expression was neutral, but I could tell from the set of her shoulders that she was tense.

"Melanie's already here. She's in the interview room down the hall. Are you ready?"

I nodded, my stomach twisting into knots. With a deep breath, I followed Berry down the corridor. The fluorescent lights above buzzed, the sound setting my teeth on edge. The walls were painted a dull, institutional green, and every step I took echoed loudly in the narrow hallway.

Berry stopped outside the door with a small, rectangular window and glanced back at me. "Take your time. If you need me, I'll be right outside."

"You aren't coming in with us?"

"I think she will open up to you more without me there. But

I am right outside the door, in the hallway. Okay?"

I nodded, though my palms were clammy, and my pulse thundered in my head. She opened the door and stepped aside to let me in.

The room was small and sparsely furnished—a metal table, a few chairs, and a recording device in the corner. And sitting in one of the chairs was Melanie.

I froze in the doorway, my breath catching. She was older than I remembered, but then again, it had been years. Her hair was dyed a coppery red and tied back in a loose ponytail, and faint lines etched her face, hinting at the life she'd endured since we last crossed paths. She had the same sharp eyes, and for a moment, I felt like a teenager again—scared, vulnerable, and completely out of my depth. *Maybe this was a mistake*, I thought as my hands trembled.

"Grace," she said, her voice calm but tinged with something I couldn't quite place. Guilt, maybe? Sadness? "You've changed."

I stepped inside and took the seat across from her, my hands clutching my bag like it was a lifeline. "I'm not sure if that's a compliment or not," I said, trying to inject a little humor into my shaky voice.

Her lips twitched, almost a smile. "It is. You look... stronger. Healthier."

I didn't know how to respond to that, so I simply nodded. The silence stretched between us, heavy and uncomfortable, until Melanie broke it.

"I wasn't sure you'd even want to see me," she said, her voice dropping. "But I've been wanting to reconnect for a while now."

"I didn't know if you'd want to see me," I replied. "Honestly, I wasn't sure if you'd even remember me."

"Oh, I remember," Melanie said quietly, her eyes dropping to the table. "You were one of the sweetest ones. You didn't belong there—not that any of us did, but you, you still had that light in you. Even after all you had lost in your accident. I remember thinking it wouldn't last. We all become broken. It was just a question of how long it would take." She swallowed hard, her fingers fidgeting with the edge of her sleeve. "And then it was gone. Your light was burnt out the second Smithick had his turn with you."

Her words hit me like a punch to the gut. "You lured me in, didn't you?" I asked, my voice wavering. "You were the one who... Who..."

"Who made the call? Yeah," Melanie admitted, her voice thick with shame. She wouldn't meet my eyes. "That was my job back then. Find the pretty, young girls. The ones who looked like they didn't have anyone to miss them. I didn't have a choice, Grace. I was just as trapped as you were. Smithick began assaulting me when I was fifteen. I was so scared of him. By the time I had met you, I had been his property for eight years."

"Oh, my God. I had no idea you were in that long. Where did you find me? What was I doing?"

"You were in a bar. Not the fancy nightclub type, but the dirty, hole-in-the-wall type where all the shady people hang out. Like me. The Rusty Knob, I think. I sat next to you at the bar and ordered you a drink, even though I could tell you already had a few. You looked like you had been crying, so I asked what was wrong. You told me all about your accident and how you just got out of prison."

Melanie paused for a moment; her chin was quivering. Then she continued, "I thought to myself, this girl has no one. She won't be missed. So, I called Smithick. He sent Lenny to the bar, and we convinced you to snort some coke. That's how we get the girls hooked and to trust us," she said as her eyes became glossy with tears. "Then Lenny went home with you to continue the party."

I didn't know what to say. Part of me wanted to scream at her, to ask her how she could have done that to me, to anyone. But another part of me—maybe the part that understood what it was like to be powerless, to be used and discarded—wanted to believe her.

"You knew what they were going to do to me?" I asked, my voice quivering.

Melanie flinched, her hands curling into fists on the table. "I did," she said, her voice raw. "And I hated myself for it. I still do. But once you were in... you weren't my responsibility anymore. You went to Smithick." She shuddered, her eyes clouding with memories. "He always took the new ones. Took them on 'test drives' as he called them, so he raped each girl first. He especially liked the virgins. He told me to keep my eye out for the youngest girls I could find.

"After raping them and getting his fill, he put them in the box. He did it to me when I was fifteen. He did it to you. That's how he gained control over all of them."

My stomach turned. The box. I had hoped it was just a nightmare, but it was real. I pushed that memory to the far corners of my mind and prayed I would never have to think of it again. The dark, cramped space, the suffocating heat, the way the walls seemed to close in until I thought I'd lose my mind. I could still hear the sound of my screams, muffled and ignored.

"How long ago did you get out? Do you know if they are still in operation?" I asked in quick succession.

"I got out six months ago, but Sasha..." She dropped her eyes. "Sasha was still working for them. Demetrie was our pimp."

"I knew it. I just knew Demetrie worked for Smithick," I said, enraged.

Melanie looked up at me, her expression filled with remorse. "I'm sorry, Grace. I know that doesn't mean anything, but I am. I wish I could go back and stop it from happening. To you, to all of us."

I swallowed hard, blinking back tears. "We can't change the past," I said, my voice steadier than I expected. "But maybe we can stop him from doing it to anyone else."

Melanie nodded, wiping at her eyes. "Yes. What do you need from me?"

I hesitated, my mind racing. And then, like a flash of lightning cutting through the darkness, a memory surfaced—a location. A place I dreamed about not long ago. A place I hadn't thought about in years, but now seemed so clear it was as if I'd just been there.

"The warehouse," I said abruptly, my eyes locking onto Melanie's. "Do you remember the warehouse? The one with the blue door?" I asked with urgency.

Melanie's eyes widened, and she nodded slowly. "I don't know the address, but that's where they kept the girls before moving them. And the drugs. But Grace, it's been six months since I've been there. Smithick knows he's being looked at by the police, so it's probably been cleaned out by now."

"Maybe, but maybe not. If there's even a chance that something's still there..." I trailed off, glancing toward the door.

Melanie followed my gaze, understanding dawning in her expression. "We need to tell Berry."

I nodded, my heart pounding. For the first time in years, I felt like we were one step closer to justice. We both stood and walked back out into the hallway, where Berry was waiting.

"I know it's not a lot to go on—a warehouse with a blue door—but it's something," I said to Berry, my voice steady but tinged with doubt. The lead wasn't exactly solid, but after weeks of dead ends, it felt like a thread worth pulling. Berry nodded, her brow furrowed as if mentally cataloging the information. Beside her, Melanie stood with her arms crossed, her expression unreadable, though her eyes conveyed a flicker of unease.

We stood near the doorway of the dimly lit office where the meeting had dragged on for over an hour. Theo and the kids were still waiting for me in the car, Theo likely listening to the radio or reading a book, ever patient. I shook Berry's hand, her grip strong and reassuring, as if she were silently telling me we'd figure this out. Then I turned to Melanie.

I hesitated for a moment before leaning in to hug her. It wasn't a warm hug, not really, but it was something; an offering. A truce. Whatever resentment I'd been holding onto toward her was too heavy to carry anymore. She stiffened at first but then returned the embrace.

"I forgive you," I whispered in her ear.

She let out an audible sigh and murmured a soft "Take

care," as we pulled apart.

With that, we went our separate ways. I stepped into the crisp evening air and made my way to Theo's car, my body and mind both heavy with exhaustion. The meeting had drained me, and all I wanted was to be home, wrapped in the small comforts of my normal life. I was starving, though. *When was the last time I ate?*

On the way, Theo drove through a fast-food joint. The aroma of salty fries and burgers filled the car as we drove in silence, the night's events replaying in my mind. I knew I couldn't sit on the memory of the blue-doored warehouse for too long—it might be flimsy, but it was the closest thing to a lead we'd had in weeks.

I'll email Maddie when I get home to let her know about my meeting with Melanie and what we remembered. Maybe she can schedule the interview with me tomorrow, I thought, sipping from my soda as Theo drove us through the quiet streets. The idea of talking to Maddie about it made me feel lighter, as if simply sharing the information might make it feel more real, more actionable.

When we finally got home, I brought in the mail. There was a letter addressed to me with no return address. Theo put Michael in his bouncer. Emily lay down on the rug to play with Cappy. I sent the email to Maddie and then flopped down on the couch with Theo. I opened the unassuming envelope and read the contents.

It was so nice to meet the children and see how much you love them. That kind of love is rare. Precious. It makes what's coming all the more... meaningful.

Courage is Grace under pressure.

Sherri

My body started trembling. Theo looked over at me inquisitively. I handed him the letter without a word.

"Who sent this?" he asked.

"There was no return address, but it was signed by Sherri, the lady who is supposedly the kids' aunt," I said quietly, trying not to show my anxiety. That last sentence bothered me greatly. I had heard it before. But where?

"We need to call Sarah Ward and tell her about it. She's not supposed to be contacting us directly," Theo said, his voice giving away his anger.

"I'll call her in the morning, first thing. The office is closed now," I said, trying to push my swirling thoughts to the back of my mind. It was a losing battle. The kids, Sherri, the blue door, and Smithick.

Smithick! That's it. That's where I had heard that saying. He had said that when he was arrested. Sherri, or whoever she is, had to be working for him. Something was off about her. She had been in my home, sitting on my couch. She had even held Michael. This was a threat.

I tried to calm myself down and think rationally. The letter could mean nothing. Sherri could have been trying to convey gratitude, but instead, my brain took it as a threat. We still didn't know if she really was a relative or not. The agency was checking on it. I just needed to wait and see. Theo was right, though. She wasn't supposed to contact us directly; that was the agency's policy.

34

Melanie

The next morning, I was jolted awake by a thunderous banging on the front door. My heart leapt into my throat as I shot upright in bed, adrenaline instantly coursing through my veins, making me shake all over.

Theo stirred beside me, groaning. "Who the hell is that?"

"I don't know," I muttered, throwing on one of Theo's hoodies and rushing to the door. The banging didn't stop. It was loud and insistent, like someone on the verge of panic.

I opened the door to find Maddie standing on the porch. Her face was pale, her expression tight with urgency. She didn't even say hello; she pushed past me, stepping into the house and slamming the door behind her.

"What are you doing here?" I asked, startled by her abruptness. "Are you wanting to get an early start on that interview?" I tried to lighten the mood with a grin, but Maddie didn't smile.

Instead, she turned to face me, her eyes wide and filled with something I couldn't quite place. Fear? Shock? Anger? My stomach twisted.

"Melanie is dead," Maddie blurted, her voice sharp and trembling, her words crashing into the room like a tidal wave.

For a moment, I couldn't breathe. The air turned thick and suffocating, pressing down on me as though the walls were closing in. The room tilted, my vision narrowing. I blinked hard, trying to focus, but her words echoed in my mind, their meaning too terrible to grasp.

"What?" I whispered, shaking my head wishing I hadn't heard her correctly. My voice cracked on the single syllable. My hands instinctively gripped the front of my hoodie as though it might keep me from slipping into a bottomless void.

Theo stumbled around the corner, pulling a T-shirt over his head in hurried, disjointed movements. His expression was full of urgency and confusion. His eyes darted between Maddie and me, wide with confusion and growing panic. "What's going on?" he asked, but I couldn't answer. My voice had deserted me.

"Dead," Maddie repeated, her voice breaking now. "There was a car accident last night. Her brakes... they were cut."

The words hit like stones hurled directly at my chest. My mind scrambled to reject them, to rewrite them into something less horrific. "No," I muttered, barely audible. "No, that's not possible. I just saw her. She was fine. She was—" My voice broke, and I sank onto the couch, my legs giving out beneath me.

My mind reeled, scrambling to piece together the impossible. Melanie, dead? *Dead?* The Melanie I'd hugged just hours ago, whose voice still echoed in my ears? It didn't make sense—it couldn't make sense.

Maddie crouched in front of me, her hands gripping my forearms like claws, her face close to mine. Her eyes were sharp, intense, but there was a softness there, too, a desperate attempt to keep me grounded.

"Listen to me," she said firmly, her voice cutting through the fog of my panic. "I need to know everything she said to you last night. Everything. Did she seem scared? Nervous? Did she mention anything, *anything*, about someone following her to the police station?"

"She didn't..." My voice faltered as my thoughts scrambled back to our last conversation. It felt like reaching through smoke, trying to grab hold of something solid. Her words kept looping in my head: *Melanie is dead. Melanie is dead.*

"I don't know," I said finally, my voice low and unsure. "She didn't say anything like that. She was... She seemed normal. Except for her anxiousness over testifying in the trial. She knew to be extra careful. That's why we met at the police station." I shook my head, frustration and fear clawing at me. "Do they know who did it? I mean, Smithick has to be behind this, right?"

Maddie stood abruptly, the urgency in her movements filling the room with tension. She started pacing, her arms crossed over her chest. "No, they don't know who did it," she admitted, her jaw tightening as she spoke. "But you're right, this wasn't random. The brakes had been tampered with. It has to be Smithick or one of his men. She was targeted." Maddie paused mid-step, turning to look at me. Her silence spoke louder than any words, her expression heavy and full of dread.

I swallowed hard, the room swaying again. "How do you even know the brakes were cut? What if it was just—just a car accident?"

Maddie exhaled sharply, running a hand through her hair.

"I sent a news crew to the crash site. It wasn't an accident, Grace." Her voice was grim, her words precise. "Witnesses saw her car blow through a red light at a busy intersection. She didn't even try to stop—no skid marks, nothing. She went straight into a tree." Maddie hesitated, as if bracing herself for the rest of what she had to say.

"Mark, my cameraman, overheard the officer at the scene say, 'Either she was trying to kill herself, or the brakes failed.' Mark crawled under the car to check—he used to be a mechanic, and he knows what he's looking for. And he saw it. The brake lines were cut. He showed the officer, and they're processing it now."

Her words painted a horrifying picture, and I felt the floor beneath me shift again. My hand flew to my mouth, trembling. "I can't believe this is happening."

Theo stepped forward; his voice was urgent but calm. "Maddie, can you stay with her while I run out and get an alarm system and cameras? We're not taking any other chances."

Maddie nodded without hesitation, placing a steady hand on his arm. "Of course. I'll stay."

Theo leaned down, pressing a kiss to my forehead. "I'll be back as soon as I can." He grabbed his keys and hurried out the door.

I stood abruptly, desperate to keep moving, to distract myself from the storm inside me. I walked toward the kitchen to get us some coffee, but I was already shaking from the news. What I really needed was a beer. "Did you bring your recorder? We could do the interview now," I said, the words tumbling out in a rush. "I have one if you didn't bring one."

Maddie studied me, as if weighing whether to push back. Finally, she nodded. "I did. Are you sure you're up for it?"

I wasn't. But I nodded anyway, turning toward the kitchen as I asked, half to myself, "Coffee? No sugar, just cream, right?" My voice was shaky, the words spilling out like water over a broken dam.

"Yes, just cream," Maddie replied, her tone patient.

In the kitchen, I gripped the counter tightly, trying to steady my hands. My head was spinning, my heart pounding so loudly it felt like the whole house could hear it. I couldn't stop picturing Melanie's face, the remorse in her eyes, her timid smile, her determination to do the right thing. And now... she was gone.

I finished getting our coffee and walked back into the living room.

"Come and sit on the couch with me and try to relax," she said as she sat and patted the couch cushion next to her. Cappy took that as an invitation and jumped up into the spot. His gold eyes met hers, and he bumped his forehead into her hand. She stroked him from head to tail, and then he plopped down against her and began kneading imaginary biscuits in the air. I glanced at Cappy and couldn't help but give a weak smile.

"You made a new best friend, it looks like," I said, handing Maddie her steaming mug. I started tearing up while I looked at him. "He has helped me get through so much. Even when I had no one and nothing else but him." Tears were now running down my cheeks. Maddie pulled a handkerchief out of her pocket and handed it to me. I sat down in the armchair so he could stay by her side.

Maddie gave me a faint smile, but her eyes were sharp with

focus. "We'll get through this. We're going to nail this bastard, Grace."

She pulled out her slim digital recorder, clicking it on. "This is Maddie Piper with the *Daytona Daily Tribune.* Today is Tuesday, October 3rd, and it's eight twenty-six A.M. I'm here with Grace Christopher, a thirty-three-year-old white female. Grace, please tell us your story."

I started at the beginning, as far back as I could remember, starting with Joseph's death. I was no saint, and I wasn't going to try to minimize the fact that I had broken the law, caused a death, and did time for it.

I gave every detail about Smithick that I knew, including the birthmark in the shape of a heart on his groin area. I listed all the pimps and Johns that I could remember. I finished by talking about the two girls who lost their lives trying to get him put behind bars.

"Sasha and Melanie were victims who were trying to do the right thing, so he couldn't hurt any more girls. And now they are both dead. I am worried that I will be next. So, if I turn up dead, look at Smithick," I said, fighting back tears. Maddie clicked the recorder off and reached over to hug me. I let out a deep, shuddering sigh, feeling like I'd emptied my soul into the room.

We sat in relative silence for a few minutes Theo's voice came from outside. "It's me! My hands are full!" he hollered.

I opened the door, my face still tear-streaked. He dropped the bags and immediately cupped my face in his hands. "Everything is okay," I whispered, my voice cracking. "I finished the interview. It just... brought up a lot."

Theo pulled me into his arms, holding me steady. For the

first time since hearing the news, I let myself lean into his strength, hoping it would be enough to hold me together. He then knelt in the middle of the living room and began to unpack the equipment for the alarm system. The coffee table was cluttered with wires, sensors, and tools. He worked methodically, his jaw set in quiet determination.

"Maddie," he said, glancing up as he tested the weight of a sensor in his hand, "do you think Melanie was killed because of what she knew?"

Maddie stood by the window, arms crossed, her face shadowed with worry. She hesitated for a moment before speaking, her voice grim. "I just think we can't rule anything out. It's too much of a coincidence that Sasha was killed, and now Melanie—and that they were both set to testify against Smithick." She exhaled sharply, shaking her head. "This is getting too close, Theo. You and—" her eyes flicked to me, "you both need to be on high alert."

Her tone made my stomach twist.

"I'm going to try to get some answers about that car," Maddie continued, gripping the strap of her purse tightly, as if bracing herself. "But until then, I need you to stay here. Lock the doors. Keep your phone with you at all times. And don't go anywhere alone. Do you understand?"

Her gaze pinned me in place, and I nodded, though my chest felt heavy with unease. "I understand." I understood completely. Whether I was going to stay at home, though, was something completely different. Now that she had my story and could share it with the world, I could take some risks. This was not about just me. I had to do everything in my power to stop them.

Maddie didn't leave right away. She lingered in the doorway for a moment, her sharp eyes scanning the room like she might spot some invisible threat. Then, with a curt nod, she stepped outside. I followed her to the door and locked it behind her. The solid click of the deadbolt would normally give me a sense of security, but now anymore.

For a moment, I stood there, my hand resting on the cool metal knob. My mind reeled, replaying her words. Sasha. Melanie. Murder. My stomach churned as I thought about the blue door at the warehouse, the meeting with Melanie, and the web of danger we seemed to be caught in. Everything felt like a piece of some larger, sinister puzzle that I had to put together.

I pressed my forehead against the door, closing my eyes. Theo came up behind me and wrapped me in his arms. "Berry probably doesn't know anything for sure yet," I murmured. "She'll call when she does. She's so busy—I don't want to bother her, but..."

A sudden cry pierced the stillness, yanking me from my spiraling thoughts. Michael. Theo went into the kitchen and started making a bottle.

I hurried to the nursery, where Michael stood in his crib, clutching the bars with chubby little fingers. His wails softened as soon as he saw me, his big brown eyes wet with tears. Theo came in and handed me the bottle. "Alright, buddy," I whispered, handing him the bottle I had made. He grasped it eagerly, already holding it on his own. He was getting so good at that.

I leaned against the crib, watching him, but my thoughts

crept back to the danger looming over us. An intrusive voice in my mind whispered its doubts. *I can't do this. I can't adopt these kids. I'll only put them in more danger.*

My throat tightened, and I gripped the rail of the crib. *What am I thinking?* The thought of leaving them felt like a betrayal, but wasn't staying worse? *How do you even begin to draw the line between being stubborn and doing what's best for them?*

Michael gurgled around his bottle, pulling me from my trance. His tiny hand reached out toward me, beckoning to be picked up. The other hand clung to the bottle, as if he'd figured out he didn't need to choose between the two. He gazed up at me with a grin so wide it crinkled his eyes into crescent moons, his chubby cheeks looking like peaches.

"Oh, Michael," I whispered, my heart squeezing. I scooped him up and held him close, pressing a kiss to his soft forehead. He smelled of baby lotion and formula. One of his hands gripped the bottle, and the other grasped firmly into my ponytail. His eyes met mine, and I felt tears welling up. My eyes got blurred. *I don't want to let you go. I can't give up on you and Emily.*

But the doubts lingered, gnawing at me from the edges of my mind. Then suddenly I remembered something. *Shit! I haven't called Sarah about the letter yet!* I took out my phone and called her.

"This is Sarah," she answered.

"Hey Sarah, I received a letter yesterday without a return address. All it says is, 'It was so nice to meet the children and see how much you love them. It will be even better to see them taken away.' I can't be certain who it's from, but it was signed by Sherri. It's very concerning," I said with Michael babbling in my ear. The sound made my heart swell, despite the nature of the phone conversation.

"I agree. I will look into it and get back to you. Thank you for letting me know," she said and hung up. I couldn't gather my thoughts. They were all running in different directions. Who was this Sherri person? I knew she wasn't the kids' aunt, and I had a bad feeling about her.

When we came back through the hall to the living room, Emily was perched on the floor beside Theo. She was still in her pajamas—a unicorn-print set that was a size too big—but her expression was all business. With her hands on her hips and a serious look on her face, she leaned over to "help" Theo set up the alarm system.

"You have to put the wires *here* so the bad guys can't get away," she explained, pointing at random pieces of equipment.

Theo smiled at her, his patience never wavering. "Oh, is that how it works?" he asked, nodding with mock curiosity.

"Yup!" Emily said with enthusiasm, her head bobbing up and down.

I couldn't help but smile at them. Emily, with her wild confidence and untouchable certainty, stood on tiptoes beside Theo, pointing out random wires and components like an expert in crime prevention. She was so sure of herself, so unshakably brave, even in a world that felt like it was teetering on the edge of chaos. Her tiny hands flew through the air as she explained her "security plan" with the kind of logic you could imagine from a five-year-old.

Theo, ever patient, nodded along as if she were imparting the most groundbreaking wisdom. "That's how we can catch the bad guys, huh?" he asked with mock seriousness, his lips curling into a faint smile.

"Yup! No more bad guys!" Emily said, her curls bouncing as she nodded vigorously.

For the first time today, the tightness in my chest eased, a little. Watching them—this fleeting, fragile moment of innocence and connection—was like stepping into a pocket of air while drowning. It was enough to remind me, however briefly, why I couldn't give up. Not yet.

Still, the nagging unease in the back of my mind refused to let go completely. I pulled out my phone, staring at the blank text message screen for a long moment. Calling Berry felt too demanding; she was always so busy, and I didn't want to push. But a text? That was safer. Noncommittal. No rush. *Let me know when you can.*

My thumbs moved quickly over the keyboard as I typed:

> I heard about Melanie. Any updates on her car, the unknown number, or Smithick?

I hesitated for a beat, then pressed send.

The response came faster than I expected. My phone buzzed in my hand, the screen lighting up with Berry's reply:

> The unknown number is not traceable. Still nothing concrete on Smithick, and so far, processing the car has given us zilch.

I read her words twice, feeling the unbearable frustration

settle on me. My pulse quickened when I noticed the familiar typing indicator, the three little dots, on the screen. She wasn't done. I waited, my hand tightening around the phone.

A second message popped up:

Meet me at the park near your house at 3 p.m.

The park? My brows furrowed as I stared at the screen. It was only a few blocks away, but why did she want to meet me there instead of calling or texting? The question gnawed at me as I held the phone out to Theo, who was in the middle of mounting the sleek touchscreen control panel for the alarm system.

"She wants to meet at the park."

Theo glanced at the message and nodded. "We'll all go," he said, as though it was already decided. "I'll play with the kids while you two talk."

35

The Mole

By two forty-five, we were on our way to the park. The weather was deceptively perfect—one of those golden afternoons that felt too peaceful for the kind of danger I knew we could all be in. The sun hung high in the sky, and giant, cotton-like clouds drifted lazily overhead. The air was chilly, settling into a crisp sixty degrees that made me want to believe everything was right in the world as long as I had a cardigan.

I pushed Michael's stroller, my fingers white-knuckled around the handle, while Emily skipped along beside Theo, her tiny hand wrapped in his. She had to pick up her pace to match his long strides. Her giggles bubbled up every time she stumbled and caught herself.

When we reached the park, Emily made a beeline for the swings. She was already halfway there before Theo could even unbuckle Michael from the stroller. Laughing, he scooped Michael up and carried him over to the baby swings. I lingered by a bench near the playground, my eyes constantly flicking between them and the parking lot.

A few minutes later, Berry pulled up in her unmarked car.

She was alone, and even from a distance, I could see the worry etched into her face. As she approached the bench, my stomach twisted. She looked nothing like her usual self. Her hair, normally pulled back in a precise, no-nonsense bun, hung loose around her face, wavy and disheveled. Dark circles shadowed her bloodshot eyes, making her look like she hadn't slept in days.

"I'm sorry for making you meet me like this," she said, lowering herself onto the bench beside me. Her voice was low and tired. "I didn't want to talk over the phone. I think there's a mole at the station, and I don't trust anyone there right now. I couldn't take the chance that your house may be bugged."

My breath caught. "Bugged? A mole? What makes you think that?"

Berry scanned the park, her eyes darting to the far corners of the lot and then back to the playground, as though expecting someone to materialize from the shadows. She leaned closer, her voice dropping barely above a whisper.

"Someone on the inside must have known that Melanie was going to be at the station yesterday. She was lying low, just like you. Nobody even knew where she was staying; she made sure of that. I was the only one who had her phone number, and she wanted it that way."

Her hands fidgeted with the strap of her bag, her fingers pale and trembling. "After I found out her brake lines were cut, and the car was wiped of fingerprints, I knew it wasn't an accident. It was deliberate. She was on her way home from the station last night when she wrecked, and it's just too damn convenient."

Berry paused, glancing over her shoulder again before continuing, her voice even quieter now. "So, I pulled the security footage from the station's parking lot onto my flash drive before anyone else could get to it. When no one was around, I reviewed it."

"What did you see?" I asked, my pulse pounding in my ears.

Her lips tightened into a thin line. "Someone in a hoodie, but I could tell they were thin and lanky. They went into the lot, messed with her car, but you can't see what they did exactly, then looked into *your* car before heading back inside.

"They probably saw the kids and Theo and got scared off," I said with relief.

Berry nodded, then continued, "They knew exactly where the cameras were—never showed their face. The lot was dark, so it's hard to tell exactly what they were doing, but it's clear they had a plan. And I think it was someone from the station. Or someone from the station had a helper."

My blood ran cold. My hands trembled in my lap. "Oh my God," I whispered. "I knew it was connected, but... I didn't want to believe it." *Jason was right!*

"I didn't want to believe it, either," Berry admitted, her voice hardening. "But the more I think about it, the clearer it becomes. It has to be someone who knew about Melanie coming to the station. Someone who had access to the building and knew exactly what to look for. It could be a cop, a detective... hell, anyone. Smithick's reach might be even deeper than we thought." Her hands balled into fists. "How far do his fucking tentacles go?"

"Do you really think my house could be bugged?"

"I don't know. Nothing is impossible. We just need to be cautious," she said.

All I could do was sit there, her words crushing me as I stared out at Theo and the kids. The playground, bathed in sunlight, suddenly felt like the most dangerous place in the world.

"That smug bastard keeps showing up while I'm on duty, threatening to sue me for libel," Berry said, raising her hands in exasperation. "He knows we don't have any evidence against him. He comes in and demands to speak to the chief while his eyes are fixed on me. I heard him yelling in the chief's office that all we had were a couple of 'cracked-out whores' who were probably out for revenge for putting them or their drug dealer boyfriends in jail. He wanted me to hear him," she said, looking down at her hands, which were beginning to shake.

"I feel like he is out to get me, too, because I won't drop this. But without any physical evidence, I don't know what we can do, because right now it's his word against yours."

"We need to find that warehouse with the blue door. It was a gray concrete building with big shipping bays and a blue door that went into an office space." I said, my excitement building. I paused for a moment, thinking, then added, "God, I wish I knew where it was. I think I was blindfolded when I was being driven there and back because that is all I can remember. The blue door and a floral scent." I looked at her with hopeful eyes.

Berry stood and slung her bag back over her shoulder. "I will look into properties or businesses that he owns. Anything that might be a warehouse. Please be careful. Oh, and if you need to get in touch with me, email me here. It's my personal email," she said as she pulled out a pen and a small notepad. She jotted her email down and handed it to me as she shook my hand.

"I will. Take care of yourself, too, Berry."

Berry turned and walked back to her unmarked car and drove away.

Theo and I grabbed the kids and headed back to the house. Emily had to be carried—she had worn herself out. Once we returned to the house, Theo and I started getting dinner ready. I caught him up on everything Berry and I spoke about.

"Well, the alarm system and cameras are up and running," Theo said, as he sliced some carrots for a roast.

"We can't stay inside forever, though. What if we are still living like this when Emily starts school next year?" I looked at him, starting to panic because I had not thought about that until this very moment.

"I can take her and pick her up while you stay here."

"What about your work schedule?" I fretted.

"The hospital will let me switch up my hours. I can just grab some extra hours on Saturdays. It will be fine," he said with a comforting smile. He finished cutting up the veggies, placed them in a pot with the roast, and slid it into the oven. "Now we wait," he said, looking back at me.

"Maybe you should take the kids to your apartment. Until things settle down," I said, trying to sound brave, but my voice exposed my fear.

"I will not leave you here alone, Grace," he said firmly.

"This is happening because of me. I can't have you be collateral damage. Especially without a gun to defend ourselves." I paused, waiting for his reaction. But he looked betrayed. "This is my fight. I don't care if I die, as long as you all are safe," I pleaded. Tears filled my eyes.

"I can't leave!" he said as he wrapped his arms around me. "We just need to be careful until he gets arrested again," his voice beginning to waiver."

I pulled away and raised my eyes to his. "What if that never happens?" I said with a scoff and turned away from him.

"Grace!"

I threw my hands up in surrender as I walked into the bedroom to check on Michael, who was down for a nap. He was sleeping soundly. My phone chimed. It was a text from Jason telling me he posted bond and asking if I needed anything. I walked over to the bed and sat down next to Cappy. I stroked his long fur, but my skin was so dry, the fur was catching on my hand. I opened the nightstand to get some lotion, and something caught my eye.

That key.

The key that I had found months ago, when I thought I was dreaming. I picked it up and examined it. There was nothing special about it, but it didn't go to anything in the house. To my knowledge, I had never owned a small key like this one. It had the word "Master" stamped into each side.

That's a padlock brand! "Master Lock," I thought. I certainly did not own a Master Lock padlock. My mind was racing, trying to dig out the darkest, deepest buried memories I had, but nothing came to mind.

I grabbed my journal off the nightstand and erratically flipped through the pages until I found the ones that mentioned the warehouse.

I gasped. "That's it! This must be the key to the box at the warehouse. The nightmare box that was used to torture us." I ran back into the living room and grabbed my phone. I took photos of the key and attached them to an email to Berry's personal email account:

"Subject: Smithick

I found a key on my bedroom floor. Might be nothing, but I think it goes to the torture box in the warehouse. Let me know if you find any buildings that might be it."

I put the key in my pocket. The smell of pot roast was saturating the room. My mouth began watering. *Honestly, I can't remember if I ate today*, I thought. I got up and went to the bedroom to check on Michael. He was starting to stir. I picked him up, and we went to the kitchen. I put him in his highchair, and Theo called for Emily as he started setting the table. Emily ran around the corner with her arms outstretched, making a loud *"vroom"* sound like she was an airplane, and plopped into a chair.

After we finished a near-silent supper, Theo and I cleaned up, also without a word. I pulled out my phone to see if Berry had responded to my email. She had. Her message read:

"Wow. Alright. I was about to email you, actually. I found some buildings in his name. Do any of these look familiar?"

I clicked on each of the photos. There were three, but only one looked promising. I responded to her email:

"Just the last one. Where is it? Can we go see it in person? I feel like I will know for sure if it's the right one if I can go there. Is it an actual business with employees there?"

I put Michael in his bouncy walker. He couldn't walk or even stand on his own, but he loved to bounce around in that thing. In front of him were brightly colored shapes that twirled, rattled, and squeaked. Emily still sat at the dining room table coloring in a mermaid coloring book.

I checked my phone again. Her new message:

"From what I can tell, it is an active business, but this late, there's probably no one there. It's on Third Street and Carswell Avenue. I know it's getting late, but I wanna nail this bastard. I could come get you in 20 minutes. Remember, this is just to identify the building. We would be in and out. No investigating or trying to get inside. Let me know."

"I need you to watch the kids while Berry and I check out a warehouse," I said with urgency in my voice.

"Berry can do it herself," he challenged.

"She's never been there. We don't know if it's the correct one, and we won't know until I can go see it. All I remember is the blue door, and there was a faint smell of orchids. Once I verify that, we'll leave. Besides, Berry will keep me safe; she's a police officer.

"Alright. Only if you promise to come back in one piece."

I messaged her back:

343

"Let's go!"

"She'll be here soon," I said. Theo was sitting on the couch, and he reached out his hand to me. I grabbed it, stooped down, and kissed his forehead.

He glanced up at me and smiled. "Please be safe and hurry back. I love you!"

I bent down, placed my hands on the sides of his face, and kissed his lips. "I love you too, so much."

I sent Jason a text giving him the address and telling him we were going to take a look. He told me to be careful and to let him know if I needed anything. About ten minutes later, a car I didn't recognize rolled up to the curb in front of my house, its headlights slicing through the darkness. It could be Berry's personal car, but I had never seen her drive it. I didn't know if I should walk out there or—my thoughts were interrupted by my phone vibrating. It was a text from Berry.

I'm in front of your place in my red sedan.

My mind was instantly put at ease. I stepped outside into the cool night air, the faint hum of crickets in the distance the only sound. My chest tightened as I crossed the sidewalk and slid into the passenger seat. The car smelled of old leather and spearmint gum.

"I'm sorry, I should have told you earlier that I would be in my car. I am trying to take every precaution for our safety." Berry said, glancing over at me. "Since the mole probably works in the station, I was worried my unmarked sedan might have a tracker on it. I hardly ever drive this old thing. It's my spare."

"Yeah. Better safe than sorry. If you don't mind, can we drive in silence? I'm going to close my eyes on the way and just see if the route feels familiar," I said, as I buckled my seatbelt, suddenly hyper-aware of the faint tremor in my hands.

Berry glanced at me, her sharp eyes unreadable in the glow of the dashboard lights. "Good idea. Get those ears and nose good and woken up," she replied, her voice low, measured. Without another word, we pulled into the street, the tires crunching softly on the gravel.

The drive felt like an eternity, the silence inside the car pressing down on me. I kept my eyes closed, trying to focus on every bump, every turn, the rhythmic whoosh of the tires against the road. My heart thudded steadily; my body coiled tight with nerves.

"We're here," Berry finally said as the car slowed to a stop. Her voice startled me, and I blinked my eyes open.

The warehouse loomed in front of us, its massive frame shrouded in shadows. It looked exactly as I'd imagined—cold, industrial, forbidding. I unbuckled my seatbelt as Berry killed the engine, the sudden silence amplifying every creak of the cooling car.

"It felt like the right amount of time," I murmured, mostly to myself.

We stepped out together, the night air wrapping around us like a damp sheet. The streetlights above cast a pale, flickering light across the empty parking lot. We scanned the area. No movement. No sound. Just stillness, oppressive and watchful.

The side of the warehouse facing us was blank, windowless, but I spotted two large roll-up doors on the left and a smaller blue door on the right.

That door. My chest tightened.

I moved toward it, my feet feeling heavier with each step. Behind me, Berry whispered, "We can't go in, Grace. We're just here to look."

"I just want to see it. And smell it. This is where they would take off the blindfold," I whispered. My fingers brushed the cold, scratched surface of the door. Blue paint flaked beneath my touch, revealing dull gray beneath. A silver kick plate was bolted near the bottom, its edges worn smooth from years of use.

I took a deep breath through my nose. A faint, unexpected scent of orchids hung in the air, sweet and out of place. My stomach turned. "This is definitely the door. I remember the orchids," I whispered, my voice hollow.

"Okay, good. Let's go," Berry said, urgency sharpening her tone. She motioned toward the car with one hand, the other resting on the butt of her service weapon. Her movements were tense and measured.

I nodded, stepping away from the door. I glanced around. We were still all alone. The car was about eighteen feet from the door of the warehouse. We both started walking back toward the car but were a few feet away from it when we both froze. The low rumble of an engine cut through the silence.

We turned in unison to see a black sedan pull into the lot, its headlights clicking off before it rolled to a stop directly behind Berry's car, boxing us in. My pulse spiked. The door opened, and a man stepped out. The high-pressure sodium lights above created an orange aura around his head, swallowing his face in shadows. He was thin and tall. The way he moved—calm, deliberate—sent ice down my spine.

"What are you doing here?" a low, grumbling voice cut through the air.

I stiffened. My mind went spiraling. Who is he? Jason? Smithick? Another one of his goons? Or am I overreacting to a security guard just doing his job?

The man took another step forward and lit a cigarette. The lighter briefly illuminated his face. His voice sharper this time, "I asked you a question. What are you doing here?"

That voice. I knew that voice.

The name barely formed in my mind before Berry let out a breath. "Schammel? Oh, Schammel! You scared the shit out of me!" She exhaled hard, pressing her hand to her chest. "Jesus."

But I didn't relax. I couldn't. Something was wrong—off. I was never comfortable around him. What was he doing here? Why had he followed Berry?

Schammel didn't answer Berry's remark. He kept walking, still in shadows, his steps echoing unnervingly against the pavement.

Then he stepped into the warehouse perimeter lights, and I saw his eyes. I could feel the hatred inside them, and something inside me told me that he was the mole. He worked for Smithick.

My blood ran cold.

He had a gun in his hand. The lights above glinted off the metal barrel. He was already raising it. His movements were steady and deliberate.

Berry stepped in front of me, shielding me.

"Berry!" I started to shout—

The crack of the gunshot shattered the night. Berry staggered back, her eyes wide with shock as she crumpled to the ground. Time slowed, my vision narrowing as Schammel turned his weapon on me. I turned, instinct kicking in, but there was no cover, nowhere to go.

A second shot rang out. Pain exploded in my temple as I fell to the ground. My head hit the pavement hard, and for a moment, all I could hear was a deafening ringing.

Through the haze, I heard two more shots—quick and sharp. My vision swam, but I forced my eyes open. Schammel lay sprawled on the ground a few feet away, his gun still clutched in his hand. I didn't know who had fired. Was it backup? Was it Berry? She was right next to me on the ground.

Blood pooled beneath me, warm and sticky, soaking into my clothes. My breaths came shallow and fast. My mind raced.

I'm going to die. The thought hit me like a freight train. A rush of warmth spread over my entire body, and I knew there wasn't much time.

No. *No*, I couldn't let him win. If I died, he'd get away with everything.

The key. I needed to get the key to Berry somehow, if she was even still alive. If anyone found the key in my pocket, they wouldn't know the significance.

The colors of my surroundings began fading.

With trembling fingers, I fumbled in my pocket and pulled it out. My vision blurred, my strength fading, but I forced myself to move. I brought the key to my lips and swallowed it, the

348

jagged edges scraping my throat. The pain in my temple burned hotter, sharper, as the ringing in my ears began to fade. The world around me dimmed. The glow of the parking lot lights softened to nothing.

I prayed silently, desperately. Please don't let me die. Please, God.

And then, everything went silent.

36

The Playground

When I opened my eyes, I was standing in the playground near the house, where the air always smelled of fresh-cut grass and rusted metal. But something was wrong. The familiar laughter of children was absent. The merry-go-round creaked in the breeze, spinning slightly, though no one was there to push it. The slide gleamed under a dull, purple and pink sky.

I knew this place, but I didn't belong here. I had dreamed of this playground before—back when I thought I lived in Chicago. But this was different. The air was heavy, the colors muted, as if the entire world had been drained of life. *Am I dreaming?*

In front of me stood a swing set with two swings. One swayed lazily, though the wind wasn't strong enough to move it. A man was sitting on the other one with his back toward me. He cradled a baby in his arms, rocking back and forth as the chains groaned and squeaked. For a moment, my heart leapt. *Theo and Michael!* I thought. I eagerly stepped forward, my footsteps crunching on the gritty ground, a burst of relief rushing through me.

But as I approached, the man turned his head slightly,

enough for me to catch his profile. My breath caught in my throat. It wasn't Theo. It wasn't Michael. It was Cameron, and he was holding Kara. They looked as they had the last time I dreamed about them, but now, I knew they weren't real.

He smiled when he saw me, his face lighting up in a way that was genuine, even tender. "Grace," he said warmly, his voice soft yet echoing strangely in the space around us.

Before I could react, Cameron stood and walked toward me, the baby nestled against his chest. His gait was slow but purposeful, as if every step had been choreographed long before I arrived. When he reached me, he lovingly placed Kara in my arms. Her tiny fingers wrapped instinctively around a strand of my hair.

Then he hugged me, his cheek resting against my forehead. They both felt as real as ever, and I was again swallowed by the fantasy. "Oh, Cam," I sighed.

For a fleeting moment, I closed my eyes, allowing myself to sink into the comfort of it, letting the chill of the playground melt away. But when he pulled back and stepped away, I looked up at his face, and I froze. *This is a dream. This isn't real*, I thought.

"I'm so glad you're back," he said, his voice soft but wrong, like it was coming from somewhere deep inside the earth. "Now you can stay with me forever."

As the word *forever* slipped from his lips, a transformation began. His eyes sank into his skull, the sockets darkening and hollowing until they were nothing but deep, black pits. His skin grew loose, sagging as if it were melting like candle wax, sliding down his face and clinging to his chin in grotesque folds.

I stumbled backward, still clutching Kara tightly against my chest.

His lips fused, melting into the misshapen mass that covered the lower half of his face. The nose disappeared entirely, leaving only two gaping holes, and his head began to bulge, forming lumps that stretched the skin unnaturally. His hair fell out in clumps, landing silently on the ground. His hands swelled, the knuckles grotesquely large, his fingers twitching as if they belonged to some alien creature.

Cameron kept walking toward me. His twisted body moved with an eerie fluidity, his head lolling to one side as if his neck couldn't quite support its weight.

For a moment, I was frozen solid. *This can't be happening!*

I glanced down at Kara, desperate for some sense of normalcy, but her face was contorted with fear. She was crying, the sound high-pitched and piercing, like nails dragging across glass. I tried to comfort her, my tears falling freely now.

Then she stopped crying. Her wide, terrified eyes locked on mine, and her tiny lips began to move.

"Why are you crying, Mommy?" she asked, her voice impossibly clear for a baby. "You don't want to stay here with us?"

I blinked, horrified, unable to process the words, confused by everything that was happening. "Where is *here*?" I stammered. Did I even want to know?

"It's the world where your soul goes when your body is asleep," she said simply, her small hands gripping my shirt. "The place you were writing about in your dreams, back when you still loved us. You did get one thing wrong, though, Mommy. You can't do whatever you want and be whoever you want all the time, because sometimes there is a higher power that won't let you." Her voice grew quieter, almost reverent. "You are not always in control here," she whispered, glancing over my shoulder. My entire body trembled in fear.

"You aren't real. This is just a dream world," I told her. Kara's face began to change, too. Her cheeks sank inward, her bright eyes dissolving into empty, yawning voids. Her soft baby skin sloughed off in sheets, exposing the uneven lumps forming beneath her skull. Her tiny mouth twisted grotesquely as patches of hair fell away, leaving her head deformed and patchy.

I screamed louder than I had ever screamed in my life, and in utter shock, I dropped her to the ground. I turned and ran, my breath coming in shallow gasps. Kara, or what used to be her, began to crawl after me.

I stopped and yelled, "You are not real!" and she, or rather it, dissolved into dust. I hadn't taken more than a few steps when I collided with something solid.

It was a door.

The door stood in the middle of the playground, massive and painted a deep, unnatural red. There were no walls around it, nothing to anchor it to reality. It just stood there, an impossible barrier. I grabbed the handle and twisted, but it wouldn't budge. I pushed against it with all my strength, slamming my shoulder into the wood, but it wouldn't give. *This door has me trapped here!* I thought.

Panicking, I glanced around. I tried to run around the door, but it was as if an invisible wall extended outward, preventing me from moving past it. It felt as if I was in a fish tank, banging on the glass and screaming my head off.

Then, my eyes shifted to the view beyond the invisible wall, and I could see the other side—a hospital room. *My* hospital room. My body lay in the bed, surrounded by machines, the rhythmic beep of a heart monitor barely audible over the sound of my own panicked breathing.

Theo was there. He stood beside my bed, holding my limp hand, his lips moving as if he were speaking to me. I couldn't hear him. I pounded on the door, trying to get his attention, but he never looked over to me.

I pressed my hands against the invisible wall, desperate to get to him. I could feel his touch as he held my hand—the hand attached to my sleeping body. It was faint but real, as if he were reaching through the barrier to comfort me. But I couldn't reach back. His head was bowed as if in prayer.

I ran my fingers along the edges of the door and the invisible barrier surrounding me, searching for an opening, but there was none. The smooth, solid surface encased me completely.

I pounded my fists against it, screaming. On the other side, Theo glanced up, his face full of anguish. His lips moved again, and this time, I could hear him faintly, his voice breaking through the barrier:

"Come back to me, Grace."

The hospital room was quiet. I could feel the stillness pressing down on me like a heavy blanket, suffocating in its weight. Theo sat beside me, his head again bowed, his fingers clutching my hand like it was the only thing anchoring him to this world.

I wanted to tell him I was here, to squeeze his hand back, to comfort him, but my body wouldn't obey. I was a prisoner, boxed in by unresponsive flesh. My body lay there, empty, but I was here on the other side.

"What is happening to me?" I shrieked.

A chill swept through me, though I felt no body to shiver with. The truth hit me all at once, sharp and suffocating:

My soul has separated from my body. It's being kept alive by machines. My consciousness is here. Is this heaven? Another dimension? My body is unresponsive, and I'm in a coma.

I watched as the Dr. spoke, his voice muffled at first, like I was underwater. Then, slowly, it grew clearer. I strained to hear what he was saying.

"She's not responding to treatment," the Dr. said, his tone clipped but softened by pity. "We've done everything we can, but her injuries were too severe. It's only a matter of time."

"No," Theo said, shaking his head. His voice cracked. "You're wrong. She's strong. She'll come back to us. She has to."

The Dr. lowered his eyes and said, "I'm sorry."

"There's still time. She can still come back! Can't she? Hasn't that happened before?" Cameron asked in anguish. His hands were on the top of his head. Tears were streaming down his face.

"I'm sorry, but not with the type of damage she has." The Dr. put a hand on Theo's shoulder.

Theo hung his head and began to sob.

"I'll stay with her," he said finally, his voice quieter now. "I'm not leaving her alone."

"Theo!" I shouted. "I'm right here! I can hear you! Why can't you hear me?"

I was stuck and feeling utterly helpless.

I stood there in utter silence, trying to make sense of my situation, when—

"Mommy?"

The meek voice startled me, light and sweet like a bell in the distance. I turned—and there she was. Kara. At least I thought it was Kara. Her form was no longer that of an infant but of a pre-teen.

She stood by the swings in the park, her small frame silhouetted by the pale glow of the sunlight. She was different now—no longer twisted or deformed like before. She was whole, radiant, her curls bouncing as she cocked her head to the side and smiled.

"Kara?" I whispered, though I wasn't sure if the words came out loud. My breaths were ragged. My chest heaved.

I sat on the worn wood of the playground's merry-go-round, staring out at the gray fog that wrapped itself around the swings and the slide like a suffocating blanket. My legs dangled, useless in this dreamlike state, but I couldn't shake the weight in my chest. The red door loomed in the distance, and I could feel it pulling at me even when I wasn't looking at it.

Kara's hands were fidgeting nervously with the hem of her dress. Her curls framed her round face, and her big, dark eyes seemed even larger than they should be. But they weren't filled with warmth. They glistened, filling with tears.

"Kara," I said softly, guilt swelling into my throat. "Sweetheart, I—"

"I'm not Kara," she interrupted, her lips trembling. Her voice cracked, and she bit her lower lip, as though trying to hold back more tears. "Why would you call me that, Mommy? You saw Kara dissolve into dust after you dropped her, remember?"

I opened my mouth to speak, but no words came out. I was utterly mystified. I tried to gather my thoughts.

"She wasn't real. She was made up in your mind," she added.

Who is this? Is she trying to trick me? "I'm sorry," my voice was quiet and unsure. "What is your name?"

She sniffled and wiped a tear from her cheek with the back of her hand. "You didn't get the chance to give me one. I'm not Kara, who you remember from your dreams. I'm the baby you never got to meet."

My jaw and stomach dropped simultaneously. "You can't be! My baby died!" I wailed. I don't..." I shook my head, struggling to find the words, trying to grasp what was happening. "I don't understand any of this. This can't be real—it's too strange, too..."

The girl crossed her arms, her bottom lip jutting out in a stubborn pout. "I am your baby. Joseph is my dad. He and I died together in the crash. This is your new reality now. It's not a dream. It just feels like one because it's not the same as before."

"Before?" I echoed, my voice shaking.

"When you were awake," she explained, as though it were obvious. "When your body was awake."

Her words were like a punch to the gut. "My body..." I whispered. The fog around the playground seemed to thicken, pressing in on me.

The girl nodded slowly. "You're sleeping, but not like normal sleep at night. It is the deep kind of sleep, the kind where your body stops but your soul keeps going. And this..." She spread her arms, gesturing to the playground, the fog, the red door. "This is where your soul is now, while your body lies in the hospital bed."

"My soul?" I repeated. My soul had separated. My body was an empty vessel.

"Yes." She stepped closer, her face tilting up to meet mine. "This is real. You keep saying it's not, but it is. You are the mommy I never got to meet." Again, waves of guilt crashed into me. I didn't know how this was happening, but she knew about Joseph and the crash. I tried to calm myself down.

"W—what should I call you?" I stuttered.

"Everyone here calls me Aniela."

37

My Baby

I thought about the baby that had been inside me at the time of the car accident. She would be about twelve or thirteen years old now if she had lived.

Aniela reached out to take my hand in hers. Her fingers were warm, and the touch sent a jolt through me—a sensation I hadn't felt in what seemed like forever.

Tears welled in my eyes, blurring the hazy playground around us. I squeezed her hand, my throat tightening. "So, I am your mom, and Joseph is your dad?" I said, trying to wrap my head around the idea.

"Yes," she nodded. "Dad is here too. You will be able to see him soon."

"You're right," I said, my voice cracking. "You are real, Aniela. I'm so sorry. I didn't mean to hurt your feelings. I didn't know what was happening to me. I still don't."

Aniela's lips curved into a small, tentative smile. "It's okay. It's confusing at first. But you're not alone, Mom. I'm here to help you."

I knelt in front of her, my trembling hands gripping hers.

"Help me how?" I asked. "How do I get out of this place? How do I wake up?"

Her smile faltered, and she shook her head. "That's the thing. You're not going to wake up—not the way you think."

The words hit me like a blow, my breath catching in my throat. "What do you mean?"

"You're not going back, not physically anyway," she said, her voice soft but steady. "This is your reality now. It's different, but it's still real. You just have to learn how to live in it. You don't have to worry about your physical body holding you back now."

I stared at her, my heart pounding, but she didn't flinch. Her face was calm now, her earlier tears gone, replaced by a strange, almost unsettling wisdom.

"Live in it?" I echoed. "But I'm not alive. Am I?"

"You're alive in a different way. Your body is in the hospital, but your soul is here. Beyond the red door is where you can be with the people you love who have passed away. While you are here, your soul can leave this realm and return to the realm your body is in. If you wish."

I closed my eyes, Aniela's words swirling in my head. My soul. My new reality. This place was real. She was real.

When I opened my eyes again, Aniela was smiling at me. "You're starting to understand," she said.

"I think so," I whispered. "But I don't know how to move through this. How to... exist here. How to enter that other realm."

"I'll teach you," she said, squeezing my hand. Her smile widened, and for the first time, it wasn't just sweet, it was confident. Reassuring. "You're my mom. I want to help you."

"I need to make sure Smithick goes to jail. I can't stay tethered to the hospital room forever. How do I go back to that world where my body is?" I asked her.

"You're stuck," she said knowingly.

I nodded, "I know, sweetheart. I don't know how to get out."

"I can teach you," she repeated. You just have to let go."

"Let go of what?"

She laughed, a light, musical sound that melted some of the fear lodged in my mind. "Of *your body*," she said, pointing to the bed through the glass of the red door.

I followed her gaze and saw my body, pale and still, lying beneath the tangle of wires and tubes. The sight should have horrified me, but instead, I felt... disconnected. Like it wasn't me at all, just a shell.

"How do I let go of it?" I asked.

Aniela smiled again, her hand reaching for mine. When I took it, warmth rushed through me, like sunlight breaking through clouds.

"Through astral projection. Close your eyes," she said, "and think about the place you need to be. Think about it really hard. Imagine yourself there. Forget about your earthly body, and then just... go."

Of course! Just like in the research paper that I dreamed about. My soul could go wherever it wanted. There was no limit.

I did as Aniela said, closing my eyes and letting the hospital room slip away. The sterile beeping of the machines and the muffled voices of the doctors melted into silence. I pictured the warehouse, the cold, cavernous space I'd walked through before everything went wrong. I focused on the chipped blue door, the faint smell of orchids, and the rough texture of the concrete floor beneath my feet.

When I opened my eyes, I was there. The air was heavy, stifling, carrying the faint metallic tang of rust and oil. The overhead lights cast a harsh light across the vast room. Crates and pallets were stacked high along the walls, their labels marked with shipping numbers and destinations that I didn't recognize.

It was clear the warehouse was still active, appearing on the surface to be a legitimate shipping company. Forklifts sat parked along the far wall, and a clipboard hung on a nearby hook, listing delivery schedules in tidy, professional handwriting. If I didn't know better, I might have believed this was a regular operation.

Maybe it is now, I thought. It was over three years since I had been here.

I walked further into the room, my footsteps soundless in this strange, detached state. My eyes scanned every detail, looking for something, *anything*, that would lead me to the box. If the girls were still being held here, they'd already moved them to a more clandestine area of the warehouse. But I wasn't here for the girls, not now. I was here for the box. I had to know if *that* was still here.

The air grew colder as I moved deeper into the warehouse, the rows of shelves casting long shadows that seemed to stretch and flicker in my peripheral vision. Toward the back of the room, I noticed a wall that seemed out of place. Unlike the rest of the open, industrial space, this wall was solid, clean, and reinforced. There was a single door embedded in it, sleek and modern, with a keypad mounted beside the handle.

This looks promising, I thought, stepping closer.

The keypad blinked red, and I hesitated for a moment, knowing I couldn't physically interact with it. Instead, I leaned forward, just far enough to pop my head through the door. On the other side of the door, I saw a typical office. Why was there so much security for an office? There's barely anything in here.

When I was about to give up, my eyes caught a strange dust pattern on the floor. There was a thin layer of dust covering the floor, except for one area in the shape of a semicircle next to the wall. Now I was curious.

I entered the room, passing through the doorway. I examined the wall and noticed cracks. Man-made, purposeful cracks that were even, straight, and about the size of a person. There was no handle, but this appeared to be a hidden door. I again leaned my head in to see if there was anything in there.

What I saw on the other side made my stomach turn.

The wooden box was there.

It sat in some type of crawl space. The walls were unfinished. There were electrical wires stapled along the studs. They had some rudimentary shelving studs on the walls. No one would think this would be back here. Smithick knew Berry was getting close, so he had hidden his torture box.

The longer I glared at it, the more it resembled a coffin. Its wood was dark, splintered in places, with deep scratches etched across its surface. The sight of it sent a cold shiver down my spine, memories flooding back unbidden—the stories the victims had told. I had been in the box before, too, but my mind would not go there. This wasn't just a box. It was a nightmare.

And it wasn't alone.

The shelves lining the room were filled with plastic bags of white powder stacked neatly in rows, alongside scales and other equipment. It didn't take much to piece together what this clandestine room had become. The box was still here, but they'd moved the drugs into this space as well, consolidating their horrors into one hidden chamber.

I stepped closer, the details of the room sharpening as I did. There were faint stains on the floor near the box—dark smears that could have been oil but probably weren't. The air in this room was different, thicker, carrying a faint, acrid smell that made me feel like I was suffocating.

They never stopped, I realized, my chest tightening. They just got better at hiding it.

The box loomed in front of me now, larger than life, its very presence radiating menace. I wanted to turn away, to run, but I couldn't. I had to know if it held the evidence Berry would need. I leaned forward, peering at the box.

There was a padlock on it, old and worn, with the word "Master" engraved on it. My thoughts immediately went to the key, the one I'd swallowed before I fell. My stomach twisted at the memory of the sharp edges scraping my throat, of the desperate prayer that it would make a difference.

The key... It has to be for this.

I stood there for what felt like an eternity, staring at the lock, willing it to open. But it didn't. I had done everything I could in life to protect the key. Now, all I could do was hope Berry would find it before Smithick or one of his men moved it.

I glanced back at the door I'd passed through, half-expecting someone to burst through it at any moment. The thought of possibly seeing Smithick sent a chill down my spine. Was he still using this place? Did he even know I'd been here the night I was there with Berry?

Oh, God! What happened to Berry? I saw her get shot, and after I collapsed, I heard more shots. I focused on Berry. I needed to know if she was still alive. I took a deep breath and closed my eyes. The warehouse faded around me. I began to hear beeping and machines whirring.

Just like that, the hospital room came into focus. The light that was streaming through the window was softer, golden, the kind of light that signaled the end of a long day.

Berry was there this time, standing beside Theo, who sat in a chair next to the bed. He was holding my hand. Berry's face was drawn, exhaustion etched into the lines around her mouth and eyes. Her arm was in a sling. She had been crying, her eyes still puffy and red. Theo kissed my hand and stood. "I need to go get some coffee. Do you want anything?" he asked solemnly.

"No, thank you, Theo. I'm just going to talk to her for a while, if you don't mind," she said, wiping a tear off her cheek. When Theo left the room, Berry sat in the chair and grabbed my hand. She squeezed tightly and dropped her head.

"I'm so sorry. I shouldn't have put you in that situation." She paused and sniffled. "I shouldn't have let you come!" she cried, her voice breaking. "Schammel followed me from the station, then to your place, and the warehouse. I thought there was a mole, but I never would have suspected my damn partner." She

365

took a tissue from the box by my bed and wiped her nose and eyes.

"I killed him, Grace," she said, almost as if confessing to me. "Schammel got me in the shoulder, but I was able to get two shots off at his chest. He won't hurt anyone else. But Smithick—he's still out there. He's running scared now, but he'll slip up. I'll find him. I swear I'll finish this."

I could hear the resolve in her voice, and for the first time, I felt something like hope. If anyone could stop Smithick, it was Berry. She stood up and was rummaging around in the clothing I had been brought in. At first, I didn't understand what she was doing, but then I realized she was looking for the key I had told her about. The one I found on my bedroom floor. She didn't know I swallowed it at the last minute.

38

Goodbye

Theo walked back into the hospital room as Berry was walking to the door to leave. Her movements were stiff, almost mechanical, as though the weight of everything was crushing her from the inside out. She glanced at my motionless form in the hospital bed before looking away, her jaw tightening.

"I'm going to finish him," she said, her voice low but filled with conviction. "I will not let her suffer in vain." She stepped toward the door, her gaze locked straight ahead, unwilling or unable to meet Theo's mournful eyes.

Before she could leave, a figure appeared in the doorway. It was the doctor. His face was grave, a quiet sorrow etched into the lines around his mouth. The room seemed to hold its breath.

Berry froze, turning slowly toward him. Theo stiffened, and I could see his hands curl into fists at his sides. They both knew. The moment they saw the doctor's expression, they understood.

The doctor hesitated, as though weighing how to soften the blow. He finally spoke, his tone steady but heavy. "I just got the most recent brain scans back. I'm so sorry to have to tell you this, but she is not going to recover. The machines are the only thing keeping her here."

The words hung in the air like a physical thing.

The doctor stepped closer, resting a hand on Theo's shoulder. "Does she have any other family that might want to come say goodbye?"

Theo's shoulders sagged under the question, his whole body deflating as the reality of it sank in. "We were fostering a couple of kids," he said quietly, his voice trembling. "But I don't want them to see her like this. It would scare them." He paused, swallowing hard, then added, "There's a friend I should call, though. Maddie Piper—her boss. And her friend."

His voice faltered as he said the word *friend*, as though it brought fresh pain. He rubbed the bridge of his nose with his fingers, blinking rapidly as his emotions threatened to spill over. "After she has a chance to see her, I'll be ready to..." he broke off, his voice cracking, and lowered his head. For a moment, he didn't move, just breathing deeply, trying to gather himself. "To say goodbye," he finished softly, the words barely audible.

With shaking hands, he pulled his phone from his pocket and dialed. His voice was rough and uneven as he spoke to Maddie. "It's time," he told her. "You should come."

When the call ended, he slipped the phone back into his pocket. He stood there for a moment, silent and unmoving, before finally whispering, "She's on her way."

The doctor gave him a sympathetic nod. "I'll come back in an hour or so to see if you're ready," he said compassionately, then stepped out of the room, leaving them alone.

Berry cleared her throat, her voice breaking the silence. "Is it alright if I stay here?" she asked. She hesitated, gripping the back of the chair she'd been sitting in. "I know I'm not... a close friend. But I'm the reason she's—the reason she's..." Her voice wavered, and she couldn't bring herself to finish the sentence.

Theo turned to her, his expression softening. "Yes, please stay," he said quickly, his tone firm but kind. "None of this is your fault."

Berry shook her head, her jaw tightening again. "I shouldn't have let her come with me that night," she said bitterly, her eyes fixed on the floor.

"She would have gone regardless," Theo replied, his voice steady but full of emotion. "You know that as well as I do. She was determined to stop Smithick so no other girls would get hurt. Even if you hadn't driven her, she would have found her way there. That's just who Grace was."

Berry blinked rapidly, fighting back tears. She nodded but didn't say anything else, her guilt hanging in the air between them.

Moments later, Maddie came rushing down the hallway, slightly out of breath. She hesitated in the doorway, her eyes immediately landing on me. Her hand flew to her mouth, and for a moment, she didn't move. Then she stepped forward, her movements slow and deliberate, like she was afraid the reality of the moment might shatter her.

She lowered herself into the chair beside the bed, her hand trembling as she reached out to touch my shoulder. Her fingers lingered there, as though trying to bridge the gap between life and death.

"Do you need time with her alone?" Theo asked, his voice

full of quiet respect. "We can step out if you'd like."

"No, no," Maddie said quickly, shaking her head. "You're fine." Her gaze never left my face, her expression a mix of heartbreak and disbelief.

She took off her glasses, folding them carefully and placing them in her lap. Her other hand gripped a tissue, and she dabbed at her eyes. Her voice, when it came, was raw and trembling.

"I'm so sorry this happened to you, Grace," she said, her words thick with emotion. "You are a beautiful soul. A beautiful soul who lost her way and was stomped on, abused, and used. You didn't deserve any of that."

Her voice cracked, and the tissue crumpled in her hand as fresh tears spilled down her cheeks. Theo walked over to her and placed a comforting hand on her shoulder.

Maddie's grief was too much to contain. She wept openly, her hand still resting on my arm. Her words were a flood of pain and love and regret, pouring out as if trying to fill the unbearable silence.

After Maddie quieted, she took a step back. Theo leaned down and took my hand in his, his grip firm but gentle. His voice broke as he spoke.

"Goodbye, my love," he whispered, his tears finally spilling over. "I'll take care of Cappy, I promise. And I'm going to apply to adopt Michael and Emily on my own. They're going to be taken care of, Grace. You don't have to hold on anymore. I love you so much. So, so much."

The room was filled with the sound of sobbing—Maddie, Berry, Theo—all of them bound together by their shared grief and love for the woman they were losing.

I wished I could speak to them, to let them know I was still here, that I could hear them, feel their love. But I couldn't. Their sorrow pressed down on me, and I couldn't bear it any longer.

I drifted back into the dream world, the hospital room fading into gray mist around me. The playground was waiting for me again, quiet and still. The swings hung motionless, their chains creaking in the breeze.

The red door stood in the distance, waiting. A silent reminder of what lay on the other side.

Time had no meaning here. There was no day or night, no minutes ticking by. I didn't know what time it was in the hospital room, or how long it would take for them to perform the autopsy. All I knew was that I was no longer tethered to my earthly body. I could feel the machines being turned off, one by one, and the final ties holding me to the world were slipping away.

I sat on the merry-go-round, my hands clutching the peeling paint of the metal bar. It spun slowly, though I hadn't moved it.

"I feel it. My body is dying," I said aloud, though the word felt foreign, heavy. The air in the dream world seemed to ripple, as though reacting to the truth I'd spoken.

No one answered, but the world around me shifted. The merry-go-round stopped spinning, and the red door seemed closer now, looming like a shadow that wouldn't leave me.

"You're not done yet," Aniela's voice came from behind me.

I turned to see her standing near the swing set, her hands clasped in front of her, her eyes wide and serious.

"I know. I need to see what happens next, and know that she finds it. I need to see Smithick go down."

Again, I closed my eyes and focused all of my attention on where I needed to be. When I opened my eyes again, I wasn't in the hospital room or the playground anymore. The air was colder, sharper. The light was harsher, too white, bouncing off stainless steel surfaces that gleamed with an unfeeling kind of precision.

I was in the morgue.

My body lay on a steel table, covered by a white sheet. The medical examiner stood beside me, his gloved hands moving methodically as he worked. What felt like minutes to me had to be hours on Earth.

I drifted closer, curious and strangely detached. There was no fear now, only a quiet kind of acceptance.

The examiner pulled back the sheet, revealing my still, pale face. His expression didn't change; he was calm, clinical, and his hands moved with purpose, almost reverently.

He began the autopsy, his movements precise and practiced. My stomach twisted when I saw him reach into my abdomen, but I couldn't look away.

And then he froze. His brow furrowed, and his hands stilled as he pulled something small and metallic from inside me.

The key.

"What the hell," he muttered, holding it up to the light. He turned it over in his gloved hands, inspecting it carefully before placing it in a small evidence bag. He labeled it and set it aside, his expression thoughtful.

I felt a strange mix of relief and urgency. The key had been found. It would lead Berry to the warehouse, to the torture box, to everything that could bring Smithick down. But I couldn't leave yet. I had to make sure Smithick got what he deserved.

He took one glove off, picked up the phone, dialed a number, and put it on speaker. His still gloved hand held the clear plastic baggie containing the key.

"Detective Berry," she answered, her voice sharp.

"Detective, this is Dr. Hayes at the medical examiner's office," he said, his tone professional but tinged with curiosity.

Berry didn't need to ask who this was about. Her stomach dropped. She finally found her voice and quietly said, "Grace."

"Yes, I just finished her autopsy," Hayes said, pausing briefly. "There's something unusual you need to see. Something we found... inside her."

Berry gasped. "Inside her? What do you mean?"

"It's better if I show you," Hayes replied. "Come down to the morgue as soon as you can."

Berry arrived shortly. The air in the morgue was cool and sterile, and her boots echoed on the tiled floor as she entered. Dr. Hayes was waiting, standing beside a steel counter where an evidence bag sat. Inside was the key—small, tarnished, and completely ordinary, except for the context.

Berry gripped her stomach as she approached. She didn't look at my covered body on the table, keeping her focus on the medical examiner instead. "You said there was something I needed to see," she said briskly, her voice steady but tense.

Dr. Hayes nodded and picked up the evidence bag. "We found this in her stomach," he said, holding it up. "Swallowed, probably not long before she was injured, as it didn't yet make it to the intestines."

Berry stared at the key, her mind probably racing. She gulped. The pieces must be clicking into place, "Grace knew she wasn't going to make it, and she'd hidden the key the only way she could," she said, in a whisper, to herself. "She... swallowed it," Berry said, a bit louder.

"Yes," Hayes confirmed. "It's unusual. Do you have any idea why she'd do that?"

Berry didn't answer right away. Instead, she reached for the evidence bag, her fingers trembling as she took it. She studied the key; her eyes became glossy with fresh tears.

"She was trying to protect it," Berry finally said, her voice low. "She knew this was the only way for her to get it to me. She swallowed it after she was shot."

Hayes nodded solemnly. "I'll file this with the rest of the evidence. But if you think it's connected to your case..."

"It is," Berry said firmly, slipping the evidence bag into her pocket. "I'll take it from here."

Dr. Hayes pointed to a chain of custody document on the table. "I'll need you to sign that." Berry complied and left the office.

I needed to follow her.

I focused on Berry—her sharp eyes, her no-nonsense voice, the way she always carried the weight of the world on her shoulders. I thought of her determination, her promise to finish this.

I drifted into Berry's office like a ghost. I guess that was what I was now. Transitioning between places was becoming easier. I was being carried by some invisible force that tugged me toward her. The morgue had dissolved into mist, and then I had been there, in Berry's office.

Berry sat at her desk, her head in her hands, surrounded by chaos. Her desk was covered with an explosion of papers and open files, notes scribbled in messy handwriting across loose sheets, and those disposable coffee cups she never threw away. She always worked like this—surrounded by the evidence of her drive, her stubborn refusal to quit. But this time, there was a heaviness in her posture I hadn't seen before.

On the corner of her desk, it sat; the key. The key I had swallowed in my final, desperate act to stop Smithick. It was in a clear evidence bag now, reflecting the dim yellow light of the desk lamp. She stared at it for a moment before burying her face back into her hands.

"I have the key," she muttered to herself, her voice low and rough. "But I need probable cause to get into that warehouse." Her words stabbed me like a knife. I wanted to scream at her, to tell her the key *was* the reason. That everything she needed was just behind that door. But I couldn't. I could only watch.

She shook her head, her frustration bubbling to the surface. "I *had* probable cause when Grace was here because she could testify." Her elbows rested heavily on the desk, her fingers digging into her hair. "How do I get into that warehouse now?" she growled, the sound raw and guttural, filled with guilt and helplessness.

I stepped closer, standing in front of her desk, my consciousness buzzing with the ache of wanting to comfort her, wanting to tell her not to give up. But she couldn't see me. She couldn't hear me. I was nothing more than a shadow in her world.

The phone rang suddenly, its shrill tone cutting through the silence. Berry startled, but then reached for the speaker button, pressing it without even lifting her head fully.

"Detective Berry," she said, her tone flat, as if bracing for another dead-end lead.

"Detective Berry, this is Maddie Piper," said a familiar voice, one that made my heart clench. "I met you at the hospital a few days ago. You gave me your card."

"Maddie," Berry repeated. She straightened in her chair, her expression shifting to something softer. "Of course, I remember you," she said, her voice tinged with genuine concern. "How are you holding up?"

"I'm pushing through," Maddie replied, though I could hear the cracks in her voice through the speaker. "Trying to be strong for Grace, you know." She paused, and I could almost see her taking a deep breath, steadying herself for whatever she was about to say. "Listen, I have something. An interview I conducted with Grace shortly before she passed away."

I froze. Yes. The recording. Maddie has come to save the day, I thought.

Berry sat up straighter, her focus sharpening instantly. "An interview?" she asked.

"Yes. She was worried something might happen to her, so she made sure to give me some details, specific ones. Things that can be verified." Her voice grew stronger as she spoke, the conviction behind her words replacing the tremble from before.

Berry leaned forward in her chair, her elbows on her desk, her fingers inching closer to the evidence bag with the key. She stared at it as though it might start speaking to her, and I could feel the shift in her energy, cautious hope breaking through the despair.

"Details?" Berry asked, her tone tight with anticipation.

"Yes. Grace wanted to make sure the investigation could move forward, even if she couldn't... be there. She talked about the warehouse, about Smithick, and what was happening there."

I wanted to cry. Maddie had listened. She had cared enough to record me, to keep my words alive even after I couldn't be.

"Can you send me the audio?" Berry asked, her voice quieter now but filled with that same unyielding determination that had brought us this far.

"Yes, of course. I'm at my computer now," Maddie replied. "I can send it to you right away."

There was a pause, and then Maddie's voice dropped, quiet but raw. "Get that bastard," she said, her words trembling. "Grace needs to know he's been put away before she can move on. I feel her spirit now and then."

My breath caught in my chest, even though I didn't have a physical body.

Berry's jaw tightened, and she blinked hard, her hand brushing the corner of her desk like she was holding herself together by sheer force of will.

"Me too," she admitted quietly, her voice breaking. She stared at the key again, her fingers brushing the evidence bag. "I want to give her justice more than I've ever wanted anything." Her words hit me like a tidal wave of emotion, and I saw just how much she cared, how deeply she felt the devastation of my loss. "I will get him, Maddie. I promise you."

Maddie exhaled shakily. "Thank you, Detective Berry. Take care of yourself."

"You too," Berry replied, her voice softer now. "Get some rest. I'll keep you updated."

The call ended, and the room fell silent again. I stood there, watching Berry as she sat motionless in her chair, her hand resting on the phone. Then, slowly, she turned back to her computer, opening the email Maddie had sent.

I drifted closer, my consciousness drawn to the sound of the audio file as Berry pressed play.

The recording crackled softly, and then my voice filled the room.

"This is Grace Christopher," I heard myself say, and the sound of my name in my voice made something ache deep inside me. "If you're listening to this, it means something's happened to me."

Berry leaned forward, her eyes narrowing, her hands trembling as they hovered over her keyboard. I could feel her determination, her focus sharpening like the edge of a blade.

"Smithick has a unique birthmark on his groin, in the shape of a heart," the recording continued. "I saw it several times as he assaulted me. He has a pimp working for him named Demetrie who uses a hot branding iron in the shape of a D to brand his girls. Smithick tortures girls by placing them inside a wooden box—after he rapes and beats them. Then they are shoved into the dark, coffin-shaped box where they can't move, or have food, or water.

"There's a padlock on the box. I know all this from experience. You start to fear the sound of the padlock because you know you're going to be raped and beaten again. That's how he breaks them. After they are broken, some of them are recruited to find other girls and bring them to him. The rest are assigned to a pimp. Mine was Lenny."

Berry's eyes flashed with recognition, her jaw clenching as she absorbed every word.

"Smithick has contacts everywhere, but I don't know how deep his reach is," I said in the recording. "But since he is a circuit judge, I am very fearful that there are many more high-power people involved. He's been good at covering his tracks and silencing witnesses like Melanie, Sasha, and, if you're hearing this, me. But if you're careful, if you follow the evidence... You can stop him. Just don't let your guard down. He's dangerous, and he'll do whatever it takes to protect himself."

When the recording ended, Berry let out a shaky breath. "Who needs probable cause when you have reasonable suspicion. We can go straight for the warrant now," she muttered to herself as she typed up a search warrant affidavit. She grabbed the key and turned to her phone, dialing quickly.

"This is Detective Berry," she said, her voice steady but laced with urgency. "I have new evidence that warrants a search of the warehouse on Eighteenth Street. I need a warrant immediately. I am emailing you the search warrant affidavit now."

A faint, bittersweet sense of peace settled over me. She was going to finish this. My death wouldn't be in vain.

39

The Warehouse

While Berry waited for the warrant, I followed her as she moved with purpose, her determination an almost tangible force. She left her office and began gathering a team—her sharp voice cutting through the murmurs of the precinct, snapping others into motion. They didn't know what she carried inside her, how every step forward was weighted with guilt and exhaustion. But I did. I could feel it radiating from her like heat from a dying fire, flaring whenever someone looked to her for leadership.

Among the faces she called upon was a young man named Perez. He was new—too new, I thought, with a pang of dread. Berry knew it too; I could see it in the way her sharp eyes lingered on him, assessing his readiness. But she didn't have the luxury of being choosy. Not tonight.

Perez stood stiffly, clutching a notebook in one hand like it was a shield. His uniform was crisp, his face boyish despite the grim set of his jaw. I thought he was in his mid-twenties. He glanced around nervously, his gaze bouncing from one seasoned detective to another, as if trying to mirror their calm.

But the truth was written all over him: he wasn't ready. Not for Smithick. Not for what they might find behind that warehouse door.

"Perez," Berry said, her tone sharp enough to make him flinch. He snapped to attention, his hand dropping the notebook onto the nearest desk.

"This isn't a desk job. We're raiding a warehouse tied to Smithick. It could get ugly." She let the words hang there, heavy with meaning. "You understand?"

"Yes, ma'am," he said, his voice firm but not quite steady.

I drifted closer to him, studying his face as he spoke. His eyes gave him away, there was fear there, raw and unfiltered, but also something else. Something quieter, deeper. Determination. I wanted to believe that meant he'd be okay, that he could handle whatever came next. But the cynicism I'd carried in life was harder to shake in death. Fear could be a liability. And in Smithick's world, liabilities didn't last long.

Berry didn't coddle him. She nodded curtly, already moving on. "Grab your gear. Evidence bags, gloves, flashlights, evidence tape—whatever we might need. Make yourself useful."

"Yes, ma'am," Perez repeated, a little louder this time, as if trying to convince himself.

As Berry continued assembling the rest of the team, Perez turned toward the supply room. I followed, drawn by the nervous energy radiating off him like static electricity. His hands moved quickly but not efficiently, fumbling as he grabbed items from shelves: gloves, bags, evidence markers, rulers, flashlights, a digital camera, and a tripod.

He even snagged a roll of evidence tape and a box of

disposable booties, though he hesitated over it, as if wondering if it was truly necessary. But then he nodded as if he was telling himself, "Yes, just in case."

His movements were deliberate, almost mechanical, like he was clinging to the simple, repetitive task as a way to calm his nerves. I hovered near him, watching as he checked and rechecked the supplies. He double-counted the bags. Tested the flashlights. Stacked the boxes just so. He turned on the camera and verified that the date and time were correct and that there was a brand-new SD card in the camera. There was a desperation to his precision, a need to feel in control of something, no matter how small.

And I couldn't blame him. I'd been there once, new to a team, trying to fake confidence while the fear ate away at me. When I was at the newspaper, I had extreme impostor syndrome. I wanted to tell him it would get easier, that one day he'd feel like he belonged here. But that wasn't true. In this career, it didn't get easier. Not with cases like this. Not when you stared into the abyss and found it staring back. And I could feel it now—the abyss waiting for him, for all of them, inside that warehouse.

"Perez," Berry's voice snapped from across the room, drawing his attention like a whip. He nearly dropped a flashlight in his haste to turn toward her. "You've been briefed on Smithick, haven't you? You know what kind of man we're dealing with?"

"Yes, ma'am," Perez replied, setting the flashlight down carefully before stepping forward. His back straightened, his voice steadier than it had been moments ago. "He's dangerous.

A predator. A man who's been protected by his position for too long. And we're going to stop him."

Berry studied him for a moment, her expression unreadable. Then, with a nod, she said, "Good. Stick close to the others. Follow their lead. And keep your eyes open. This isn't just about bagging evidence. If Smithick or his people show up..." She let the words trail off, but their meaning was clear. *Things could go sideways. Quickly.*

Perez nodded again, his jaw tightening. "Understood."

He returned to his task, his movements slower now but no less methodical. I could still feel the doubt lingering in him, clinging to him like a shadow. It made me ache in a way I didn't expect, seeing someone so green, so untested, about to walk into the heart of something dark and twisted. And there was nothing I could do to help him. I couldn't tell him anything that would help to prepare him.

I turned my attention back to Berry as she gave last-minute instructions to the rest of the team. Her confidence was unshakable, her movements precise. She'd done this a hundred times before, but I could see the tension in her shoulders, the tightness in her jaw. She felt it too. The seriousness of what they were about to do. The risks. The stakes.

The team was almost ready. All that remained was the warrant—and the small, metallic key Berry carried in her pocket like a lifeline. I followed her as she paced near her desk, the key a constant, heavy presence that tethered her to the task ahead.

I wanted to tell her to hurry, to push for the warrant, to move faster. Every second seemed like a lifetime, like another chance for Smithick to slip away. But all I could do was watch. Wait. Hope.

And pray that when they stepped into that warehouse, it wouldn't already be too late.

Berry checked her email yet again, and this time there was a new message. "I got it!" she yelled out. "Let's go!"

I pictured the warehouse in my mind and drifted there alongside Berry. I could feel her energy. She emitted determination and bravery, but there was also some fear inside her that she was fighting. The police department faded behind me, and now, the cold, industrial space of the warehouse stretched before us.

All my senses were heightened. I could hear the slow drip of a faucet and the hum of industrial air handlers. The smell of orchids wafted in from the front door. My memories of this place surged forward, unbidden: the blue door, the box, the horrors this room had held. My memories were no longer hindered by my physical body, and everything was at the forefront of my mind. I understood why I had blocked so much out. The torture, the rape, and the forced drug use had been absolute torment.

Berry moved with purpose, but she wasn't alone. A small team of officers followed her, their footsteps echoing against the concrete floor. Flashlights bobbed as they spread out, their beams cutting through the shadows and illuminating pallets, shipping crates, and the high shelves that lined the walls.

"We clear?" one of the officers asked, his voice low but firm.

"For now. But peel your eyes and glove up before touching

anything," Berry replied, her hand gripping her service weapon tightly. She turned back to the group; her flashlight held steady. "Stay alert. I want every inch of this place searched. Photograph everything. Don't forget to place an evidence marker on items of interest and photograph them with and without rulers— anything that seems out of place, bag it and tag it."

The officers nodded and split off, their movements deliberate but cautious.

I stayed with Berry, my consciousness tethered to her as she moved toward the back of the warehouse. I knew where she was headed, and my chest tightened with each step. She had no idea where the torture box was, but she was headed in the right direction. She would not leave without seeing every bit of the warehouse.

The office door came into view, its silver doorknob catching the light from her flashlight. I saw her jaw tighten as she approached it, her fingers flexing before reaching for the handle. She saw the security panel. She paused, glancing over her shoulder.

"Perez," she called out. "You're with me. The rest of you, keep searching."

Perez nodded and jogged to her side, his flashlight raised. His sharp eyes darted to every corner of the room. He stopped beside her, pulled his gun, and gave Berry a knowing nod.

"You went to school for electronics, didn't you?" Berry asked.

"Yes, actually, I did. Computer shit is my jam," he said in a chipper voice and with a smile. Berry stood there, expressionless. Prez dropped his smile and continued, "You need a way to bypass the security panel, right?" Perez asked.

"Yeah, and I have no idea how this thing works."

"This is definitely in my wheelhouse. I have a tool that we can use. It's a code cracker. The device connects to the keypad and uses an algorithm to input every possible code combination. For a simple numeric keypad like a four- or six-digit PIN, it could crack the code in minutes if no advanced encryption or timeout lock is in place, but if the security panel has a 'lockout' feature after too many failed attempts, the brute-force cracker could trigger it, sealing the door or activating an alarm."

Berry stared at him, deadpan. "You might as well be speaking Greek to me. I knew you came from the IT department at the crime lab, that's why I wanted you on my team."

Perez straightened with confidence. His face was full of determination, and he couldn't help but display a little grin after what Berry said.

Berry continued, "We have to try. If Smithick's thugs come blazing in here, we'll just have to be ready for them. You work on the code. I'll warn the others to be ready."

Perez pulled the code cracker device out of his bag and connected the USB cable to the panel. LED lights on the code cracker blinked on and off while it attempted different codes.

Berry came back to the door with Perez and watched as the code cracker worked. Her face was flushed with suspense as it beeped with red light after red light. Berry glared at Perez with intense eyes.

"How much longer?" Berry snipped.

Perez took a breath in and was about to respond when they

heard a beep and saw a green light.

The door was unlocked.

Berry took a deep breath and pushed the door open with her gloved hand. It groaned on its hinges, the sound low and hollow, sending a shiver down through me. The air inside the room was laced with the faint smell of chemicals. She and Perez exchanged glances, seemingly confused about the lack of items in the room.

One small desk and chair, a notepad, and a calculator.

"What the fuck?" Berry said. "Why is this room behind so much security?" She raised her arms in confusion. Berry turned around and started walking out of the room.

"Wait, wait!" Perez whispered rapidly.

Berry turned back around, waiting for an explanation. Perez was bent at a ninety-degree angle, shining the flashlight horizontally across the dusty floor.

He sees it! I thought!

"Look at the dust pattern there, and those cracks in the wall," he said. Berry bent down to his angle. Her jaw dropped.

"Holy mother of God, you're right," Berry exclaimed. She went back into the room and traced the crack with her fingernails. It wouldn't move.

"I need something. A butter knife, a letter opener, something."

Perez walked over to the small desk and checked the drawers. Berry was watching him intently when he pulled out a long, thin, metal staple remover. He handed it to Berry with a grin. She cracked the makeshift door open and popped her head inside.

"Call forensics now," she said solemnly.

Perez called for the forensics team and followed Berry into the room.

Her flashlight swept across the shelves, catching on rows of plastic bags filled with white powder. Scales and measuring equipment sat neatly organized on metal tables. It looked like a drug operation, but I knew that wasn't all this room held.

"There," Berry murmured, her light landing on the corner. The box.

40

The Box

It sat in the back of the office, the dark, splintered wood reinforced with steel bands. It looked harmless at first glance, like something you might find in an old storage unit. But as the flashlight's beam lingered on it, its presence filled the room like a physical force.

Berry's breath hitched. She stepped forward, motioning for Perez to follow her. He drew his service weapon and asked, "What do you think's inside?" His gun pointed at the box.

Berry didn't answer. With her flashlight fixed on the box, she placed her free hand on the gun Perez was holding and lowered it.

"What if there is a girl in there?" Berry whispered. Perez nodded.

I hovered behind Berry. My mind raced with the possibilities of what might still be inside. I could sense Berry's dread as if it were my own.

What did the box hold? Evidence? A body? A terrified girl?

Berry knelt in front of the box, handing her flashlight to Perez to focus on the lock.

She reached into her pocket and pulled out the key that had been pulled from my dead body.

She hesitated, the key hovering above the lock. Her lips pressed into a thin line, and I could feel her steeling herself for what she might find.

Perez shifted behind her. "You sure you don't want to wait for forensics before you open it?"

"No," Berry said firmly. "If something in here can lead us to Smithick, we need to know now."

She slid the key into the padlock. *Click.*

The lock fell away.

She whispered under her breath, "Please, God, don't let it be a body."

She took another deep breath. Slowly, she lifted the lid, the hinges creaking. Perez shifted closer, his flashlight aimed at the box.

The light revealed the contents, and Berry's breath hitched audibly.

The top layer was filled with photos, ledgers, and documents. There were photos of young girls, their faces pale and hollow, their eyes wide with fear. Some of them looked only a bit older than Emily.

Berry's hand hovered over the photos for a moment, her face frozen in a mixture of horror and determination. Her body tensed as she picked up one of them, holding it under the beam of her flashlight.

"Jesus," Perez whispered.

Berry set the photo aside and reached for the ledgers. The pages were filled with numbers, dates, and names—names that tied everything together. Smithick, Schammel, Demetrie, as well as others. Berry's shoulders sagged under the weight of the discovery, but her jaw tightened again, her determination pushing her forward. She flipped through the pages quickly, her flashlight illuminating transaction after transaction, each one a sickening reminder of the lives that had been bought and sold.

But that wasn't all.

As Berry flipped through the papers, her flashlight caught something at the bottom of the box. Her movements slowed, and her brow furrowed as she leaned closer.

"Wait," she said sharply, her voice cutting through the stillness.

Perez stepped forward, his flashlight joining hers. The bottom of the box was stained—dark, dried stains that spread across the wood in uneven patches. Berry's stomach churned visibly, and a wave of nausea rolled through me too.

"Is that...?" Perez started, but he didn't finish the sentence.

Berry nodded grimly. "Apparent blood and perhaps other bodily fluids," she said, her voice tight. "We'll need a forensic team to test it, but if we can match it to any of the victims..." she trailed off, her jaw clenching.

She straightened, turning to Perez. "Bag everything. Photos, ledgers, all of it. And show the forensics team where this is ASAP. I want samples taken from the bottom of this box and tested for DNA."

Perez nodded, already keeping an eye out for the team.

Berry stayed kneeling for a moment longer, her hand resting lightly on the edge of the box. Her head dipped as though the discovery had finally caught up with her. I could see relief settle on her face.

"You did it, Grace," she whispered, her voice barely audible. "You got them."

I felt a surge of emotion at her words—relief, sadness, pride—all swirling together in a way I couldn't untangle.

This was it. The evidence we needed. Smithick wouldn't be able to hide behind his money and connections anymore. I wanted to tell her it wasn't just me. That it was her too. That it was all of us. But of course, she couldn't hear me. She took the key out of the padlock and slid it back into her pocket.

She stood, her movements slow and deliberate, as though what she'd uncovered had physically drained her. She turned toward the door, grabbed her flashlight from Perez, and did a quick sweep across the room one last time.

"Let's finish this," her voice firm. I followed her, my consciousness lingering behind her as she left the room. Justice was so close I could feel it, like a faint hum in the air.

Smithick's time was up.

Moments later, the distinct rumble of the crime scene van shattered the uneasy silence outside. It pulled up to the warehouse, its headlights cutting through the gloom like twin beams of resolve. Two technicians exited the vehicle, moving with the practiced precision of people who had walked into countless horrors before.

I drifted closer as they began suiting up, their motions deliberate and ritualistic, as if donning armor for battle. From head to toe, they encased themselves in white, disposable coveralls—what detectives called "bunny suits." Goggles gleamed over their eyes, blue bonnets snugly covered their hair, and N95 masks obscured their faces. They were faceless soldiers of science, walking into the aftermath of Smithick's darkness, carrying their tools like weapons.

Each technician carried their gear: a heavy-duty camera slung over the shoulder of one, a field-testing kit in the hands of the other, along with evidence collection boxes and a scattering of smaller tools. They exchanged a few brief words, voices low and calm, before they approached the warehouse like explorers stepping into an uncharted abyss.

They began in the main storage area, their flashlight beams slicing through the stale air, catching on shelves and discarded crates. The technicians murmured something to each other before moving deeper into the warehouse, their footfalls muffled by the disposable booties they wore over their shoes. It wasn't long before they entered the office. My heart lurched as they stepped inside. The scene here was different. Charged. A quiet storm of chaos and evidence waiting to be uncovered. They worked slowly, methodically, like surgeons preparing to cut open the heart of something sinister.

Their first order of business was to map the scene, every detail measured, sketched, and photographed. The camera clicked rhythmically, its flash momentarily igniting the shadows in the room. The sound was almost comforting in its familiarity, but there was no comfort in this place, not with what waited for them here.

The box.

The box that had haunted me in life and lingered with me in death. Cheaply made, its wooden panels were roughly nailed together, but its true horror lay in its function. It was Smithick's tool of control, a cage of suffering and fear. But now, it would be something else. Now, it would be the beginning of his undoing. That box, that vile, disgusting box, was about to become the metaphorical nail in his coffin.

The technicians approached it with care, circling it like it might suddenly come to life. They photographed it from every angle, capturing its warped edges and the scratches carved into its wood. When they finally saw what was inside, I could feel the tension in the air thicken, as if the room itself was holding its breath.

Inside, the stains told a story. A grotesque, damning story that Smithick would never be able to deny. Blood. Each stain was a story of the suffering he had caused, the lives he had destroyed. One of the technicians knelt by the box, his gloved hands moving carefully over the interior surface. He dabbed at a darkened area with a testing strip.

His partner, leaning over his shoulder to watch, asked, "Is it human?" His voice was clinical but tinged with an edge of tension.

The blood analyst dabbed a sample onto a stick, similar to a pregnancy test, and paused, waiting for the test to react. Then, as the red line appeared, he gave a grim nod and confirmed, "It's human."

My chest tightened, a strange mix of fury and vindication coursing through me. The blood was human. Of course, it was. It had to be. It was mine. It was theirs. It had come from everyone who had ever suffered because of that monster. But now, finally, it was evidence.

The two of them worked in silence for a while, documenting

each stain with an almost reverent precision. Every stain was measured, catalogued, and sampled. The first technician sketched the scene inside the box, marking the location of each stain inside. I hovered closer, drawn to their calm professionalism, their quiet dedication. They weren't just collecting evidence, they were reconstructing the truth, one fragment at a time.

Their voices were low as they spoke, almost murmurs, but I could hear every word. "We've got a variety of patterns here," one of them said, shining a flashlight along the side of the box. "Drip stains, transfer smears, and pooling. Looks like a lot of activity, over a prolonged period."

"Think it's enough for DNA analysis?" the other asked, not looking up from his sketch.

"It's enough," the first replied with confidence. "And then some."

They didn't stop with the box. Moving deeper into the office, they turned their attention to the drugs scattered across the desk. One of them unpacked a small field-testing kit, laying out its contents like an artist preparing to paint. He opened a plastic vial and scraped a small sample of powder into it, shaking it gently before holding it up to the light.

"These field tests won't be super specific," he said, half to his partner, half to himself. "Mass spectrometry back at the lab will give us the full picture, but this'll at least narrow it down."

The other technician chuckled dryly. "They sent the right team for this one, huh? Blood guy and drug guy."

"Damn right." the first replied. "And Smithick doesn't stand a chance if any of the blood is his."

I couldn't help but feel the flicker of hope that rose within me at their words. They were good at what they did, both of them. Professional. Precise. Unshaken by the horrors they faced. They continued their work, their movements deliberate and steady. Even as the enormity of what they were uncovering began to settle over the room like a heavy fog.

And I thought to myself, Yes. You'll get him. You'll make him pay. Every last one of his secrets will be out for all to see, and he won't be able to hide behind his judge's robe.

The box. The blood. The drugs. Piece by piece, they were building a case so airtight that not even Smithick's power, money, or connections could save him. I couldn't touch the evidence. I couldn't speak the truth anymore. But these two, along with Berry, were my voice now. My hands. My hope.

Berry stood outside the warehouse door, waiting for the technicians to finish. When they walked out with all of their gear and evidence bags, Berry shut the door behind them.

"Let me know the second you have identified the DNA, any of it. I have an arrest warrant already made up for Smithick, just waiting on the results. Oh, and put a rush on it. We could all be in danger."

"I will," the blood guy said. "I want to get this guy. As soon as I get back to the lab, I will start on it."

41

DNA

Berry sat slumped at her desk, surrounded by chaos. Papers, files, and empty coffee cups spilled over the edges, a testament to her relentless drive and sleepless nights. Her head rested against her forearm, her dark hair a tangled mess over the glowing screen of her laptop. She looked like she hadn't left the office in days. Early morning light trickled through the blinds, casting pale stripes across the cluttered desk. Around her, the precinct was beginning to stir—officers and detectives filtering in for the day, chatting softly, shaking off sleep. But Berry barely moved.

She had poured everything she had into this investigation. Too much, probably. The dark circles under her eyes, the tension in her posture, the jittery way she tapped her fingers against the desk, all of it screamed exhaustion. She needed a break. She needed time to breathe, to reclaim a piece of herself that she had given up for this investigation—but I knew she wouldn't take it. Not while Smithick was still free. Not while there was even a chance that he could be out there, hurting another girl.

I moved closer to the desk, my attention drawn to the papers scattered in front of her. One caught my eye, a list of the evidence from the warehouse.

The branding iron. Demetrie's tool of cruelty. My stomach turned at the thought of it, at what it had been used for, the pain it had inflicted on the girls who had the misfortune of crossing paths with this sick, twisted network of men.

Nearby, other files sat stacked haphazardly, labeled with names and numbers. Jane Doe cases. Berry was piecing it all together, trying to match faces to the nameless, giving them back their humanity. Were these girls Smithick's victims, or did they belong to Demetrie? Or maybe Lenny? It didn't matter. Smithick was the puppet master. He controlled all of them— Demetrie, Lenny, and the victims. No one escaped his grip unscathed.

I couldn't help but glance at one of the files on top. The address listed for the body was a short distance from the warehouse, deep in the woods. A homeless camp had been nearby, Berry had noted. I wondered if anyone from that camp had seen something, anything, but if they had, would they even have come forward? People like that didn't trust the system. Not when the system had failed them so often.

The sudden shrill ring of the phone cut through the quiet hum of the precinct. Berry startled awake, jerking upright as though she'd been caught off guard by her exhaustion. She blinked rapidly, brushing her hair out of her face before punching the speaker button, her voice hoarse but quick. "This is Berry."

A man's voice came through the line. "Hey, this is Marvin

from the lab. We have a match on the DNA."

Berry froze, her tired expression sharpening into something laser focused. "How many profiles were there? And is one of them Smithick?"

"We compared the DNA collected from Smithick when he was arrested to the samples taken from the box at the warehouse," Marvin said. "Smithick's DNA is all over it—not just touch DNA, but semen. There were several older, degraded profiles mixed in, but five stood out as more recent. Two of them matched your Jane Does. The other three? Melanie Stringer, Sasha Woods, and Grace Christopher."

Berry's hand hovered over her keyboard as the weight of those names settled over her. Grace Christopher. Sasha Woods. Melanie Stringer. Names that weren't supposed to be on that list. Lives that weren't supposed to end like this.

Marvin continued, his voice grim. "We may be able to isolate additional profiles if we can get samples from other potential victims. But that's what we have for now."

Berry exhaled slowly; her voice was tight. "What about the rape kits on the Jane Does? Did the perp leave anything behind?"

"Oh yeah. Smithick left his calling card inside both of them. Also, I spoke with the M.E., Dr. Hayes. He said one of the Doe girls was pregnant when she died. We ran the fetus's blood. It's Smithick's."

Berry pressed her lips into a thin line, her fingers curling into a fist. "How did they die?"

Marvin's answer came after a pause, his tone heavy. "The pregnant girl was strangled. The other one? Hayes thinks it was malnutrition. He suspects she died in that box. There were splinters under her nails, consistent with her trying to claw her way out."

Berry closed her eyes for a moment, her chest rising and falling as she fought to contain her fury. When she opened them, her gaze was colder, sharper. "And the branding iron?" she asked.

"Demetrie Volkov's touch DNA was all over the handle," Marvin replied. "It's consistent with his prior arrests for domestic battery. His DNA's in the system. But nothing usable on the hot end—too degraded."

"Got it," Berry said curtly. "Marvin, I need that report emailed to me ASAP. I'm drafting a new arrest warrant now. Thank you for rushing this."

"You got it, Detective." The line went dead.

Berry leaned forward, typing furiously, her fingers moving like a blur as she pulled all the pieces together. When she finished, she flagged the email to the district attorney with one word: "URGENT."

Berry pushed back her chair with a loud scrape, the sound grating through the relative quiet of the precinct. She stalked around the corner, her boots striking the tile floor with quick, purposeful steps. Her voice cut through the murmurs of the early morning like a blade.

"Hey, Sarge?"

"Yeah?" came the gruff reply from the next office over.

Berry didn't hesitate. She stopped in the hallway, standing tall despite the exhaustion etched into her face, and locked eyes with him. "I need a team to go arrest Smithick and Demetrie," she said, her tone sharp enough to make two nearby officers pause mid-conversation and glance in her direction. Her no-nonsense demeanor brooked no argument. It was the kind of voice that made everyone in earshot straighten their backs.

The sergeant stepped out of his office, his expression darkening as he took in Berry's demeanor—the unrelenting fire in her eyes, the exhaustion tugging at the corners of her mouth. It was clear that he had seen her like this before. She wasn't going to stop until this was done. "I'll pull two officers now."

Berry nodded sharply, her jaw tightening. "Good. Because we need to move fast, before Smithick gets wind of this and bolts. I'll take Perez with me to Smithick's place. Have the other two pick up Demetrie."

The sergeant hesitated for half a second, then nodded and stepped back into his office. Berry didn't wait to see if he followed through. She was already turning on her heel, heading back to her desk to grab her jacket and badge.

Every second mattered now. The clock was ticking, and she wasn't about to let Smithick slip through her fingers—not this time.

"Perez, let's roll," she barked as she passed his cubicle.

Before she even reached the door, Perez was already there, adjusting his holster and keys. "On it," he said, giving her a sharp nod. I could see that he had worked with Berry long enough to know when she was in this mood—focused, fierce, unstoppable. There was no room for hesitation.

I followed them. I had to. I couldn't miss this. Not the look on Smithick's face when he realized he couldn't slither out of this one. The first time he'd been arrested, it had been for human trafficking—an airtight case, or so everyone had thought. But one by one, all the witnesses had mysteriously turned up dead, and the charges evaporated. He'd smirked his way out of the courthouse like he owned it.

This time, though, there was physical evidence. DNA. Unshakeable, undeniable. This time, the arrest warrant wasn't just for human trafficking—it was for *murder*.

Berry's unmarked black sedan wound its way through the suburban streets, past manicured lawns and pristine driveways, before pulling up in front of Smithick's disgustingly ostentatious house. It stood out like a sore thumb among the others. The fountain in the circular driveway glistened in the early morning sunlight, a pretentious spectacle of excess.

A fucking fountain.

As they got out of the car, Berry's eyes skimmed over the ridiculous scene. A three-car garage. Their sprawling lawn was perfectly trimmed. A doormat on the front porch that read: Wipe Your Paws," dotted with cutesy paw prints. She sneered.

"Perez, take the back," Berry ordered curtly, nodding toward the side of the house. "If he runs, cut him off." Perez moved wordlessly, circling the property with practiced ease.

Berry approached the front door alone, her hand ready on her hip near her holstered gun. She knocked, the sound echoing through the still morning air. A moment later, the door swung open, revealing a well-dressed, middle-aged woman with perfectly styled hair and an apron tied neatly around her waist. She was like a modern-day June Cleaver, complete with the faint scent of lemon polish wafting from the house behind her.

"Can I help you?" the woman asked, her voice pleasant and

polite.

Berry flashed her badge. "Detective Berry. Is William Smithick home?"

The woman tilted her head back toward the interior of the house, raising her voice just enough to call inside, "Will! Honey, it's for you!"

From somewhere deep inside, a gruff voice responded with a groan. "Someone probably needs a warrant signed," he muttered loudly enough to be heard.

A moment later, William Smithick appeared in the doorway, shuffling to take the place of his wife, who slipped back into the house with barely a glance at Berry. Smithick looked as smug as ever, with a perpetual smirk plastered on his face. He was dressed casually in tailored slacks and a crisp button-up shirt.

Berry grabbed her radio and spoke into it as soon as she saw him. "Come on back, Perez."

Smithick's expression flickered for a moment, a hint of confusion clouding his smug demeanor before he covered it with a scowl. He turned back toward the house. "Dear, will you and Robert head upstairs, please?" he called over his shoulder, his voice oddly soft, almost gentle.

Then, as he turned back to Berry, "We need privacy," he said sternly. Stepping fully onto the porch and pulling the door shut behind him with deliberate quiet. He glanced back through the glass to make sure his wife obeyed before leveling a sharp glare at Berry.

Perez rounded the corner, jogging up the porch steps to stand beside Berry.

Smithick's tone sharpened. "What's this about? We both know all your witnesses are dead—how tragic. So, unless you've got a medium on your payroll, I don't see how this is going anywhere."

Berry didn't blink. "DNA speaks louder than words," she said calmly, her hand moving to her cuffs. "William Smithick, you are under arrest for murder, human trafficking, and drug charges. Turn around and put your hands behind your back."

Those words. I had waited so long to hear those wonderful words. This time, the charges would stick, and my family would be safe.

For a moment, Smithick froze. His eyes narrowed. His jaw twitched, and his hands ran over his salt-and-pepper hair in one smooth motion. He let out a sharp, frustrated gasp before finally turning around, his movements slow and deliberate.

"Do you know who I am?" Smithick huffed. "I'll have your job for this, bitch!" he shouted over his shoulder. He sounded desperate, like a trapped animal.

Berry's face remained stoic as she recited his Miranda rights and cuffed him. Her tone was steady and firm. Smithick didn't say much—just the same refrain, muttered under his breath like a mantra. "I want my lawyer."

Perez moved to escort him down the steps while Berry lingered on the porch for a moment, her gaze following the man, who had eluded justice for far too long. *Not this time*. This time, he wasn't walking away. Berry's lips curled into a smile for mere seconds, then it went back to a straight line.

As soon as they arrived back at the station, Smithick was escorted into one of the smaller, windowless interrogation rooms. The air in there always smelled of bleach and stale coffee, a suffocating mix that clung to the walls. Berry let him sit alone for two hours, telling Perez that she wanted to make him sweat a while. The walls had that institutional shade of off-white, almost beige, and they seemed to close in the longer you stayed in there. It didn't matter how tough you thought you were; those rooms worked on you.

Berry had to wait for his attorney anyway, and it gave her time to let the anticipation build. Everyone knew when Smithick's lawyer finally showed up because his entrance was anything but subtle. He threw the double doors open like they were parting just for him and stormed inside, his voice loud enough to echo down the entire hallway.

"Where is my client? What are the charges?" he barked. His arms were thrown up in theatrical exasperation, his gold pinky ring catching the sunlight and flashing like a tiny, angry flare. His diamond-encrusted watch gleamed, as though it was part of the act—a small fortune wrapped around his wrist. He looked like he'd stepped out of a 1940s crime film: a sharp three-piece suit so well-tailored it seemed painted on, a pocket square folded with surgeon-like precision, and a gray fedora tipped just so on his head.

This guy wasn't just an attorney. He was *the* attorney—the kind who charged for breathing in his direction, the kind who made deals behind closed doors and got guilty men walking free on technicalities. Everything about him screamed top-tier defense, loud, arrogant, untouchable.

Berry leaned casually against the wall, holding a cup of coffee. She gestured toward the interrogation room with her free hand. "He's in here."

The lawyer turned to face her, his sharp jaw tightening. "I hope you waited to question him until I got here!" His voice was gravelly, the kind that made you think of unfiltered cigarettes and scotch.

Berry opened her mouth to respond, but he cut her off before a single word escaped. "We need to speak privately first, if you don't mind." His hand shot up between them, palm out, the universal signal for "shut up." It hovered there for a second, inches from Berry's face, before he swept into the room without waiting for her answer.

The door clicked shut behind him, and Berry took a long sip of her coffee. "Nice guy," she muttered under her breath, then made her way over to Perez's cubicle, which had a direct line of sight to the interrogation room door.

"Let me know when those girls are done gabbing, will ya?" she said with a wink, her tone dry but amused. Perez nodded and snickered, already anticipating the headache this lawyer was about to give her.

Time dragged. Nearly an hour passed before Perez knocked on the doorframe of Berry's office. "They're done," he said, his lips twitching with the beginnings of a smirk.

Berry grabbed a slim file folder from her desk. Inside were the photos, the evidence, the kind of things you didn't want to look at for too long, you'd see them every time you closed your eyes. Carrying her coffee and the folder, she walked briskly to the interrogation room and stepped inside.

The lawyer was leaning back in his chair, legs crossed, the picture of smug confidence. Smithick, on the other hand, had his elbows on the table, his hands fidgeting, tapping a rhythm against the metal as if he were trying to drum the nerves out of his system.

Berry slid into the chair across from them and dropped the file on the table with a soft thud. She didn't say anything at first. Instead, she opened the folder and began pulling out the photographs one by one, laying them out like playing cards.

Smithick was the first to speak. His lips curled into a twisted smile, a smirk that didn't quite reach his eyes. "It's too bad about your last witness passing away," he said, his tone mocking. "But you were fond of her, weren't you?"

Berry didn't flinch. The lawyer leaned in, his face tightening. "William, please stop talking," he hissed under his breath.

Berry didn't react. She didn't flinch or scowl. Her expression was a blank slate, her eyes cold and steady as they bored into Smithick. She raised her coffee to her lips and took a slow sip, the silence stretching long enough to make him shift in his chair.

"I didn't have anything to do with what happened at the warehouse," Smithick said finally, his voice steady at first but gaining volume with each word. "Whatever Demetrie was doing with drugs or girls, that was *his* operation. I wasn't involved!"

Berry remained silent, but I moved closer, hovering over Smithick's shoulder. If he could feel my presence, he didn't let on, but I could see the pulse hammering in his neck. His skin was growing shiny, a sheen of sweat forming along his hairline.

Berry pulled a photograph from the stack and slid it across the table. It was the torture box: battered, crude, horrific.

"Recognize this?" she asked, her voice calm, almost conversational.

"Don't answer that," the lawyer interjected, leaning forward, his eyes flashing with warning.

"No!" Smithick blurted, a little too quickly. "It must be Demetrie's."

Berry tilted her head, her expression unreadable. "Then why is your semen and touch DNA all over this box?" she asked, her tone sharp now, cutting through the tension like a blade. "Along with DNA from about a dozen girls, five of whom are dead?"

Smithick stammered, anxiety eating away the last shred of composure. "I—I don't—"

Berry leaned forward, the faintest smile curling at the corners of her lips. "You know what the best part is?" she asked. Her voice dropped, almost conspiratorial, like she was letting them in on a secret.

Smithick and his lawyer both froze, their confusion obvious.

"It's the little key," Berry continued, her smile widening. "The one Grace told me about before she died. She said she thought it was the key to the padlock on the torture box in the warehouse. She was so sure of it that she swallowed it after she was shot in the head. I got it back after her autopsy. We all know we could have gotten into the box without the key, of course. But the key proves you were in her house. This key connects you to a dead woman."

The words hung in the air like smoke, suffocating and inescapable. Smithick's face went pale, as sweat pooled on the table from his splayed fingers. His lawyer leaned back in his chair, his mask of confidence slipping enough for Berry to catch the flicker of worry in his eyes.

I drifted closer to Smithick, willing him to feel me, to know that I was there. My anger burned bright, a flame that didn't waver, and for a moment, I thought I saw his hands tremble ever so slightly. Good. I wanted him to squirm. I wanted him to be haunted.

Berry didn't break eye contact as she leaned back in her chair, her coffee cup cradled in her hand. "We're just getting started."

42

Arrest

I thought about the red door in the middle of the playground, the strange, solitary object that seemed to call to me without words. As I focused on it, the clouds surrounding me began to shift, thinning out like smoke caught in a breeze. Slowly, the door emerged, vivid and solid, standing stark against the muted colors of the playground. It was as if the world was being painted into existence by my thoughts.

Here, thoughts weren't just thoughts. They were tangible, powerful. All I had to do was think of a place, or a person, and I could be there.

Aniela sat on the swings, her legs dangling as she looked up at me with bright eyes, her hair fluttering in an invisible breeze. She was the picture of happiness, her voice light and cheerful as she called out, "Hi, Mom!"

I walked past the red door, its glossy surface almost glowing, and sat down beside her on the swing. My hands brushed the cold chains.

"What's behind the red door?" I asked, my voice wavering.

"Behind the door is eternity. It's your afterlife with us,"

Aniela said simply, kicking her legs to make her swing rock gently.

"So... Heaven?" I asked, my mind grasping at the concept.

"Yes. Your Heaven. Everyone's Heaven is different," she said, her voice full of certainty in the way only a pre-teen's voice can be.

"What is this place called?"

"The Veil," she said matter-of-factly, as if she were telling me the weather. "This is where you go until you're ready for Heaven."

I swallowed hard. "So, while I am in the Veil, I can take care of my unfinished business?"

"Yep!" she chirped, hopping off the swing with a small thud as her feet hit the soft, sandy ground. "If you try very hard, the people you love can sense you when you visit them."

"So, am I a ghost?"

"We call them spirits here. But yes. Your spirit can go anywhere and do anything. You can visit whoever and make your presence known if you want. It is all possible because your spirit is no longer attached to your physical body."

Aniela's simple explanation settled over me, both comforting and overwhelming. I did have unfinished business. There were so many loose ends I needed to tie up, so much left undone. I wasn't ready to open the red door. Not yet.

The first thought that came to me was Smithick—the man who had hurt so many, including me. I had to make sure he went down, that he would never again see the light of day or harm another soul. And then there were the people I loved. I needed to know that they would be alright, that they would heal and carry on.

For the first time in what felt like forever, I allowed myself to believe in justice. To believe in hope. To believe that, somehow, all of this—everything I had been through—was leading somewhere. I knew deep in my soul that when my unfinished business was done, the red door in the middle of the playground would open, and I would be ready to walk through.

But for now, my heart pulled me in a different direction. I had to say goodbye.

I thought of Theo, the kids, Maddie, Frank, Janie—so much love welled up in my heart that it felt like it might burst. These people, the ones who had stood by me and shaped me, made up for every dark and terrible thing I had endured. The playground began to dissolve around me, the vibrant colors of the swings and slides fading into the soft gray of memory.

And then I was there. At my grave site.

The cemetery was quiet, the air heavy with a solemn stillness. The soft murmur of wind rustled the trees as I stood near the small gathering of people. They were all there, huddled close together as my casket was being lowered into the ground. I didn't feel the way I thought I might—I was not afraid or desperate, but filled with an aching love for the people I was leaving behind.

Maddie stood with a few of my coworkers from the newspaper. She dabbed at her eyes with a tissue. Her nose was red, but I wasn't sure if it was from crying or the cold. Her curly hair was shifting in the chilly October air. The smell of a bonfire nearby wafted in the air. Theo was there, standing tall and steady, holding Michael in his arms. Frank and Janie sat nearby. Janie was curled close to Frank like a baby bird taking shelter beneath its mother's wing. I couldn't help but smile at the sight of them together—Frank, ever the protector, and Janie, quietly soaking up his warmth.

Even Detective Berry was there, her presence a quiet reminder of the justice I had fought for. And Nurse Ben—strong, dependable Ben—stood near the back, his hands clasped in front of him, his expression one of quiet grief.

There were tears, yes. But there was something else, too. As I moved closer, listening to the soft murmur of voices, I realized there was laughter—gentle and bittersweet—as they shared stories of our time together.

I wanted so badly to touch each of them, to hug them, to tell them how much they had meant to me. But all I could do was watch. I tried to exude my spirit energy to them all, letting them know I was here with them. I hoped they felt the love emanating from me.

I drifted toward Theo, who stood a little apart from the others, holding Michael close. Michael's small hands were clasped around a stuffed bear, but as I moved closer, his bright, curious eyes locked onto me.

"Hi, baby," I whispered, even though I knew he couldn't hear me. To my surprise, Michael's face lit up with a big smile, and he reached out toward me, babbling excitedly.

"You see me, don't you?" I whispered. I believed that children weren't clouded by disbelief. He could see me, maybe hear me, too. "Hi, baby. Be a good boy. I love you."

Michael giggled, as if he understood, and my heart swelled.

My arms ached to hold him. I turned to Theo, who was staring off into the distance, his face lined with grief but full of quiet strength.

"I love you, too," I said, tears streaming down my face. "So much. I can't thank you enough for everything you've given me. You kept me alive when I wanted to give up. You gave me hope when I thought there was none left."

Theo didn't respond, of course, but for a brief moment, I thought I saw him tilt his head, as if he had heard something faint in the wind.

Emily was sitting next to Theo with a solemn look. I stooped down as if on one knee, "I'm sorry for how this turned out. I love you! Take care of your baby brother."

A single tear streaked her cheek as she picked up her stuffed bunny and held it tight.

The service was small and intimate, the way I would have wanted it. As it came to an end, everyone stood in silence, wiping tears and hugging one another. There was no rush to leave—only the slow, tender unfolding of goodbye.

I floated above them, watching, as a thought crept into my mind like a whisper: If I had never lost my way after Joseph died, I would never have met any of these beautiful people.

The realization hit me like a wave, warm and bittersweet. Maybe everything had happened for a reason. Maybe the pain, the chaos, the struggles—they had all been leading me here, to this love, to this peace. The last time I felt love like this was when I was with Joseph.

I focused my attention on the playground.

The Veil stretched around us like an endless twilight, its air heavy with the sounds of whispers that might have been dreams or voices, I wasn't sure which. Aniela sat perched on the rusted merry-go-round, one leg curled beneath her while the other lazily pushed against the ground, spinning herself in slow, circles. The creak of metal echoed, the sound impossibly small in the vastness of the Veil.

I turned my gaze toward the red door, its edges glowing in the distance like a beacon pulsing through the haze. It wasn't time yet, but it would be soon. The thought tightened something in my chest, but it didn't crush me the way it once had. I wasn't afraid. Not of what was behind the door. Not of what waited on the other side.

I was almost ready.

Aniela stopped spinning, planting her bare foot firmly on the dusty ground. She smiled at me. Her freckles danced across her cheeks when the faint light shifted, and her sky-blue eyes studied me like she could see straight into the cracks of my soul.

Aniela tilted her head, her golden curls catching the faint light of the Veil's strange atmosphere. She stared off toward the red door with a solemnity that didn't belong to someone so young.

"Where is Joseph?" I asked her, my voice quieter now.

"Behind the red door," she said simply, her eyes still focused on the door.

"Can I talk to him?"

Her small hands gripped the poles of the merry-go-round as she stilled completely. The light surrounding us seemed to dim, and the haze grew thicker. I felt her hesitation like a ripple through the air, a warning I didn't understand.

"Once you go through the door," she said, then paused. "After you go through and leave the Veil, you can't come back out."

The words hung between us, as sharp and unforgiving as shards of glass. My heart twisted. "Why are you still in the Veil, baby?" I asked, the question tumbling out before I could stop it.

Her eyes flicked back to me, and for a moment, she was both my little girl and something far older. Something ageless. She smiled, but there was sadness in it. "I was sent here to be your guide," she said, matter-of-factly, as if the answer should have been obvious.

My throat tightened, and I reached for her hand. "You came for me?"

She nodded, her curls bouncing with the motion. "Aniela means 'messenger of God.' He sent me here because you weren't ready, Mommy. Not yet. Someone had to help you find your way."

Her words settled over me like a blanket, both comforting and suffocating. I stared at her for a long moment, memorizing the soft flush of her cheeks, the tiny freckles that dotted her nose, the way her eyes seemed brighter than the Veil itself.

"Thank you," I whispered, my voice cracking.

She leaned forward and kissed my forehead, her touch light as a feather. "You'll do fine. You just have to be brave, okay?"

The air seemed to hum with anticipation, and the haze of the Veil swirled around us, stirring like it was alive. I wanted to ask more, to hold on to this moment a little longer, but Aniela slid off the merry-go-round and landed lightly on her feet.

She smiled up at me, "Are you ready now, Mommy?" she asked, her voice as soft and sweet.

I crouched down beside her, brushing invisible dirt off my palms as if that small, grounding gesture could steady me. "Almost, baby," I murmured. "I just want to make sure Berry gets the bad guy."

I focused my attention on Berry.

43

Finally

After months of grueling court proceedings, media scrutiny, and sleepless nights, the case finally came to a close. The trial of William Smithick had been one of the most high-profile criminal cases the city had ever seen, and the courtroom had been packed every day with reporters, families of victims, and curious onlookers hoping to witness justice served.

In the end, Demetrie Volkov had taken a plea deal. It wasn't out of remorse—he had none—but pure self-preservation. Faced with the overwhelming evidence against him, his attorneys advised him that his only hope of avoiding life in prison, or the death penalty was to cooperate.

Under the deal, Demetrie agreed to testify against Smithick in exchange for a reduced sentence: twenty years for his role in the prostitution ring and the torture of women and girls, with a chance of parole after fifteen years. He also received an additional five years for distributing cocaine, bringing his total sentence to a minimum of twenty-five years behind bars.

His testimony, though self-serving, cracked the case wide open. Demetrie named names. He identified the two Jane Doe victims, finally giving them back their identities. They had been his girls, and he had branded them, but he testified that Smithick was the one who killed them.

He detailed the extent of Lenny and Detective Schammel's involvement in the criminal enterprise. He described how Lenny, Smithick's enforcer, had followed orders without question, and how Detective Schammel—a man sworn to uphold the law—had used his badge as a shield while committing heinous acts. Schammel had helped Smithick get rid of evidence, diverted investigations away from Smithick, and even silenced witnesses.

It was the murder details that shook the courtroom. Demetrie testified that Detective Schammel had killed Sasha Woods. He described how Schammel, paranoid that Sasha might turn informant, shot her in cold blood, then dumped the gun in the Halifax River to destroy the evidence.

The most damning testimony, however, was about Smithick himself. Demetrie recounted, without an ounce of regret, how Smithick had strangled one of the Jane Doe victims, the pregnant one, when she threatened to expose him. "She said she was going to talk," Demetrie said on the stand. "She was going to ruin everything. He couldn't risk it." His words chilled the packed courtroom. She was the Jane Doe with Demetri's brand that I had recognized, so it's no wonder that Schammel didn't pass the information to Berry.

When it came time for sentencing, the jury was not unanimous on the death sentence. Smithick was given life in prison without the possibility of parole. His crimes were too heinous, too systemic, too deliberate for any leniency. The evidence against him, bolstered by DNA, forensics, and Demetrie's testimony, had been ironclad. Smithick's high-powered defense team had done everything they could—arguing technicalities, trying to poke holes in the evidence, even attempting to smear the victims—but it hadn't been enough.

The day the trial concluded, the atmosphere in the courtroom was electric. Families of the victims sobbed quietly, holding one another as the judge delivered Smithick's sentence. The reporters scribbled furiously in their notepads, cameras flashing as the judge's gavel slammed down for the final time.

Smithick and his attorneys filed appeals almost immediately after his conviction, citing errors in procedure and claiming that the testimony of a co-conspirator like Demetrie was unreliable. But the appellate courts upheld the original verdict. The evidence was overwhelming, and the jury's decision had been sound.

Smithick would never see the light of day again. The courtroom, moments before buzzing with muted whispers and the shuffling of papers, had fallen utterly silent after the verdict. The weight of the words—*life without parole*—hung heavy in the air, thicker than smoke, pressing down on everyone in the room. You could feel it on your skin, like a suffocating fog, wrapping itself around you and making it hard to breathe.

Smithick sat there motionless, his face unreadable. Not a flicker of emotion crossed his features, though his jaw twitched—a hint, perhaps, of the frustration or fury boiling underneath. He had built a reputation as a man who showed no weakness, and he was determined to maintain that façade, even now. His hands, cuffed and resting on the table, didn't even flinch as the words "no chance of parole" were read. He was going to rot behind bars until the end of his days.

It was a grim triumph. Justice, yes, but justice that came at a terrible, almost unbearable cost. Nothing could undo the damage he had already done. Five women were confirmed dead, *confirmed* being the cruel operative word. Five lives stolen, their families left broken and bleeding, with gaping holes that could never be filled. But we all knew that those five women were just the tip of the iceberg.

Detective Berry had warned us of that early on. No one knew exactly how many people Smithick, or his network of thugs, had killed. We didn't even know how many had simply vanished, their bodies never found, their names fading into whispers. Berry thought the number of victims could stretch into the hundreds, maybe even thousands. Torture, rape, drugs, trafficking, murder—his operation had been vast, intricate, and ruthlessly efficient for years before anyone dared to take him down.

I used to lie awake at night wondering if Smithick would ever be caught. A part of me feared he was untouchable. Men like him were often protected by money, power, and a web of corruption that stretched far beyond what most people could imagine. But everything had changed the day I met Detective Berry.

She had this quiet, unshakable determination about her, the kind of resolve that made you believe, even in the darkest moments, that there was still hope. She didn't just want to bring Smithick to justice—she *needed* to. It was personal for her, though she had never said so directly. I had placed my full confidence in her from the start. She was relentless, methodical, and, above all, fearless. She became my hero.

As the judge's voice faded into the heavy stillness of the room, I let out a breath I hadn't realized I'd been holding. My chest ached from the tension, but it was nothing compared to the relief that washed over me. I glanced over at Theo, and the look on his face mirrored exactly what I felt. Relief. Gratitude. Exhaustion. He took a big breath in as if a crushing weight had been lifted. He wiped his face with his hand, though I couldn't tell whether it was to clear away a tear or just out of pure exhaustion.

Then, slowly, he turned to Berry. His lips quivered for a moment, as if he couldn't quite find the words. Finally, he managed to mouth the words, "Thank you." His voice didn't need to carry for her to understand—his expression said everything.

A single tear rolled down his cheek, though he didn't bother to brush it away. He stared at her, his gratitude raw and overwhelming. *You can rest now*, I thought. *You don't have to protect me from him any longer.*

Berry's response was as understated as ever. She gave him a small, solemn nod, her face stoic, though her eyes betrayed a flicker of something deeper—perhaps satisfaction or perhaps sorrow for all the lives that had been lost. Her hands were folded tightly in front of her, the only sign of the tension she still carried. This wasn't a win to her. It was simply a step—a necessary one, but one that could never undo the horrors of the past. I wondered, briefly, if she would allow herself to rest now. Somehow, I doubted it.

When the officers moved to escort Smithick out of the courtroom, his face was twisted into an ugly sneer. He turned his head enough to glare directly at Detective Berry, his dark eyes filled with hatred. For a moment, it seemed like he might say something, but he didn't. Instead, he smirked, as if daring her to.

Berry didn't waste any words on him. She didn't flinch. She met his stare with unflinching calm, her lips curling into a faint, knowing smile. Her expression said it all: "You lost. You'll never hurt anyone again."

As the officers led Smithick away, Berry allowed herself a deep, steadying breath. It was over. He was gone. For good. Smithick was led out of the courtroom in chains, flanked by two towering officers who didn't so much as glance at him. The clinking of the chains against the floor echoed as he shuffled away.

Theo exhaled deeply. Berry stood motionless, watching Smithick being led away until he disappeared through the door at the back of the courtroom. Only then did she let out a soft sigh, so quiet I almost missed it.

Once the courtroom emptied, Berry stood in the quiet, her fingers brushing against the stack of papers she had carried with her for the past year, or longer. There were case notes, transcripts, photos of evidence, and the lives of the victims etched into every detail. She let her hands fall to her sides and stood motionless for a moment, her eyes fixed on the now-empty chair where Smithick had sat.

A single tear escaped down her cheek, and she quickly wiped it away, unwilling to let anyone see. Her job was done, but the cost had been high. Too high.

I hovered near her, watching as she stood in the aftermath of the case that had consumed her life. I had been there every step of the way, watching her fight for justice, watching her push herself past the point of exhaustion again and again.

"You did it," she whispered to herself, her voice breaking. "You got him, Grace."

The sound of my name startled me, and I wondered if she could feel my spirit near her.

Berry's fingers brushed her cheek as though wiping another tear, and then she added under her breath, "If it wasn't for that key, we might never have gotten here."

I felt a wave of bittersweet pride. The key, the one I had hidden so desperately in those final moments, had been the thread that unraveled everything. It had been enough to connect the dots, to reopen cases that had seemed unsolvable.

Berry slipped her badge back into her pocket and gathered her things. I could see the relief in her face, see the sheer weight of her accomplishment settle over her, but so did the weight of everything she couldn't change—the lives lost, the families shattered, the women who would never be the same.

As she walked out of the courtroom, I followed her. This wasn't just her victory, but it was mine, too. And as much as she couldn't see me, as much as she would never know I was there, I would stay with her, my silent thanks hanging in the air like a whisper: "You found the truth. You brought them justice. You gave us peace."

It was over. Finally, it was over, now that the head of the snake had been cut off.

There were still trials pending for the other members of the trafficking ring. Detective Berry had identified and arrested four others who had worked for Smithick. They'd find their way to this same courtroom soon enough. But after months of testimonies, harrowing accounts, and evidence that had stolen the sleep of even the most seasoned detectives, it was clear— Smithick had been the puppet master, the one pulling the strings. The branches of his operation were rotten to the core, but now that the trunk had been cut down, the rest were withering and falling, piece by piece.

Smithick wasn't some shadowy figure operating in the margins of society, hiding in the dark like a cliché villain. No, he wore a robe. He held a gavel. He was a circuit judge—a man who swore to uphold the law, to seek fairness and truth. All the while, he had been exploiting that power for his own depraved purposes. Who was supposed to hold him accountable?

Why had he thought he was above the law? Maybe because, for a long time, he was. He sat untouchable and smug, thinking he was smarter than everyone else. Untouchable. Unstoppable. Until he wasn't.

I glanced over at his family during the verdict. His wife sat directly behind him, her shoulders slumped as if someone had physically crushed her spirit. His teenage son—God, he couldn't have been older than sixteen—stared blankly at the floor, his hands twisted together in his lap. I wondered what they had thought of him before all of this. Had they known, even in some quiet, unspoken way, that something was wrong? Or was this a complete shattering of the man they thought they knew?

When the word "guilty" was read, Mrs. Smithick had let out

a sound I'd never forget. It wasn't a cry—it was a howl, guttural and raw, the kind of sound that made your stomach turn because it was so nakedly human. Her husband had destroyed lives—dozens of them, maybe more. But he'd destroyed hers, too. His son's life was also collateral damage. His selfishness had ripped through his own family like a fire, consuming everything in its path, leaving only ashes behind.

She collapsed into herself, I felt something unexpected: pity. Not for Smithick—never for him—but for her. For the boy. I hated Smithick, but I pitied the people who were left in the rubble of what he had done. They were both seemed to be in complete shock and had no clue he was Jekyll and Hyde. I couldn't imagine what they were going through. Thinking you had this wonderful life, but the person you loved was the boogeyman.

And yet, Smithick had proven something that terrified me. One person *could* change the world. It only took one, like a single drop of rain falling into the ocean, sending ripples across the surface. His ripples had reached further than anyone could have imagined, corrupting the innocent, dragging down the guilty, and tainting the waters for miles. It's terrifying how much destruction one person could unleash.

I thought about that now. My own life, as I knew it, was over. I had made my choices, done things I could never take back, things that had brought me to this point. Was I any better? How big was *my* ripple? Did it counter his in some small way, or was I just another part of the same storm?

The thing about a raindrop was that once it hit the water, you couldn't tell where it went, it became indistinguishable from the ocean it had joined. I wondered if my drop would leave anything behind, any evidence that I had tried, in my own way, to set something right. Or would I be another wave in an endless sea, lost and forgotten before the tide even turned? So many questions remained in my mind. I wanted to make sense of my life. I needed the nightmare I had lived to have had a purpose.

44

A Place of Truth

My mind drifted to the playground, and in an instant, I was there. It happened as effortlessly as the blink of an eye, the shift between places as natural as breathing. The Veil was strange like that, time and distance didn't matter anymore. It obeyed only the laws of thought and memory.

The playground was almost empty, bathed in a muted twilight that seemed neither night nor day. Aniela sat on the swings, her feet brushing the ground. She wasn't swinging exactly, just swaying back and forth, her toes stirring little clouds of dust in slow, deliberate circles. Her head was bowed, her long, blond hair obscuring her face. She didn't need to speak for me to feel her thoughts pressing against the space between us. There was heaviness in the air—a somber, weighted quiet that seemed to settle over both of us like a heavy blanket.

While I watched her, my heart was aching deeply and bitterly. Aniela hadn't known life on Earth, not really, not beyond the brief months she existed inside me. Yet here, in the Veil, a soul untouched by the complications and corruption of earthly life. Somehow, she was the one teaching *me* how to let go, how to move forward into whatever came next. It was cruel, almost backward, for her to bear the burden of guiding me when it should have been the other way around.

"What are you thinking about?" I finally asked, my voice soft, almost tentative. Aniela didn't look up, but her swaying slowed to a stop. She hesitated for a moment, then lifted her gaze to the horizon.

"Just thinking about..." she started, then paused. Her voice was light and lilting, like wind chimes stirred by a breeze. "Eternity."

I swallowed hard, the lump in my throat rising painfully.

She was the daughter I never got to know. She existed only here, in this strange in-between, because of my mistakes. Those dreams I used to have, the ones where I was twenty-two-year-old Grace from Chicago, they had been just my subconscious trying to fill the void. A fabrication, a bandage over a wound that would never fully heal. In those dreams, I had been whole. In those dreams, I had had everything I'd lost: Joseph, our daughter, a life untouched by tragedy.

But that wasn't reality. Reality was the accident. Reality was the fact that I never even knew I had been pregnant. The truth burned like a fresh wound every time I thought about it. If I *had* known, everything would have been different. I wouldn't have taken even one sip of alcohol that night. I wouldn't have slid behind the wheel, drunk and blind to the road ahead. The accident wouldn't have happened. Joseph would still be alive. Aniela would have lived. We would have had our happily ever after.

But then, another thought wormed its way in, the same one

that had haunted me ever since I crossed over into this liminal space. If the accident hadn't happened, if I had gone on living that perfect life, would Smithick have been caught? Would those girls, those fragile, broken lives, have been saved? Would Melanie and Sasha still be alive?

I'd been at the right place at the right time to uncover everything. It was a bitter truth, but it was a truth nonetheless: my choices, my mistakes, had led to his downfall. Without the crash, without everything that came after, he might still be out there, hurting more girls, destroying more lives.

It was a terrible dichotomy to wrestle with. What did it all mean? Had it been my destiny to crash that car, to lose Joseph, to lose Aniela, just so my daily journaling and memories could guide me to Smithick's web of lies and depravity? Or had it all been just a coincidence, a meaningless chain of events that only seemed connected because I desperately needed them to be?

The Veil didn't answer questions like that. It didn't offer clarity or comfort. It left you with your thoughts, your regrets, and a silence that was sometimes unbearable.

I turned back to Aniela, who was watching me now with her dark, unblinking eyes.

"You think it was destiny, don't you?" I asked her, though I wasn't sure if I wanted an answer.

She tilted her head, considering me. Her expression was soft, but there was a flicker of something sharp and knowing in her gaze.

"Does it matter?" she asked.

The question hit me like a blow. Did it? Would knowing the answer change anything? Would it bring Joseph back? Would it bring *her* back?

I looked away, my eyes drifting to the horizon where the muted light of the Veil seemed to stretch endlessly. My chest was heavy with everything I'd done and everything I hadn't. Aniela's voice broke the silence again, gentle but firm.

"You're here now," she said with a smile. "That's all that matters."

I turned back toward her, but she was already moving, her feet lifting from the ground as the swing began to sway again. The breeze stirred her hair, and I wished I could have gotten to know her in life.

I stayed there, watching her, trying to make sense of the ache in my heart and the questions spinning in my mind. Maybe I would never have answers. Maybe that was the point.

Aniela stood up from the swings and walked toward me, her feet soundless on the soft ground of the playground. The twilight sky above us seemed to dim as she approached, the edges of the horizon blurring into a muted haze. She stopped just in front of me and tilted her head back, her dark, innocent eyes meeting mine.

She held out her hand. It was so delicate, like a porcelain doll's, but warm and solid.

"Are you ready to go now?" she asked. Her voice was soft but steady, with a calm certainty that both comforted and unsettled me.

I stared at her outstretched hand, unsure of what to do. Was I ready? Would I *ever* be ready? The truth was, I didn't know. There were so many unanswered questions, the regrets, the guilt that clung to me like a shadow. Maybe going through the door would give me some answers.

I reached for her hand, hesitating for only a moment before my fingers brushed against hers. Her grip was surprisingly firm.

"I'm scared," I admitted quietly, the words trembling as they left my lips. I wasn't even sure what I was afraid of. The unknown? Eternity? The idea of seeing Joseph again—the man I loved, the man whose life I had stolen?

"It's okay," Aniela said, her voice filled with a gentle certainty that steadied me. "I will be with you." She gave my hand a small, reassuring squeeze, melting my fear away.

We began walking together toward the red door. It loomed larger and larger as we approached, its glossy surface gleaming like wet paint in the dim, ethereal light. It was strange, out of place, yet it felt as though it belonged here, as though it had been waiting just for me all along.

When we reached it, I paused. My free hand hovered over the brass doorknob, the metal cool and polished beneath my fingertips. The air seemed to hum a low vibration that resonated in my body. I thought I could hear faint whispers coming from the other side of the door. Familiar voices, distant and distorted, like echoes traveling through water.

Before I could even twist the knob, the door began to open on its own. It knew I was ready even before I did.

It swung inward slowly, creaking softly, revealing a light so bright it made me flinch and shield my eyes. But it wasn't harsh—it was warm, golden, and inviting, spilling out from the doorway like sunlight breaking through clouds. My pulse quickened, my breath catching in my throat as I tried to understand what lay beyond.

The playground dissolved around me, fading into the light as though it had never existed. Aniela's hand remained steady in mine, her presence anchoring me as the brilliance of the afterlife unfolded before us.

And then I saw him.

Joseph stood just inside the threshold, his figure bathed in the golden glow. He looked exactly as I remembered him—his kind brown eyes and his warm smile. His presence was so achingly familiar that it brought tears to my eyes. He didn't speak, but he didn't have to. The love in his gaze, the forgiveness etched into every line of his face, said more than words ever could.

I froze, my guilt crashing over me like a tidal wave. How could he be here, waiting for me, after everything I had done? How could he *forgive* me?

As if sensing my hesitation, Aniela tugged on my hand.

"It's okay, Mom. This is where you're supposed to be."

I took a shaky step forward, my eyes still locked on Joseph. He opened his arms, and the tears spilled over as I let Aniela lead me closer. The warmth of the light surrounded us, and for the first time since the accident, the unbearable heaviness began to ease.

As I crossed the threshold, something incredible happened. Suddenly, I felt lighter and at peace.

The guilt, the grief, the hatred, the self-loathing that had consumed me for so long—it didn't disappear, not completely, but it began to shift. It was still a part of me, but it no longer defined me. It was as though it had been absorbed into the light, transformed into something softer, something I could carry without it crushing me.

And at that moment, I understood.

The afterlife wasn't a beautiful, generic heaven or the fiery pits of hell. It was what you brought with you, what you chose to see, what you were willing to let go of. It was a place of truth, of reckoning, of healing.

As Joseph's arms wrapped around me, Aniela's hand still holding mine, I realized I had been given a second chance. Not to undo the past, but to make peace with it. My head rested on his chest. He placed a hand on my head and caressed my hair. It was as if we had never been apart. As he held me tight, he said three little words I never thought I would hear.

"I forgive you," he whispered.

My knees started to buckle. I was trembling and crying. I held him so tight, and I never wanted to let him go. I finally found the words that were swirling in my head: "I love you, Joseph. I never stopped loving you."

"I love you, too," Joseph whispered, gripping me harder.

I felt completely whole. The fear had slipped away like a distant memory. I didn't even have any more questions. None of it mattered anymore.

And as the light enveloped us completely, I knew that this was my heaven. It was not the eternal nightmare I thought I deserved.

ABOUT THE AUTHOR

Maggie D. Purvis is a versatile new writer with a passion for blending genres in unexpected ways. Holding degrees in forensics and working in law enforcement, Maggie brings a unique perspective to her writing, often drawing inspiration from her love of true crime and the paranormal. When she's not exploring the mysteries of the world, Maggie enjoys spending time with her husband, two dogs, and cat. Whether delving into the darker side of human nature or unraveling the unexplained, she's always looking for the next great story to tell.

Thank you for reading Maggie's debut novel. Please write a review on Amazon and keep an eye out for more books to come!

Get in touch at MaggieD.Purvis@gmail.com or follow on X @MaggieDPurvis

ACKNOWLEDGMENTS

To my editor, Marios Pagonis, who is extremely talented as well as patient, thank you!
Thank you, Lindsey Romig, for your supreme editing skills and suggestions, and Christopher Evans for your vast knowledge and insights on working girls.

REFERENCES

Gray, T. (1742). Ode on a Distant Prospect of Eaton College.

www.ingramcontent.com/pod-product-compliance
Lightning Source LLC
Chambersburg PA
CBHW021842010726
47493CB00005B/1508